HEART OF STONE

TOR BOOKS BY DEBRA MULLINS

Prodigal Son
Heart of Stone

HEART OF STONE

DEBRA MULLINS

A TOM DOHERTY
ASSOCIATES BOOK
NEW YORK

HEART OF STONE

Copyright © 2014 by Debra Mullins

All rights reserved.

A Tor Book
Published by Tom Doherty Associates, LLC
175 Fifth Avenue
New York, NY 10010

www.tor-forge.com

Tor® is a registered trademark of Tom Doherty Associates, LLC.

The Library of Congress Cataloging-in-Publication Data is available upon request.

ISBN 978-0-7653-7614-5 (trade paperback)
ISBN 978-1-4299-4288-1 (e-book)

Tor books may be purchased for educational, business, or promotional use. For information on bulk purchases, please contact Macmillan Corporate and Premium Sales Department at 1-800-221-7945, extension 5442, or write specialmarkets@macmillan.com.

First Edition: October 2014

Printed in the United States of America

0 9 8 7 6 5 4 3 2 1

For Josh,
who feels so deeply and has enriched my life with his presence,
much love always

HEART OF STONE

PROLOGUE

Faith Karaluros watched the minivan in the distance, skis and a snowboard fastened to the rack on top, as the vehicle wound its way along the mountain highway. A chill swept over her, and it had nothing to do with the dusting of snow on the frozen ground around them. So normal. Not what she'd imagined the enemy to look like.

"They're going skiing," she said.

Michael glanced over at her. Even in the shadows of the leafless trees where they hid, her husband's green eyes gleamed, always so startling against his sun-kissed, angular features. "That's what they want you to think. It's a great cover."

"Are you sure they're the ones? I mean, that van looks like it belongs to a soccer mom."

"Like I said, a great cover." He stroked her cheek with one finger. "Our intelligence says these are high-ranking officials, Faith. They have the info we need, and we have to detain them."

Her nerves calmed a bit, and she nodded, breaking from his comforting touch and turning her gaze back to the approaching van. She pushed aside any lingering doubts. This was her first mission, and he had much more field experience than she did. She must come off like a total rookie. Just first-time jitters, nothing to worry about.

She shook her head. She knew how dedicated he was to the cause. Even before their marriage two years ago, he'd been urging her to come with him into the field. This time, she'd finally agreed. She wanted to share every part of his life, not just those weeks when he wasn't on a mission.

"Be ready," he said, and closed his eyes.

Slowly she stripped off her gloves. Despite the nip of winter in the air, her hands weren't cold. No, they were hot and getting hotter, warmed by both Michael's rising energy and the tattoos spidering down her fingers and past her wrists, throbbing like twin heartbeats. Her energy and Michael's linked and blended as they had for years. The familiarity, like a cozy fire on a snowy night, calmed her. She shoved the gloves in her pocket, along with her misgivings. If she got in over her head, Michael would take care of her. He always did.

"When they get closer, push those rocks down into the road." He indicated a bunch of boulders perched awkwardly on the mountain opposite them. They sat in a teetering pile, like a child's blocks haphazardly stacked. Strange and beautiful formations like it peppered all the deserts of the Southwest. Normally the rocks would stay exactly like that, just one more oddity on a remote New Mexico highway.

Unless something—or someone—pushed them. She blew out a long, slow breath.

"Showtime, babe." Michael flashed her that crooked smile she had always thought so charming. And though her heart still skipped a beat, for some reason his bared teeth didn't seem quite so cute this time.

Were they doing the right thing?

"I don't know about this," she whispered, then immediately wished the words back.

"Hey." He captured her gaze with his. "You know it has to be done. They're *Seers*, Faith. Their kind tried to take all the power of our homeland and enslave the rest of us. They destroyed Atlantis doing it."

"I know." How many times had she heard the story? "But that was our ancestors. Thousands of years ago."

His face settled into a grim mask. "They're still a danger." When she said nothing, he smiled again, though this time it seemed forced. "Look, we're doing this to protect ourselves, to protect our children. We're just going to take them back to camp to find out what they know." He reached out a hand to tweak her chin. "Don't chicken out on me now, babe. You can do this. Trust your training."

"All right." She sucked in a breath and let it out slowly, closing her eyes and opening to the energy around her. She was just going to block the road. Michael wasn't a zealot like some of the others. No one would get hurt.

She would make sure of it.

She reached for the power that simmered all around them, housed in the sturdy protection of stone and earth. She was a Stone Singer, able to channel and utilize the energy stored in any kind of rock, everything from gemstones to the mountains around them to the Earth's core. The power rose at her command, swelling and gathering. A hum erupted from her throat, a song unknown and unwritten, yet tuned perfectly to the vibrations of the forces rising around them. Her tattoos burned and throbbed with her heartbeat as she focused on the rocks across the way.

The power flowed easily between her hands. She had to time this perfectly. She opened her eyes and watched the van come closer; she didn't want to crush it.

A dog stuck its head out the window, tongue hanging out the side of its mouth. Her lips curved. Didn't want to crush him, either.

Then a second head poked through the window. A child. A little boy who laughed as the dog licked his face, then tugged the animal's collar to pull him back inside. Now she could see the flicker of a movie running on a DVD player, the outline of a car seat. There were children in the van.

She hesitated. The flow faltered between her hands.

What are you doing? Michael's mental voice snapped through her mind.

There are children down there.

Seer spawn. So? You know what we have to do.

"Put children in danger?" She shook her head. "I'm sorry, Michael. I'll never be ready for that."

"The Elders are counting on us. You've been training for this." He said the words with hard deliberation.

"Training, yes. But not for *this*." She held up her hands. "I don't want to take the chance of hurting those children. I don't care who their parents are."

"Then I have no choice."

Earth energy roared forth, fed like a flame fueled by gallons of gasoline, out of her control, out of her hands. Suddenly Michael's essence was in her, part of her, *taking the reins of her power from her.* She struggled against his mental invasion. Michael was an Echo, a Channeler whose talent was to augment the gifts of others. Always before, he had guided her abilities. Enhanced them. Supported her as she learned how to handle them. But now he was taking it a step further. Now he was stealing her power from her, taking control of it, leaving her helpless to watch any destruction he cared to wreak with it.

And through their joined minds, she saw the truth of his intentions. Her stomach lurched. He'd never planned to take these Seers prisoner; he had always intended to assassinate them. Wipe them from the Earth like a scourge.

Cold crept through her. Who was this man? Not the husband who'd loved her since they were teenagers. Not the gentle teacher who'd coaxed her into confidence in her abilities. She did not know *this* man.

His obsession ate at him like acid. After all the times they'd linked, how had he managed to hide this from her?

Never mind how. Just the fact that he had hidden it at all spoke volumes.

She couldn't breathe. A heaviness weighed on her chest, squeezing her breath from her lungs. A gaping hole tore open inside her, shattering her heart and sucking away the gentle flower of love she'd nurtured all these years.

He truly believed these people evil, truly thought in the depths of his warped conscience that their ancestors were responsible for taking something from him, from all Channelers and Warriors of Atlantean heritage. Truly believed they deserved to be annihilated.

And he expected her to stand there and watch him do it. Be the docile, obedient student she had always been, while he demonstrated the carnage her abilities could bring. Marrying her, training her—it had all been part of his *mission*.

Her tattoos seared like hot coals. All Stone Singers had tattoos made from ink derived from minerals. It linked them to the Earth, made them stronger Channelers. She glanced at Michael's hands, ungloved and unmarked. He was an Echo. He had no power of his own; he was forced to direct the power of others. And right now, she was letting him steal hers to commit murder.

She gathered the torn and throbbing remnants of her heart and encased it in diamond-hard stone. Any tenderness, any sorrow, any regret, got entombed behind the impenetrable walls of her mental fortress. Michael wouldn't hesitate to pounce on the slightest weakness. She knew that now, just as she knew she had a battle before her.

She hummed. Immediately the stream of energy flickered. He scowled and glanced at her. She hummed again, listening to the song born within her, releasing it into the air. Summon the energy back. Control it. Don't let him win.

The energy flickered again.

Stop!

His mental bellow rattled her nerve endings, but she would not relent. She kept singing the song, and the Earth listened as she slowly coaxed the power out of his hands and into hers. He fought her, and the stream jerked and flared and nearly came apart more than once.

The van below passed by safely, the teetering rocks solid on their perch.

Michael whirled on her. "Look what you've done!"

She struggled to hold her power in check. He'd amped it to a level she'd never experienced before. "I'm no killer."

Hands fisted, he stepped forward. "So much power at your command, and you refuse to use it."

She stepped back. "Maybe we just disagree on how I should use it."

"You're a Stone Singer. You don't get to choose."

He jerked at the energy again, but she held it fast.

"I can't let you kill those people."

He smiled, his voice softening, but the rage still simmered beneath the coaxing tone she'd heard so many times before. "Babe, I told you—"

"You lied." She fisted her pulsing hands as his eyes narrowed. "When you linked with me, I could read your thoughts, Michael. Usually you're more careful, but not this time. I know exactly what you were trying to do. And don't call me *babe*."

He stepped closer, and she retreated. She didn't like that light in his eyes, and he'd masked his thoughts.

She masked her own. She knew she'd have to leave him. She couldn't stay with him, not now. Not when she knew what he truly was.

But first she had to get to safety.

She turned her back on him and started down the path, flexing her fingers to keep the energy close, just in case. Her legs trembled, but she forced them to move forward.

"I didn't say you could leave." He grabbed her by the arm and spun her around to face him, eyes burning with unmasked fury. "What makes you think you're in charge here? You have no idea how to use your power. You're nothing without me. You're like a kid with training wheels."

"The training wheels have to come off sometime." She jerked at her arm, but his grip only tightened.

"Not until I say so." He leaned closer. "*Babe*."

"I'm leaving, Michael." She jerked at her arm again, but he hauled her closer.

"Oh, yeah? Go ahead and try it." He leaned in, his scent familiar, his demeanor a stranger. "They say sex amps our powers, but that never happened with us. And I finally figured out why." He caressed the bare fingers of her left hand. "Your wedding ring. You never wear it when you work energy."

He knew. Still, she played it off. "Any other stone is a distraction and might disrupt the flow. You know that."

"Nice try. The wedding ring's a blocker, isn't it? To keep you safe from other people's powers. All the times we've made love and never once did our powers merge. Not. Once."

"Michael, we can talk about this at home." She tugged at her hand, but he held it fast.

"And I can't help but think about where you got that ring, who made it for you. *My dad*." He shook his head. "The two of you felt you needed some sort of protection from me. From *me*!"

The edge in his voice warned her he was losing control. She couldn't predict what he'd do next. But she wasn't playing his game anymore. "Yes, your father made it to my specifications, and I sang the energy into it."

He reared back, astonished enough to let her go. "You admit it?"

"Your father told me how your mother died. It was just a precaution." At the time she'd thought Ben had been overreacting. Now she silently thanked her father-in-law for his foresight.

"My mother? She died in childbirth."

"Yes, she did."

"What's that got to do with—"

"She burned to death," Faith said. "Burst into flames. They

15

told your father that the strain of the birth must have activated your powers—"

"Which amped up hers. Wow." A slow smile crept across his face.

She recoiled. "Michael, your mother died a horrible death!"

"I did that, and I was just a baby." His grin widened.

She shouldn't have told him. He seemed too well pleased with this news that would have horrified a normal person.

"I'm all grown up now," he whispered, snagging her wrist before she could dart away. And slammed into her mind with the full force of his gift.

She screamed. He seared through her mental defenses—defenses *he* had taught her—as if they were tissue paper, boring into her mind like a white-hot laser. She yanked at her wrist, tried to avoid his relentless invasion, turned away as far as she could, straining to get free. He grabbed her long hair and jerked her face around to kiss her, plunging his tongue into her mouth with a force she'd never experienced at his hands. The physical, sexual contact flared the power between them, his ability slicing its way to the core of hers with the precision of a scalpel.

His lust for domination, to be respected, to be feared—it all polluted her like the sludge of a strip mine. He would stop at nothing to get what he so desperately craved.

She could not let him win.

She lifted her hands, her tattoos throbbing and burning with the molten power of the planet's core, and grabbed his head, the song vibrating in her throat a high-pitched, keening wail. She opened up the channel full-on and let the Earth speak.

He screamed and reared back, his eyes wide, but her hands glowed white-hot, and he could not break away. For her, it all seemed to happen at a distance. Some part of her, the spark that made her who she was, stood apart, her emotions sealed within the protection of earth and rock. Her heart felt like a hunk of ice in her chest, the confusion of emotion removed, the dispassionate power of the Earth taking over as she let the energy flow through her and into him, doing what must be done. Distantly she could feel him fighting to free himself, but the sheer strength of the force flowing through her held him in unbreakable manacles. His eyes glowed like hot emeralds, his body stiffening as she ripped through the channel he had opened and tore back what he had stolen.

He screamed. The shriek echoed off the mountains around them, and she released him, her song dying in her throat as his body crumpled to the ground.

She stood staring, her limbs trembling, as the power ebbed back through her, settling like a calm sea where moments before an ocean had raged. The dam holding back her emotions burst, and she choked on a sob, her knees giving way as she sank down beside Michael. Her husband. Her first love. She pressed shaking fingers to his neck, but she already knew, could tell by his staring eyes. He was dead.

She was a killer after all.

CHAPTER ONE

Old Town Albuquerque, New Mexico
Three years later

The bear figurine glowed in the rosy light of the setting sun streaming through the window. Faith set down the soft black pouch in which the gift had arrived, unable to take her gaze from the polished stone in her hand. Lovingly carved of caramel-colored travertine with little turquoise eyes, the fetish warmed in her palm, sharing both her body's heat and its energy. Like a whisper, the carving's song trickled into her mind, soothing and protective.

Her eyes stung with tears, and she closed her fingers around the stone figure as she absorbed the love and caring infused in the stone by its maker. Ben Wakete still worried about her, had made this to protect her, and she couldn't stop the curve of her lips. A harmony rose in her throat, a counter to the sweet song of the stone.

"Faith, are you still back there?"

Lucita's raspy voice jerked her back to her surroundings. Sucking in a shaky breath, she blinked and looked around. She was in the rear room of the shop, unpacking the newest delivery of handmade jewelry and crafts from the pueblo. Her father-in-law, Ben, had brought the box himself, smiling that mysterious smile of his and reminding her of their dinner date as he'd slipped the pouch into her hand and disappeared.

18

He'd kept her sane these last three years after Michael's death, always supportive yet letting her find her own way.

"Faith?" Lucita appeared in the doorway from the front of the shop, her gray-threaded braids and weathered, bronzed skin a testament to her mixed Spanish and Native American heritage. She took the part of Old Town merchant seriously, dressing in long skirts and a multicolored shawl for the tourists, though Faith knew darn well she wore jeans and sneakers when not at work. "Didn't you hear me, child?"

"I did. Sorry, Lucita. I was wool-gathering." She slipped the fetish into the pocket of her jeans. She knew Ben had made this for her, not to be sold in the shop. The energy he'd woven into it spoke volumes. "I'm almost done here."

Lucita snorted. "More than likely you were dazzled by whatever gorgeous things Ben brought. Well, we'll have to admire everything tomorrow. It's closing time."

"I don't mind staying a little later, Lucita."

"No, you won't. You know the rules. We close at sunset." She peered at Faith with knowing dark eyes. "You aren't going to live your life for work, child. Not while I'm breathing. A young girl like you needs to enjoy life. See friends. Go to parties." She winked. "Maybe have a little romance."

"Romance? No way." Faith gave a laugh. "You're the only friend I need, Lucita."

"Bah." Lucita waved a hand. "I'm old. You need friends your own age. Go dancing. Be happy and silly and young."

Faith shook her head. "Not interested."

Lucita pursed her lips, clearly weighing her words. "I'm going to say something, child, and then I'm going to never mention it again. When Ben asked me to give you a job, I knew you were running from heartbreak."

"Lucita—" The other woman held up a hand, and Faith fell quiet.

"Losing a husband like you did is bad, no doubt about it, but you can't let tragedy cut your life short before it's begun. Things happen, child, and then you have to live afterward."

Faith started repacking the new merchandise, unable to look Lucita in the eye. The shop owner thought her a grieving widow, and while Faith hated lying to her, the omission of certain facts kept Lucita safe. "I am living," she said. "Living it up here in the big city."

"I'm serious." Lucita shook her head. "Big city or not, working here is a job, not a calling, Faith. You can't shut yourself away. Life—and love—has a way of finding you, like it or not."

"What if I don't want to be found?"

Lucita laughed. "Good luck with that in this world. Not a day goes by you're not leaving a trail on the Internet or being tracked by the GPS in your cell phone or being caught on a traffic cam somewhere. I think the days of being able to truly hide are gone."

"Still, it would be nice." Faith paused with her hands on the flaps of the box she was about to close. "You know, if you want to head home, I can lock up. I'm meeting Ben for dinner down the street."

Lucita gave her a long, hard stare, seemed as if she wanted to say more. Then she shrugged. "All right, then. I've said my piece, and I can see you don't want to talk about it. That's fine. But I'm still your boss, and I'll be checking up to make sure you weren't here all night. You know how I feel about all work and no play." She wagged a finger. "And I have my spies."

Faith managed a grin. "I'll be gone in ten minutes, tops. I promise."

"Then I'll see you in the morning. Good night." Lucita turned away.

"Good night." Faith closed up the last of the boxes, listening to her boss's quiet steps as Lucita headed to the front of the shop, then the tinkle of the bell as the older woman left the building. The front door shut with a click of the latch, letting Faith know she was finally alone.

She stopped where she was, hands clenched on the edges of the last box, and closed her eyes, inhaling a slow, deep breath. Lucita meant well, but the older woman had no idea about the complications of Faith's true heritage. Friends? Romance? Not for her. Not as long as the Mendukati pursued their mad obsession for superiority. Not as long as they saw a Stone Singer as an important key to obtaining their goals.

She wanted no part of this war and never had. Being a Stone Singer made her a target, and she longed to disappear, where those looking to take advantage of her powers could never find her. There had to be a place, even in this world of constant surveillance.

Michael had not been the first Atlantean to try and manipulate her into using her powers for his gain, but he'd been the most clever. She'd never seen it coming, just blindly followed his lead as he "helped" her learn about her abilities, believing all the while he had her best interests at heart, that he loved her. But as he'd demonstrated on that ridge three years ago, all that had been a lie. He'd just wanted to exploit her powers for his cause. And he'd died for it.

Her heart still sank like a rock in her chest as she remembered his staring eyes.

If not for Ben, she might have gone mad that day. He'd dealt with the body, protected her from the backlash of Michael's death with her people, helped her move away from the Mendukati to the human world in Albuquerque. And he'd forgiven her, though she'd killed his only child. He knew Michael's nature. He'd tried to talk them out of getting married, but she wouldn't hear of it. So he'd made her that ring. And even after that day on the ridge, he'd continued to protect her. To watch over her as if she were his own flesh and blood.

But even he couldn't save her from the stain on her soul. The way the act had changed her. What she had become.

A murderer.

A laugh sounded from outside, and she jumped. Just tourists. Her shoulders relaxed. Normal foot traffic in Old Town. Nothing to worry about.

Shaking her head at her own edginess, she turned off the light in the back room and headed into the front. Glancing at her watch, she leaned down to get her purse from beneath the register. She was looking forward to a nice, peaceful dinner out, and maybe a beer to go with it. She'd missed Ben. Her father-in-law's trips to Albuquerque were becoming less and less frequent as he traveled to more galleries and art shows in other states to sell his work. He could certainly have sent his handmade jewelry and carved fetishes along with one of his younger cousins or nephews. But she knew the only reason he made the trip at all anymore was because he still worried about her.

The bell on the door chimed while she was still bent behind the counter. She sighed, shoved her purse back into the small cabinet, and straightened. There was almost always a last-minute tourist who stumbled upon the tiny shop at the end of the Old Town street just as she was trying to close up.

"May I help you?" she called to the woman perusing the pottery near the door. "I was just getting ready to close."

The woman turned and smiled, a baring of teeth that lent an edge to her girl-next-door, blond good looks. "Hi, Faith."

Cold swept over her. "Corinne."

"Long time, no see." Corinne sauntered toward her, hands clasped behind her back—always a dangerous sign for a lightning thrower. "Took awhile to find you."

"Didn't know I was hiding." She knew why Corinne had come. Faith glanced down at the case in front of her, at the turquoise and tiger eye and boulder opal jewelry displayed there. She could pull power slowly from the gems without being obvious about it. Hopefully Corinne, with all her flash and flare, wouldn't notice something so subtle.

Hopefully Faith wouldn't need the power to defend herself.

"Oh, come on, now. You practically fell off the Earth after Michael died." Corinne clicked her tongue. "Understandable, I guess. What was it again? Energy overload?"

"That's what they said."

Corinne flashed her a knowing look from cat-green eyes. "Occupational hazard for an Echo."

"I guess."

"I understand the whole mourning thing." Corinne waved her hand as she spoke, a swath of crackling light, like an Independence Day sparkler, trailing after the movement. "You two got married so young. First love and all that. I get having to go lick your wounds, work through the pain of watching your husband die." She paused and tilted her head, chilling and predatory in her stillness. "But, Faith. You. Didn't. Come. Back."

She bit off each word like a chunk of ice.

Faith glanced down, monitoring the flow of energy from the jewelry in the display case. Her hands trembled, but the resilience of the stones slowly hardened her resolve, and the tremors ceased. She looked Corinne in the eye. "That life—it's not for me. Never was."

"Not for you?" Sinuous as a feline, Corinne edged toward the counter. "You're a Stone Singer, Faith. What kind of life did you expect? This?" She swept her hand at the displays. "Running a gift shop for tourists? Are you kidding me?"

"I like it. It's simple." Faith kept her voice calm.

"Well, get ready for complicated. We've found the second Stone of Ekhia." Corinne laughed. "You should see your face! It's true. We found it. The third can't be far behind." She did a little twirl and stopped on a dime, her every muscle under supreme control.

Faith shook her head. "Every few years someone thinks he's found one of the missing stones, and it's always a fake."

"But we did find it! Don't you get it?" She cocked a hip. "Time to come home, Faith."

"No, Corinne." Faith braced herself, harmonies slipping into her mind as the gemstones around her hummed. "I won't help you kill anyone else."

"What is wrong with you?" Corinne surged forward, gripping the edge of the counter as she got up in Faith's face. "They're Seers," she hissed. "Greedy murderers who destroyed our homeland."

"Thousands of years ago. Who are they hurting now? No one."

Corinne narrowed her eyes, her tight mouth pulling her features taut. "And they won't be allowed to. We have to protect what's ours."

"I won't be a part of it." The song gathered in her mind, power swelling around her. "Go back to them, Corinne, and tell them to find another Stone Singer."

"There isn't one. Wei Jun died two weeks ago. You're the only one who can finish his work." She held Faith's gaze. "You're the last Stone Singer alive."

The silence stretched between them for a long moment. She knew Corinne had been sent to bring her back, willing or not. But Faith had changed in the years since she'd stood on that ridge with Michael.

She would never be used as a weapon again.

"I'm sorry you came all this way," she said, watching the rage flare in Corinne's eyes, "but you've wasted a trip. Tell the Elders I'm not going back."

"The Elders? They're not the ones you have to worry about." Corinne gave a knowing little smile. "It's Criten. He's sent Azotay for you."

Faith's blood chilled at the name. She'd heard of Azotay; who hadn't? In the island nation of Santutegi, where many refugees from Atlantis had settled, Jain Criten, their leader, ruled with equal amounts intimidation and ruthlessness. If Criten wanted something from you, or wanted you to disappear, he sent Azotay to handle it.

But she'd been with the Mendukati long enough to learn the truth about Criten. He personally commanded the forces of the Mendukati in their quest for blood vengeance against the Seers. Though he smiled for the cameras and played politics on the surface, in reality he wielded Azotay like the whip's lash Azotay had been named for, mercilessly destroying his enemies and bending others to his will with icy callousness. The merest mention of Azotay made even the most hardened mercenaries uneasy. No one dared cross Jain Criten, or if they did, they didn't live to tell about it, thanks to Azotay.

Corinne was watching her closely. Faith hoped she looked mildly interested rather than terrified. "Azotay is here, in the United States?"

"Oh, yeah, he's here. Flew in a few days ago. President Criten was ambushed by the Seers who stole the second stone. He escaped, but he had to get back to Santutegi, so he sent Azotay to get the stone back."

"I thought you said you had the second stone." Faith watched some of the glee fade from Corinne's expression.

"We know where it is. We'll get it back." She smirked and pointed at Faith, electricity crackling and flowing around her fingers, along her arm to her elbow. "And my orders are to bring Azotay the Stone Singer."

Never. Two of the three Stones of Ekhia had been missing for centuries, ever since Atlantis was destroyed. If Criten were to get his hands on all three and harness their power . . .

Well, Armageddon just wasn't a strong enough word to describe what would happen.

Her heart thundered in her chest, her blood roaring in her ears. She could not let them use her like that. They'd tried to make her a weapon before. Wei Jun was dead, so without her, they had nothing, just a bunch of rocks. It had to stay that way.

"No." Faith pulled her own simmering power with a rush, the songs of the stones around the shop whirling in her mind like a choir. Her tattoos glowed and throbbed, and she held up her hands so Corinne could see. "How smart is it, really, to threaten a Stone Singer in a shop full of stones? Leave, Corinne. While you still can."

Corinne's lips peeled back in a growl. She whirled, firing lightning blasts all around the room. Woven blankets on the walls caught fire. Pottery shattered on shelves, and jewelry in glass cases exploded. The turquoise and tiger eye and onyx in those rings and bracelets and earrings shrieked their death wails in Faith's mind, ripping through the power stream she'd summoned and flashing back on her. She staggered, bile rising at the death of the stones.

Corinne spun back to face her, advancing with an obvious rage flaring her power even hotter. The lightning coiled all the way up her arms like snakes. "Who's the smart one now? You haven't learned anything about combat, Faith. But I—" She thumped her chest with one crackling hand. "I've been training for this my whole life."

"I'm not going with you, Corinne."

"Oh, you will." The blonde leaned closer. "I've orders not to kill you, but all bets are off for Michael's daddy. You don't come, he pays."

Faith's breath caught. No way would she let them hurt Ben. Not after all he'd done to help her, both before and after Michael. He was all she had. She would die first. If she were dead, they wouldn't be able to use the stones. And they would leave Ben alone.

She slid her hand into her pocket, touched the stone bear fetish. Power surged through her body at the brief contact, borne of love and woven especially for her. Its song swelled inside her, fighting to explode.

She let it.

. . . . .

"I've dreaded this day." Ben Wakete sat with his hand curled around his beer mug and gave the other two men at the table a solemn look, the light of dusk carving shadows around his strong Native American features. "She's happy now. I don't want to ruin it for her."

Darius Montana tossed back another swallow of his bourbon, ice clinking in his tumbler. As with most humans, Ben's emotions batted at him like moths trying to get to a glass-encased flame. Being here in a big city like Albuquerque had just about tested his empathic limits. So many people, so many feelings. But there had been no choice. In order to survive this war, they had to chase down this woman.

This *Atlantean* woman. The Stone Singer.

The notion still threw him for a loop. All his life he'd believed that only his ancestors had escaped the destruction of Atlantis. A few weeks ago he'd discovered that not only were there others, there were *many* others, and not just Seers like his family. Channelers, who could manipulate energy and matter, and Warriors, who had super strength and speed and, in some cases, the ability to implant suggestions to make a person do whatever the Warrior wanted. And some of those blamed the Seers for the destruction of Atlantis. They called themselves the Mendukati and had made it their mission to murder every Seer alive.

Six weeks ago the leader of the Mendukati had broken into his family's home and tried to take them all out.

Darius took another swig of bourbon and longed for the days when life had been simple.

"Are you sure about this?" Ben asked. "She's in danger?"

Adrian Gray, a Warrior and the one who had known Ben for

years, lowered his voice. "Absolutely sure. We just got word the other Stone Singer has died. This war is starting, Ben, and Faith is right in the middle of it."

Ben let out a harsh sigh, then glanced around the restaurant and lowered his voice before continuing. "These people will stop at nothing. They're crazy. She got away once, and she wants to stay away."

His concern was genuine, the love he felt for his daughter-in-law bringing a very real lump to Darius's throat as the emotion swept over him like a gentle tide. But sharp fear peppered the swell like broken seashells, and having experienced his own encounter with the radical Atlanteans, Darius couldn't blame the guy for being scared.

"She can't stay away anymore," Gray was saying. "They've had one of the stones of power in Santutegi for centuries now, and a Stone Singer working with it to keep it balanced and charged for when the war comes. Now with the second stone that we have, and their guy dead, I don't think there's any doubt. The war is here, and they're going to come for our stone next. And Faith."

"I didn't want this for her. I've done my best to protect her."

"I know, but now you can't do it by yourself. Help us convince her to go with us." Gray held the older man's gaze. "We need to know what this stone can do, how to prepare. She's the only one who can connect with it and tell us what to expect."

Ben shook his head, the desire to help and his need to protect his family clashing like waves against the rocks. Darius took another swig of bourbon.

Gray leaned in. "If it's not us, it will be them. At least with us, you know she'll be safe. We can protect her."

We hope, Darius sent telepathically.

Gray's mouth tightened. *Not helping,* he sent back before continuing aloud. "Ben, your people and ours have been allies for centuries. Hell, you and *I* have been friends for years. I need you to trust me."

"Which is the only reason I'm even talking to you about this." Ben shoved aside his beer. "Our peoples have learned from each other and helped each other since the earliest times. My wife, Alishka, was of the Zaindari, and I lived among the Zaindari for many years, teaching the children to respect balance and the harmonies of our world. But this group . . ." Ben shook his head. "They claim to be Zaindari, but they are different. Evil."

Darius sent a question to Gray. *Zaindari?*

Gray didn't take his attention from Ben. *Guardians. It's what Atlanteans called themselves long ago.*

"She is the only one who can help us," Gray said out loud to Ben, "and by doing so, we can stop these guys. And maybe all stay alive."

Darius flicked a glance back at the older man. He was wavering; Darius could feel it. The hope that he could save his daughter-in-law when he had failed to save his own son had kept the old man going all this time.

For a second Darius's connection to Ben wavered. It came back again almost instantly, and then, before relief could take hold, it flickered again.

Darius frowned at Gray. *You using your powers to convince him?*

The other Atlantean turned to scowl at Darius. *We've never used our powers on them. They're our allies. We would not disrespect them so.*

Ben looked from one to the other. "Is something wrong?"

Gray shook his head. "Not at all."

Darius could feel that Gray was annoyed with him, and for an instant the emotions of both men clamored front and center in his senses. Then they faded, everyone's emotions faded, leaving only . . . music.

The notes swelled in his mind, not instrumental, not really verbal, as if the world itself had a voice and had raised it in song.

Even as the thought formed, the melody faded. He turned his attention back to Gray and Ben.

And his every sense exploded with an ethereal sonata that took his breath and set his heart to racing.

Where was it coming from? He looked around, but no one seemed to even notice them—well, except for one hungry-eyed waitress near the bar. One quick glimpse into her man-eating heart told him she was not the source of the music.

Where the heck was it coming from?

Something wrong? Gray sent the question telepathically, though anyone watching would think he was focused on what Ben was saying.

I don't know yet. Darius got to his feet and grabbed his cane where it leaned against an empty chair. Ben stopped talking, and both men looked at him with inquiring expressions.

"I need some air," Darius said. "I'll be right back." Without waiting for a response, he headed for the door. As he limped through the restaurant, he could sense the waitress's gaze on him. Her sexual interest faded, replaced first by disappointment as his injuries became obvious, then pity. He looked straight at her. She glanced away.

They always did.

His lips twisted. *Yeah, don't stare at the cripple.* Even his former fiancée hadn't been able to look at him at the end. He left the restaurant, lured by a siren song apparently only he could hear.

． ． ． ． ．

Corinne shot lightning in Faith's direction, but the bolts flew wild, shattering more pottery. Faith didn't even flinch. Most Atlanteans could not use their powers on one another; they just didn't work. As far as she knew the only exception was an Echo like Michael, a Channeler whose ability was to enhance the powers of others.

So Corinne couldn't electrocute her, but she could certainly use the lightning to set the store on fire or bring the roof down on Faith's head. To that end, Faith used the energy she had pulled from the stones to reinforce her personal barrier. Corinne had always been a hothead, and control was definitely not one of her strong points.

She was, to put it simply, bat-shit crazy.

"I'm not going back, Corinne."

"It's not that simple, Faith. You can't just leave. Sure, we knew you were torn up after you killed your husband, and the Elders were giving you time to grieve. Now Wei Jun is dead, and Azotay is here." Breathing hard from temper, Corinne rounded the edge of the counter. "Time's up."

"Just leave, Corinne. You've had your hissy fit. Why don't you call it a night?"

Corinne laughed, throwing her head back in clear, maniacal glee. "You really have forgotten everything, haven't you? Do you really think I came here alone?"

Silently, Faith cursed. She *had* forgotten. The Mendukati always went on missions in pairs. "Call your pal," she said. "Let's get this out in the open."

"My thoughts exactly." Corinne propped her hip against the counter and folded her arms, blocking Faith's only exit. "I already called him."

Him. Azotay? Faith sucked in a slow breath to calm her churning stomach. No, Azotay wouldn't come himself. Rumor said he only stepped in personally in the most extreme circumstances, so it was probably someone else. Another Mendukati soldier. A Channeler like her and Corinne, or a Warrior? She'd have a shot against another Channeler, but a Warrior, blessed with super-human strength and speed, was a different story.

The bell tinkled as the door opened. Faith tensed, and Corinne looked over, her smug expression fading. "We're closed."

The man filling the doorway tilted his head, his stylishly cut, long brown hair just sweeping his massive shoulders. Handsome in a chiseled-cheekbones-sexy-mouth kind of way, he had tempered being too pretty with a rakish-looking mustache and goatee. His casual khakis and the navy blue polo shirt hugging his broad chest tagged him as a tourist, a well-to-do one based on the pricey watch on his wrist. Any other time Faith would have admired the view, but not with Corinne hair-triggered to do some damage.

"You do know the place is on fire, right?" he said.

"It's under control," Corinne said. She flexed her fingers, lightning rippling around her hands behind the counter.

Corinne, don't. Faith sent the thought telepathically. *He's just a tourist.*

A tourist in the wrong place at the wrong time.

"Let me help you." The man sent Faith a steady look, his eyes a stunning blue against his olive complexion, his smile coaxing. "I couldn't call myself a gentleman if I left ladies in distress."

"It's all right," Faith said. "We're leaving." *Just go,* she pleaded in her thoughts. *Get out of here before Corinne decides to toast you.*

She might be surprised.

The decidedly masculine voice in her mind made her gasp.

Corinne narrowed her eyes. "You know this guy, Faith?"

Slowly Faith shook her head. "No." Blue eyes. Brilliant, topaz-blue eyes, and he could hear her thoughts.

Seer. Had to be. She'd never seen one up close before.

She spoke directly to him. *Go, Seer. She'll kill you.*

A shadow appeared behind the Seer. Corinne smiled.

"Look out!" Faith cried just as Corinne's partner shoved the Seer into the shop. The Seer stumbled and caught himself on a display rack, and for the first time Faith noticed his cane as it clattered to the floor. Corinne's partner followed him in, shutting the door behind him.

"We don't have time for this," Corinne snapped. "Take her, Erok, and I'll clean up here."

Erok. Faith remembered him from the Atlantean orphan camp where she'd grown up. He'd come into his impressive size early in his teens and had enjoyed terrorizing some of the younger kids before he'd been enrolled in formal combat training. His penchant for killing made him the perfect soldier for the Mendukati.

He pushed past the Seer and headed toward them, his gaze cold and black like an icy abyss. She shuddered. She'd had a close encounter with him once, caught alone in the woods when she was fifteen. She'd escaped then only because Michael had come looking for her. This time she wouldn't be so lucky.

Erok's orders didn't allow him to kill her, but she might wish he had.

The Seer slowly bent down to pick up his cane. "I'm not sure what's going on here, but we're all going to die of smoke inhalation if we don't get out of this place."

Corinne came out from behind the counter and moved past Erok toward the Seer. "It's all under control." She raised her hands, energy crackling like a live thing up to her shoulders. "Just hold still, and this won't hurt a bit." She laughed. "Wait, who am I kidding? It'll hurt . . . a lot."

With a whoop, she thrust her arms forward and fired the lightning at him.

* * * * *

The blonde was a nutcase.

Darius didn't need his empathic abilities to know the lightning lady was unhinged; the pure delight she took from his imminent demise said it all. But it also gave him something to work with.

The lightning bolts curved past him as if jerked by invisible strings, striking a display of brochures behind him. She frowned and fired again. The same thing happened. The brochures went up in flames.

"What—?" She scowled at him.

He smiled, snaring the red whorls of her anger as if they were cotton candy and he were the candy maker, weaving them into something new and bending them to his will. He sensed when she realized what was happening, when she struggled to retain control of her own emotions. But she failed. He was an empath, and this was his domain.

Now, now. This won't hurt a bit.

Her eyes widened at his telepathic taunt, then narrowed as she studied his face. He sensed her realization of what he was. Her fear. Her struggle to conquer that fear. He wove it all into the emotional cocktail he was brewing.

"*Seer,*" she hissed, and dove at him with nails extended.

Out of nowhere a song swelled in his mind, the same melody that had led him here. He fell, one arm blocking the blonde's attack. He shoved her off him and rolled to trap her beneath him, snagging her wrists as she tried again to claw his face. Then he locked his gaze with hers and shoved her emotions back at her, amping up the wrath he had captured, turning up the heat on the fear, dosing her with the mickey of emotional poison he had conjured just for her.

The music in his mind played harmony to his abilities, somehow enhancing them and honing his aim to perfect precision.

Corinne shrieked, tears spilling from her eyes as she struggled beneath him. He released her, reaching for his cane and getting to his feet as she convulsed on the floor. She tore at her hair, curling away from him, sobbing, screaming, ripping at her clothes, lost in the labyrinth of irrational rage into which he had led her.

He cut his connection. As his mind cleared, he realized the floor was vibrating, the jewelry around him rattling in its display cases. The song that had lured him here no longer whispered only in his mind; he could hear it audibly now, and it was coming from Faith.

The huge guy who'd shoved him—Erok—had Faith cornered against the cash register. But when he tried to grab her, his hand bounced back as if he'd hit a wall. Erok's frustration struck Darius in waves as the Warrior shot his fist toward her over and over again, each time looking as if he would succeed in striking her. But her defenses held, and each blow ricocheted back.

The bitter taste of Corinne's fury still lingered, and his own temper sparked as he started forward. "Hey, leave her alone."

The Warrior spared him a glance. "Back off."

"Can't do that." Darius smiled as Erok glared. "Pick on someone your own size."

The Warrior looked Darius up and down. He shook his head and smirked as he turned back to Faith. "Let me know if you see anyone who fits that description."

Please, Faith said into his mind, *just go before he realizes what you are. I can hold him.*

Don't worry, he sent back, and fired off a quick, telepathic SOS to Adrian Gray.

He awkwardly picked his way past the debris on the floor until he stood in front of the counter. "In case you haven't noticed, King Kong, you're flying solo here." He gestured toward Corinne. "Your partner took a powder."

Erok frowned at Corinne, still curled in a ball and alternately raging and weeping. "Corinne! Quit your bawling and get up."

The woman remained on the floor, lost in her private torment.

"You won't reach her," Darius said. "She's done."

The Warrior snarled and leaped over the counter with one bound, landing in front of Darius with the grace of a cat. Darius tilted his head back to keep eye contact. The guy had to be six five if he was an inch, and bloodlust exuded from his pores like potent perfume. Darius clenched his fingers around his cane, hard enough for his nails to dig into his palm. Primitive emotions like bloodlust tapped the most basic drives of the body, and for the empath who succumbed to those instincts, the urge to commit mayhem could be nearly impossible to control.

Pain helped, but Faith's song seemed to augment his ability to absorb emotion somehow, making it harder to resist the bloodlust. He shook his head to clear it, to focus.

Erok grabbed Darius by the shirtfront and jerked him off the floor so their eyes were level. "What did you do to her?"

The discomfort of his shirt pinching under his arms helped Darius resist the urge of his primitive side. Erok wanted to be feared, so he responded with insolence. "She was tense. I helped her out."

Erok roared and lifted him higher. "Tell me the truth! What did you do?"

Erok's murderous urges spiked, and Darius grabbed hold of them, twisting them and blocking their escalation. He knew it wouldn't hold for long, and killing rage was not something he wanted to send back to this guy.

He reached for Gray. *Hey, where the heck are you? I've got a homicidal Warrior here.*

Almost there, Gray responded. *Had to do some crowd control.*

Erok shoved his face close to Darius. "Answer me!"

The haunting music stopped.

"Erok," Faith said. "I told Corinne, and I'll tell you: I'm not going. Now get out of here before someone calls the cops."

"Let them." Erok shook Darius and gave him a deadly smile. "Someone will have to clean up the mess when I'm done with this one."

Faith, get out of here, Darius sent. *I've got this.*

Faith jerked, her green eyes widening. "How do you know my name?" she whispered.

Her burst of panic flooded his mind and spiked his heart-beat. *It's okay. I'm here with Ben.*

She didn't respond, though he could feel that the mention of Ben had calmed her a bit.

"What are you . . . Wait a minute." Erok glanced from Darius to Faith. "You can't be talking to me; I've known you for years. So that means—" Erok stared deep into Darius's eyes. "That means she's talking to you."

Guilty.

Erok's grip loosened at Darius's telepathic response, his shock weakening his concentration for just an instant. But he recovered quickly. "Really blue eyes and telepathy . . . You're a Seer." His mouth split in a delighted grin, perverse pleasure flooding through him and leaving a sour taste in Darius's mouth. "I've always wanted to kill a Seer with my bare hands."

"Get used to disappointment," a new voice said. Erok's head whipped around—right into Adrian Gray's fist. Erok took the punch with barely a stagger. He dropped Darius, who landed on the floor with a hard jar to his bad knee. Erok turned to face the new threat. Gray was a Warrior as big and badass as Erok was himself.

Badder, actually.

Leaving the psycho to Gray, Darius made his way over to Faith. She'd resumed her song, and he could sense her struggle to contain her fear, to maintain her defenses. She looked up as he slipped around the counter. Her green eyes stood out in stark relief to her pale face and short dark hair. Her lacy white top dipped just enough to hint at the small breasts underneath, and her jeans emphasized the delicate curve of her hips and the length of her legs. Her head didn't quite reach his shoulder, but that didn't lessen her impact to his senses.

Strong. Capable. Female. The primitive instincts roused in battle surged to the fore, sparking a dangerous desire deep inside him. He couldn't look away from her, from the curve of her ear or the sweet slope of her shoulder. Her scent entranced him. Her song fed his hunger, luring him like a siren's call. He longed to touch her, craved her like oxygen. Wanted to claim her as his woman. Fast, hard, *now*.

He frowned and gave his head a hard shake. Where had *that* thought come from?

He must still be absorbing pieces of Erok's primal emotions. How else could he explain this sudden caveman madness to possess a woman he'd only just met? Or the very real physical reaction tightening his pants in the middle of a battle?

With all his will, he tamped down the raging urges and focused on survival.

We have to get out of here. He spoke telepathically so she would hear him over the crashing of the fighting Warriors and the keening of Corinne. He took her hand.

Her song cut off on a gasp at his touch. Her pulse skittered beneath his fingers, awareness flaring as she jerked her gaze to his. For one moment, heat ripped through both of them, reflecting back on him doubled as he absorbed her emotions. She jerked her hand free. Her panic careened through his senses like a pinball headed for tilt as she pressed back against the cash register, and her wail echoed through his mind. *No. No, it's not possible!*

She was headed for a full-on meltdown. He could feel it building up in her, like a geyser about to erupt. Smoke stung his eyes and made it harder to breathe as the fire spread. They would all be in big trouble in a few more minutes if they didn't get some fresh oxygen. He had to get her out of there.

Faith. He took her chin in one hand and forced her to look at him, his fingers trembling against the urge to stroke her soft skin. *I know this is a lot for you, but you have to hold it together a few minutes more. We have to get out of here. Ben is outside waiting for us.*

She locked her gaze with his. *Ben?*

Yes, he's outside. Let's go.

She jerked free of his hold and bent to yank her purse out of the cabinet beneath the counter. Slinging it over her shoulder, she shoved past him.

Follow me.

· · · · ·

Faith raced through the storage room and out the side door into the paved alleyway alongside the store. The cool evening air embraced her, a balm to her perspiring skin and burning lungs. She inhaled deeply of the sweet, clean oxygen before she turned to face the Seer. He had hobbled out behind her, leaning heavily on his cane. He bent over, coughing, clearing his airways as she had hers.

Now that they were alone, she realized her legs were trembling. Tonight's events had shredded the safe little life she had built. Corinne and Erok tracking her down had not been entirely unexpected. But Wei Jun, dead? Azotay, here? And now him, the Seer. How had he slipped through her defenses back in the store? Even Erok hadn't been able to penetrate her Stone Shield, that protective bubble she spun from the Earth's energy, but this guy had simply reached through it like it wasn't even there. And when he'd touched her . . . Her hand still tingled from his caress. She'd never reacted to a man like that, not even Michael.

That made him dangerous—more dangerous than even the Mendukati or Criten or Azotay.

She could slip away now while he was unguarded. With his disability he wouldn't be able to keep up with her if she ran full speed and got her car from the lot next door. She could disappear. She took one tiny step back.

He looked up, those amazing blue eyes pinning her like a butterfly to a board. "Just to get things out in the open, I'm Darius

Montana. I know you're thinking about running, but I'd appreciate it if you didn't. I've already overextended myself more than I should have tonight."

She edged away another step. "Thanks for the help, but I'm fine on my own now."

"No, you're not." He straightened to his full height, a good head above hers, his broad shoulders and muscular torso an odd contrast to the presence of the cane. "Look, you and I both know that those people aren't going to stop until they get what they want from you."

"And what about you?" She slipped her hand in her jeans pocket and touched the bear Ben had carved for her. The fetish warmed her fingers and still vibrated with the melody humming in the back of her mind, like a gun cocked and loaded. "Maybe it's time you told me what *you* want from me."

CHAPTER TWO

The fire crackled behind them, smoke twisting like a serpent into the air. The streetlights cast her features into relief, but even through the falling darkness he could see her eyes, green and piercing like a cat's and just as wary. Her short dark hair emphasized her cheekbones, her skin nearly alabaster in the dim lighting. She kept her hand in her pocket, her lean, athletic body poised to run at any second. Her uncertainty pricked at him, so different from the calm he usually inspired in others. Obviously trust was not her strong point, and though she might feel cornered, she wasn't going down without a fight.

He could respect that. Admire it. And had to admit that her grit just added the cherry on top of the attraction he'd been trying to ignore since he first saw her.

And attraction was as far as it could go. Relationships weren't for him. He scratched the itch with occasional, no-strings-attached sex. But not with her, not with the Stone Singer. She was off-limits.

A couple of streets over, a siren wailed. "Guess someone finally dialed 9-1-1," he said.

"You didn't answer me. What do you want?"

"I need your help."

"My help?" Sarcasm edged her words. "I'm the last one to help anyone, pal. My place of employment is going up in smoke, and I'm pretty sure I won't have a job tomorrow. Find someone else."

"There is no one else. You're the last Stone Singer alive."

"And I intend to stay that way." She turned away.

"You could hear me out."

She laughed, a brittle sound that implied the cynicism of a survivor. "No, thanks." She started walking toward the end of the alley.

He scowled after her. His leg ached like a bitch and his back promised he would pay for his athletics inside the store later, and now she was leaving him in the dust? "Listen, lady," he called after her. "I just risked my butt to get you away from the crazies in there. That should count for something."

"Appreciate it!" She waved a hand, not even looking back as she kept walking.

He cursed under his breath and went after her, half hobbling. "They'll never leave you alone, Faith. You know that. Don't you want to be free from them?"

She spared him a glance as he caught up to her. "Of course. Which is why I'm out of here."

"Hey." He took her arm.

She jerked from his grasp. Stumbled back a step. He reached out to catch her and froze when her green-eyed gaze pierced like a blade. "Don't. Touch. Me."

He held up his hands. "Just trying to get your attention."

"You have it." Muscles tensed, she focused on him with unnerving intensity. Her defenses had slammed into place with an almost audible clang, but not before he'd caught a taste of what she was trying to hide.

She was afraid of him.

More than *you're-a-stranger-I-don't-know-you* afraid, but just a hair away from bone-deep *I'm-scared-you-might-kill-me* afraid. He'd seen the last in his volunteer work at the homeless shelter. Battered women, abused children, rape victims. That type of terror lingered on the tongue like a mouthful of coffee grounds, never forgotten.

Who had hurt her?

A familiar tune barely reached his ears but drifted loud and clear through his mind. She was gathering power to shield herself, coaxing it from the Earth. The energy transfer rippled like seductive hands over his body . . . which responded in the most inappropriate way possible.

He tamped down on the unwanted sexual urges. Residual Warrior emotions. Had to be. And even if it wasn't, he refused to jeopardize their objective by hitting on the only person who might be able to tell them anything about that mystical stone sitting at home in his family's vault.

The Stone Singer was too important to risk.

He stepped back to give her space. A loose rock sent his foot skidding, wrenching his leg at exactly the wrong angle. His knee seized up, jagged shards of pain twisting his nerves into barbed wire all the way up his spine. He muttered a curse, blinking to keep the blackness at bay, and grabbed his knee, massaging the swollen flesh around it with one hand as he tried to balance himself on his cane with the other.

The melody faded in his mind, and he glanced up at her. She watched him, still poised for flight but a little less scared. His lips twisted. Guess he didn't pose such a threat after all. Kinda hit a guy right in the ego. But if it got her to trust him, he would roll with it.

And if any of this was going to work, he needed her to trust him.

He straightened slowly, his vertebrae clacking into place like a roller coaster climbing the first incline. His leg protested, his muscles rebelling against his commands to straighten, to stand. But damned if he was going to end up flat on his back.

"I didn't know you were hurt."

"Old injury." He shrugged. "Hand-to-hand combat wasn't on my agenda this morning, and I should have known better. Some ice and anti-inflammatories will fix me right up."

She scowled, glanced from the burning store and back. "I can't leave you here. You have no idea what they're capable of."

"Actually I do. I've had my own encounters with the Mendukati."

She gave a harsh laugh. "Well then, you know exactly how dangerous they are, especially to a Seer. I know they won't kill *me*. Can't say the same for you."

"No, they won't kill you. They need you. There's a war on, Faith, and you're the key to it."

"Is that why you're here? To convince me to help the Seers?" She shook her head, holding up her hands. "No way, pal. Not taking sides. I want no part of this. I just want to be left alone."

She was going to bolt. He could sense it. "Do you think that's reasonable?"

"To not want any part of a war?"

"No, to think they'll actually leave you out of it."

She pressed her lips together. "They can't force me to do anything."

"Can't they?" He glanced back at the store. "That was just a building. What if they come after people next? What if they threaten Ben unless you do what they want?" Her expression didn't change, but he knew he'd touched a nerve. He pressed on. "We can protect both of you."

"Oh, yeah? How do you propose to do that?" She propped a hand on her hip and tilted her chin in challenge. "Can Seers make me invisible?"

"Of course not. But we can take you someplace where the Mendukati can't get to you."

"I doubt anyplace like that exists."

"It does now. Look, we've seen what they can do, and we've upped our security to deal with it." When she said nothing, he added, "We can even pay you, if that's what it takes. It's that important."

She frowned, but he could tell he'd caught her interest. "Pay me? How much?"

"Enough to disappear, create a new identity. Get off the Mendukati's radar."

"Really. And what would I have to do to—"

A charcoal gray compact skidded to a halt at the end of the alley.

Faith backed away. "Who's that?"

He started toward the vehicle. "Our ride."

The passenger's side window rolled down, and Ben stuck his head out, relief evident on his face as he waved them closer. "Faith! Come on!"

Darius felt the anxiety drain from her at the sight of her father-in-law. Ben hopped out of the car and opened the back door, gesturing to Faith.

She glanced at Darius. "We're not done talking, Seer."

He nodded, and she ran to the car and climbed into the backseat. Ben slid in beside her. Darius followed more slowly and eased himself and his cane into the passenger's side.

"Did you take him out?" he said to Gray.

"Bastard got away, but I got a couple of shots in."

Darius slammed the door. "Get us out of here."

"Your wish is my command." Gray hit the gas.

. . . . .

"Okay, Seer. Start talking." Faith reached for Ben's hand, a comfort she hadn't realized she craved until he twined his fingers with hers.

Darius met her gaze in the rearview mirror. "Like I told you, my name is Darius Montana. This is Adrian Gray. My family recently acquired one of the Stones of Ekhia."

Her heart skipped into triple time at his words, and she forced herself to breathe in and out slowly for a moment until her pulse calmed. Corinne had said something about finding a stone. Could he really have one of the three sacred stones that were the legendary power source of Atlantis? All but one had been missing for centuries.

But if it were the real deal . . .

"Are you kidding?" She gave a shrug to hide her excitement. "Every couple of years some wacko comes around claiming they have a stone. I heard someone even had one for sale online a couple of months ago. I'm sorry, but yours has to be a fake."

Darius shook his head. "I don't think so, and neither did Jain Criten. He went to great lengths to try and steal it from us just a few weeks ago."

"Criten?" Her heart pounded. "You said 'tried.' I assume he wasn't successful."

"No. We have the stone well protected."

"Where? That safe location you were talking about?"

"Do you want the job?" he countered.

"Depends. What do you want me to do?"

"We want you to talk to it or charge it or sing to it . . . whatever Stone Singers do. We need to know as much about it as you can tell us. Maybe even how to use it." He turned his head to look at her. "You in? Like I said, we'll pay you well. And we'll protect you."

Those sharp blue eyes seared through her like a laser, raising doubts. Something about him encouraged her to trust him and, strangely enough, she wanted to, even though going off with a Seer seemed the height of madness. But she'd trusted others, her own husband among them, and it had ended badly every time. "Protect me, huh? How do I know you can? The Mendukati are ruthless and powerful. They always get what they want."

"Not always," Darius said. "Last time we saw Criten, he was riding in the back of an ambulance after tangling with us."

The words should have terrified her, but instead she took comfort from his certainty. And if the stone they had was real . . .

She tried to play it cool. "You said you'd pay me. How much? I can't just vanish to parts unknown at the drop of a hat."

"Not parts unknown," Darius said. "Sedona." And then he named a dollar amount that made her blink.

Money like that meant she could disappear where the Mendukati could never find her. Buy land far away, build a house, get a new identity, hire security, or maybe even just disappear to an island in the Pacific somewhere. She tamped down the hope springing to life inside her, tried to appear composed. "I need to stop at my place and get some clothes. And Lucita—"

"No, they'll be looking for you there. We'll buy you whatever you need. Think about it," Darius said. He faced forward again and leaned his head back against the headrest. "We'll be at the airport soon."

"But—" She cut off what she was about to say when Ben squeezed her fingers.

"I can call Lucita, tell her what's happened," he said. "It's all right. These men are Zaindari, but not like the Mendukati. They need your help."

"I must be crazy," she said. "You know I never wanted any part of this war."

"They're trying to end the war. Maybe you can help them. Besides, I worry about you. The Mendukati won't stop until they get what they want, and they will kill to get it."

She shook her head. "They won't kill me. Apparently I'm the only Stone Singer alive now."

"That's even worse. To get you to cooperate, they might harm the people close to you—Lucita, me. Better you go with these men. You'll be safer there."

"And what about you? You're coming with us, right? I can't leave you alone to face them."

"Don't worry about me." Ben gave her one of his cryptic smiles. "You can't deny what you are, daughter of my heart. You sing the song of stones, and they have a stone whose song you need to hear. Go with these men to Arizona. See the stone; hear its song. Then you will know your true path."

She cast a glance at the silent men in the front seat. Darius's head lolled against the headrest as if he were sleeping, and the other kept his eyes on the road. "I don't know them."

"I do. My people and theirs have been allies for centuries, and I've known Adrian for many years." He raised their clasped hands and enclosed her one between the two of his. "Trust me in this, daughter."

"Why won't you come with us? I'm frightened for you, Stone Bear."

Tenderness swept over his expression at her childhood nickname for him. "I can't, not right now. I have a show in Santa Fe in a couple of days. I can't cancel it. You know half my yearly income comes from that show, and my family is counting on me."

"I'll split what they're paying me with you. Come with us, Ben. Please."

"A generous offer." He patted her hand, then released her. "One I cannot accept right now. You have your path, and I have mine. But if it makes you feel better, I can come visit in a week or so, after the show."

"A week or so?" Her voice rose louder than she intended, so she lowered her tone. "You expect me to be there that long?"

He shrugged. "You must stay as long as it takes to find your path."

"And if that never happens?"

"It will. I have faith in you." He grinned. "I have faith in Faith."

She rolled her eyes as her only relative chuckled at his own pun. "At least in Arizona I won't have to hear your bad jokes."

"Not true. There are always text messages."

. . . . .

After giving Faith his pitch, Darius closed his eyes and drifted into a light healing trance, focusing on easing the pain of his joints and not on the bumps in the road. He heard the murmuring voices in the backseat as if from a distance, but he didn't try to make out the words. In fact, he shielded himself from the other passengers, needing this time to recharge as much as he could. His body was trying to shut down, and he had to stay functional, at least for a while. He'd just drifted into a doze when the car came to a stop. He opened his eyes to see the airport and the small private plane waiting for them.

Gray slid out from behind the wheel and came around to open Darius's door. He extended a hand. "Let's go, old man."

"I'm younger than you are," Darius said. "I think."

"But with more wear and tear."

Gray steadied him as Darius climbed out of the car. His spine creaked like an unoiled hinge, his knee objecting as he slowly extended his leg. His nerve endings protested every movement, and he knew that once he sat down again, he might not get up for a day or two. Faith and Ben climbed out of the car and watched with concerned frowns, their worry snapping at him like whips.

"Why don't you two come on board while he gets settled?" Gray said. He held out a hand to Faith. "We haven't formally met. Adrian Gray."

She shook his hand. "Faith Karaluros. But I never actually said I would accept the job."

"You're here, aren't you? We'll talk on the plane." Gray flashed his movie star smile, and Darius could feel Faith waver. Of course she did; Gray used charm with the skill of a fencing master to get whatever he wanted. Normally it didn't bother Darius, just made him shake his head. But today—

Today he wanted to slug those perfect pearly whites right out of Gray's mouth.

The force of his reaction stunned him. He'd seen Gray smile at dozens of women, even Darius's own sister Tessa, and had never experienced even an inkling of this violent rage. What the hell was wrong with him? Had to be the pain. It must be addling his brain.

Because it sure couldn't be the woman. He wouldn't let it be.

"I'm not going with you," Ben said as Gray opened the trunk and took out two overnight bags. "I have a show in Santa Fe on Wednesday, and I need to finish up my inventory."

Gray paused. "That's a mistake, Ben. You know they'll probably come after you to get to her."

"Then I can lead them away from her."

"No." Faith laid a hand on her father-in-law's arm. "I couldn't bear it if anything happened to you. Please come with us."

Ben smiled. "I already explained why I can't. Times are hard, and my family depends on the money I make at this show. It's the biggest one of the year."

"What if I go with you?" Adrian said. "I have to get these two to safety, but I can come back by tomorrow."

Ben nodded. "I would welcome your company."

"It's a deal then. Since you're staying, would you mind taking the rental car back for me?" Gray slung Darius's duffel over his shoulder and tossed the keys to Ben.

Ben nodded as he caught them. "No problem."

"Ben." Faith reached out a hand.

"It's all right, Faith. This is what is meant to be." He leaned in and kissed her cheek. "Do you think I would let you go if I thought you were in danger from them?" he murmured in her ear. "They will protect you from the Mendukati. Let them."

"But—"

"Trust them." He stroked her cheek with his thumb before he turned to shake hands with Gray and Darius. "Keep her safe. She is my heart."

"Of course." Gray hoisted both bags and turned toward the plane. Darius followed, but Faith lingered near the car.

"Go on." Ben climbed into the driver's seat and turned the key in the ignition. "You have my number. If anything goes wrong, you can call me." With a last wave, he pulled away, leaving Faith standing there on the tarmac looking after him.

Darius paused at the bottom of the stairs. She watched the car go, her hands flexing at her sides. Then she turned toward him, raising her chin and straightening her shoulders.

"I guess I'll take the job," she said.

Though she looked ready to handle anything, her nervousness rippled through her facade, affecting Darius like lemon juice on a bleeding wound. He clenched his hand around the head of his cane. She felt a little abandoned by Ben and less than trusting toward him and Gray, and that uncertainty tangled with his physical pain until his empathic senses throbbed just as much as his body. He swayed on his feet.

Gray dropped the bags and rushed to his side, catching him by one arm before his legs collapsed out from under him.

Faith hurried over and shoved herself under Darius's other arm. Her concern wrapped around him like cotton, and he wanted to rub his face in it, like you would clean, soft sheets fresh from the dryer. He caught a whiff of some kind of floral scent from her hair as she staggered beneath his weight, her small breasts pressing into his side.

"Darius." Gray peered into his face. "Can you make it with Faith's help? Or do you need me to get you inside?"

Damned if he was going to let Gray carry him like a baby, not with Faith there.

"I can make it," he muttered through clenched teeth.

"Faith, what about you?" Gray asked. "Are you okay getting him on the plane by yourself? I can bring the bags."

"I think we're okay. Right, Darius?"

"Yeah." Darius made himself take a step with her help, just to prove to himself that he could. Luckily, her worry for him had blunted her doubts. But he still hated her seeing him this way. Some rescuer he was.

"See you on board," Gray said. He fetched the bags and jogged past them into the plane.

I thought you didn't like to be touched, Darius murmured into her mind.

She kept her eyes on the path before them. *You're leaning, not touching.*

He gasped a quick laugh, but even that hurt. He concentrated on the challenge that lay before him: putting one foot in front of the other, climbing the stairs to the plane, and getting himself into a seat before his body went on strike. He hated that he had to lean on Faith to accomplish such simple tasks, but he couldn't object to the sweet feminine curves pressed up against him.

One step at a time, he began the arduous climb to board the plane.

. . . . .

The interior of the private plane looked nothing like a passenger jet. Instead of the usual rows of cramped seats, the aircraft had four chairs the size of recliners around polished wooden tables, a couch along one wall and two flat-screen TVs hanging on either side. The decor of earth tones and leather gave a homey feel that commercial airlines never managed to convey.

Faith was sweating by the time she helped Darius into one of the plush seats on board. "This place looks like a flying living room."

He shrugged, his eyes closed as he slowly stretched out his bad leg. "It does the job. Where's Gray?"

"I think he's up with the pilot." She crouched beside his chair. "Is there something I can get for you? Water? Aspirin?"

"I need my bag." He opened his eyes, and she could see the pain he was trying to hide. "Check the overhead."

She stood and opened the compartment, yanked out the black bag Gray had put there, and dropped it in the seat beside him. "I know you said this was an old injury, but I still feel responsible."

"Don't. This wasn't your fault." He unzipped the duffel and rummaged until he pulled out a brown prescription bottle and a small, black drawstring bag.

She frowned as he shook a pill into his hand and closed the bottle. "You sure you don't want water?"

"I'm fine." He flipped the pill into his mouth and swallowed it dry. Tossing the bottle back into the duffel, he nodded his head at the seat across from him. "You should buckle up."

"Don't we have to stow the bag or something?"

He jerked the zipper closed and dropped the duffel on the floor between them. "Shove that under your seat if you're worried."

She bristled at his terse tone. "I know you're in pain," she said, grabbing the duffel and swinging it back into the overhead, "but that's no reason to be snotty." She slammed the compartment door and dropped into her own seat, pulling the ends of the seat belt to buckle it.

"Snotty?" He chuckled, but the sound had an edge to it. "I don't think I've ever been called that before."

"I'm shocked."

"I doubt that." He gave her one of those looks again, as if he could see all her secrets. And for all she knew, he could. He was a Seer, after all . . . whatever that meant.

He picked up the little drawstring bag and dumped the contents into his hand before setting the bag aside. Her senses flared, her tattoos tingling as she stared at the pentagon-shaped stone in his palm. Delicate veins of white traced paths through deep blue-green.

"Amazonite."

He nodded. "I guess a Stone Singer would know her stones on sight."

"Sometimes. Or they tell me."

"The stone tells you?"

"Stones tell me all sorts of things. It's beautiful." She leaned closer, unable to help herself. The energy of the stone hummed in the air, its melody teasing through her mind. "May I?"

He raised his brows but held out the stone. She spread her fingers above it, connecting to its essence. "You've been using it extensively. For healing? Yes, for healing." Her eyes drifted closed as the stone sang its song to her, of cold and fire, darkness and light, pain and healing. Her tattoos throbbed, the minerals in the ink synching to the rhythm of the amazonite. The stone wanted to heal, longed to heal, but its energies had been depleted over time.

Melody rose in her throat, bursting free with power and pain, death and rebirth, a keening homage to creation and destruction and everything alive. She lowered her hand and closed it around the blue-green beauty. Reaching for the Earth, she lost herself in the age and knowledge, the hot, molten core of the planet, the icy cold of the darkness. She pulled that energy forth, channeling it into the stone, hands hot and heart bursting as she sang the amazonite back to life.

· · · · ·

His hand burned, but he stayed still, rapt in the presence of the Stone Singer.

The pain in his bones and muscles existed, but seemed unimportant. Joy flooded him, coming from her, he knew. The amazonite glowed white, its energy filling spaces that had once been empty. In him, in the stone. Her song filled the cabin, haunting, compelling. He wanted to sing the notes, but they had no words and slipped from his memory as soon as he tried to capture them. He hungered to be part of this spell she was weaving; it tasted of earth and magic and everything that made her.

The engines rumbled. The plane eased forward, creeping toward the runway for takeoff. She didn't seem to notice, so caught was she by the stone. What would happen when they left the ground? Would the connection to the Earth sever? Would it lash back on her?

He closed his fingers around hers. Her flesh was feverish, her tattoos searing like brands. He could sense her consciousness, still embedded in earth and stone. He squeezed her hand and spoke her name, with his voice, with his mind. "Faith."

She opened her eyes, and he could tell part of her was yet distant, miles away and buried in the earth. Her singing trembled in the air between them. Faded. Her cloudy eyes slowly cleared to gemlike green, her fingers quivering beneath his.

And the stone glowed as if lit from within, warming their palms with healing power.

"We're taking off," he murmured. Her skin had taken on a translucence that mirrored the amazonite. He stroked a hand over the spidery tattoos on her hands, watching embers of energy sparkle along the inked lines like an electric current. His body hummed with the echoes of what she had done. Somehow she had jump-started the amazonite like a car battery, and the nearly drained stone throbbed with new, vibrant energy.

The hunk of rock wasn't the only thing throbbing.

She met his gaze, and his spit dried up. Their hearts beat together in the same rising rhythm, blood heating, awareness like a live wire between them. She licked her lips, and he focused on her mouth. The emotions she'd sparked tasted like cinnamon and bourbon, spicy and sweet, woodsy and tangy.

The intercom crackled. "Prepare for takeoff."

Faith jerked at the pilot's voice, breaking eye contact. She pressed back in her seat, her hands clutching the armrests, and stared out the window. He sensed her defenses slam down. She thought she'd broken their connection.

But her feelings flowed free, like warm water beneath ice. The attraction he'd been fighting had flared flame bright between them, touching an answering fire in her. She'd felt the chemistry between them just as he had, and knowing it existed forged a bond neither had sought. Five years ago, he might have acted on the passion that flickered between them. But now he knew that wasn't possible, not for him.

He closed his eyes and opened himself to the healing power of the newly charged stone.

· · · · ·

They called him Azotay, those who dared speak of him. The name meant "whip's lash," and it pleased him, for it summed up his existence nicely. He was the weapon of Jain Criten, a stinging and sometimes deadly reminder that Criten's will would be done no matter what the cost. As he regarded the two soldiers cowering before him in his spacious office at the Mendukati camp, he pondered their fates.

"Tell me again," he said, "why you failed to recover the Stone Singer."

"We were ambushed," stammered the one called Erok. The youth tended to emphasize his own importance in a loud and frequent manner, but had seemed competent enough—at first.

"Explain," Azotay said. The young pup had bungled badly, but Azotay did not betray his growing ire in either voice or body. Control of oneself was a path to power too often overlooked by most.

"It was Seers," the whelp spluttered. "They did something to Corinne."

Azotay glanced at the female. She'd serviced him with great enthusiasm his first night here with the Western unit. He knew well that most of her hunger had stemmed from who he was more than physical attraction, which pleased him. He stroked a hand over the carefully groomed stubble that couldn't quite hide the thick scar beneath his jawline. They'd both found release and had gone their separate ways, satisfied.

But this . . . The whimpering creature with matted hair and broken nails crouching on the floor, rocking back and forth with her arms wrapped around her bent knees, bore no resemblance to the sexually adventurous wildcat who'd left bite marks on his thigh.

He walked over to her and lifted her chin, peering into her wild eyes despite her futile struggles to smack him away. He speared both hands into her hair. "How many?" When no one answered, he turned his gaze on the cowering cub. "I said, 'how many?'"

The young man startled, paling. "Sorry, sir. I thought you were talking to Corinne."

"Hardly." With a quick twist, Azotay snapped the female's neck. She crumpled into a heap. Azotay spared her a glance, one second of regret for the waste of future raunchy sex that would never come to pass, then signaled to one of his guards to remove the body. When he turned back, the runt was, literally, shaking.

Azotay smiled, wondering if the kid would piss himself before the night was through. "Now," he said. "You were telling me about an ambush."

CHAPTER THREE

Darius hadn't said a word the rest of the flight, not when they were in the air and not when they'd climbed into the chauffeured black SUV that picked them up at the airport.

Maybe it was better that way. After she'd charged his healing stone, Faith had sunk into a light doze, recharging her own energies. She couldn't imagine what waited for her at the other end of this journey, but the money and the opportunity to finally escape the Mendukati could not be denied. Besides, Ben trusted these men, so she would go along with it. Unless they proved themselves untrustworthy.

She hoped that day would never come.

The SUV wound its way upward, the mesas of Sedona masked by the inky night, mere hulking shadows against the stars. Around them pine trees stretched to the skies, at times hiding the heavens from view. They turned left into a well-concealed driveway, passing a pair of stone pillars as they continued up the mountain. The road curved right, and suddenly iron gates blocked further progress. Their driver stopped, lowered the window, and reached through to hit a button on the speaker box outside.

"Yes?" came a disembodied voice.

"Darius Montana," the driver replied.

The gates rolled slowly, silently, open.

Faith tensed as they passed through the portals, her stomach sinking as if she were entering somewhere from which she would never return. She glanced back over her shoulder and watched the massive gates close behind them.

"Don't worry," Adrian said from beside her in the backseat. "Everything's going to be fine."

She gave a rough laugh. "Then why do I feel like the fly walking into the spider's parlor?"

The Warrior's teeth flashed white in the darkness. "Could be worse."

"Says you." She caught her first glimpse of the house, well-lit from the tall lamps around the circular driveway. "Wow."

The place was enormous, with what looked like a multi-car garage and a fountain that ran even this late in the day, clever lighting changing the water's color from blue to pink to green like something out of a Disney movie. The luxury of a running fountain existing here in the desert spoke of the family's wealth and status, but the house's many windows blazed with warm welcome.

The SUV pulled up in front of the door, which immediately opened. A middle-aged Hispanic woman wearing jeans and a simple, short-sleeved pink blouse stepped out, pushing a wheelchair. She wheeled it down what appeared to be a ramp cleverly concealed by shrubbery, and stopped at the edge of the driveway. As soon as the vehicle stopped moving, Adrian was out and moving to open Darius's door.

"Darius, come on. You're home, pal." He shook Darius's shoulder.

"What . . . ?" Darius stretched his legs and hissed in obvious pain. "Aw, hell."

"I've got you. Can you get out of the seat belt?"

"Yeah." Darius pushed the button and shrugged out of the harness. "I feel like I went ten rounds with the world champs of wrestling. All of them."

"You're home now. Let's get you inside."

Faith climbed out of the backseat and stood by as Adrian

helped Darius down from the high vehicle. Darius landed with a jolt, and his knee buckled. Adrian swept in, quick as lightning, and slung Darius's arm around his shoulder before the Seer hit the ground. Faith darted forward.

"No." Darius stopped her with the sheer force of his gaze. His features hardened, like the stone of the mountains around them. "I've got this."

Left with no choice, she trailed after them as Adrian helped Darius hobble the few feet needed and eased him into the chair. The sight of such a strapping man in a wheelchair, all wide shoulders and broad chest, struck her as *wrong*. When she'd met him just a couple of hours ago, he'd seemed so vital, so capable. He'd fought beside her and won. He'd rescued her, at least for the moment, from Azotay. Brought her to a temporary sanctuary.

Now he could barely move under his own power, dependent on an appliance that seemed an insult to everything he was. An old injury, he'd said. From where she stood, that injury appeared to be way worse than a simple bad knee. The grimace creasing his face every time he moved any part of his body made it clear the damage was extensive. And the fact that his home had a wheelchair standing by spoke volumes.

Their shared connection with the amazonite on the plane told her he was a proud man. It must be torment for him every time he had to use that chair. Her heart ached for him.

He jerked his head up and glared at her as if she had spoken aloud. His ferocity stole her breath, and she nearly stepped backward before she stopped herself. She wasn't going to be intimidated by him. Let him growl and scowl all he wanted; she could only imagine what it did to a man like him to be confined to a chair like that.

The woman behind him grabbed the handles of the chair. He broke the searing eye contact and glanced over his shoulder, his expression softening. "That's okay, Lupe. I've got it."

"Are you sure, Mr. Darius? I can push you."

"No, that's fine." Darius tossed Faith one more hard look before, with an expert spin, he turned the chair and wheeled himself up the ramp and into the house.

Lupe sighed before turning to them. "So stubborn, that one. Please, come inside. Mr. and Mrs. Montana are waiting."

"Faith, this is Lupe," Adrian said. "She keeps this place running with rather terrifying precision."

Lupe shook her head, a smile flirting across her lips. "And this one with his silver tongue. I'm the Montanas' housekeeper. If there's anything you need during your stay with us, just let me know."

"Thank you," Faith said.

"Come on, Faith," Adrian said, following Lupe to the front steps. "Let me introduce you to your hosts."

· · · · ·

Pity.

Darius wheeled down the hall with skillful speed, his jaw clenched, his throat tight. He'd seen it on Faith's face, felt it through his empathic link. One glance at the blasted chair and she got all gooey with sympathy, just like every other woman he'd met since the accident. Well, he wasn't a charity case. Just a couple of hours ago, he'd held his own against a crazy lightning girl and a Warrior. He'd saved their butts and gotten Faith away from the Mendukati.

Funny how she forgot that as soon as she saw the damned wheelchair.

He sped across the spacious kitchen and stopped at the sliding glass doors. He lifted a hand to the door latch, then left it there, resting his forehead against the cool glass. He hated that it hurt him, how she saw him. How any woman saw him.

Poor Darius. He was so big and strong . . . once.

He sucked in a shaky breath. It caught on the knot of emotion clogging his throat, bursting out in a harsh hiss. The sound echoed through the empty kitchen, bouncing back at him. He sat up with a jerk. Stared at his reflection in the pane of glass and the black night outside. And forced the unwanted despair back to its shadowy corner.

This was a temporary situation. He'd overtaxed himself, and even with the short-term pick-me-up of the amazonite, he needed several hours of therapy and meditation at minimum to get back on his feet. He knew what to do, had spent years learning the art of healing himself. He'd walked out of that chair once and, damn it, he'd do it again.

Opening the sliding door, he wheeled out onto the patio and headed toward the cabana by the pool.

. . . . .

Faith walked into the foyer of the house just as Darius disappeared down the hallway. She frowned after him.

"Don't worry about Mr. Darius," Lupe said, smiling at Faith. "He has his moods, but he'll be fine in a little while."

Before Faith could answer, footsteps from the opposite hall claimed her attention, and a man and woman entered the foyer. They looked to be in their fifties or early sixties, as evidenced by the silver sprinkling the man's black hair and the crinkles around his brown eyes. The woman had strands of silver in her dark hair as well, but that seemed to be the only indication of her age. She glanced at Faith with wariness in her stunning blue eyes—the same color as Darius's—and clung to the man's hand a bit more tightly than Faith would have expected. But when the woman looked at Adrian, the suspicion disappeared.

"Adrian, you're back!" She let go of the other man's hand and embraced the Warrior. "Tell me you're staying."

"Not this time." Adrian returned the woman's hug, then stepped back and held out his hand to the other man. "John."

"Adrian." They shook. "I've made some more modifications

to the estate's security systems," John said. "I'd like you to test them when you have time."

"Definitely." Adrian turned to Faith. "Allow me to introduce Faith Karaluros. She's the Stone Singer. Faith, this is Maria and John Montana, Darius's parents."

"Hello." Faith held out her hand. Maria hesitated only a moment before shaking it.

"Welcome," she said, and stepped back.

John reached out to shake hands, staring her down with an assessing gaze that made her think of a cop sizing up a suspect. "Thanks for coming," he said. "I hear you can tell us something about this stone."

She shrugged, fighting the urge to shove her hands in her pockets. "That's the hope."

"If you'll excuse me," Lupe said, "I'm going to get dinner started now that everyone is here."

"Thank you, Lupe," Maria said. The housekeeper left the foyer.

"Speaking of which, where is everyone else?" Adrian asked.

Maria's lips curved in a knowing smile. "You mean Tessa?"

"I mean Rafe."

Maria laughed. "If you say so. He and Cara are on their way down." The mirth faded from her expression as she addressed Faith. "Rafe is my other son, and Cara is his fiancée."

"Congratulations." Faith searched for something else to say. "When's the wedding?"

This time genuine amusement lit Maria's eyes. "Well, that's the question, isn't it?"

"They haven't set a date yet," John said.

"Rafe insists on completing his Soul Circle before the wedding," Maria said. "If you can't stay today, Adrian, you must come back for that." She wagged her finger. "I insist."

"I'll do my best."

"What's a Soul Circle?" Faith asked.

Maria and John exchanged a long look.

"It's a coming-of-age ceremony for Seers," Adrian offered. John sent him a sharp glare.

Faith nodded, uncertain what else to say. She could tell from the way the Montanas were acting that they were uncomfortable in her presence. She sent a thought to Adrian. *Why are they acting so strange?*

Maria's family was hunted by the Mendukati for generations, came the reply.

They know I was with the Mendukati while I was married to Michael, don't they?

Yes.

The simple answer explained everything. No wonder the Montanas watched her as though she might steal the silver. As far as they were concerned, she was a nightmare come to life, staying in their house, in their lives. All things considered, Maria was treating her with more class than Faith might, were their positions reversed.

"I was with the Mendukati for just over a year," she found herself saying. "But I left. I didn't like what they were doing."

She could tell she'd surprised them. John and Maria exchanged another glance.

"You say that now," came a new voice. A slender, blond woman clad in a white blouse and jeans emerged from the hallway where Darius had disappeared. "But how do we know you're telling the truth?"

"Tessa!" Maria gave Faith a tight smile. "Please forgive my daughter, Ms. Karaluros."

"Faith," Faith corrected.

"I'm just saying what everyone else is thinking." Tessa came to stand beside her mother, folding her arms. "What did you do to my brother?"

"Tessa, please," John said. "This situation is hard enough as it is."

"Oh, come on, Dad. Dar can barely move. He's in the chair again. He was fine when he left here." Tessa moved closer to Faith, her striking violet eyes fierce. "What did you do to him?"

"It was the Mendukati," Adrian said. "I was there. They tried to take Faith."

Tessa swung to face him, chin raised. "How do you know she didn't want to go?"

"She had no idea we were coming," Adrian said. "I don't consider Faith a threat and neither should you."

"She did something to Darius."

"I did not." Faith came forward, her own temper sparking. "Your brother helped me escape some agents who were sent to bring me back to the Mendukati, willing or not. I didn't ask him for help. In fact, once I realized he was a Seer, I begged him to leave. I didn't want them getting hold of him."

"So you say," Tessa sneered.

"So I say," Faith agreed. "Your stubborn brother wouldn't leave, and he took on a lightning thrower and a Warrior until Adrian got there."

"A lightning thrower? Come on." Tessa rolled her eyes.

"Yes, a lightning thrower," Adrian said. "A very dangerous type of Channeler."

"You're serious?" Tessa's perfect brow wrinkled as she looked from Adrian to Faith and back again.

"Very." Adrian tugged a lock of her hair. "Remember, you don't know much about the Atlantean world, princess."

She shoved his hand away. "Darius had no business getting into a fight in his condition."

"I got there as soon as I could," Adrian said. "You can't protect him forever. He's a grown man."

"Then he should know better!"

"Tessa," Maria warned. "Enough."

Footsteps sounded on the stairs. "That's Rafe and Cara," Tessa said, and turned away, hugging her arms tightly against herself.

Faith watched a dark-haired man and a fair-haired woman descend the staircase, holding hands.

"Sorry we're late!" the woman called. She wore her long, caramel-colored hair in a curly ponytail that bounced as she walked. "Rafe was practicing for the Soul Circle."

The couple reached the bottom of the steps and approached the group. As Rafe came closer, the tattoos on Faith's hands began to heat. A stone was nearby, a powerful one. But the song whispering in her mind sounded off-key, disharmonious. She glanced around the foyer but saw no stones in evidence.

"Well, well," Rafe said, extending a hand. "Adrian Gray. You bring my brother home in one piece?"

Adrian shook. "Mostly."

"Not mostly," Tessa said, coming back to the conversation. "He's in his chair again."

Rafe frowned. "What the hell did you do, Gray?"

"Not me, the Mendukati."

"And *her.*" Tessa jerked her chin toward Faith.

All gazes turned to her, and Faith froze as if she had been shoved on stage naked and ordered to sing. Rafe narrowed his eyes, the same gorgeous blue eyes shared by his mother and brother. "So you would be the Stone Singer?"

"Yes." She gathered her courage and extended her hand. "Faith Karaluros. I'm afraid we had an encounter with the Mendukati, and Darius took the brunt of it."

"Did he now?" Rafe shook her hand. "What happened?"

"Your fool brother took on a lightning thrower and a Warrior by himself," Adrian said. "Messed himself up, so he's back in the chair for the moment."

"He's holed up in his cabana with his healing stones," Tessa said. "Won't talk to anybody."

Rafe snickered. "You mean he won't talk to *you.*"

"By the time I showed up," Adrian said, "he'd neutralized

the lightning thrower and was keeping the Warrior busy until I could get there."

"He did all that, even with a bum knee and a cane?" Rafe grinned. "Way to go, big bro."

"I told him to leave," Faith said. "He wouldn't go."

"I bet not." Rafe's shoulders shook as he chuckled. Faith caught the glint of a chain around his neck, beneath his shirt. A pendant of some sort? Maybe with a stone in it?

She longed to ask, but didn't dare. They were already suspicious enough without her probing them about stones of power.

"Oh, for pity's sake." The woman with the ponytail shoved Rafe back a step with a palm to his solar plexus and extended a hand to Faith. "Hi, I'm Cara McGaffigan. I'm engaged to Chuckles over here." She scowled at Rafe. "Your brother being hurt is not a laughing matter."

Rafe rubbed his gut where she'd pushed him. "I'm laughing at Tess, not because Dar was hurt."

"You think he'll be all right?" Faith asked, trying to focus on the conversation and not the persistent cry of the stone. "I'd hate it if he was permanently injured because of me."

"Thank you for your concern," Maria said, "but we'll take care of him."

Cara smiled at her. "You look beat. Did you want a few minutes to freshen up before dinner?"

"Oh, my, *yes*." Faith winced. "But I didn't bring anything with me. These guys pretty much packed me on the plane with the clothes on my back."

"That doesn't surprise me." Cara glared at Adrian.

He held up his hands. "Hey, the bad guys were out for blood. We had to get out of town, fast."

"I have something you can borrow for tonight," Cara said. "Tomorrow we can go shopping for some clothes."

"Hold on a minute," Rafe said. "If the Mendukati are after her, you can't just jet off to the mall like nothing's wrong."

Cara whirled on her fiancé. "And what do you suggest we do? The woman can't go around naked." She pointed a finger. "And don't even think about making any kind of smart crack, pal."

Rafe came closer to catch her hand in his, opened her fingers, and dropped a kiss on her palm. "Yes, dear." Cara's face softened for a moment. Rafe pressed her fingers closed. "You hold on to that," he murmured.

His proximity to Faith left no doubt; Rafe had the discordant stone somewhere on his person.

Maria stepped forward. "Why don't I show you to your room, Faith?"

"I'll do it." Cara stepped away from Rafe with only a hint of reluctance and smiled at Faith. "I know what it's like to be the new kid around here."

Something that might have been relief swept across Maria's face. "Thank you, Cara."

"Come on, Faith." Cara swept her hand in a "follow me" gesture. "You're upstairs."

Faith turned to Adrian. "I want to thank you for your help today. And to ask you . . . well, please keep Ben safe. I'm scared for him."

He nodded. "Don't worry. I'll take good care of him."

She exhaled with relief. "Thank you."

"Who's Ben?" Tessa demanded. "Boyfriend?"

Faith narrowed her eyes at Darius's sister. "Family." Turning her back on the rude young woman, she followed Cara upstairs.

"What'd I say?" she heard Tessa grumble from below.

"Too much," Rafe replied. "As usual."

Cara said nothing until she and Faith reached the top of the curving staircase, and she led Faith down a hallway. "Don't mind Tessa," she said over her shoulder. "She's very protective of Darius."

"I got that."

"I'm fairly new here myself, but from what I've seen and what Rafe has told me, Tessa took it hard when Darius got injured. Apparently she idolized him." She stopped in front of a door halfway down the hall. "This is your room. It has its own bathroom. All the bedrooms in this palace have their own bathrooms." She opened the door and waved Faith in.

The bedroom, expertly decorated in desert tones of sage green, sandy beige, and dusky rose, boasted a queen-size bed and what promised to be a spectacular daytime view of the red rock formations of Sedona through the panoramic windows. Sturdy wooden doors to the left indicated closets, and Cara turned the knob to open a smaller door on the right, flipping on a light.

"Bathroom just has a shower, no tub, but it's big enough for a family of five." She shook her head. "The Montanas sure like to be comfortable."

"It's a lovely room." Faith set her purse on top of a low dresser. "Do you mind if I ask you something?"

"If I can answer."

"I'm sorry," Faith hurried to say. "I understand if they told you not to tell me too much—"

"No, no! That's not it." Cara gave a little laugh. "What I meant is, I'm new here myself, not just to this house but to the West in general. I'm from New Jersey and just moved out here permanently a couple of weeks ago. Still getting acclimated, so I may not know the answer to your question, that's all."

"Oh." Faith rubbed her forehead. "Maybe I'm just hypersensitive. Adrian told me the Montanas were hunted by the Mendukati for generations, and I was a member of that group for a short time. I just assumed they don't trust me much because of that."

"That's probably true," Cara said. "From what I understand, some members of Maria's family were killed by the Mendukati, including her mother. I can't imagine it's easy for her, having you here."

Faith's stomach clenched. "I had no idea. I lost my mother when I was nine. You never quite get over it."

"I lost mine in a car accident when I was in college," Cara said. "And I agree. It stays with you, no matter how much time passes."

"No wonder she doesn't want me here."

"She's cautious," Cara corrected. "She's spent the past thirty-something years protecting her family from the Mendukati. You can't blame her for being concerned now that a former member of the Mendukati is staying in their house."

"No, I can't." Faith sighed. "I wish there was someone else, but I'm the only Stone Singer alive right now. If they really do have one of the Stones of Ekhia—"

"Oh, they do." Cara's friendly face settled into sober lines. "Jain Criten himself came after it. Held me hostage and threatened to kill my stepbrother unless I gave him whatever artifacts from Atlantis the Montanas have."

A different slant to the story Corinne had told her. "Since I'm here, I assume he didn't get the stone."

"Oh, he got it. My brother had it—long story—and even though Criten got his hands on the stone, he couldn't resist coming after the Montanas. That's what did him in."

Faith frowned. "Did him in? What are you talking about? I thought Jain Criten is still alive."

"Yeah, he's alive. But he left here on a stretcher with a fractured neck. He won't be getting around under his own power for a while."

The news sent Faith reeling. Darius had mentioned an ambulance. And she remembered Corinne telling her Criten had been ambushed by Seers. More like driven back by Seers defending their home. And wounded? It didn't surprise her that Criten had hidden that little weakness from his Mendukati soldiers. If he was unable to walk or fight . . . "That's why he sent Azotay," she murmured to herself.

"Who's Azotay?"

Faith met Cara's gaze. The other woman's light brown eyes nearly matched the shade of her hair, and a kindness lived there that could never exist in a person who had seen the loss and death Faith had. She didn't want to dim that optimism. "It's probably better if I tell everyone at the same time."

"As long as you tell them. Keeping secrets is probably not a good idea, considering."

"I agree."

"Okay, then." Cara slapped her hands together. "I'll go get those clothes for you, and tomorrow we can go shopping. Dinner should be ready soon. You can just come down when you're ready." She turned toward the door.

"Cara." Faith waited until the other woman faced her. "What happened to Darius? You know, for him to end up in a wheelchair."

For an instant, she thought Cara wasn't going to tell her. "He was shot," Cara finally said. "Spine damage. He didn't walk for quite a while."

"So the wheelchair—"

"Is his," Cara confirmed. "I've never seen him use it, though. Not until today."

"Was it . . ." Faith forced the words through stiff lips. "Was it the Mendukati?"

"No." Cara gave her a gentle smile. "Plain old human with a gun. But that's another story. I'll go get those clothes now."

She left the room, shutting the door with a soft click and leaving Faith alone before she could ask about Rafe's fractured stone.

CHAPTER FOUR

Hours later, Faith entered her bedroom again, her nerves stretched to fraying. Adrian Gray had departed right away to go back to New Mexico and Ben, leaving her alone to face an awkward dinner that had been punctuated by stilted silences and halted small talk from the Montanas, and dagger glares from Tessa. Only Cara appeared easy with casual chatter, and to a lesser extent, Rafe.

Darius never showed.

What was it about that man? Why did she care if he came to dinner or not? She'd just met the guy today. Yes, he'd saved her life. So had Adrian Gray, and while the Warrior certainly deserved a second look from any female with a pulse, it was Darius who haunted her thoughts. And that was dangerous.

She glanced at the clock. Though darkness had fallen outside, it wasn't too late yet to do what she had been dreading. She let out a sigh, dug her cell phone out of her purse, and selected one of the few numbers in her contacts list. The phone began to ring on the other end of the line and was quickly picked up.

"Hello."

"Lucita?"

"Good heavens, child, it's about time you called!" The older lady's familiar voice soothed away wrinkles of anxiety. "I nearly had a heart attack when I thought you'd been caught in that fire."

Faith squeezed her eyes shut. "I'm sorry. I should have called sooner."

"That's all right. Ben called me, told me what was going on."

"Oh, good. He said he would."

"Well, he kept his word. Listen, Faith, don't you fret about what those friends of your husband's did. I'm insured."

Friends of her husband's? Accurate enough. "I still feel terrible. I want you to know I didn't go looking for this—"

"Of course you didn't! Ben told me all about it, how those troublemakers have been pestering you since Michael died. Some kind of cult wasn't it? Beats me how a levelheaded man like Ben has a son who falls into a cult, but there you go."

Faith smothered a snort. Yes, the Mendukati could certainly be considered a cult, from a certain point of view. She rolled with the story Ben had given; it was as close to the truth as any. "He told you about that?"

"Now, don't be embarrassed. Wasn't your fault your husband got mixed up in all that. Ben told me way back when he asked me about hiring you. Wanted me to know the risks, just in case."

That quickly, the tickle of humor evaporated. "I hate that you took that risk. If you hadn't hired me, they wouldn't have trashed your store. And I'm worried they might be back."

"They'd better not be." The older woman's voice caught. She cleared her throat. "I'm investing in one of those state-of-the-art security systems with cameras and all that."

"Lucita." Faith's eyes stung. "I'm so sorry. You worked so hard to build your business, and all this is because of me."

"You stop that talk right now, you hear me?" Lucita snapped. "This wasn't your fault! Did you burn up all the weavings, shatter all the pottery? Did you set my store on fire? No, you did not. This is on those cult punks who came looking for trouble. Well, they found it."

"But they targeted you because of me."

"What did I just say? I have insurance, and I'll get the store rebuilt. It's going to take some time to restock, and the paperwork's a headache I didn't need. Am I furious? Yes. Hurt to see the business I built from the ground up trashed? Yes. But unless you struck the match or broke all those pots, you better stop acting like you did. You got nothing to feel guilty about, and it's starting to tick me off."

Faith bit back another apology. "Well, I don't want to do that."

"You bet you don't. Now you let me take care of the store. What's important is that you're safe and out of the reach of these *locos*. I'm glad those friends of Ben's could put you up for a while."

"But what about you? These people aren't reasonable, Lucita, and I'm scared they might come after you. I hate that my problems are causing you so much grief."

Lucita snorted. "Child, I've seen my share of grief in my life, and this doesn't even come close. Just a bunch of idiots trying to flex their muscles, and they'll get what's coming, if there's any justice in the universe. But I appreciate that you're worried about me."

"Can't you go somewhere for a while, just for a couple of weeks? Maybe while the store is being repaired?"

"Turns out I'm overdue for a visit to my sister in Vegas. Once I get all the insurance nonsense out of the way and the construction company contracted, I'm taking a little vacation. Should be playing slots before you know it."

"Oh, good."

"I'm touched that you're worried about me, Faith, but I'm a tough old gal. I'll be fine. I've been on you to have some fun, and it looks like Heaven agrees with me. These friends of Ben's got a pool?"

Faith smiled through the tears. How like Lucita to focus on the positive. "Yes, they do."

"Any good-looking men around?"

Faith thought of Darius. "As a matter of fact."

"Well, then. Like I told you, you can't hide forever. Life has a way of finding you. Guess it did."

"It's not like that—"

Lucita snickered. "Not yet, but I have hope. Now why are you on the phone blathering with an old woman when there are handsome men to flirt with? Get on with you, and don't let me down. I expect you to have some good stories when I see you again."

Faith swiped her damp eyes with the back of her hand. "Okay, if anything exciting happens, I'll tell you all about it."

"That's my girl. Bye now." She hung up.

Faith checked her phone to make sure the call had disconnected, then dropped it back in her bag. Why had she encouraged Lucita's fantasies about romance? Guilt? She'd only have to disappoint her later when she had to confess that nothing romantic had happened. She simply would not allow herself to form any personal attachment to Darius Montana. She would do the job he'd hired her to do, and he'd give her the money she needed to disappear. A nice, tidy business relationship.

Then why did she keep thinking about him, and in a non-businesslike way?

She dropped on the bed, staring at the ceiling as she wrestled with her persistent fascination with the man. She'd learned the hard way not to trust anyone who knew about her abilities, and it seemed that the motivations of a Seer would be doubly suspect. The fact that she was clearly an unwelcome guest in this house should only add to the list of reasons why she should be on guard. Sure, he was a good-looking man, and at first he'd seemed friendly enough. But that attitude had evaporated as soon as they'd gotten to Sedona. Or, more to the point, as soon as he'd gotten in that wheelchair.

Her heart ached as she remembered the image of him, so broad and strong, undone by a simple mobility aid. How did he stand it? The sympathy and concern of his family must grate on his male pride like sand. No wonder he'd sealed himself away.

And no wonder she couldn't stop thinking about him. His isolationist ways echoed her own.

Okay, she had to stop that line of thinking right now, before she started writing their initials in glitter on red paper hearts with doilies. Maybe they did have something in common, but that was no reason to start speculating about any kind of romantic nonsense. The one time she'd truly opened herself up to a man, she'd married him and he'd nearly killed her for her powers. Darius was a Seer. What was to prevent him from doing the same, especially now that she had moved into the lion's den? She would have to step carefully.

But as she closed her eyes, she couldn't help but wonder what he was doing in that little cabana by the pool.

. . . . .

Darius set out new healing stones, having drained the first ones. He'd learned, after nearly four years of intense practice, to always have a backup set. While his control had improved and he'd needed the healing stones less and less over the past several months, he still kept to old habits. His first attempts at these healing rituals after being discharged from the hospital had seen his injuries absorbing the energy as soon as he began directing it.

Tonight reminded him of those early days.

He settled into position in the chair, bad leg extended, good one bent at the knee, and both hands palm up on his thighs. The exertion of the fight against the Mendukati had certainly weakened his body, and he could admit he'd overextended himself. But the physical damage couldn't compete with the emotional drain on his empathic powers. Albuquerque was a big city, and while Old Town was only a small part of it, the large number of people and emotions had required all his skill to manage. Only another empath could understand how insidious emotion could be, how feelings that did not belong to you could nonetheless take hold, even direct your actions before you realized it.

Like his intense reaction to Faith. Clearly Erok's lust for battle had channeled itself into Darius's uncharacteristic sexual hunger for Faith. Why else was he so drawn to her? She had once been Mendukati, and if the fiancée who'd loved him hadn't been able to live with his injuries, how could he expect a former enemy to do it?

And where had that crazy thought come from? Why was he thinking about Faith that way at all?

He closed his eyes and let out a long, slow breath. His brief healing on the plane had served to hold him together like a field dressing on the battleground, but it was a far cry from the complete recovery he needed. Each session with fresh stones only made him stronger. Soon he would be back to normal levels—at least as normal as he ever got these days.

The warmth of the stones' power swept over him like bathwater, and he sank deeper into concentration. He'd learned to let his mind drift, to not think too much during the rituals. To allow his subconscious to go wherever it needed to go.

And it went back to Faith.

He drifted as images formed in his mind. Faith, as he'd first seen her. Lacy white top, curve-fitting jeans. He'd thought a lot about the sexy body beneath those clothes, though he knew nothing could come of it.

He stopped the idea right there. *No negativity. Just go where your mind takes you.*

His mind apparently wanted to take him to forbidden places. Resistance would cause more negativity, which would make this whole exercise futile.

He surrendered.

Lips curving with mischief, the Faith in his mind slid a finger along her collarbone and beneath the shoulder of the top, pushing it down to reveal one creamy shoulder. The top drooped, caught on her breast. Her hard nipples poked against the light cotton. He wanted to put his mouth there, dampen the material over those peaks.

She slid her fingers down her stomach, popped the snap of her jeans. His mouth dried as she shimmied them down her legs. Naked. She wasn't wearing any underwear. Her grin absolutely wicked, she stripped the shirt over her head and bent in front of him, dabbing at a bead of sweat that trickled from his temple. Her breasts bobbed in front of his face, succulent and irresistible. He leaned forward, tasted one nipple with his tongue.

Naughty. It was her voice, but her lips never moved, never changed from that seductive smile. *Let me help you.*

She picked up two of the smooth amazonite healing stones, each as big as her fist, round and polished and glowing. As soon as she touched them, the glow intensified. She slid them down her body, over her breasts and stomach and thighs. They blazed from the contact, nearly blinding him. He put up his hand to shade his eyes.

She crouched in front of him and placed the stones in his hands, holding them there palm-to-palm. Heat flooded his body, blunting the pain.

You need more. Her voice again, though she never spoke the words. She leaned forward, braced herself on his thighs to stand, straddled him. Her sex brushed his leg, the scent of a ready woman jerking his attention away from his aching muscles.

She sank down. Somehow he was naked, too, and she slid onto his hard cock as if they were two parts of the same whole, smiling that sinful smile as she began to move. His fingers clenched around the stones in his hands. They burned into his flesh, just like she did.

Leaning her head back, she began to sing.

·　·　·　·　·

Faith woke the next morning to the sun streaming in her window and a looseness in her muscles she hadn't felt in a long, long time. A smile curving her lips, she stretched, enjoying the softness of the sheets against her bare skin.

The thought stopped her cold. Bare skin? When had she lost her clothes?

She jerked back the covers. Yup, buck naked. She sat up and looked over the side of the bed. The nightshirt Cara had lent her was nowhere to be seen. She rummaged first through the pillows, then the blankets. She found the garment tangled in the sheets on the other side of the bed. Since when did she do a striptease in her sleep?

Since she started having erotic dreams about Darius Montana, that's when.

The memories of her nocturnal imaginings came rushing back. She'd been wondering what he was doing in that cabana. She'd sensed the energy of healing stones and had drifted to sleep to the lullaby of their songs. Then, apparently, her subconscious had taken over and manifested the various fantasies she'd been secretly weaving about Darius.

She dropped her face into her hands, cheeks burning as the carnal images replayed in her mind. Clearly, three years was too long for a healthy young woman to go without any kind of sex at all if healing energy could get her hot . . . and for a Seer, at that.

This had to stop. If he even invaded her dreams, no telling what could happen if she allowed herself to think of him as anything but an employer . . . or a potential threat. She'd bought into Michael's lies all those months, willfully believing whatever he told her, and look how that had ended. Her gullibility had turned her into a killer.

Even today, she could still see Michael's staring eyes.

That couldn't happen again. Better to stay neutral—businesslike—here in the lion's den. Keep alert. She had no intention of being fooled again. Or of hurting anyone else.

She glanced at the clock: 8:00 a.m. She and Cara were

supposed to meet downstairs at nine to go shopping for clothes. She slid off the bed. She had just enough time for a shower.

She'd make it a cold one.

. . . . .

Darius woke up, put on a swimsuit and a T-shirt, and made his way to the kitchen. He found his father at the kitchen table, dressed for work in his business suit and with a cup of coffee and a file folder on the table in front of him.

"Good morning," his dad said. He gave an approving look at the cane. "I see you are, literally, up and about early today."

"Yeah, I feel tons better." Darius sat down across from his father. "I'm going to swim my laps, but before I get started, why don't you tell me what you're waiting here to tell me?"

John Montana regarded his son with a half smile and took a sip of coffee. "Guess I can't hope to put one over on an empath. But you could at least pretend once in a while."

Darius leaned his cane against the table and sat back in his chair. "I used to when I was a teenager. I knew you wanted to feel like you had some kind of control over us kids."

His dad laughed. "Gee, thanks. And you're the oldest. Maybe that's why you always seemed to be the good, well-behaved child compared to your brother and sister? Inside intel?"

Darius kept his poker face and shrugged. "I have no idea what you're talking about."

"Yeah, okay. Play it that way." The senior Montana pushed the file folder across the table, his face falling into more sober lines. "You know I wasn't about to let anyone who even smelled suspicious in this house, not after what happened back in September. Especially not someone who was part of that Mendukati group."

Darius laid a hand on the file but didn't open it. "This is your background check on Faith?"

"Delivered to me early this morning."

"Look, I know you were against bringing her here, Dad, but we need her. We're getting dragged into a war, and if we have any chance at surviving it, we need every advantage we can get."

The senior Montana shrugged. "Well, if the other side wants her, then it's definitely good strategy to get her on our side first. I can live with that, as long as she doesn't betray us."

"About that. She didn't want to come at first."

His dad's brows lowered. "Is she still loyal to that other group?"

"No, it's that she doesn't want to choose any side. She wants to stay out of this thing."

"And how does she think she can do that? From what Adrian has told us, the Stone Singer is a key player in this fight."

"She doesn't want to be. I had to provide incentive."

His father narrowed his eyes. "What kind of incentive?"

"Money. And the promise we'd help her disappear after her part is over."

His father stayed silent for a long moment, then got up. "I'm getting another cup. You want one?"

"Not before I swim. Dad—"

"You know how your mother and I feel about monetary compensation for using your powers." His father poured himself another cup of coffee and reached for the sugar. "We've always been against it. We believe these gifts were created to help people, not to get rich. You may recall how angry we were at your brother for using his abilities to work as a bounty hunter in Vegas."

"Well, he had separated himself from us. He had no other marketable skills and didn't want to touch his trust fund. But, Dad, Faith is desperate. She wants nothing to do with the Mendukati. The offer I made her gives her the resources to disappear. And that's what she wants more than anything."

His father added cream and stirred his coffee. "I can't argue with her desire to avoid war, but like I said, it may be a little naïve of her to think she *can* avoid it, especially if she's the only

Stone Singer alive, as we've been told. Then again, what if this is all an act? What if it's a ploy by the Mendukati to get their hands on our stone?"

"I'd know," Darius said. "She wouldn't be able to hide that from me."

"Which is the only reason she's here. Read the file, son. Then tell me what you think."

Darius flipped open the pages of the report. Much of it was stuff he already knew about Faith. Born in New Mexico, father died when she was five, mother when she was nine. Raised in foster care. Married just under five years ago to Michael Wakete, son of Ben. Widowed three years ago.

His dad and Alishka came to stand beside Darius's chair, his dad sipping his coffee as he regarded the file over his son's shoulder. "Looks like she didn't get involved with the Mendukati until she got married, so it was a short time. Go to the last page. That's where the interesting stuff is."

Darius skipped to the last page as instructed and found himself looking at a coroner's report for Michael Wakete. "Twenty-eight years old, and his heart just stopped?"

"He died up there on that cliff with no one but Faith around. Even if we were talking about normal humans, it would seem suspicious. Atlanteans? We don't know exactly what she can do."

Darius closed the file and looked up at his father. "You think she killed him? Is that what you're saying?"

His dad shrugged. "I'm saying I don't know what happened. But you should be careful."

Darius got up and grabbed his cane. "Thanks for the warning, but like I said, Faith doesn't mean us any harm, at least none that I can sense."

"Still, be on your guard."

Darius scowled. "There's one thing you're forgetting in your little conspiracy theory: Atlantean powers don't work on other Atlanteans. Gray told us that."

"Yours does. So does your mother's."

"We're exceptions. We've always known that. There's a reason Tessa doesn't see anything about either of us, why Rafe couldn't locate us if we were lost. Both Mom and I have powers that stem from empathic abilities, and those work on everyone."

"I'm only saying be careful. You're our best defense against betrayal." His father sipped at his coffee, appearing unruffled by his son's reaction, but Darius could feel the concern he kept deep inside.

"I don't think Faith will betray us." Darius headed for the patio doors. "I'll be in the pool, just in case anyone else wants to warn me about our houseguest."

His father said nothing, but he didn't have to. Concern followed Darius outside and lingered long after he'd left his dad standing in the kitchen.

. . . . .

Thirty minutes later, showered and dressed in Cara's borrowed jeans and shirt, Faith made her way downstairs. She wandered into the kitchen, hoping for coffee, and found Lupe sitting at the informal kitchen table, writing a grocery list.

"Good morning," Faith said.

Lupe looked up and smiled. "Good morning, Miss Karaluros. Can I get you something for breakfast?"

"Coffee, if you have it," Faith said. "And please, call me Faith."

"Coffee is made early around here, Miss Faith." Lupe indicated a coffee machine on the counter. Beside it stood a stack of disposable cups with lids, a sugar bowl, and creamer. "Help yourself. There are muffins there, too, and cereal, or I can make you some eggs."

"Coffee and a muffin sound great. I didn't think anyone else would be up this early."

"Mr. Montana just left for his office, and Mr. Darius is always up with the sun." She laughed. "That one gets grumpy without his morning coffee."

Faith paused in reaching for a cup. "Darius is up?"

"Oh, yes, always this early. He's in the pool."

Faith poured her coffee and added sugar and creamer. Putting a lid on the cardboard cup, she used a napkin to grab a blueberry muffin out of the basket on the counter. Despite her efforts to resist, she found her gaze drifting toward the windows overlooking the pool.

"You can eat on the patio if you want," Lupe said. "It's a beautiful morning."

"Thank you," Faith replied, and found herself sliding open the glass door leading outside.

The brilliant Arizona sun shone in a cloudless blue sky, revealing the stunning view of flat-topped red rock mesas and craggy buttes in the distance, which had been hidden by darkness the previous night. The formations rose like monoliths from the lush green sea of juniper, oak, and pine trees that carpeted the landscape. No matter which direction she turned, the panorama took her breath away.

A splash caught her attention and she turned her gaze to the large, natural rock pool in front of her and the man swimming laps in the clear depths. He sliced through the glittering water like an arrow, his wake sending ripples across the pool. Unable to tear her eyes away, she managed to sit down at a wrought-iron table in the shade of an umbrella before her knees gave out.

Difficult to believe the guy speeding through the water was the same man who'd required a wheelchair the night before. She looked around and saw no evidence of the chair, but his cane rested against a nearby table. A dark blue towel had been tossed over a patio chair, and a pair of men's flip-flops lay kicked aside on the ground nearby.

He completed his lap and pushed off the far side of the pool, streaking toward her, tanned, muscular arms propelling him through the water toward the shallow end where she sat. He came to a stop and stood, water swirling around his waist. He shoved his long wet hair back from his face with both hands.

She'd known he had a powerful build, but the muscles rippling beneath the sun-kissed skin of his naked shoulders and chest sent a little tingle through places inside her that hadn't tingled in years. He strode toward the steps, a half-nude personification of Neptune with his dripping long hair and blue eyes that matched the sky above him. He climbed the stairs, slowly, deliberately, grasping the metal rail with one strong hand. Water whooshed over him, running down that hard body to puddle on the patio. He picked up the towel and rubbed it over his face.

Faith took the opportunity to check out the rest of him, her gaze hovering over the no-nonsense navy blue swimming trunks, clearly designed for aerodynamics and not fashion. The close cut of the bathing suit left little to the imagination, and she swallowed hard as she realized her estimations of his physique in the dream seemed to be pretty close to reality.

And her estimations had been generous.

She darted her gaze lower, touching briefly on the scars on his one knee. Clearly the injury had been traumatic. The crisscrossed white lines from surgeries stuck out like chalk marks in his dark tan, bisecting a thick starburst of a scar that could only have come from a bullet.

He slung the towel around his neck. "Do they bother you? The scars," he clarified when she didn't answer. "I usually keep them covered up, but I wasn't expecting company out here this morning."

"No, they don't bother me."

"You sure?" He turned his back and braced himself on the sturdy iron table as he slid his feet into his flip-flops. Two more puckered bullet scars marred his otherwise smooth back, one near his hip and one closer to the base of his spine. More white scars from surgeries crisscrossed the smooth, rippling muscles of his lower back.

What fortitude it must have taken to recover from such crippling injuries. What strength of character. That he had suffered and come out on the winning side only made him more attractive in her eyes.

She lifted her gaze to his face as he turned around. "I'm sure. You seem better."

"Compared to yesterday? Oh, yeah. Sorry to disappear like that, but I needed privacy for my ritual."

"I understand." She flashed another quick glance over his physique. "Seems to have worked."

"So far, so good." He scrubbed the towel over his face and goatee. "I hope you slept well last night after all the excitement. I know I did."

"Um . . . yes. Yes, I did. Sleep well, that is." She followed the play of his muscles on his chest and arms as they flexed and flowed, clenched and relaxed. "The room is very comfortable."

"Hope you had sweet dreams."

Heat surged into her face. "I don't remember."

"I did. At least I think I did." He flashed a grin at her. "It's all kind of a blur, but I woke up very relaxed. De-stressed. They say some dreams do that."

"I don't know. Like I said, I don't remember." She cleared her throat and looked down at her muffin.

· · · · ·

Darius ducked his head and rubbed the towel against his hair, hiding his face. He knew Faith was lying.

While the Seer ability to see truth or lies in another's eyes did not work on other Atlanteans, his empathic powers did. And his senses told him she'd not only remembered her dreams of last night, but was aroused by them. Aroused by *him,* right here, right now.

The knowledge kindled an answering fire in his own body.

He couldn't remember the last time a woman had felt genuine desire for him, not since before the accident, not since his fiancée, Becca. Sure, ever since Becca had broken off their engagement, there'd been women. Some. But they'd all been quick, serviceable flings to scratch a sexual itch. Most women interested in the long term took one look at his limp and scars and made a fast retreat. Even Becca. Her leaving had hurt the worst, pouring salt into some already grievous wounds. She'd loved him, he'd felt it, but she couldn't face living life with a disabled husband. She wasn't strong enough.

Last night, Faith's pity had ticked him off. The last thing he wanted was more sympathy, especially from an ex-Mendukati agent. The family had made Faith his responsibility for the length of her stay and, as a precaution against betrayal, had wrangled his promise not to tell her about his empathic abilities. Essentially, he was supposed to empathically spy on her, which stuck in his craw just a bit, though he accepted the necessity of it. It was the only way he'd been able to talk them into letting her come.

Yes, they were fighting a war, but he would do whatever was necessary to protect his family.

His father's warning from this morning rang in his ears. He didn't think Faith had cold-bloodedly killed her husband. Having tasted the crazy of a true Mendukati believer in Jain Criten, he knew Faith wasn't like the rest. Something had happened on that ridge, all right, but he didn't think it was premeditated murder. He simply did not get that vibe from her.

Last night he had felt her heart soften when she'd seen him in the wheelchair. But pity had nothing to do with the way she eyed him now. Even after she saw his scars, he only felt admiration and attraction from her. As he relished the hum of desire, he wondered what she'd dreamed about. If it was the same thing he'd dreamed about.

"Do you always forget your dreams?" Finger-combing his hair, he slung the towel around his neck again, pulled out the patio chair, and sat down at the table with her. He stretched out his bad leg, deliberately bumping her sandal-clad foot with his.

She jumped, scooting her foot away with satisfying speed. "Sometimes."

"I dreamed, but I wasn't sleeping. It was more of a meditative state." He leaned back in the chair, folding his hands behind his head and watching how her gaze followed the movement. She didn't seem to be aware of the heat in her eyes or the effect it was having on him. His bathing suit didn't hide much, and any minute his reaction to her flattering perusal could become blatantly obvious. He pulled the towel from around his neck and dried his chest and shoulders before crumpling it strategically into his lap. "So, I was thinking we could get started this morning."

"Started?"

"Yes, on the stone. Remember, the reason you're here? We could use my workroom to examine it. No one will bother us there."

"Of course. The stone." A blush swept her cheeks, and damned if the sight of that sweet pink didn't turn him on even more.

"Why don't we plan on doing that after you're done eating? I'll get dressed while you finish your breakfast."

"All right."

He leaned closer, unable to resist her little intake of breath, the swell of emotion—part alarm, part thrill—that exploded from her like tart peaches bursting on his tongue. He made her nervous, but he excited her, too, and the heady mix left him drunk with wanting. What would she do if he flirted with her? Touched her hand? Kissed her? He looked at her mouth, wondered what she would taste like.

"Faith, are you ready to go?"

The swoosh and click of the sliding glass door closing flooded his system like ice water. Darius sat back as Cara crossed the patio, her sandals scraping softly against the tile. He'd been so focused on Faith he hadn't felt Cara coming, but now her curiosity tugged at him like an insistent puppy on a leash.

"Hey there, Darius." Cara did a quick scan of his face and nodded. "You look better. And apparently in a good mood for a change."

"Yeah." Darius frowned, putting lie to her observation. "What's going on?"

"Faith and I are headed out this morning to get her some things. You guys basically grabbed her with the clothes on her back and nothing else." She glanced at her watch. "We'd better get going, Faith."

"Wow, I almost forgot. Let me get my purse." Faith popped a piece of muffin into her mouth and washed it down with a swallow of coffee, not meeting Darius's eyes.

"You can't go alone," Darius said.

"We're not," Cara assured him. "One of your dad's security guys is coming with us."

"Good."

Faith got up from the chair and finally looked at Darius. "Maybe you can show me the stone when I get back?"

"It's been waiting for centuries," he said with a shrug. "It can wait a couple more hours."

She smiled, but he could sense the uncertainty behind it. "I'll be back as soon as I can. I'm glad you're feeling better."

"Thanks."

The two women headed for the house, chatting along the way. Darius stood. Faith looked back at him, just a quick sideways peek as they went into the house, but the heat and curiosity in that glance seared him to his toes. As soon as she was out of sight, he tossed the towel on the chair, kicked off his flip-flops, and dove into the cool, bracing water.

And hoped like hell it would wake him up from any more impossible fantasies about the Stone Singer.

· · · · ·

Azotay strode into the Mendukati training camp refreshed from his hike over the nearby terrain. It was his habit to rise with Ekhia, the sun, and greet her with a meditation, followed by vigorous exercise. The Warriors of his family had always sought focus in this manner since before great Atlantis had sunk beneath the waters, and he cherished this tradition that linked him to his ancestors.

He needed focus now, for the Stone Singer had eluded the ones sent for her and taken shelter with, of all creatures, the Seers. The foolish one, Erok, had said she left willingly. But had she? What if the Seers held her captive even now? What if they wanted to use her powers on the stone they had stolen?

He had to get her back. Their very world depended on her.

He headed for his quarters. The many trees hid half the wooden cabins from view of the road, and the sun-bleached sign that creaked on ancient hooks over the gate to the compound read DIEZ REYES CAMP FOR THE GIFTED. Children dotted the landscape in every direction, Atlantean youth working with energy or sparring in a ring, all being trained in their gifts and in the doctrine of the Mendukati. His master, Jain Criten, would approve of the disciplined schedule.

"My lord!"

Azotay stopped as one of the instructors approached him, an Elder named Quillan. Like all Warriors, Quillan had dark brown eyes, but his curling hair held more gray than red these days. He taught tracking and hunting to the youngest boys, preparing them for the more advanced classes that would come later. He had lost his wife and daughter in a battle against Seers and had sworn blood vengeance—*mendeku*—until his dying breath.

"Quillan," he said by way of greeting, not slowing his pace.

He'd learned the identities and histories of all the Elders before he'd left Santutegi to come to the United States.

"My lord Azotay, we have word about the Stone Singer."

Azotay paused. "Go on."

"She has been taken to the house in Sedona, Arizona. The one where President Criten was attacked. We also believe this is where they are keeping the stone."

"I see. As I recall, this house is extremely well fortified."

"Yes, sir. And my sources report that security has been increased." Quillan scowled. "Last time, the only way they were able to get in was to use one of the Seers' people against them. And I would think they'll probably be on the lookout for that gambit again."

"Agreed." Azotay stroked his chin, traced the scar on the underside of his jaw with his thumb. "Summon the other Elders to meet in my office ten minutes from now. The Stone Singer must have a weakness we can exploit. Bring everything you have on her."

"Yes, my lord." Quillan bobbed his head. "We already know of one weakness. A father-in-law. They are very close."

"The father-in-law, is he Atlantean? Maybe we can turn him."

"No, my lord. Human."

"Even better. Capture him, bring him here." Azotay started to walk away.

"There may be a problem with that."

Azotay spun back. "What did you say?"

"The father-in-law. There may be a problem." Quillan visibly shrank as Azotay loomed over him. "Surveillance from yesterday indicates he may be protected by a Warrior."

"What Warrior would dare?"

"None of ours, certainly. We suspect he might be a member of the lost temple of Mneseus. They've been seen in this area in the past."

"Mneseus!" Azotay grabbed Quillan by his shirtfront. "Are you certain?"

"No, no, we're not, my lord." Quillan's hand hovered over Azotay's, though he clearly dared not touch him. "That's what I'm saying. It's all speculation."

Azotay hauled the other Warrior closer. "Get me facts!" Shoving Quillan aside, he stormed down the path. "My office! Ten minutes!" he shouted over his shoulder.

Mneseus. The name echoed through Azotay's mind, waking dark memories from a cold, forgotten place. A young boy. The mother he adored. The father he longed to please. And *him*, Prince Perfect.

His hands curled into fists. Mneseus. He would take pleasure in destroying the temple and everyone in it—especially the prince himself.

CHAPTER FIVE

Adrian Gray opened his eyes as he came back to himself, his mind, body, and soul at peace with the completion of his meditation. Poised on one leg, the other bent at thigh and knee, and his arms reaching toward the sky, he'd held this last position of the *orekatu* until he'd finished fully balancing his energies. He'd have to be at full strength for the coming battles.

He lowered his leg and arms, shaking out his straining muscles, and reached for the towel he'd draped over the rail of the deck. The exquisite precision required of the ritual not only worked his body but also honed his control over the tiniest of movements and enhanced his ability to remain utterly still. Despite the chill in the early morning air, sweat misted his skin. He rubbed the towel over his face, then down his bare arms and chest.

The peaceful energy of the pueblo settled over him. Whenever he came to visit a friend here, he stayed at this inn for that very reason. Not that it was silent. Beyond the inn, he could hear the high-pitched calls of children as they headed for the school bus stop. The crunch of tires on dirt roads. Birds calling. The barks of the many dogs running loose throughout the pueblo. Absent were the intrusive sounds of the urban city: no car horns, shrilling cell phones, or street vendors. Delicious smells came from the main building of the inn, where breakfast for the inn's guests was being prepared.

His stomach growled. Blue corn pancakes, the inn's specialty, sounded really good about now.

He slung the towel over his shoulder. Footsteps sounded from the courtyard below him. He froze, listening intently. Though there were three other rooms that had access to the wooden deck of the inn, no one had disturbed him thus far. The deck was on the second floor and was surrounded by trees, so it offered some privacy, but it could also hide anyone sneaking up on him. He stayed still until he heard the murmurs of a male and a female voice, the squeal of a child. One stealthy step got him to the rail, where he was able to peer through the trees to the courtyard. The family of three walked along the pebbled path toward the main house, where breakfast awaited.

He smiled. No threat there. He headed back to his room, a shower and pancakes on his mind. His cell phone was ringing as he entered the room. He reached for it, but it fell silent. He checked the missed calls list, noted the familiar number, and hit redial, mentally moving blue corn pancakes further down on this morning's to-do list. If his superior at the temple was calling him, it had to be important.

The call was answered immediately. "Hey, Adrian. I was just leaving you a message."

"Now you won't have to. What's up, Von?"

Von's voice grew heavy. "A family of Seers was killed yesterday."

"Who?" Adrian sat on the edge of his bed. "Not the Montanas?"

"No, a relative. A cousin of Maria Montana's, Lorinda Torrez."

"What happened?"

"She and her husband were taking their twin boys out for pizza after basketball practice when their van exploded."

Adrian hissed a curse. "Are they sure it wasn't just mechanical failure?"

"The van was brand new, and witnesses reported smelling sulfur."

"Flame Walker. Damn it."

"My thoughts exactly," Von said. "The Mendukati have been training Flame Walkers as assassins for years. Where are you now? Still in Arizona?"

Adrian got up and began to walk around the room, cooling down his recently worked muscles. "No, New Mexico. The Stone Singer is safe with the Montanas in Sedona. I'm guarding Ben Wakete."

"Wakete? The father-in-law?"

"There's a strong possibility the Mendukati might leverage him to pressure Faith into helping them. I'm going to make sure that doesn't happen."

"Glad you're on that," Von said. "Because guess who's in town? Azotay."

Adrian halted. "Where?"

"Your neck of the woods. New Mexico area."

"Hell, Von, you got any more good news for me? Maybe an asteroid is going to hit the planet?"

"Not that I know of. Just keep your eyes open, Adrian. You know how slippery that bastard is."

"I've heard. Thanks for the heads-up, Von. I'll keep you posted." Adrian ended the call. Azotay's presence on the heels of the death of a Stone Singer and the reemergence of a new Stone suddenly made sense—in a sick, apocalyptic way. The Mendukati were upping their game.

He scrolled through the contacts on his phone. Finding the number he sought, he tapped to call it and brought the phone to his ear, listening to the ringing on the other end.

And braced himself to tell Maria Montana that another member of her family had been murdered.

· · · · ·

A couple of hours after Faith left with Cara, Darius entered the family *tenplu* on the top floor of the house. The Montana temple area had been constructed in the traditional Atlantean style with a greenhouse roof to let the sun in and—his mother's touch—bright, flowering plants thriving in boxes on either side of the large room. To his left lay a door that led out to the rooftop garden where his mother grew herbs and where members of his family often went to meditate, soaking in the rays of blessed Ekhia, the sun, to recharge their powers. Before him stretched an expanse of sand dividing the room. Seven short marble pillars lined a path through the sand, each one holding a colored stone signifying one of the chakras. On the other side of the sandpit, embedded in the far wall, stood the door to the vault.

Darius set off across the sand, a hum of power sweeping him like some kind of sensor as he passed the pillars. The Agrippa Boundary, a mystical energy field that guarded the vault against intruders, recognized him as both a Seer and a Montana and allowed him to pass unmolested.

Anyone not recognized by the Agrippa Boundary would experience a nasty surprise as the energy of the standing stones defended the vault, usually sending the intruder flying with a hard jolt of energy. Most did not rise again immediately.

Darius got to the other side without incident. He entered the code into the keypad of the first security measure and inserted his hand into the reader. When a green light flashed, he looked into the retina scanner. A flash of red into his eyes, another green light, and the vault lock clicked.

"Darius."

He paused in pulling open the heavy door as his mother crossed the sand. Each of the seven stones flashed as she walked by, as if recognizing her. Which made sense, since she had tuned and set the Agrippa Boundary herself. "Hi, Mom."

She stopped beside him and glanced at the partially open door. "You're getting the stone."

"Cara called and said they were on their way back from

shopping, so I thought I'd get it ready." He waited, sensing her turmoil. "Is that okay?"

"Yes. No. I don't know." She rubbed her forehead. "I'm sorry. I've had some upsetting news."

He stepped away from the door, her distress swamping him. "What happened?"

"Adrian called. He said—" She took a deep breath. "He said a cousin of mine was killed."

"A cousin? I didn't think you had any more family." A sudden burst of guilt from her brought understanding. "But you do."

"Of course I do." She raised damp blue eyes to his. "Years ago my family made the decision to scatter and not contact each other as a way to throw the Mendukati off the scent. It worked, mostly. I married your father, and when you were born, when we realized you were a Seer, he built this house to protect us all." She stared somewhere over his shoulder, clearly reliving some old memory. From the burned-coffee-grounds-and-chalk taste of her emotions, he knew the memory was a bad one. "You have no idea what it was like, being hunted by them. Homes burned, battles fought, family killed. I didn't want you to know."

He bit back bitter words. He'd forgiven her, mostly, for the secret she'd kept from him and his brother and sister until just a few weeks ago, about the Mendukati and their mission to murder Seers. But now and again, that hurt still flared. "I know you were trying to protect us, Mom, but I hope you can see now that ignorance wasn't the way."

"Yes, yes, we've been through this. And you're right, I do see that now. At least if you know the enemy exists, you can watch for them."

"Exactly." He came to wrap his arms around her. "I'm sorry about your cousin. What was her name?"

"Lorinda." She clung to him for a moment, then stepped back, brushing the tears from her face. "We played together as children, but I hadn't seen or heard from her in over thirty years. She was a little younger than I was. She had a husband, children. They were all killed in the same car fire."

"And they're certain it wasn't just a random accident?"

"Adrian seemed sure." She sighed. "I guess this really is war."

"That nut Criten breaking into our house and trying to kill everyone back in September kind of made that clear for me."

His wry tone brought a weak smile to her lips that immediately disappeared. "You're right. I didn't want it to be true. I wanted to believe that time of my life was over. But maybe it will never be over."

"It will be if we stop them. If we can figure out how to use this stone against them."

"That's why we need the Stone Singer. I understand." She laid a hand on his arm. "I was on my way to talk to you when I got Adrian's call. I have something to say, but it's difficult, so I need you to listen."

Her inner conflict batted at him like tiny fists, a whirlwind of fear and hope on top of her grief. He let go of the door. "This is about more than your cousin, isn't it?"

"Yes. There's something else I need to tell you, but I don't know how."

"Mom?"

She turned to face him but didn't come closer. "You were very angry with me, all of you were, for keeping the danger of the Mendukati a secret from you all these years. I don't want you to think I'm keeping things from you again."

"Keeping what things?" Her turmoil increased, splashing his empathic senses like hot vinegar. "Mom, you're scaring me. What else haven't you told us?"

"Not us. You." She gripped her pendant in her hand, the symbol of the *apaiz nagusi*, the high priestess of the Seers. "You know my primary power."

"Yes, matchmaking." The hesitation in her eyes and her trepidation suddenly made sense. "No. Not me."

"Do you think I want this?" she snapped. "Matchmaking is very much like empathy, and I have no more choice in what is revealed to me than you do when the emotions of others are revealed to you. And when it involves one of my own children—"

"No, I'm not buying it." He turned back to the door, started to pull it open, then stopped again. "Becca loved me. I know she did. You can't fool an empath."

"You're right," his mother agreed. "Even though she was not your destined mate, she would have made you happy."

"Destined mate." He gave a harsh laugh. "She left because she couldn't handle being married to a cripple, and if *she* couldn't hack it, the woman who truly loved me, then who could? Who could possibly be my so-called destined mate, especially now?"

"Faith."

"What?" He literally fell back a step. "I've known the woman for twenty-four hours. And there's a whole bunch of reasons why it would be stupid to get involved with her."

"I see what I see," his mother snapped. "Do you think I want this for my son? That he should be matched with a member of the group who murdered my mother? Killed my cousin and her children? I wanted to tell you, to warn you, so you could be careful."

"Careful. Everyone's telling me to be careful." His mind whirled with the implications of what she was telling him. His mother was never wrong about these things, so if she said Faith was meant for him, then she was, at least on a certain level. "You'd think your power would take into account things such as she used to work for the enemy of the Seers."

She threw up her hands. "It is what it is. Just be careful around her. Maybe it will all work out."

"You don't sound too confident about that."

She sighed. "I hope I am wrong, that she truly means us no harm. But it's hard to forget."

He reached out to squeeze her hand. "I know, and I'll be careful."

"That's all I can ask. Perhaps you will know more after you've seen her work with the stone. How it reacts to her may tell us whether she can be trusted or not. Either way, I don't want her at Rafe's Soul Circle on Saturday."

"Wait, what? Saturday? Rafe's walking his Soul Circle *now*? Surely he's not ready yet."

"When I told him of the murder of my cousin and her family, he grew very quiet. Very grim. I've never seen him like this before. He said that we all need to be at the top of our games to beat these people, that this was necessary." She shook her head. "I tried to talk him out of it, but he's determined. He said that if he's not ready now, he never will be. He won't be satisfied until he completes the ritual, no matter the risk."

"And the risk in this case is him losing himself to his powers completely, ceasing to be Rafe." Darius frowned. Rafe's abilities included channeling a being called the Hunter, a primeval fighter who took over Rafe's body and could wreak carnage if given the chance. Rafe himself seemed to disappear when the Hunter fully manifested, making it even worse on his brother when he came back to himself. The Hunter held the key to Rafe's ability to find anyone, anywhere.

And Darius's injuries were the direct result of one of the Hunter's rampages.

"He says he has better control of it now since he formed the mating bond with Cara," his mother was saying. "But I don't know. I'm afraid for him. You saw what happened when Jain Criten tried to kill all of us right in this very room."

"Rafe's Hunter stopped him," Darius said.

"With the help of his mating bond with Cara. It took a lot

out of both of them, remember? Your brother was in the hospital for days."

Her fear washed over him, and he pulled her close for another hug, then leaned back to look into her eyes. "Mom, stop borrowing trouble. Rafe does have Cara to help him. And if *I'm* willing to trust him—"

"I just wish he would take more time, practice. Hone his abilities. But he's sworn to master this, to be able to defend us. I don't want him to rush. It could be dangerous." She shook her head again, turned away from him and paced a couple of steps.

"This war is speeding up a lot of things," Darius said. "And your cousin's murder, that brings it closer to home. Try to be positive. What if Rafe is successful and achieves total control over his powers? That could only help us."

"I know, I know. I will try to visualize that outcome. Perhaps it will help. Now." She waved a dismissive hand. "I don't want to think about any of it anymore." Her tension eased enough that he felt it as she shored up her emotional control. "Now let's get that Stone. I never tire of seeing it."

· · · · ·

Close to noon, Faith came downstairs after stowing her new clothes in her room. Cara had insisted on paying, their security escort watching every move but saying nothing. Faith had protested, but Cara had stated that since Faith was there to help the family and had arrived with nothing through no fault of her own, the Montanas felt it was only right they provide her with a few necessities as part of her payment for the job she was there to do. They'd given Cara money to do just that, and nothing Faith said would dissuade her.

Besides, if Faith tried to use her credit card or get cash out of an ATM, she might leave a trail for the Mendukati to find her. So she had acquiesced. In Albuquerque Darius had mentioned buying her whatever she needed, and it was good to see he kept his word, at least in this.

She went through the empty kitchen and out the sliding doors to the patio, then stopped. Though it was mid-October, it had been unseasonably warm this week, and Tessa had apparently decided to take advantage. She lay stretched out on a lounge chair near the pool, wearing sunglasses and a white bikini that accented her athletic build and already amazing tan. She appeared to be sleeping, and Faith was content to leave her that way. She started toward the cabana, which she had been told was Darius's workroom.

"Faith."

Faith stopped and looked over at Tessa, who hadn't moved. Her bronzed skin gleamed with oil or sunblock that made her appear gilded in gold, like some ancient statue. Faith ignored the twinge of jealousy only the very fair felt when confronted with those who could brown instead of burn. "Nice tan," she said, since Tessa had thus far been civil.

"Thank you." Tessa leaned up on one elbow and pushed her sunglasses on top of her head with the other hand. "Heard you went shopping."

"I had nothing to wear. They didn't give me time to pack."

"Convenient. So you get a new wardrobe out of this arrangement, too."

"Part of the deal."

"I bet." Tessa's tone said otherwise.

Faith strode up to the lounge chair. "Look, I was pretty happy with my life in Albuquerque until your brother showed up. I didn't ask for this."

"But you took it." Tessa swung out of the lounge chair and landed on her feet, inches away from Faith. "You saw an advantage—and maybe you already knew who my brother was just from his name—and jumped right on it."

"You bet I did." Faith got a hint of satisfaction from the

surprise on Tessa's face. "The Mendukati were after me. They were going to drag me back in whether I wanted it or not. So when your brother offered me a way out, yeah, I took it."

"A lucrative way." Tessa's lip curled.

"You bet your ass," Faith shot back. "I won't apologize for it. I need that money, and if the work I can do here takes a bite out of the Mendukati's power, all the better."

"Of course you would do it for money," Tessa said. "What else can be expected from someone like you?"

"What's that supposed to mean?"

"Faith." Darius's voice had both women turning. He stood outside the cabana, leaning on his cane and frowning. "You ready?"

"Yes." Faith slanted Tessa a look and walked away from the other woman toward Darius.

Darius addressed his sister. "Back off, Tess."

"You know what she is," Tessa shot back.

"Yes," Darius said. "I do. Better than you do." As Faith got to him, he indicated the open door to the cabana. "Sorry about Tess," he murmured.

She paused in the doorway and replied in the same low voice. "It's fine. She doesn't trust me. I get it."

"It's not just that. Our family lost some more members yesterday."

Faith's breath froze in her lungs. More murders? The Mendukati? Please, not that. But her gut churned. "I'm so sorry, Darius. Was it—?"

"Yes, they think it was Mendukati. I'd rather not talk about it." The words came as if chipped from ice.

"Okay." She didn't know what else to say. She, more than any, knew how murder changed people.

"As for Tess, she knows why you're here and how important it is."

She nodded as he neatly shelved the topic of murder. "Well, I can't blame her for wanting to protect you."

"I don't need people looking out for me. I can take care of myself."

"Yes, you can. I saw that for myself yesterday. But you also overdid it, didn't you? That probably scared her."

His mouth tightened. "I'm fine." Again he waved her into the cabana. She walked in and he followed, shutting the glass door behind them.

The instant she fully entered the room, the residual power hit her. She stood completely still as he closed the blinds on the door and limped around the cabana, doing the same to the windows. Whispers of stone song lingered in the air, vibrating like a guitar string that had just been plucked. Her tattoos tingled. He'd performed some powerful stone energy here, and recently, too. His healing ritual, no doubt.

This was why she was here, to do a job, to work with stones of power. Not to become emotionally involved with the Seers—no matter how much her heart ached for them.

Darius closed the last blind, sealing them into the dimly lit room. Sunshine eked in around the edges of the window coverings, but no one could see in, which Faith assumed was the point. As cabanas went, this one looked to be top class, with comfy couches, tables, and a bar with a mini fridge behind it. She stepped farther into the room, then stopped when she saw the armless chair and burned-down candles in a cleared section of the floor at the far end, beyond the sofas. Beside the chair and candles rested a wooden chest. *Just like in her dream*. If she opened the chest, would she find the amazonite healing stones she'd imagined? The ones she'd rubbed against her body in the dream before she—

"That's where I do the healing ritual," Darius said, coming up beside her. Her skin prickled at his nearness, her senses painfully alive. Her tattoos reacted to the remaining hints of energy quivering around them, and her pulse to the scent of him, the warmth of him. The images from her dream slipped into her mind, the two of them naked, joining in passion and power. Her head spun. It seemed so real. But it couldn't be.

Could it?

"So." She turned away from the view of the chair and candles and gave him a smile that felt as falsely bright as it probably looked. "Where's this stone?"

He gave her a puzzled look. "Right here." He walked to a tall storage cabinet. Faith let her gaze drift down his body as he walked away. Broad shoulders tapering to slim hips and tight buttocks. Even his limp couldn't take away from the inherent sexiness of the man. He leaned his cane against the cabinet and opened one door, the muscles of his back and shoulders flexing with the movement. She remembered the pool, the way he'd sliced through the water with such control.

Remembered the dream, his strong hands guiding her movements as she rode him. Every female fiber in her body softened like melting caramel.

He set a small wooden box down on a table, raising those amazing blue eyes to meet hers. "You okay?"

"Yes." She made herself inhale, made herself approach, though she shook with the desire to touch him. This was not the time, not the place.

What was she thinking? There could not *be* a time or place, not for that. Not for them. This was business. Her body disagreed with her brain, but she ignored it. She'd trusted a man before, and he'd made her a murderer. Darius had lost family. There had been enough bloodshed, for both of them. "So this is one of the Stones of Ekhia?"

"You tell me." He opened the lid.

Power. The stone *thrummed*, its song compelling yet unintelligible. Faith staggered back, her tattoos flaring like fresh brands. She could barely breathe. Could barely understand the notes and melodies fighting for her attention, cramming into her mind like too many people in an elevator. The dull roar made her want to cover her ears, but she knew that would do no good. The music wasn't audible; it was mental.

Darius shut the box, but the connection had been made. The stone hummed in the back of her mind, no longer silent now that it had found its path. "Faith, are you all right?"

She managed to nod. "It's okay," she whispered, her throat suddenly tight. "I've just never felt anything that strong before."

"Maybe this wasn't such a great idea." He reached for the box. "We wanted you to connect with the thing, tell us more about it, how to use it, but not if it's going to hurt you."

"I need to do this." She stopped him with a hand on his arm. The contact of flesh on flesh sizzled, rippling up to her shoulder. But she didn't let go. "Darius, you know I'm the only one who can."

"We can try something else."

"No, I'm okay. Just overwhelmed. But I know what to expect now." She took a bracing breath, then lifted the lid on the box herself.

This time when the force swept over her, she opened her senses wide, accepting the essence of the stone. It was *old,* centuries old. Eons even. She started to reach for it, then paused and looked at Darius. He nodded. She lifted the bloodred crystal pyramid out of the box. It fit in the palm of her hand, warm and alive. Its energy throbbed with the steady assurance of a heartbeat. She closed her fingers around it.

Memories clamored in her mind, the stone's memories, some of them thousands of years old. Images flared before her eyes like strobe lights—quick, blinding, blurred together like a smeared watercolor. Song erupted from the stone, swamping her senses. The notes rose in her throat, bursting free like molten magma trapped beneath the earth for too long. The here and now melted away. She was earth, she was fire, she was power. She lost herself in the stone, deeper and deeper, connected with its consciousness.

And sang a song too long unheard.

So many had touched it, eager to learn its secrets. Imprints of all of them, what they looked like, who they were, the emotions they felt; all of the information slammed into her like an ocean wave. She struggled to sort it out, but the knowledge flew at her like bullets, as if the stone had not been able to talk to someone in so long that it wanted to tell her everything all at once.

The memories twined together like different-colored threads in her mind, the newer ones bright white, the older ones deep blue and bright green and shiny black. All of them tangled together in a big knot. She would have to pull the strands one at a time to separate them, to organize them. She wondered how long it had been since a Stone Singer had tuned this stone. Balanced the energy.

Too long. The raspy mind-voice could only belong to the stone.

An image flared in her mind, a young Stone Singer with tattooed hands and a green tunic. His name had been Ja-Red, and he'd lived in Atlantis. He'd died there, too, on the day of destruction.

She nearly dropped the thing. Never before had she received such clear images from a stone, even a stone of power. Any lingering doubts disappeared. This was indeed one of the three Stones of Ekhia.

More images flowed into her thoughts, as if it had simply needed a path. *I am the Stone of Igarle, the prophet maker.* The ancient whisper swept through her mind with impressions and emotions, a sense of knowing rather than being told. She could detect layer upon layer of old patterns within the stone, patterns imprinted by those who had tried to tap its power. Untangling all that was going to take some time.

For now, she picked one bright white thread and tugged.

Female. Maternal instinct, great love, and equally great power. Maria Montana, Darius's mother. She'd held the stone briefly, then set it in the box and stored it away in the vault. Other emotions swelled on top of the first, like a series of waves breaking on the shore. Regret at lies of omission. Anger at the attacks on her family, both now and in the past. Fear that there might be more. Worry that she would not be able to stop them. Disbelief that the stone existed, and awe of the same. Joy that finally, after ages untold, one of the Stones of Ekhia had been returned to its rightful owners.

Encouraged, Faith plucked at another white thread.

Male. Furious. Wronged. Arrogant. Great power but also great needs and desires. The hunger for vengeance infected everything, from his first breath in the morning to his last thought at night. The Seers must die to restore order to the world. Faith threw up a barrier to repel the toxic energy. Who was this?

Jain Criten. President of the Atlantean homeland of Santutegi and leader of the Mendukati.

As if the last thread had opened up a floodgate, more information rushed at her, drowning her in images and emotions and identities. She struggled to keep her head above water, but they kept coming, thousands of years of pent-up human energy. She couldn't sort through them quickly enough to discharge them, from either the crystal or herself.

Faith. Darius's mind-voice. She could pinpoint him like a lighthouse in fog, a shining beacon of clear blue in a sea of churning white and green and black. She reached for that fragile link, grasped on to it. With eons of other people's residue flooding her, she knew he was the here-and-now, her only link to the real world.

Help me, she sent.

Let go of the stone. Warm hands covered hers, prying at her fingers' grip on the crystal. She focused on releasing it, on coming back to the present, to her own reality. The stone protested, its song shifting to a soaring wail of denial. Inch by inch, she pulled her fingers away. The stone fell from her grasp. She stumbled backward.

Darius grabbed her upper arm, preventing her from falling on her butt. She gripped his arm with her other hand as the visions slowly receded from her mind. When she could see clearly again, she noticed that the deep red color had disappeared from the crystal pyramid, leaving it clear and glowing with bright white light in his palm.

"When did it start doing that?" She made to touch it, but he moved it out of her reach.

"Enough for today. I thought for a minute there we weren't going to get you back." He set the stone on the table.

"I've heard legends about Stone Singers getting lost in a stone, their consciousness trapped." She frowned at the now harmless-looking pyramid as its color slowly darkened to its previous crimson shade. "Wonder why it changes color?"

"I thought you could tell me. I noticed it goes clear when one of my family touches it. It was going clear with red swirls of energy when you held it." He eased his grip and rubbed the area where he'd clenched her arm. "Sorry about grabbing you. You looked like you were going down."

"I was." She tried for a nonchalant smile, caught as usual by the striking blue of his eyes. She fought the pull. "You saved me from an embarrassing spill my first day on the job."

"No worries." He dropped his hand and turned to the stone. The sudden absence of his touch triggered an echo of emptiness in her core, as if a piece of her had broken away.

Oh, boy, this was a problem. Being attracted to a Seer was definitely not on her to-do list, especially if a fleeting touch left her aching like a woman brought to the brink of orgasm and then abandoned. Ignoring the chemistry between them was the best thing to do.

It was the only way she would get through this.

· · · · ·

What had just happened here?

Darius perused the stone, which had returned to its original crimson hue. One moment Faith's emotions had been front and center, plain for him to see. The instant she'd touched the stone, gone. Like having the world suddenly fall silent.

He had to admit, he'd been reveling a bit in her genuine attraction to him. She had watched him with those cat-green eyes, half wary and half curious, her pink lips parted and a slight flush in her cheeks. His vision from the night before had played over and over again in his thoughts, hot and urgent, the two of them naked and entwined in the candlelight.

His parents' warnings had slipped into his mind. She'd been with the enemy once and might still be. But when he'd told her about Lorinda's murder, he hadn't sensed satisfaction. He'd only gotten the same sort of distress he himself felt that yet another innocent life had been snuffed out by the Mendukati, and even a hint of guilt that she'd ever been associated with them. That spoke of her innocence as far as he was concerned. Alleviated any guilt he felt at being so attracted to her.

At wanting to turn that vision last night into reality.

The truth of it had unnerved him, even as his jeans had tightened and his hands shook. He liked what he was feeling from her, how she stroked him with her eyes even as she tried to appear disinterested. After so many years of women dismissing him with pity, it was heady stuff indeed to be genuinely desired.

Then she'd gotten lost in the stone, gone deeper even than when she'd charged his healing stone for him. He could tell by the way she'd paled, by the glazed look in her eyes. Could sense her distress.

He'd spoken to her verbally, but she hadn't responded. He'd realized all she could see or feel was the stone, so he'd touched it to try and reach her. And the emotional trail had winked out, like a plug pulled from a lamp.

He chewed the inside of his cheek, trying to moisten his dry mouth as he remembered. He'd never been so scared. Had they really found the last Stone Singer alive, only to lose her essence in the very stone she was here to examine?

He'd tried to reach her, but his empathy would not respond. After a lifetime of always knowing how everyone was feeling all the time, to have it simply stop working like that had been like losing his hearing or his sight. But he'd lost things before, like his ability to walk. And he'd fought and found new avenues of doing things. This was no different. It couldn't be.

They . . . he . . . couldn't lose her now.

After the longest moments of his life, he remembered what his mother had said, that Faith was destined to be his mate. When Jain Criten had attacked them a few weeks back, he'd watched, helpless, as Criten had sucked away his brother's power with a wave of his hand. But Rafe had rallied, fueled by the mating bond he had with Cara, and won.

Did he want a mate? No. He wasn't ready, especially for an ex-Mendukati agent who happened to be the only person alive who could balance this damned stone. But in that moment when he'd thought he'd lost her, he'd gone for the Hail Mary and looked for the bond that should be there, provided his mother was right.

And she was. He'd found it, a fragile thing, still new, a slender sliver of silver that connected him with Faith. He'd called to her, his knees nearly weakening when she'd responded. He knew he had to separate her from the stone.

The instant he'd touched it, the swirling red had washed away, and the pyramid had glowed with brilliant white light. He'd guided her back with his mind-voice, prying at her fingers to get her to release the stone and come back to him.

"Darius? You okay?" She touched his shoulder, and he turned. There she was with her big green eyes and pretty mouth. His empathy had come back to life, and he could feel her concern for him, and the ever-present attraction.

"Sorry. I guess I was jazzed from the energy in that stone." He glanced at the now dark red crystal sitting on the table. "That was something else."

She hugged herself and rubbed her arms. "That was definitely crazy, different than anything I've ever experienced. If you hadn't pulled me out of there—"

"But I did, so we're all good. I'd advise always having someone nearby when you're working with it, though, just in case."

She nodded. "Good idea."

"So now that we're both back on Planet Earth, what was it like?"

"Oh, wow." She forked her fingers through her short hair. "There are so many layers in there, so much emotional energy, so many memories. Centuries of them. Maybe even more than that. It's going to take several days of intense bonding to even begin sorting everything out and balancing the stone so it can be used properly."

"Memories?"

"Of anyone who ever handled the stone." At his confused frown, she continued. "The Stones of Ekhia are different from other stones. They are living entities, in a sense. Not like how you and I are alive, of course, but sentient on a different level. All memories are connected with some kind of emotion, and the stones absorb emotions. Every person who has ever handled the stone has imprinted upon it, but the patterns are all tangled up. I need to sort them all out."

"You realize how crazy that sounds. Living stone?"

She shrugged. "Now you know why there are Stone Singers."

"To what . . . clean up these stones?"

"In a way. We clear out negative energies, balance and charge and tune the stones so they can be used to fuel and filter Atlantean powers. You understand; you work with healing stones." She stared at the crystal on the table. "There are many kinds of Stones of Power, but the Stones of Ekhia are the strongest in the world. In ancient times, it was the job of the Stone Singer to keep the three Stones of Ekhia in top condition so the people of Atlantis could communicate with their Creators."

"Okay, now you're losing me. I confess I don't know much about the Atlanteans. I just found out a few weeks ago that my ancestor was not the only survivor."

Her mouth dropped open. "You're kidding."

"No. Long story." He waved a hand in dismissal. "Back to the Stones of Ekhia. What else do you know about them?"

"I know they belong to the Seers."

"What?"

She shrugged. "The Seers are the only ones who can use them to contact the Creators. Others have tried and failed. Some died. In ancient times, the head priestess was the guardian of the stones."

"The *apaiz nagusi?*"

He felt her surprise even as it registered on her face. "I thought you said you didn't know anything about Atlantean history?"

"I know about this. My family is descended from Agrilara, the last High Priestess of Atlantis. And my mom is the current *apaiz nagusi.*"

"Oh." She blinked. "Guess that makes you royalty or something."

He laughed. "Hardly. Anyway, that's enough excitement for today. Why don't you relax for the rest of the day, get your balance back." He picked up the stone and returned it to its box, closing the lid.

"Good idea. Maybe I'll give Ben a call." Her expression softened. "Thanks for coming after me in there."

"No problem. Go call Ben."

"Yes, sir." She headed for the door.

"Don't call me sir. Darius is fine. Or Dar. Or Dumb-ass. Just not sir."

"Got it. Stick with the D's." With a cheeky salute, she let herself out of the cabana.

Darius looked down and shook his head. As his luck would have it, he'd been handling the stone when she'd given him that dewy-eyed look. His empathy had cut off again until he released the stone, so he had no idea what emotion was behind it. Was she just being a wise guy, or had there been some softer feeling there, something more personal?

He tucked the box under one arm and took up his cane with the other hand as he headed for the door. "Forget about it, dumb-ass," he muttered. "She's too important to risk with an affair, no matter what Mom says."

CHAPTER SIX

It was barely four in the afternoon when Darius bumped into his father in the kitchen. He stopped short and glanced at the clock. "You're home early."

"Your mother called me."

"About her cousin."

"Yeah." His dad frowned at the cup of coffee in his hand, having apparently forgotten about it, and set it down, untasted. "Nothing like this has happened for a long time. We thought we were safe." He let out a harsh laugh. "I should know better than that. Security is my business."

Darius could sense the warring emotions churning in his normally focused father. Taste them. The peppery heat of self-anger. The char of frustration. The bitter burn of fear.

"You can't blame yourself for this," he said. "Did you even know Mom had a cousin?"

"Yes, yes." His father waved a hand and began to pace. "I met Lorinda years ago. Your aunts, too."

"I have aunts?"

"And uncles. And more cousins." He rubbed his forehead. "I thought they were all protected."

"Hey." Darius laid a hand on his father's shoulder. "You did what you could. At least we're all safe."

"But for how long?" His father shrugged off Darius's hand. "This house is my security masterpiece, yet Criten was still able to waltz in here and try to kill my family."

"Key word is 'try.' He failed."

"He'll be back. One thing I've learned about these bastards is they don't give up. That's why I keep upgrading the security, why your buddy Adrian Gray tests it for me. I figure if I can keep him out, it should work for those other Warriors. But Gray keeps getting right through it."

"Bet it takes him longer each time."

That sparked a hint of a smile from his father. "Yeah, it does."

"That's progress then."

"But is it enough?" His dad rubbed the back of his neck. "First Criten and this stone. Then the Stone Singer—a former Mendukati agent—living in our home. Then these murders. And in the middle of it all, your brother decides to walk his Soul Circle."

"Yeah, it's a lot. As soon as that stone surfaced, all hell broke loose. That was the kickoff."

"It was, and now we're in an all-out war. There's bound to be casualties. That's what scares me the most."

His father's fear spiked, jagged and visceral. Darius snagged that harsh energy and softened the edges, quietly feeding it back to the source as calmer concern rather than primitive panic. "It's definitely a lot, Dad. But together we can beat this."

"That's the key, isn't it?" His father smiled. "I think we need to remind ourselves of that—that we're a family, and together, we can do anything. I think we need to have a barbecue."

"A barbecue? Uh . . . this doesn't seem like the best time to invite people over."

"Not people, just us. Tonight, six o'clock. And the Stone Singer, Faith. She can come. Maybe seeing us together will make her think twice about pulling anything."

"Damn it, Dad, I keep telling you—"

"I know, I know. I'm sorry. But with all that's happened, I have to consider anyone who isn't one of us to be a potential threat. There's every possibility I'm wrong about her." He paused, then added, "But since we're talking about it, your mom doesn't want Faith anywhere near Rafe's Soul Circle. He'd be vulnerable then, and it would be the perfect time to strike."

"Dad, it's a private family ritual. She has no reason to be there or even want to be there."

"Still. I'm having Mendez keep an eye on her while we're all in the temple."

"Fine."

"I'll let your mother know. And I'll take this up to her." His dad picked up the cup of coffee he'd set down and headed out. He paused in the doorway. "By the way, thanks for whatever you did just now. I'm feeling calmer. Better able to deal with all this."

Darius kept his expression bland. "Don't know what you're talking about."

"Of course you don't." His father gave him a nod and left, a smile playing along his lips.

Darius shook his head and turned toward the coffee machine. The murder of Lorinda's family had them all shaken up. His family had already been on edge about allowing Faith into their home, about letting her have access to the stone. But the alternative would be to meet Faith on the outside and bring the stone to her, and that was unacceptable. This way was safer for everyone and kept the stone contained. Out of Mendukati hands. Though to hear his dad tell it, Faith *was* the Mendukati. Darius knew she wasn't like that. No one would be able to hide that kind of fanaticism from an empath. But how could he convince the rest of the family?

Maybe once enough time had passed without Faith doing anything suspicious, everyone would settle down. Maybe they'd finally believe him when he told them she wasn't a threat.

As he poured himself some coffee, he pondered how he was

going to tell Faith that she would be under guard Saturday morning.

. . . . .

The Stone of Igarle continued to whisper to her throughout the afternoon.

Faith called Ben, but he couldn't talk for long; he and Adrian were loading Ben's truck for the trip to Santa Fe. He reassured her again that he would be fine, that he would see her soon.

After she hung up with him, she tried reading some of the magazines she found in the living room to entertain herself, and when that didn't work, she tried TV. She was used to being active all day, working at the store and walking around Old Town on her lunch hour. This sitting around twiddling her thumbs didn't do anything for her. And she wasn't ready to confront the stone again, not so soon.

Since she didn't mind being alone, she decided to take a walk on the grounds of the Montana estate. The raw beauty of the surrounding red rock formations and green trees never failed to take her breath away. As she wandered the paths hewn out of the underbrush, she became aware of an underlying hum vibrating from the land. She paused in a clearing, sat down on a large stone, and closed her eyes, opening her senses to listen.

Earth energy. Male. Female. Sometimes both. The humming came from the earth around her. She placed her hands flat on her stone seat. *What is this?*

The answer came right away: the vortexes. Sedona was famous for them.

Information flooded her mind from the stone beneath her and the buttes and mesas all around her. A vortex was where energy from multiple planes spiraled into set places in the Earth, creating harmonics beyond the physical ear, and Sedona was home to four of the most powerful. Vortexes supported gifts of spirit, like Atlantean powers. She'd rarely felt anything like it.

The feed from the nearest vortex touched her scarred soul. She ached for the childhood she might have had if her parents hadn't died when she was a girl. As if losing her father at age five weren't enough, her mother had been killed when she was nine. They said her parents had been murdered by Seers, but now she wasn't sure what to believe. All she knew was there was a hole in her chest that would never be filled.

Add to that the pressure of being a rare Stone Singer and the demands placed on her. If Ben hadn't taken her under his wing after she'd been orphaned, taught her everything she needed to know about minerals and rocks, she had no idea where she'd be. And because she'd loved Ben so much, it had been easy to fall for Michael's good looks and charm. By marrying him, she truly became Ben's daughter, though she had never given up her maiden name.

This house, a safe haven from the Mendukati, embodied the security she wanted to achieve for herself. And the closeness of the Montana family made her long for something she could never have—a family of her own where she belonged, was accepted for just being herself.

How could a Stone Singer ever have both? She couldn't, not as long as the Mendukati existed, and the truth shattered her, regret and grief inflaming her heart and smothering her naïve dreams.

She washed all that away in the vortex current, the past mistakes she'd made and the losses she'd suffered, and gave herself up to the healing mystical energy.

. . . . .

Darius knew Faith was somewhere nearby.

He picked his way along the pathway, avoiding rocks and tree roots in his path. He could have sent someone after her, maybe Rafe or Cara, but with Rafe's Soul Circle coming up, he didn't want to distract either of them. And Tessa was out of the question.

Which left him, not that he minded spending more time with Faith. Warnings from his father notwithstanding, ever since his mother had declared Faith his destined mate, he couldn't get the idea out of his mind. Everything seemed to be pushing them together: the attraction he had to her even in the midst of this craziness, the erotic dreams, the way he was able to lead her to safety in the chaos of the stone even when his own Seer powers were disabled.

One thing he'd learned when he'd healed himself out of that wheelchair was not to look askance at a gift from the gods.

He opened his empathic senses wider, searching for her. He felt someone up ahead, someone contemplative. He wouldn't have guessed it to be Faith except for the silver energy trail—the mate link—connecting them. After their encounter with the Stone of Igarle, the link had grown slightly stronger. He wondered if she sensed it yet. He doubted it. People tended to ignore what they chose not to see.

He came upon her in a place where several boulders had fallen centuries before, surrounded by a few trees and a stunning view of the buttes. She sat with her eyes closed in some kind of meditative state.

For a moment he enjoyed the sight of her, short dark hair gleaming in the sun, fair skin against her purple top, and the sweet curves revealed by her new jeans. His body recognized her on a basic level, tugging him toward her with an insistence he chose not to resist.

"So this is where you are," he said.

Faith jerked her eyes open as Darius descended the incline. He didn't need the visual clue of her cheeks flaring tomato red to know how flustered she was; he could feel it. Her words came out in a burst. "Are you crazy? The footing here is uneven. Treacherous. You shouldn't be here." She got up from the rock and went to meet him as he made it to her clearing.

"I've been walking this way since I was a kid. I know it pretty well." Pausing on the downhill path, Darius stared out at the breathtaking view before them, giving her time to settle. "Gorgeous, isn't it?"

"Yes, a great place to be alone."

He raised his brows at her thinly veiled annoyance. "I've disturbed you. I'm sorry. I came to tell you something, and I got distracted by this gorgeous scenery." He inhaled deeply as he looked around, then turned his most charming smile on her. "I never get tired of it."

"I doubt I would, either."

He could feel her struggle to hang on to her displeasure. She was softening. "You're unhappy with me. I didn't mean to interrupt your meditation."

She pushed her hand through her hair. Surrender. "You didn't interrupt much. Just checking out the vortexes."

"The vortexes? I'd steer clear of them if I were you. The last Channeler who tried to access vortex energy nearly fried himself."

"And that would be?"

"Jain Criten." He didn't have to sense her surprise; it was written on her face.

"Criten tried to use the vortex energy?"

"Yeah, but not successfully. Apparently vortex energy is not good for Channelers."

She raised her brows. "But it is for Seers?"

Darius shrugged. "Probably why my parents built a house here."

"So any Channelers who came at you would find their powers compromised. Nice." She glanced out at the buttes in the distance. "The vortex energy doesn't seem to bother me, but I'm a different kind of Channeler."

"Oh?"

She waved a hand. "Know how you get a Stone Singer? Mate two elementals."

"Okay, you're going to have to explain that one."

"That's right, you don't know much about our people. A lot of Channelers have specific abilities. You saw Corinne, the lightning thrower, and I've heard that Jain Criten has the power to use energy to change matter."

"I saw him change flowers into knives. That what you mean?"

"Yes." She nodded. "Those are normal sorts of channeling powers. Now, elementals are Channelers whose abilities lie with the four basic elements: wind, fire, earth, air." She indicated herself. "Obviously I identify with earth. My mother was a Wind Chanter and my father a Son of Poseidon, a water elemental. Elementals are rare, and when they produce a child, it is always another elemental, often a Stone Singer."

"What about fire?"

"Michael's mother—Ben's late wife—was a Flame Walker."

"Michael. He was your husband, right?"

"Yes. He died three years ago."

"I read about it. His heart stopped, right? Strange for a guy still in his twenties."

"That's right." She kept her gaze level with his, but her sudden alertness hit him like red pepper flakes on the tongue. His empathic senses tingled with a hint of something beneath the surface, something dark and sticky and raw. But she suppressed it too quickly for him to read it. Secretiveness, maybe. Or shame. Guilt?

Damn it. There was something she wasn't telling him. Something about her husband's death. "Was he sick for long?"

"Not a day in his life. He had an accident." She glanced away at that, another trickle of that stickiness filtering through to him. He didn't want to believe his father's speculation was right, but something had definitely happened on that ridge. Something disturbing. Was there any chance she was a danger to them after all?

"Do you want to talk about it?"

"Not really." She sent him a look, and her suspicion pricked at him. "So tell me, Darius, why is it always you handling me? Were you elected or something?"

"Something." He stroked his goatee when she raised her eyebrows at him. "I'm the oldest, right? I'm also the family . . . um . . . diplomat."

"Ah." She folded her arms. "The peacekeeper."

"I used to be. I have to admit, I've lost my patience with people since my accident. Just ask Rafe. He'll tell you I've been an angry guy lately."

"You seem fine with me."

"That's another story."

"I bet." She let out a long sigh. "Look, I'm kind of in new territory here. With the stone. With you . . . and your family," she added quickly. "Not quite sure what I'm doing."

"Solving a mystery."

"A mystery that's going to take awhile. It's been centuries, maybe thousands of years, since that stone was cleared out and tuned properly."

"Then we've got the right person to handle the job." He sat down on a boulder, rested his chin on the hand covering the head of his cane and looked her straight in the eye. "I'm glad you're here."

The thrill that he felt from her did a lot for his masculine ego. She tried to play it off. "Well, like you heard, I'm the only game in town."

He didn't smile. "This isn't a game, Faith. My cousins were killed just yesterday."

Her mirth faded. "I'm sorry. I didn't mean to seem so cavalier about all this. Of course I know it's not a game."

"My idea to bring you here . . . well, it wasn't an easy decision. I had to talk everyone else into it." He stretched out his bad knee with a slow, controlled move. "Yesterday wasn't the first time my mom's family was targeted by the Mendukati—"

"I know. Cara mentioned it."

He nodded. "Right. Your association with them was a concern. But we didn't have a choice, and I didn't know what to expect."

"I—"

"I'm not finished." Faith closed her mouth, and he continued. "Like I said, I didn't know what to expect from a Stone Singer, especially one who had been associated with the same people who keep trying to kill my family."

"I wasn't with them for that long. And when I realized what they were doing, I got out. You can't think—" She pressed her lips together, but he could feel the sting of her hurt feelings. "Of course you do."

"Don't put words in my mouth. I don't think you intend to hurt anyone." He let out a long breath. "Look, this is getting way more intense than I intended. I came looking for you to tell you about the barbecue."

"A barbecue?" She indicated her clothes. "I don't have much to wear to a party."

"It's just the family. My dad's been itching to get some burgers going, and he thought tonight would be a good reason to get everyone together. You're invited."

"I am?"

"Yes. He told me specifically to ask you to come." When she didn't respond, he said, "Come on. Is that the act of someone who thinks you're the enemy?"

"I guess not. What time?"

"About six o'clock."

She glanced at her watch. "That only gives me an hour! I should shower."

"You look fine."

"Leave it to a man to say that. I'll see you at six." She started up the path but then paused. "Do you need any help getting back?"

"No, I'm good. I'll see you there."

She hesitated, then nodded and hurried up the incline.

Darius watched her go. She was hiding something from him, something to do with her husband's death. How did a healthy twenty-eight-year-old man drop dead without a mark on him? She could just be feeling grief. Or maybe survivor's guilt because she hadn't been able to save him. He hoped that's all it was. Because his attraction to her was getting stronger.

According to what he knew about destined mates, the sexual tension built with speed and intense heat no matter what obstacles might lay in their path. Eventually they simply would not be able to keep their hands off each other.

Then again, maybe he was already there.

. . . . .

The soldiers he had were inadequate.

Azotay stared out into the night from the front seat of the lead SUV. The failed attempt to extract the Stone Singer, allowing her to escape with the Seers, of all creatures—a very poor showing. And now the rumored involvement of the Temple of Mneseus. Clearly he would have to see to every aspect of the mission himself. This Mendukati encampment had no idea what power the Stones of Ekhia could bring, the glory to be found for those who brought the new era to life. Their level of preparation fell far below what was expected by President Criten . . . and himself.

How on Earth had a Stone Singer come to exist in such a ragtag group as this? The sheer improbability boggled the mind.

Still, Azotay had gathered the best of them, sorry group that they were, and led them himself to Santa Fe to track down Ben

Wakete. Once he had the carver in his grasp, he would have the perfect leverage to obtain the cooperation of the Stone Singer.

And he could see for himself if the rumors about Mneseus were true.

Wakete was not hard to locate. The exhibition hall holding the art show in which he would be participating had advertised well, and Wakete had a reputation as a skillful fetish carver, a good draw. They located Wakete's hotel, and a call to the front desk confirmed he had checked in, but his car was not in the lot. Probably out to dinner.

It was a simple matter to send teams out to find the car, and simpler still to launch an offensive on a lonely stretch of road . . . provided he did not have an unexpected bodyguard.

. . . . .

Faith came downstairs at 5:45, showered and dressed in a turquoise blouse spotted with flowers and a new long black skirt. She wore inexpensive black sandals on her feet and dangling gold earrings that featured clear fake crystal gems in her ears. She'd also dipped into her new makeup and had a sweater hooked over her arm.

The first person she saw was Tessa, dressed in white capris and a white top, a dark blue sweatshirt, and tennis shoes. She turned away before the blonde could see her and caught sight of John Montana in a T-shirt and faded jeans behind the barbecue. Maria laughed beside him as she held a platter of burgers. Her dark hair was pulled in a haphazard up-do held with a large clip, and she also wore a turquoise shirt with her jeans and flip-flops. Rafe lay on a lounge chair, also garbed casually, as he joked with Tessa. Darius sat nearby, dressed in jeans, brown sandals, and a white T-shirt with an open, button-down shirt of slate gray over it that no doubt accented his eyes. His long dark hair looked damp from the shower.

She was overdressed. She wondered if there was time to

sneak back to her room and change before anyone saw her. She had just slipped back through the kitchen doors when Cara came into the kitchen. She, too, seemed casually dressed in jeans and a pink top with a gray hooded sweatshirt over it, her hair in its usual ponytail. She was pushing buttons on her phone when she looked up.

"Hey, Faith. Where you going?"

"I'm just going to run up and change," Faith replied.

"Why? You look great."

"No, I'm overdressed. I was going to slip upstairs and put on some jeans."

"Nah, you look pretty." Faith grinned. "Dress for anyone special?"

"Of course not." But Faith couldn't help looking out the door at Darius.

"Uh-huh. Pull the other one." Cara slipped the phone into her pocket and followed Faith's glance. "You can't fool a woman in love. Since I doubt you're ogling my man, I'm thinking you're checking out Darius."

"Don't be silly." Faith shrugged off the observation. "I just met the man."

"I only knew Rafe for a couple of days before we ended up in bed together. Those Montana men are hot, that's all I can say."

"I just wanted to fit in, that's all. I don't need more snide comments from Tessa."

Cara nodded. "I imagine it's tough being the odd man out. Take me, for instance. Except for John, I'm the only non-Atlantean here."

"But they love you. It's obvious."

"Now. I was involved in the whole Jain Criten nonsense. I helped Rafe defeat him. I guess that makes me one of the family."

"You've proven yourself. I still have to earn the trust of this family." Faith sighed and rubbed her forehead. "Maybe I shouldn't have come here."

"Aw, honey." Cara put her arm around Faith and led her to the kitchen table. "I only have sort of an idea what you're doing here, but from what I can guess, your powers are pretty rare, and you're the only one who can make sense of that stone they have."

"Basically." Faith sat on the long side of the table while Cara grabbed the seat at the end near her. "Touching it for the first time was . . . intense. No one has cleared it or balanced it properly in eons. I got a little lost in there. Darius had to pull me out."

"He did? Huh." Cara frowned.

"What?"

Cara shook her head. "It's just . . . well, I thought Seer powers stopped working when they handled the stone."

"That can't be." Now Faith frowned. "I saw him, clear as day, a blue beacon that led me out."

"I must be wrong then." Cara shrugged and smiled. "I'm still learning all the rules."

"Maybe." But Faith continued to ponder the matter.

"Nah, I must be wrong. I'm kind of rattled. Worried about Saturday, I guess."

"What's happening Saturday?"

"They didn't tell you? Oh, dear. Maybe I'm not supposed to mention it." Cara bit her lip. "The Montanas are still kind of weird about you."

"I know." And she did, though it still stung a little. But they didn't have to like her to pay her the money they'd promised. "It's okay."

"It's just that Rafe has this big test coming up. He thinks he's ready, but I'm not so sure."

"I'm sure everything will go fine." She squeezed Cara's hand across the table.

"Thanks. I'm holding on to that." Cara took a deep breath. "Now, your problems. First off, you know Maria's family was terrorized by the Mendukati for generations. These new murders have everyone rattled, especially Maria, but she's trying."

"I know she is. I appreciate that it's going to take time, especially after what happened to her cousins."

"Right. And John is protective of Maria. He runs a security company, and it's in his nature to be suspicious. Just a few weeks ago, a Mendukati sniper took a shot at Maria. If she hadn't gotten a flash of insight right at that moment, she would have been hit."

"Oh, no! No wonder they're so worried."

"Exactly. John's taking every precaution. Throw in Jain Criten's visit a few weeks back, and you just know every warning bell in the man's head is ringing twenty-four-seven."

"I can imagine."

Cara continued. "Now as for Rafe, he's been away from home for about five years, and he's been living in the real world. He's on the fence about you, waiting to see what's going to happen."

"So as long as I do my job and keep my nose clean, I should be fine."

Cara grinned. "Right. Now me, I'm giving you the benefit of the doubt. As the most recent outsider taken into this family, I know how it feels. So you have my vote, unless you hurt the Montanas, and then I'm coming after you. I'm from Jersey, you know."

Faith smiled back, though she heard the truth beneath the words. "Noted."

"Now Tessa. She has what we call limited social skills. She's great with PR for the company, writing ad campaigns and all that, but put her face-to-face, and she's lost. I told you she's protective of Darius. When he was shot, Rafe took off and left her and the family to deal with all that."

"So she's a shoot-first-and-ask-questions-later kind of gal."

"In a nutshell."

"Well, if looks could kill, I'd be dead already." Faith lowered her voice. "And she can tan. For that alone, I should hate her."

"With you on that one." Cara pointed to herself. "Irish and German here, so all I get is the lobster tan, red from head to toe."

Faith nodded. "Ditto. I'll try and steer clear of Tessa. But I'm warning you, if she starts with me I'm shooting back."

"Fair enough." Cara leaned back in her chair. "Which leaves Darius."

Faith tensed. "What about him?"

"Well, he's the big brother. It goes Darius, Rafe, Tessa. When I met him, he was a big cranky puss."

"Darius, really?" Faith glanced over her shoulder at the laughing man on the other side of the glass door. "I know he can be gruff once in a while—"

"Gruff? Honey, he could peel paint with his glare. The very first time I met him, he punched Rafe in the mouth within a minute of answering the door."

"No! Seriously?"

"To be fair, there was some bad blood there. It was Rafe's fault Darius got shot, and rather than face the music, he ran off. Some nonsense about being too dangerous to be around his family." Cara shook her head. "Long story. Requires margaritas. At any rate, there was brother anger going on there that they worked out, so Darius has gotten nicer. Less angry. Though he has his moments. He was in a wheelchair for almost five years. They told him he would never walk again. That would make anyone grumpy."

"Wow." Faith glanced again at Darius. "Guess he proved them wrong."

"Yeah, no one keeps Darius down. He's sort of the family diplomat."

"He mentioned that."

"He's the one they send in to negotiate things. He's the talker, Rafe's the fighter."

"Darius can fight. He took on two Mendukati and won." Faith warmed as she remembered it. "Adrian helped at the end."

"Wish I could have seen it." Cara glanced out the door herself. "The only thing that sets him off these days is pity. Can't stand it. He reverts to the pissed-off man I first met."

"Aha." Faith pointed at Cara. "The night we arrived, he was all angry and sped off to be alone."

"Probably thought you pitied him. He really hates that."

"I was thinking how weird it looked, such a powerful man in a wheelchair. It must have shown on my face."

"Guess so." Cara stood up. "Better now? I think you look great, and Darius is going to swallow his tongue."

Faith stood as well. "Cara, I told you—"

Cara propped a hand on her hip. "You going to deny you're attracted?"

"Well, no, but I work for the guy. I can't imagine he'd hit on the help."

Cara laughed. "I doubt that will stop him. If Darius is interested, he'll let you know. It's been awhile for him, though, so cut him some slack."

Faith followed as Cara led the way to the sliding doors. "What does that mean?"

Cara slid open the door. "Before he was shot, Darius was engaged. She left after he was injured."

"Oh, no!"

"Oh, yes." Cara paused in the doorway. "Another reason for Tessa to be rude to any woman around Darius. She's a softie and doesn't want to see him hurt again. In more ways than one."

"Thanks, Cara, for telling me all this."

"I think it's great." Cara winked. "Maybe Darius has finally found his destined mate, just like Rafe and me." With a waggle of her fingers, she left Faith standing in the doorway as she went to join her fiancé.

Faith stood frozen. Destined mate? What the heck did that

mean? She stepped outside and closed the sliding door, then glanced at Darius.

This time he gazed back. The quivering started low in her belly at the way he looked at her, and she knew.

She was in trouble.

CHAPTER SEVEN

Faith stepped outside, and Darius stood up, coming across to meet her. She stood still, caught between the instincts of fight and flight.

If she stayed, anything could happen. Maybe things she wasn't ready for.

If she fled, she might lose any small respect the Montanas had for her.

She stayed.

Darius reached her. "Don't you look nice."

"I might have gotten a little carried away. I didn't realize it was casual."

"I like it." He flicked one of her dangling earrings. The warmth of his finger so close to her neck, yet not touching it, sent an unexpected ripple through her. How did he do this, cut through her defenses until she forgot she had any?

"Hot date?" Tessa's voice reached them just as she did. She sipped at the drink in her hand and eyed Faith over the rim.

Faith opened her mouth to reply, but Darius slipped Faith's hand beneath the crook of his arm and met his sister's gaze. "As a matter of fact, she's with me."

Tessa only missed a beat. "Oh, come on, Dar. You can't be serious."

"Sure I am. Faith is with me tonight. Right, Faith?"

Faith nodded. "He even met me at the door."

Tessa narrowed her eyes. "Watch it, brother dear. This one may be more than you bargained for."

"Or more than you think she is." He stroked Faith's fingers where they rested on his arm. "Maybe you're jealous because a certain Warrior took off without kissing you good-bye."

Tessa's mouth opened and closed before she snapped, "Don't be an ass."

"I won't if you won't. Come on, Faith, let's go put in our burger orders." He led Faith away from a clearly simmering Tessa.

As they headed over to the grill, Faith murmured, "I'm sorry to be so much trouble."

Darius stopped. "You're no trouble. Tess gets on her high horse sometimes and needs to be knocked down a bit."

"Thank you for riding to my defense, but why did you lie to her and tell her I was your date?"

"Who said I lied? Now, how do you like your burger?"

. . . . .

"Thanks for dinner," Ben said as he and Adrian left the restaurant outside Santa Fe. He jingled his truck keys in his hand. "But I can't let you pay for every meal. These are business expenses. Tax deductions, my friend."

"You can get the next one." Adrian kept his senses alert. Ben may have been doing a show at a big exhibition hall in a major city, but he still stayed in a cheap motel at the edge of town and ate at a roadhouse diner. The farther away from the center of town they were, the better the chance the Mendukati could come at them on an isolated stretch of road somewhere. And the way the back of his neck itched made him think that's exactly the sort of attack that was coming.

"Faith called earlier to let me know she was okay." Ben unlocked the pickup and climbed into the driver's seat. "Seems to be settling in up there. She asked me to get her some materials."

"Materials?" Adrian opened the passenger side door and gave a long, level glance around before climbing in. "What kind of materials?"

"Different crystals, gemstones. Good harmonics." Ben laughed. "I don't know about harmonics; I just see what a piece of rock wants me to carve it into. But this is her area, and she knows what she needs. Guess she wants it to help her with that stone they have her looking at. Anyway, I picked up what she needed and sent it overnight mail after we got off the phone. She said she needed it quickly."

"Makes sense." As Ben fastened his seat belt, a shadow moved on the edge of the half-empty parking lot. Adrian narrowed his eyes, searching for any other anomalies. But the night stayed still. No more shadows stirred.

"Appreciate you coming all the way out here," Ben said, putting the keys in the ignition. "Hope it ends up not being necessary." He flashed a smile. "Either way, it's nice to have company. You can help me haul boxes and set up."

"Happy to."

"I don't pay," Ben said, "but I'll buy you a beer."

"Done."

The strike hit hard and fast, just as he'd expected.

The doors on either side of the pickup were yanked open. Between one breath and the next, Adrian was ripped from his seat belt and thrown to the ground. Ben slammed his door closed again and flipped the lock. He reached behind the seat and pulled out a tire iron.

It would buy a couple of minutes, but that was it.

Adrian flipped to his feet with a half leap and grabbed the nearest attacker, taking him down with a chop to the windpipe that left him gasping for air. The second Warrior had his back to Adrian as people came out of the roadhouse. Number Two made a gesture at the people and murmured something. They continued to their car as if they saw nothing.

Which they didn't, not when a Whisperer told them they didn't.

At least one Whisperer, four Warriors in total, one down already. Adrian charged at the Whisperer, grabbing him and slamming his head against the bed of a nearby pickup. The Whisperer slumped to the ground.

Two down, two to go.

Glass broke. Adrian whirled around to see Warriors Three and Four reaching through Ben's broken car window, fumbling for the lock, for the seat belt. Ben swung the tire iron at the face of Number Three, who'd shoved his head in the car. The Warrior fell back.

Adrian leaped over the hood of the truck, grabbed the third Warrior by the back of his jacket. Number Three slipped his arms from the sleeves and came around, fist thudding into Adrian's ribs. Adrian dropped the jacket and jumped back, sucking in air, then charged again. Number Three met his strike with his own; both blocked, both stepped back.

Adrian and his opponent faced off, circling, looking for an opening. Number Three jabbed, Adrian dodged. Adrian came back swinging, landing an elbow to Three's back. Number Three stumbled, then rounded again, grabbing Adrian's waist and taking them both down into the dirt parking lot.

Adrian was on the bottom. Grabbing Three by the shirt, Adrian flipped them both over, slamming his opponent's head against the packed dirt with the impact. He shoved against Number Three's diaphragm with both hands to heave himself to his feet, knocking the wind out of the Warrior. A hard kick to the head made sure Number Three would stay down. Adrian turned to the last man.

Number Four had managed to drag Ben from the pickup. Ben put up a good fight, but he was over fifty and no match for a young Atlantean Warrior with super strength. Still, he made it hard for his captor to haul him very far before Adrian caught up to them.

When he saw Adrian coming after them, Number Four dropped Ben in the dirt and charged forward to meet the challenge. Adrian went after him with a blur of movements that had the younger man scrambling to counter. In the end, Adrian took him out with a leaping kick to the head that snapped him unconscious. Number Four dropped like a stone.

Ben struggled to get up, and Adrian went to help him. "Well," the older man said, "I'd say you earned your beer tonight."

"I'll hold you to that. Can you drive?"

"I think so." Ben walked to the open door. "Damn, that window is going to set me back."

"I'll take care of it. If I'd been paying closer attention, they wouldn't have gotten so close."

"Ah, you did fine." Ben slapped Adrian on the upper arm. "But if you really want to pay for the window, you can probably talk me into it."

"I've got it." Adrian scanned the dark parking lot around them. The four Warriors were still down, one or two groaning, but he had the feeling they were not alone. "Let's change hotels," he said to Ben. "I don't like the security of the one we're at."

"You mean how there's no security at all?" Ben picked up his tire iron off the ground and threw it behind the seat. "I assume we're dealing with the Mendukati?"

"I'd say so."

"Then we'll do what you want to do. This is your area." Ben grabbed a rag and swiped broken glass off his seat before climbing back into the truck. "Let's get out of here before they come to."

"Agreed." Adrian went to the passenger side. Number One lay facedown in the dirt outside the truck door, just coming back to consciousness. Adrian boosted himself into the truck using the back of the stirring Warrior, flattening Number One into the dirt again. When he was seated, he pulled out his cell phone and started looking for hotels. "Head back so we can get our stuff while I arrange for a new room."

"You got it." Ben started the pickup and pulled out of the parking lot, leaving the four Warriors groaning on the ground.

· · · · ·

Azotay watched them go. Normally he would order his men to pursue, but his focus was on the Warrior who had been with Wakete. And there was no doubt this was a Warrior, but not Mendukati. In fact he seemed familiar, eerily familiar, and that last leaping head kick had clinched it for him.

He hadn't seen that kick in nearly twenty years. The specialty of the Temple of Mneseus.

He turned away from the scene, his breath caught in his throat. Could it be? After so long?

Forget the carver. He could take him when he needed to.

He had to find out more about this Mneseus Warrior who guarded him. Where was the temple now? Who was the current maisu-ra, the Master Warrior of the temple?

Heart pounding, he telepathically ordered the troops back to camp.

· · · · ·

Faith had more fun than she'd realized. She sat on a lounge chair and ate a burger and salad and laughed. Rafe and Cara kept up a lively conversation with Maria and John occasionally chiming in. Darius's parents still held back a bit, the shadow of the recent murders lingering like the scent of burned popcorn, but it was clear the family was very close. Even Tessa tossed out a comment or two, but she kept her sharp tongue silent when it came to Faith, settling for the occasional cold glance now and again.

Faith ignored her. There were other distractions that claimed her attention, such as Darius's warm body beside her on the lounge chair, his leg touching hers every now and again. He wasn't overt about it, but he would reach for things and brush against her. Subtly. Accidentally. His hand grazing her arm, his foot bumping hers.

She could have been eating sand for all she knew.

And now that she sat near Rafe, that disorienting buzz played at the bottom of her senses, like a bee flying near her ear. She knew it was a stone, but was it his or was it residuals from the Stone of Igarle? She had connected with the ancient stone, and it knew her now. Maybe it was affecting other stones around her?

She shrugged it off. She would work with the stone again tomorrow and start unraveling the chaos within it. Probably Rafe did have a focus stone of some sort that needed balancing, and that's what she sensed.

Then Darius reached past her for a napkin, his fresh-washed hair an inch from her nose, and she forgot everything else.

When he moved back to his seat, she set down her plate and sat back.

"You get enough to eat, Faith?" John asked. "We have s'mores coming later."

"Oh, then I'm glad I didn't stuff myself. The burger was great, and I was thinking about another one, but I can never turn down s'mores. Better leave room." Faith patted her belly.

John nodded. "Smart thinking."

Darius set down his plate with a half-eaten burger, his second by her count. "I think I'm going to walk some of this off before s'mores." He turned to Faith. "Want to come so I don't fall down the mountain?"

She considered for a moment. Going off alone with Darius hadn't been in her plans, but Cara had raised some questions she wanted answered. "Who could resist an invitation like that?" she said.

"Come on." He stood and got his cane, then moved out of the way so she could get off the lounge chair.

"S'mores in an hour," John announced. "If you're not here, I'm eating yours."

"Not if I get there first, Dad," Rafe said.

Darius shook his head. "My loving family. Be back in a bit." He gestured for Faith to precede him, pointing to the paved path leading off the pool area. "We'll go down there. It's an easy walk and still close enough to tackle my brother if he goes for my share of the s'mores."

"Your family's really nice," she said, starting down ahead of him. "Well, as nice as they can be, given the circumstances."

"Everyone seems to be on their best behavior. Trying to keep going despite the bad news earlier."

"I guess so," she said. "I never had siblings, though I grew up in an orphan camp with other kids. Still, it's not the same. And when my powers manifested and they knew what I was, things changed."

A section of the pavement widened and curved to reveal a bench. Darius pointed to it, and she sat down. Murmurs of conversation drifted to them from the patio area, punctuated by occasional laughter. Close enough that they didn't seem alone, but isolated enough that they could be if they wanted to.

Darius sat next to her, hanging his cane on the armrest. "So a Stone Singer is treated differently from other kids?"

"Oh, yeah. A Stone Singer's the rarest of the elemental Channelers. As soon as my powers started to flare, the elders had a ceremony and gave me these." She held out her hands with their spiderweb-like tattoos. "Every Stone Singer has borne these tattoos since time immemorial. The ink is made from minerals, the better to integrate stone with the singer."

"Sounds like you didn't want them."

"I was nine. I didn't know what I wanted." She clenched her

hands into fists and rested them in her lap. "Not that I have much choice anyway. I am what I am."

"That's the same for all of us, I think." He looked back as a laugh reached his ears. "I'm a Seer. I've always been a Seer. It's all I know. And until a few months ago, I thought my family constituted the sole survivors of Atlantis. Now I've learned differently, and I'm trying to get up to speed on this new world." He smiled. "Please forgive my questions if I get too nosy."

She shrugged. "All I know about Seers is what I learned from my people. So far, they seemed to have lied about just about everything." She gave him a sidelong glance. "Unless you really do eat small children for breakfast."

"Only on Thursdays." He barked a laugh as her mouth dropped open. "Kidding, Faith. Wow."

She flushed. "I know. You just surprised me is all."

"I think we're surprising each other."

"Yes, and I'm not sure I'm ready for that."

"What do you mean by that?"

"I'm messing this up." She dropped her face in her hands, then sat up again, smoothing her hair back. "Okay, so you know I was married."

"Yes, to Ben's son. And he died."

"Right." She swallowed. "We weren't married for long, just a couple of years, but I've known Ben since my parents died. He was a teacher at the camp. I think I gravitated toward him because he was a stone carver. At any rate, one day Michael asked me to marry him, and it seemed like a good idea."

"Maybe it was, at the time."

"I think I just wanted to belong to a family." She sighed. "Michael was an Echo. Do you know what that is?"

He relaxed into the bench, laying his arm along the back. "Never heard that term before."

"An Echo is a Channeler who amplifies the powers of others. He had no active power, just the ability to make others stronger."

"Kinda cool. Most of the time Atlantean powers don't work on other Atlanteans."

"This is an exception." She swiped her hand over her mouth. "I don't know why I'm even telling you this."

"You don't have to."

"I just want you to understand. You know, why I can't—" She shook her head. "Maybe I'm imagining things, but it seems like there's something between us. Chemistry. Attraction. Something."

"I won't deny that. I felt it the first time we met."

"Okay, so we agree there's something. Anyway, I don't know if I'm ready for that right now. Or if you're even thinking about that."

"I do think about it." He waited until she met his gaze. "I think about you. The other night, when I was meditating, I have to admit my imagination got a little . . . hot."

His little half smile added wicked dimensions to the word *hot*. Her core melted at memories of those images, at the truth of his admission, of this moment. "You were thinking about me?" Was that really her voice, so breathy and low?

"I was." He rubbed the top of the bench with his fingers. She wondered if he knew he was doing it, what he imagined he was touching.

"I had a dream about you, too, that night. And I can't believe I just told you that." She jerked to her feet, her hand clapped over her mouth.

He remained still. If he'd made a move toward her, she might have bolted. As long as he didn't pursue, she stayed where she was, her muscles quivering with the instincts to either turn to him or flee. Or maybe both.

"So we connected that night," he said.

"Maybe."

"Perhaps because I was doing such high-powered healing work with stones, and you're a Stone Singer? Maybe you picked something up?"

She calmed at that, nodding. "That's one explanation."

"And if it got . . . intense . . . maybe it's just that latent attraction manifesting."

"It was intense, all right. That is, if you had the same dream I did."

"We'll have to compare notes sometime." He grinned at the appalled look she sent him. "Oh, come on."

"I am not about to confide my secret naughty dreams to you, Darius Montana."

"Naughty, huh?"

"This is getting out of control. I came here to do a job, not to have a romance. I don't have time for it, and I don't want it. Once was enough."

"You're counting your marriage as a romance, I assume?"

"Closest thing I came to it, even if it did end in disaster."

"I was engaged once," he said. "It hurts when it doesn't work out."

She nodded. "Cara mentioned that. Said she left when you got hurt."

"Yes." He winced. "She loved me, but she couldn't deal with a husband in a wheelchair. Kind of tragic now, but at the time it was devastating."

Faith shook her head. "You're an impressive man, in or out of a wheelchair, Darius, at least as far as I've seen. I'm sorry she couldn't take it."

"So my injuries don't bother you? Not even that first night when I needed my wheelchair?"

"I was surprised, that's all. No one warned me. Seeing a big, strong guy like you in a wheelchair just seemed . . . I don't know, ridiculous at the time. Wrong. You looked like you could tie the thing into a knot with your bare hands."

"Not quite, but I wanted to once or twice. In the early days." He patted the bench beside him. "Come back here. Tell me more about Michael."

"That's a depressing conversation." She eased back down on the bench. "Why don't you tell me something?"

"Sure, whatever you want."

"What is a destined mate?"

He reared back. "You been talking to my mother?"

"No, Cara. She mentioned she and Rafe are destined mates."

"Oh, okay."

She arched her brows. "What does your mother have to do with this?"

"You know mothers." He waved a hand. "She likes to set her kids up."

"Ah, get them all settled down, huh?"

He shrugged. "Anyway, a destined mate is when two people are fated to be together, and their powers entwine to make them stronger."

"But Cara has no powers, right? She's just human."

"She's not Atlantean, no. But she is connected to Rafe through what we call the mating bond, and she has the ability to feed his powers if all else fails."

"What are his abilities? I mean, I know nothing about Seers. Do you guys just sit around looking into pools of water or crystal balls? See stuff?"

He laughed. "Not quite. Every Seer has the ability to see the truth, so if a human is lying, we know it. Some have other gifts. Like Rafe, he can find things."

"Handy. So if your car keys go missing, he's the guy you call?"

"Not exactly. He finds people. He's a bounty hunter."

"Oh." She resisted the urge to twist her fingers together, instead stretching out her fingers along her thighs. "This conversation has gone way off topic."

"I would agree, if I knew what the topic was to begin with."

The mischief in his gaze, in his voice, slipped beneath her guards like they were tissue paper. The heat of him called to her, and she curled her fingers into fists. This unexpected attraction to a Seer, of all people, had not been in her plans. But the humor quirking his mouth, the edge of danger added by his goatee and mustache that prevented him from being too pretty, the teasing and *kind* light in his eyes . . .

He was way too appealing.

"The topic is—" She cleared her throat. "I just didn't want there to be any misunderstandings. I'm here to work on the stone."

"Right." He nodded.

"The idea of any kind of . . . um . . . personal relationship is probably not a good idea."

"Probably?"

"*Not* a good idea," she reiterated. "Not just because I'm working for you. Also because, well, it's not a good idea. No romance."

"You've been thinking about this a lot, haven't you?"

"A bit, yes." She held her breath, then made herself softly exhale. "I'm not cut out for romance. It doesn't work for me. Because of who—what—I am."

"So Stone Singers have to be alone?"

"I have no idea; I'm the only Stone Singer I know. But my one attempt at romance ended in disaster." She met his gaze with what she hoped was firm resolve. "I don't want you to get the wrong idea. Relationships, well, they just don't work for me."

"So let me get this straight." He sat up, leaning forward. "Your husband had a passive power, and you are one of the most powerful Channelers out there."

"Yes."

"Did Michael want to control your power?"

"How did—" She bit back the anger, took a breath, and spoke more calmly. "It bothered him that he didn't have a more active power, something cool and flashy. That's understandable."

"It is." He covered one of her fists with his hand and eased her fingers open. "He sounds like he was competitive."

"Oh, yeah." She let him spread her fingers apart, turn over her hand until theirs were palm to palm. "He was competitive."

"I'm just taking a guess here, so let me know if I'm out of line."

She couldn't look away. "Okay."

"I suspect that he was jealous of you."

The words stung as if he'd ripped a Band-Aid from her flesh. Tears sprang up from nowhere. She blinked back the sudden moisture and raised her chin. "I tried not to do anything to make him feel that way."

"Faith." His lips curved. "I doubt you did anything wrong. Some people feel that way no matter what, and there's nothing to be done."

She swallowed and tried to ignore the squeeze in her chest. No one but Ben had ever taken her side before. "Not everyone sees it that way."

"Did people blame you for his death?"

"Some. Look, enough about this. It's a painful subject. Back to what I was saying. There's this thing going on between us, and I didn't want you to get the wrong idea. There's about a hundred reasons why we should ignore this."

"Like?"

"Oh, come on. You're a Seer."

"And you're a Channeler. So?"

She scoffed. "Seers are . . . well, they're—"

"The bogeymen?"

"Well, the way you say it makes it sound ridiculous."

"It is, kind of." He linked their fingers together. "It's like saying you can't go out with me because I have blue eyes." She opened her mouth to retort, but he held up his other hand. "Listen, I get it. You were raised to think the Seers are evil. But we're not, so let's toss that idea, okay? What else you got?"

"Well, I'm working for you. That sort of makes you the boss."

"Technically, my father is paying you, so he's your boss. You and I are more like coworkers. Office romance. Next?"

"I barely know you."

"You're living in my family's house. We'll be seeing a lot of each other. Besides . . ." He held up their clasped hands. "We survived the Stone of Ekhia together."

"Igarle." At his inquiring look, she clarified, "All three of the stones together are the Stones of Ekhia, but each one has an individual name. They're Igarle, Gerlari, and Eraldatu. You have Igarle in your possession, the stone of the Prophets."

"Prophets, huh?"

"Seers, actually. Gerlari, the Warriors; Eraldatu, the Channelers."

"Is this your way of changing the subject?"

"No, I just—" She shut her eyes. "Maybe."

"Avoiding it won't make it go away." He traced her palm with his thumb. "Look, I wasn't necessarily looking for this, either."

"We should just ignore it. There's no good way for this to end."

"Are you certain of that? Seems to me if we go into this whatever-it-is with eyes open, we should be fine." He squeezed her fingers. "You and I, we're a lot alike. We both gambled by doing things the right way with people we thought were the right ones. In both cases, it ended badly. That doesn't mean we should cash in our chips and leave the table."

"Your fiancée didn't die."

"But your husband did. I know you don't want to tell me the story, at least not yet, but based on what I know about you, I would wager it wasn't your fault."

"You're big with the gambling metaphors today."

"I'm not going to let you change the subject, Faith. You've given me a list of reasons why we should ignore this attraction between us. I'm going to give you one reason why we shouldn't."

He bent his head, staring at her mouth with bone-melting intensity. As he leaned in, she knew the smart thing to do was run.

Instead, she waited to see what it felt like to kiss a Seer.

· · · · ·

He was dying to taste her.

Darius couldn't pinpoint the exact moment it started, but somehow in the last twenty-four hours, somewhere between the Mendukati attack and his physical burnout, Faith had taken over the bulk of his thoughts. Sure, she was cute and, hey, powerful, but he suspected it was her emotional reaction to him that had ensnared him like a honeybee to a sunflower. Her genuine attraction soaked his senses and left him half drunk and wanting more.

He leaned closer, watching to see if she pulled away, empathy alert for the slightest hint that he'd misread her. But she sat firm, watching him come. Anticipation rippled over him, both from her and from himself, jacking up his pulse. She licked her lips, and he tugged her closer by their joined hands and brushed her lips with his.

It was a gentle kiss, an exploration more than a demand, yet the snap of connection between them struck like a hammer to steel. He physically jolted, nearly breaking the kiss, then cupped the back of her head with his free hand and sank into the taste and feel of her. Her stiff spine slowly relaxed, and her fingers, tangled with his, tightened and then eased. She opened for him, letting him explore. He could sense her curiosity, her tentative excitement. It fed his own hunger.

He slid further into their shared passion, intoxicated with the pure sweetness of her response, touching the mating bond and gliding along its silky length. He wondered if she sensed it yet. What she would do when she did.

She broke the kiss, flattening her hand against his chest when he would have leaned in again. Her eyes shone, her cheeks flushed an adorable pink, and her shaky breaths brushed his damp lips. "Someone's calling you."

He listened, heard Tessa calling his name, let out a sigh. Closing his eyes, he rested his forehead against Faith's and sent a mental question. *What is it, Tess?*

He hadn't tried to conceal his impatience at being disturbed, and he could sense Tessa's surprise and pique. *Dad said to come up now if you want s'mores. If you're not too* busy, *that is.*

We'll be up in a minute.

I'm timing you, came the snarky reply.

He ignored his sister and focused on the woman in his arms. "Time for s'mores, if you still want some."

She sighed, half reluctant. "That might be a good idea. This was . . . unexpected."

"And new, and we should take it slow and all that, right?"

"Probably a good idea, considering."

"Okay." He gestured toward the path. "Ladies first."

She rose and waited as he got up and took his cane from where he'd hooked it over the arm of the bench. He held out a hand. She hesitated.

"Too early for hand-holding?" he asked. "We were just necking on the bench there."

Her color deepened. "It was one kiss."

"A hell of a kiss. Come here." He took her hand and pulled her closer. "It's fine if you want to take this slow and not share it with everyone up there."

She nodded. "I think that's smart. It's all kind of fast."

"Then that's what we'll do." He pressed a kiss to her fingers. "Tomorrow morning around nine work for you?"

"To work with the stone?" At his nod, she said, "Nine's fine."

"Can't wait." He grinned. "Then we can be alone . . . you, me, and the stone."

"Heck of a chaperone."

He barked a laugh. "Go on, head up. I'll be right behind you."

She headed toward the path and said over her shoulder, "I suspect the reason men always let women go first is so they can check them out from behind."

"Of course."

She giggled, an unusually flirtatious sound for her, and started up the path. He picked his way more slowly in her wake. He wanted to delay reuniting with his family for a few moments longer, to pretend there wasn't all this tension and that he and Faith could explore this passion between them in peace and at their own pace. But he knew that wasn't going to happen. Too many very real obstacles lay in their path, and he had to navigate them carefully. Faith had been used so many times in her life, and her willingness to pursue a romantic interest was yet fragile. He would have to step carefully to avoid scaring her away.

Then there was the consideration of the mate link. That connection had proven an effective weapon for Rafe and Cara when Jain Criten had come calling, and he couldn't ignore the practical aspect of cultivating it. But he preferred to think of that as a free gift with purchase rather than the main reason for getting closer to Faith.

He thought about Michael and the scars he had left on Faith, the damage from manipulation and betrayal. He had no intention of being the next man in her life who used her for her power. He wanted so much more than that, so much that was uniquely her. But she reminded him again of those abused women he'd worked with in the shelters, and he knew that it took a lot to come back from that mindset. It would take both time and patience. He had plenty of patience, but they were running short on time.

He still didn't know exactly how Michael had died and what role Faith had played, but from where he sat, it was a good thing the bastard was dead.

Because otherwise, Darius would have had to kill him.

CHAPTER EIGHT

Thunder crashed, echoing off the walls of the shining citadel at the center of the mighty metropolis. Lightning ripped across the sky. Waves swelled above the buildings of the city, only to smash down like Poseidon's own wrathful hand, sweeping away everything in their wake. Ships split like kindling, the harbor gone without a trace. The ocean boiled.

The earth shrieked, stone and soil crumbling like ash. Those who could scurried to what boats they might find, praying they would yet escape. The marauding tide scooped up everything not fast enough to flee and even some that were: elephants and horses and merchant ships from afar. Blazing red light shot into the sky from the temple, fire without flame.

Atlantis shattered, its very foundations ripped from the earth, its glorious walls and palaces and harbors cracking into rubble, sinking into an abyss of mud and sea. All its glory, all its knowledge, lost.

But like dandelion seeds on the wind, some few escaped, drifting away on friendly tides, dodging debris and destruction to begin anew far from home. . . .

Faith woke with a gasp. It was dark. Her heart raced, and her mouth was dry. She gulped for air. Though she'd kicked the covers from the bed, fine sweat misted her skin. Her tattoos throbbed and her limbs trembled as if she'd been running.

Or trying to escape a cataclysm.

The smooth sheets beneath her palms reminded her of where she was. The Montana house. Arizona, not Atlantis.

She sat up and swung her feet over the side of the bed, reaching for the bottle of water she kept on her nightstand. Her throat burned as if she'd been trapped in a fire, or struggling for air beneath a merciless sea. Unscrewing the cap, she chugged back several long swallows, then pressed the bottle against her hot forehead. The plastic was cool from the air conditioning.

A dream. Just a dream.

She glanced over to the window, where the light from the lamps along the driveway below cast a soft glow into her room. No fire. No lightning, no thunder. No tidal waves. No getting swallowed by the earth forever.

Where had the dream come from?

Memories, came the whisper through her mind.

She knew that ancient rasp: the Stone of Igarle. She reached for the stone, just a feather-light touch. *Whose memories?*

Mine.

She took a slow, deep breath. Most stones absorbed some emotion from the humans who handled them, but she'd never heard of one that recorded events without a human link. Then again, she'd never encountered anything like this stone before.

You woke me, it whispered. *So long have I slept, never to touch another since the Before Time. Then you were there, after so long. So very long . . .*

Pressure crushed down on her chest, and her tattoos flared anew. She tried to sever the connection, but the stone clung to her like a drowning man to driftwood, sucked her in further. Swamped her with its anguish. A sob erupted from her throat. So black. So alone. Eons passing, each the same as the one before. Her eyes flooded, and tears overflowed down her cheeks. Always alone. Shouting, yet never heard. The most torturous of existences, cut off from contact with anyone or anything.

So much to share. So much to tell.

Her muscles contracted in unyielding spasms, forcing her to curl into herself, clasping her knees. Her throat tightened. She couldn't breathe. Cramped. Dark. Too much to say and no one to hear. Until now.

Images crashed into her consciousness, one after the other. She gasped for breath, tried to keep up. But the deluge hammered her brain like hard summer rain against a tin roof. Relentless. Too much at once. Couldn't see. Couldn't understand. She struggled to focus, but control slipped from her shaky grasp.

Darius, she whispered in her mind.

. . . . .

Darius burst out of his room in the guesthouse, hurrying along the pool toward the main house as fast as his damned knee would allow. The sun hadn't yet risen, and the night echoed the black anguish that had awoken him from a sound sleep, flooding his empathic senses and filling his mouth with the essence of burned coffee and rotten vegetables. Then the darkness had cut off, leaving him panting and sweaty with cold dread weighing in his gut. He'd reached for Faith out of instinct. Nothing. She'd vanished from his empathic radar.

Until she whispered his name.

He'd thrown on shorts and a T-shirt and scrambled out of his room. His body protested the impatient pace he demanded, but still he forged on, searching for the mate link. He found it, a frail, quivering silver strand. Good, she was alive. He grabbed hold of it, wrapped it around his own essence, and used it as a rope in the storm to guide him home.

Guide him to Faith.

He made it to the house, ignored his nemesis—the stairs—and went for the elevator. Whatever would get him to her faster. When he finally flung open the door to her room, his heart nearly stopped.

Faith was curled in a fetal position on the bed, shaking, her face pale and her eyes wide and cloudy. Tears gleamed on her cheeks in the dim light from the hallway.

"Faith." He said her name, with his voice and with his mind. He sat on the bed and reached for her. She remained curled in that ball, and his attempts to straighten her stiff limbs met with no success. Her muscles seemed to be locked in this rigid form, and he didn't dare try to force it, lest he hurt her.

He hauled her into his lap as she was, wrapping his arms around her, and followed the mate link into a maelstrom of memories.

His normal empathy had shut down. Everything he got, he received through the mating bond with Faith. Anguish. Desolation. But not from her. From the Stone of Igarle.

The sheer magnitude of the stone's longing for contact smothered like a wool blanket on a hot summer day. Darius pushed his way through the emotional muck as if he swam in a strong current, the bright light that was Faith flickering in the distance. He sent reassurance along the mate link, hoping to reach her. Hoping it would make a difference.

The stone must have sensed what he was doing. The black sludge grew thicker, swirling around him like tar, weighing down his arms and legs. The muck slipped into his nose and throat, drowning him. He tried to shove aside the black ooze, but it piled on even more. He couldn't walk, could barely move, could hardly breathe.

They had to break this connection.

Faith. Let go!

. . . . .

Faith heard Darius from a distance. She turned in a circle, disoriented by the tar pit–like wasteland where she found herself. How had she gotten here?

Darius?

She saw him now, far away, just as she had seen him the last time the stone had entangled her. He gave off a blue glow, with a silver ribbon leading back to him, but he was in trouble. The black goo of the stone's toxic emotions had piled on him from his feet to his chin, trapping his arms at his sides. She ran toward him, following the ribbon and dodging piles of stagnant, seething, ancient emotions. This was the second time the stone had captured her, and this time she wasn't even touching it.

It was more powerful than she'd thought. And it was ticking her off.

Faith. Darius called to her again. *Follow the link. It will lead you home.*

The stone protested. *No! Stay. I have so much to tell you, so much to show you.*

But Faith dodged the new tentacles that tried to wrap around her and headed for the blue light that was Darius.

When she reached him, the ooze had crept up his chin to his mouth. He kept spitting it out, his gaze on her. He couldn't talk without swallowing the stuff. She shoved her hands into the muck covering his chest, against his heart, and began to sing.

She sang of loneliness and forgotten times. Of bittersweet promises left unfulfilled. Of betrayal and love and the things that should have happened and didn't. Of what did happen, and shouldn't have. She sang the song the stone needed to hear, until with a nearly audible sob, the blackness melted away, releasing them.

Faith snapped back to herself in the real world. With a groan, she sat up, Darius steadying her as she stretched out her arms and legs with slow, easy movements. She heard the stone whispering, lamenting, trying to coax her back in, but she wasn't biting. As long as she didn't respond to it, it couldn't trap her again.

Trying to get the kinks out, she twisted at the waist and found her mouth inches away from Darius's. Reality hit her with a crash: his hair-roughened legs beneath her, his hands on her hips, the mouthwatering scent of his shampoo. And those eyes, those insanely beautiful eyes, soft with concern yet intent as he studied her face. "You okay?" he asked.

"I seem to be. How about you?" She eased off his lap to sit beside him on the mattress. The burning of her tattoos was starting to subside.

"I'm okay. What happened?"

She shook her head. "One minute I was dreaming, and the next the stone had linked with me. Swallowed me." She swept a hand over her hair. "I've never known a stone to be able to do that unless I was either holding it or in close proximity."

"As far as I know, the thing is still locked up tight," Darius said.

"Well, it has a far reach, like a black muck smothering me. But I don't think it meant to hurt me."

"I don't know about its intentions, but I've never encountered anything like that before."

"Strange that we were trapped together. I don't think that's ever happened to me before." She pursed her lips in thought. "Why you?"

"Beats me. That was some trip. I swear I have more gray hair now."

"What gray hair?" she scoffed. "You're not even thirty yet, are you?"

"Thirty-one in June."

"Methuselah."

"And don't you forget it." He stroked the back of his hand along her cheek. "You going to tell me how this happened? Because if you don't, I'll make up my own version, and that will be far worse."

She grabbed his hand, but rather than shoving it away, she just held it. "The stone is lonely. It's been eons since the last Stone Singer balanced it, and it's absorbed countless emotions from countless humans over countless centuries. Think of it as your crazy great-uncle who recites bad poetry when he's had too much to drink."

"Ouch."

"Exactly. Ever since the first contact yesterday it's been whispering to me, trying to get my attention."

"Why didn't you say anything?"

She shrugged. "I have stones whispering to me all the time. It's a white noise that I can ignore if I need to."

"Guess this one didn't like being ignored."

"No, it really didn't. It's going to take a lot of work to make it healthy again."

Darius frowned. "I don't want you taking any risks. As important as this thing is, it's not worth your safety."

"I'll be fine." She smiled. "As long as you keep doing your lighthouse imitation whenever I get stuck."

"What do you mean, lighthouse imitation?"

"Twice I've gotten lost in that stone, and twice you've led me out. I see you as a glowing blue light in my mind, and that shows me the way."

"I still don't like you taking these chances." He lifted their clasped hands to his lips. Goose bumps prickled along her flesh, and she had to make herself focus on his words. "Promise me you'll be careful."

"I'm being as careful as I can." Her voice came out huskier than she'd intended, and she cleared her throat. "How'd you know I was in trouble?"

"You called me. I woke out of a sound sleep because I heard you whisper my name."

"I'm glad you did, but you could have been trapped in there. I almost didn't get you free in time."

"But you did. Thank you."

She rubbed her face. "Man, I'm tired. Why can't these things happen in daylight? Why always in the middle of the night?"

"Maybe because when you're asleep, it's easier for the stone to tap into your subconscious?"

"You may be right about that." She yawned. "And now I'm beat."

"You need to get some sleep." He reached for his cane, which had fallen to the floor. "Do you want me to stay?"

Soft words in a quiet night should not have made her heart race, but they did. She'd only started to level out from the incident with the stone, and now her adrenaline streaked back to maximum again. He sat there on the bed next to her, white T-shirt stretched over that powerful upper body, long hair mussed from sleep, and watched her with calm eyes as he awaited her response.

Such patience. She wondered how patient he was in other areas. . . .

"Faith?"

"Sorry." She managed a smile.

"Do you want me to stay? You know, in case it happens again?" He tapped his knee. "These old bones probably couldn't take another dash from the guesthouse."

"I'm too big to be afraid of the dark."

"The dark can't hurt you. It's what lives in the dark that you have to watch out for." He gave her that charming grin that always made her pulse zing.

She should tell him to go.

"Or I can crash in the other guest room down the hall."

"No." The word escaped her lips before her brain could talk her out of the decision. "This sounds silly, but I really don't want to be alone right now."

"Not silly at all."

"Said the spider to the fly."

"Hey, hey." He put up his palms in surrender. "Just offering bodyguard services."

"Uh-huh." She let out a long sigh. "I would appreciate not being alone, but I'm not ready for more than that, no matter what happened earlier."

"You mean the kiss."

"Yes, I mean the kiss."

"Understood. Which side of the bed do you want?"

"Huh?"

"My chivalry may be alive and well, Faith, but my body can't handle bunking on the floor. It's a king-size bed. We should be able to sleep without even touching, if that's what you're worried about."

"Fine. Yes, okay." She got to her feet. "I get the bathroom first."

"Sure. Gentleman, remember?" He stood as well. "Now, the bed. Right or left? I'd prefer the side closest to the door." He shrugged, that crooked grin curving his lips. "Not that the stone will grow legs and attack us."

"At least not that we know of." She waved a hand. "Whatever you want is fine. I need sleep."

She wandered into the bathroom, wondering if she was making a huge mistake in letting him stay. Not that she worried about Darius pouncing on her. She trusted him to keep his word to not force anything.

It was herself she didn't trust.

. . . . .

Darius sat down on the bed and listened to the water running behind the closed bathroom door. He leaned his cane against the wall between the bed and the nightstand, then looked down at his trembling hands. For all the cool exterior he'd presented to Faith, his heart still pounded. Sweat still coated his skin. He couldn't close his eyes without seeing that wasteland of sludge and muck, centuries of human emotions broken down into pure, physical desolation.

At least that's what he thought it was. As soon as Faith had come into contact with the stone's energy, his empathic abilities had winked out. Atlantean powers were always rendered neutral around the Stones of Ekhia except, apparently, for a Stone Singer. It made sense. The Stone Singer needed to balance the stones, and she wouldn't be able to do that if her powers were cut off.

The only exceptions seemed to be any form of empathic ability, like his and his mother's, or the ability to amplify another's power, like Faith's late husband had had. Since other Atlanteans were used to their abilities not working on one another, it wasn't quite as disorienting for them when the stones rendered them temporarily powerless. But for him, whose powers always worked on everyone—he hated it.

He didn't know how to function in the world without his empathy.

The water shut off. He didn't want Faith to come out and find him sitting there as if he'd been waiting; she'd take it as pressure. Once she'd broken free of the stone's hold, his abilities had come rushing back, and he knew that while she was attracted to him and was beginning to trust him, she still had reservations.

And he had one or two himself, at least until he got the full story out of her about how her husband had died.

He swung his legs up onto the bed and made himself comfortable on top of the covers. When she stepped out of the bathroom, she glanced at him, her titillated uncertainty like spiced honey on the tongue. He didn't give any indication he was awake. She reached back into the bathroom, the light behind her silhouetting her breasts and erect nipples through her thin cotton T-shirt. She flicked the switch and the light went out.

Darius lay as still as he could while she tiptoed around to the other side of the bed and got in with a quick dip of the mattress and a rustle of sheets. The mating bond between them stretched warm and sweet like old-fashioned taffy, and he wanted a taste more than anything. She did, too, but that barrier of wariness still lingered. Until she took it down, it was hands to himself on his own side of the bed.

Besides, the remnants of her encounter with the stone still

lingered, rippling through the currents of her drowsiness like jagged driftwood, leaving splinters in tender places. He reached out with his senses, captured those shards of negativity, smoothed them into soft, warm balls of reassurance and eased them back into her fading consciousness. She drifted into a peaceful sleep.

He stared into the darkness. The oblivion of slumber beckoned just beyond his reach. Sunrise could not come soon enough.

CHAPTER NINE

Darius woke up at 6:30 the next morning, years of keeping a disciplined schedule rousing him without benefit of an alarm clock. He glanced at Faith. She appeared to be sleeping peacefully, and a quick empathic check confirmed it. No nightmares from the stone's antics last night. He grabbed his cane from the floor and slipped from the bed, trying not to jostle her.

He'd started toward the door when she made a sound. The sheets rustled, and he paused to appreciate the image of her in bed, her delicate features relaxed and her dark hair tousled. She'd kicked away the bedding, and he took a moment to enjoy her long legs revealed by the skimpy cotton sleep shorts, the inches of midriff uncovered by the cotton T-shirt that had ridden up. He imagined slipping back into bed beside her and pushing that shirt all the way up. She wasn't particularly busty, but he couldn't deny the affect her slender, athletic build had on him. The idea of nuzzling those sweet, small breasts in the early dawn hours had his body responding.

She murmured in her sleep. Could she sense his thoughts? In his mind he stroked his hands along that fair skin, sliding under her top to grasp her breasts. She murmured again and arched her back. Her erect nipples poked against the pliable cotton.

He gripped his cane. His morning erection had returned with a vengeance, and his mouth watered as he stared at those inviting peaks.

She said no, dumb-ass. He made himself turn away. He had

time for a swim, and the water would still be chilly from the evening's dip in temperature. Seemed like the most prudent option right now. He went to the door and paused again with his hand on the knob. The gentleman in him knew he should probably leave a note or something, but the raging horn dog part knew that if he moved back toward that bed, all bets were off.

He opened the door and stepped out, pulling it shut behind him with a quiet click, and headed down the hall, pondering tackling the stairs rather than the elevator. The physical challenge might help work out some of his sexual frustration. That and the pool should do the trick.

A door opened on his right. "Dar, what are you doing up here this early?" Tessa came out of her room, clad in a navy blue business suit and heels.

"You're all dressed up." He dodged her question with one of his own. "Heading into the office?"

Tessa fell into step beside him. "As a matter of fact, I have to interview someone for the part-time position we have open." She leveled a look at him, which he pretended not to see. Her curiosity scratched like a stiff tag in a new shirt.

"Going in with Dad?" he asked.

"Yes, and you didn't answer my question. You're usually in the pool at this hour. We don't see you in the main house until at least eight o'clock."

"Couldn't sleep."

"Uh-huh. Again, that usually drives you to the pool." She stopped at the top of the stairs and stared him down with those unique violet-colored eyes. Not for the first time, he took comfort in the fact that his sister's powerful ability to see the future did not work on other Atlanteans.

Didn't take the creepy out of that stare, though.

"If I didn't know better, Dar, I'd think you were sneaking home with the sunrise after some romantic liaison." She folded her arms. "But liaisons take two. Unless you're trying to do Rafe dirty with Cara, there's only one other person in this house that could possibly qualify as the other party. And I don't think you're that stupid."

"Butt out, Tess." Darius reached for the banister.

"Tell me I'm wrong, Dar. Tell me you're not betraying this family with that . . . that person."

He stopped and narrowed his eyes at his sister. "You've been a bitch to her since she first showed up here. I'm not sure what's eating you, Tessa, but I can take care of myself. If Faith had any bad feelings toward this family, I would know."

"Someone has to keep a cool head about her." She glanced back at Faith's door, then at him, eyebrows raised. "Clearly you're not."

"Don't pretend you know what's going on, Runt." He used the hated nickname on purpose. "Because you don't."

She tried to hide her flare of anger, but it seared his senses with satisfying intensity. "Whatever."

"Leave Faith alone, Tess. She's not here to hurt us. I'm sure of it." He touched her arm, sent a pulse of reassurance to ease the fear she didn't want to admit. "If you think any woman could come between me and my family, you're wrong."

Slowly she unfolded her arms and twined her fingers with his. "Be careful, Dar. I see the way you look at her."

"It'll be okay, Tess. You have to trust me."

She gave a little laugh. "I do trust you."

"That's all that matters." He grinned. "Race you down the stairs?"

"Ha, I know a sucker bet when I hear one. If you kill yourself, Mom and Dad will kill *me*."

"Then you'd better make sure I don't fall."

She rolled her eyes. "See? Sucker bet." But she stayed beside him every step until they reached the first floor. "Okay, safe and sound." She stood on tiptoe to kiss his cheek. "Stay out of trouble."

"Don't terrorize your interviewee."

"Would I do that?" Her normal confident smile in place, Tessa waved and headed toward the front door.

Darius shook his head and made his way out the patio doors in the back of the house. He'd taken over the guesthouse when he'd been confined to the wheelchair. It was easier for him to get around if he didn't have to deal with stairs, and he'd set up his private workroom in the cabana, where he could work his healing energy. Eventually his parents had installed the elevator in the house so he could get to the upper floors, especially the *ten-plu*, but he'd never moved back into his old bedroom. He liked the privacy of the guesthouse.

He heard his cell phone ringing as he reached his door. Shoving it open, he hurried as fast as he could to where the device sat plugged into the charger on his desk. He glanced at the display and answered the call. "It's not even seven o'clock, Gray."

"Sorry, Darius. This was the best time for me, and I know you're always up early, anyway."

Darius frowned at Gray's somber tone. "What happened?"

"Ben and I were attacked last night."

Darius sat down in his desk chair. "Mendukati."

"I didn't stop for interrogations, but I assume so. Four Warriors jumped us in a restaurant parking lot, tried to grab Ben. One of them was a Whisperer."

"I'd say they know Ben is Faith's weak point." Darius rubbed a hand over his face. "Ben isn't safe."

"I know, but he insists on finishing this show before he'll even talk about protection."

"Stubborn."

"Don't I know it. Listen, I'm sticking to him like glue, but as soon as his show is done, I want to bring him to Sedona."

"Absolutely. With the new modifications to security, this is probably the safest place. Even if you did eventually get in when Dad had you test them."

"Well, it took me awhile. That would buy us some time. And I know where the weaknesses are. It's still the best option."

"Okay. When is the show over?"

"It's a two-day thing. We should be on the road tomorrow night, heading to your place."

"Maybe you should fly. I can have the jet waiting at Santa Fe airport. Should be safer than the road."

"Even better." Adrian sighed. "Damn, I'm going to have to haul all Ben's equipment onto the plane. Stuff's heavy, and he won't leave it."

"Come on, Gray. I think you can handle a few boxes."

"A few boxes of rocks and rock-carving equipment. Heavy as hell."

"Man up, buddy. You've got all that super strength working for you. Call me when you're in the air."

"You got it. See you in a couple of days."

"See you." Darius disconnected the call. Tossing the phone on his desk, he wondered how he was going to break the news to Faith that Ben was in danger.

· · · · ·

Faith awoke alone in the morning. Darius was gone, with barely a dent in the pillow where he'd lain. She might have imagined the whole thing.

Except she hadn't. She remembered every bit of the journey through the stone's emotional wasteland, how it had lured her in. How lonely it was. How it had tried to consume Darius. Just the memory made her shudder. And even after several hours of sleep, she still didn't feel a hundred percent.

Something that had become clear to her afterward was how much the stone longed to be reunited with its counterparts. She didn't mention it to Darius because she didn't want to get his hopes up. Eraldatu, the Channeler's stone, was in Santutegi under Criten's guard and had been for centuries. Igarle was here.

That left only Gerlari to find, and if they did somehow locate it, perhaps with the help of this stone . . .

Criten couldn't harness the power of Atlantis with only a single stone, and while the Seers would be equally powerless having only two of the three, it would keep the war at a stalemate. Taking the plan a step further, perhaps they could even get their hands on the third one, the stone from Santutegi. With that much power in Seer hands, the Mendukati might finally be defeated.

If, if, if. All speculation.

Dismissing her fantasies, Faith got up, pushed aside the curtains of her bedroom window and gazed out. The sun shone strongly from the east, casting its light over the brilliant hues of red rock country. The jagged buttes glowed as if afire against a cloudless blue sky, cut throughout the red by the occasional streak of white or gray or beige, with spiky green foliage dotting the landscape below the peaks.

She'd lived most of her life in New Mexico, so she was no stranger to the beauties of the desert, but this place possessed an almost magical quality different than anything she'd ever known. Even now, she could sense the ancient whispering of the sandstone monoliths around her, rock that had once been at the bottom of a prehistoric ocean or simmering as molten lava. She knew that iron oxide in the mix gave the ordinary sandstone its extraordinary color. She knew the buttes and mesas were the sculptures of water and volcanic activity. But such mundane facts did nothing to dull its majesty, or her own feelings of awe.

The vortexes murmured just beneath audible hearing, like the hum of powerful machinery. She had an idea she wanted to try out using vortex energy, but she wanted to wait until Darius was with her when she did. Just in case.

Strange how quickly she was beginning to trust him, a Seer. First she was working out a plan in her mind to help him get all the Stones of Ekhia and now she was cautious about using her powers without him nearby.

She mused over the strange development as she turned away from the window and went to get her clothes for the day. She hadn't trusted anyone but Ben in a very long time, especially not after so short an acquaintance. And she certainly hadn't kissed anyone, not since Michael.

She laid her clothes out on the bed, then wandered into the bathroom and turned on the shower. If anyone had told her even a few months ago that she would be not only living in a house full of Seers but kissing one of them, she would have thought they were nuts.

She stripped off her new cotton T-shirt and sleep shorts, and stepped beneath the spray.

After Michael's death, she had retreated completely from the Atlantean world, helped along by the condemnation and suspicion of the Mendukati. They had considered Michael an up-and-coming leader in their organization, and hadn't been pleased to hear of his death. But then again, her late husband had convinced them he had her powers—and her—under his control.

And hadn't he? She faced the showerhead and let the water stream over her face. Even now her own gullibility stung. She reminded herself she had been barely twenty-one when they'd married, and younger than that when they'd dated. She'd been a child, blind to the manipulations of an ambitious man five years her senior. She knew this, intellectually, but no one wanted to be a sucker, and that's what Michael had made her.

She'd allowed him to talk her into helping the Mendukati, spinning a tale of the "misunderstood" organization that was only trying to right an ancient wrong. The Seers had selfishly hoarded the Stones of Ekhia, he said, then misused them in a greedy attempt to conquer the other sects of the Atlantean population. The Mendukati was trying to find out the truth by interrogating Seers and searching for the missing Stones of Ekhia to restore the balance. She'd bought that story, too naïve to realize the group's real purpose. It was right there in the name, and she'd missed it.

Mendukati. *Mendeku*—the Atlantean word for revenge.

She squeezed some facial wash into her hands and scrubbed her face with more force than necessary. But she couldn't wash away her own foolishness, or the memories. The Mendukati assimilated people into their ranks and led them down a path of destruction. When she'd realized Michael's true purpose that day on the hillside, she'd tried to walk away.

She hadn't meant to kill him. But he was dead and the Mendukati had won; they'd stained her soul by turning her into a murderer.

Would Darius still find her attractive if he knew?

Her throat tightened. Her eyes burned. She sniffed, denying the tears, and shoved her face beneath the water again. The green girl who'd blindly married the man she'd thought was her soul mate had died on that hill, and now she didn't know who she was. Or what she was supposed to be doing. Working for Lucita had given her a respite, long enough to begin healing, but apparently she'd been naïve again in thinking she could hide from the Atlantean world forever.

Maybe the Seers held the key to the truth.

She finished washing up, then turned off the water and stepped from the stall. As she wrapped a towel around her body, she met her own gaze in the mirror. So pale, and a haunted look in her eyes. She didn't want to be that person again, the emotional wreck Ben had taken into his home before he'd nurtured her back into someone more or less normal. She had to get her head out of the past.

She and Darius would be working with the stone again this morning. She could focus on that. She glanced at the reflection of the bed behind her, the rumpled covers and creased pillow where Darius had lain. She touched her lips. Or she could focus on this new development.

She turned away from the mirror and grabbed a second towel, rubbing it against her hair. She didn't understand this connection she seemed to have with Darius. Sexual attraction was part of it, sure. But there was something more. She'd come to trust him more quickly than she had anyone before, except maybe Michael. She was almost twenty-seven, not a kid anymore, and because of that maybe she could go into a new relationship—but with her eyes wide open—after only knowing him for a couple of days.

. And what a couple of days. Darius had defended her from the Mendukati, whisked her away to safety in the fortified Montana mansion, shared an erotic dream with her, and rescued her when she'd gotten lost in the ancient stone's energy. He'd protected her from the detractors in his family, most notably Tessa's sharp tongue, he'd calmly shot down all her reasons for not getting involved with him, and he'd kissed her in a way that made her head spin.

There was definitely something special about Darius Montana. She could see how he'd fallen into the role of peacemaker. He had a certain calmness about him that soothed those around him and inspired confidence that, whatever your problem, Darius would help you solve it.

Even she believed it.

Her hair only half-damp now, she discarded the towel and pulled out the hair dryer. Once more she caught her own gaze in the mirror. Some of the shadows had disappeared from her eyes, replaced by a sparkle that no doubt came from anticipation of the coming day, and not only because she was working with a legendary stone of power. No, the kiss yesterday had been the start of something. Her lips curved. She couldn't wait to see what revelations today would bring.

Still smiling, she flicked on the dryer and started getting ready for the day.

. . . . .

Faith ran downstairs just after nine o'clock.

She'd daydreamed too long and now she was late, with the prospect of working on the stone looming in front of her. After last night, she wanted to stay as far away from that thing as possible, but she couldn't do that. She was here to do a job, one that would pay her enough money to finally build her own sanctuary away from the Mendukati, and that was worth any sacrifice.

Besides, as long as Darius was nearby, she'd be safe.

She walked into the kitchen, lured by the smell of coffee. Cara sat at the kitchen table, her laptop open and a Bluetooth earpiece in her ear. She waved at Faith, then scowled at her computer screen.

"No, Warren. I told you I can't get the interface done for Monday. Because I'm busy, that's why. Tell the client they can have it Wednesday."

Faith made a cup of coffee and grabbed a freshly baked biscuit from the basket on the counter.

"I've warned you about promising my time before running it past me," Cara said. "Now either you fix this, or find another job." She disconnected the call and pulled the earpiece from her ear, dropping it on the table with a growl.

Faith stopped beside the table. "Is it okay if I sit down? I don't want to disturb you if you're working."

"No, I'm done." Cara closed the laptop. "I'm supposed to be on vacation, but I had to handle this." She tapped her fingers on the table. "I keep telling this moron not to promise things to customers without running it by me first. But he keeps doing it."

"Can you really fire him?" Faith tore off a piece of biscuit and popped it in her mouth.

"Yes. I own the company." Cara rested her chin on her hand.

"But it's complicated, because he's my ex. He has a wife and a newborn little girl. I don't want to be petty."

"Okay, I get that. But if he wasn't your ex, would you still fire him?"

"Maybe. I'd probably write him up first."

"Then do that." Faith washed another piece of biscuit down with some coffee. "Since he's your ex, he might be banking on some old feelings keeping you from firing him."

"Ha! As if that turkey could hold a candle to Rafe. Still . . ." Cara reopened the laptop and clicked the mouse a couple of times. "A write-up isn't a bad idea. It would let him know I'm serious, and it would be in his employment file permanently." She grinned at Faith. "Thanks."

Faith shrugged and sipped her coffee. "Sometimes when feelings are involved, it's hard to see clearly. Consider me an objective observer."

"It's much appreciated."

Lupe came into the kitchen with a box bearing the logo of a well-known delivery service. "Miss Faith, security just brought this for you. It was delivered at the gate." She put the box on the table and headed down the hall to the laundry room.

Faith took the box and glanced at the return address.

"Who could possibly know you're here?" Cara asked.

"It's from Ben." Faith grinned at Cara as she tore the tape off the box. "I asked him to send me some crystals and other things that will help me with the stone." She opened the package and pulled small clear plastic bags out of the box, each containing one or two stones in a myriad of colors.

"What do you mean, help?" Cara picked up a bag of clear quartz crystals and held it up to the light.

"Near as I can tell, it's been a long time since anyone talked to that stone. Centuries. It seems to have forgotten its manners."

Cara handed back the quartz. "Stones have manners?"

"Stones of power do." Faith closed up the box again. "Last

night that darn stone sneaked into my dreams and took me and Darius on a ride through some kind of desolate wasteland. Luckily, I was able to sing us out of there, but it was touch and go."

"I had no idea."

Faith laughed. "Stone singing is not for the faint of heart. But this stuff should help me keep a controlled environment so it doesn't happen again. The stone wants me to balance it, but it has to do it on my terms." Faith shoved the last bite of biscuit into her mouth and washed it down with a swallow of coffee. She stood and grabbed the box. "Darius is waiting, and I'm already late. See you later?"

"Sure. I'll be around . . . writing up Warren."

"Go get him." Faith returned Cara's grin and headed for the cabana.

· · · · ·

Darius waited outside the cabana, frowning as he glanced at his watch. Faith was late. She'd seemed okay this morning when he'd left, but what if something had happened since then? He reached out with his empathy to search for her. And found . . . nothing.

His blood chilled. Where was she? Had she left? Been kidnapped? Been sucked back into that damned stone?

He grabbed his cane and started for the house when he saw her come out the patio doors. She carried a small white box with her and smiled when she saw him. Waving, she quickened her pace.

He let out the breath he hadn't known he'd been holding. His knees turned to water, and he gripped his cane for balance with trembling fingers. She was okay. She was right there in front of him in her hot pink T-shirt and jeans. He hadn't realized how much he feared for her until the relief staggered him.

But why couldn't he sense her emotions? There was a big blank on his empathic radar where she should be.

"Sorry I'm late," she said as she reached him. "Overslept."

"That's okay. It was a rough night." He searched again, but still no hint of her emotional state. He could only go by subtle clues in her expression and demeanor, by the tone of her voice. How did humans survive with such ambiguous clues?

"Yes, it was a rough night." A light flush swept across her cheeks, and she glanced down at the box in her hands. "Thank you for staying with me. I feel kind of silly now in the bright light of day."

"You shouldn't."

"And thank you for not, you know, pushing things." She lifted her gaze to his again. "I wasn't ready and—"

"Faith." He reached out to cup her cheek. "Don't worry so much. Whatever is meant to happen will happen in its own time."

"I guess." She shrugged. "But thanks anyway."

"It was my pleasure." He dropped his hand. Even with his empathic senses not working, he could tell she wanted to move on to another subject. "So what's in the box?"

"Ben sent it." A smile curved her lips. "I asked him to send me some crystals and things that might help keep the Stone of Igarle in line. Once it's balanced, we won't need these safety measures, but for now, I really don't want to tour that wasteland again."

"Good idea. Can I see?"

She folded back the flaps of the box. Gems of all colors and consistencies glimmered at him. "I can set up a safety circle with these."

"Sounds good. Let's get started."

She fumbled with the box flaps to close them, and something flashed on her hand. He realized it was a ring, fashioned with Native American flair out of silver and amethyst. He'd never seen her wear any jewelry before, except for earrings.

"Nice ring," he said. "You get that on your shopping trip with Cara?"

"No, it's mine. Ben made it for me years ago." She nodded toward the cabana. "Shall we?"

"Sure." He swept a hand to indicate she should precede him. "Door's open."

"Okay, let's get this over with."

·   ·   ·   ·   ·

The arts trade show was packed within an hour of the doors opening. Adrian hauled boxes, handed out change, and chatted up customers who were waiting for a moment of Ben's time. The carver knew how to talk to people, and he positively loved conversing about his art. Adrian kept an eye on the crowd, which grew with each hour that passed. So many people, packed into a small space. Logistical nightmare.

And possible opportunity for the Mendukati.

A tall teenaged boy sidled up to the table, all shaggy brown hair, pimples, and sharp blue eyes. His black hooded sweatshirt and swagger indicated he thought he was cool, but his hands fidgeting in the pockets of the hoodie said otherwise.

"So," he said when Ben's most recent customer walked away, "you make all these?" He jerked his chin at the array of carved stone fetishes across the table.

"I did." The older man took off his glasses and cleaned the lenses with a soft cloth.

"What are they made of?"

"Different things."

"Oh." The kid chewed his bottom lip. "So, how do you know what to make? Do people like call you up and ask you for stuff?"

"Once in a while." Ben put his glasses back on. "Most of the time, I listen to what the material wants to be."

"Huh."

"Let me show you." Ben reached down under the table and pulled a palm-sized chunk of light gray marble from a box. "You see this? It's marble. Scraps from a construction site.

Someone was building a house and wanted a fancy bathroom."
Ben chuckled. "This was left over, and they sold me a box of
these because they cannot use them." He offered the stone to the
boy. "Look at it. Tell me what you see."

The young man took it and studied it. "It's a cool color. All
those black lines going through it."

"True. But look closely. You see a hunk of marble. I see a
bear." Ben pointed at a small triangular part that protruded
from the short side of the stone. "This is his nose. And the way
this longer part curves looks like his back." He grinned at the
boy. "The stone tells me what it wants to be."

"I see it now! Yeah, kind of." He handed the marble back.
"Cool."

"When I am done, it will look like one of these." Ben indicated his display of bear fetishes. "The bear is very important.
He is the protector of the West."

"That's so awesome." The boy grinned from ear to ear. "I
gotta find my mom and bring her over here." He darted away.

"Looks like you've got a fan," Adrian said.

Ben chuckled. "I just showed him what he didn't know to
look for." He picked up his water bottle and downed the last sip.
"Adrian, would you please get me another bottle of water? All
this talking's making my mouth dry, and my doctor wants me to
stay hydrated. There's a soda machine out in the hallway."

"I don't like the idea of leaving you alone."

"You'll only be gone a minute."

"A minute is all it takes for someone to grab you."

"I'm not taking this lightly, my friend, but we can't both go
over there together with all my work on display. Please, would
you just get me another bottle of water? Or maybe get a couple
so we don't have to do this again."

"I still don't like it."

"Look at all these people." Ben indicated the crowd. "Certainly one of them will sound the alarm if they see me in trouble."

"Unless they don't notice you're in trouble." *Like if a Whisperer tells them they don't see anything.*

"Adrian, in the time we've been arguing, you could have gone to the hallway and come back again."

"Fine. I'll go get water. I will be back in two minutes."

"Thank you."

Scowling, Adrian headed for the exit.

· · · · ·

Azotay watched the Warrior walk away. What a fool to leave his charge here, unguarded. Anyone could infiltrate the crowd and take the old man by surprise before the bystanders even noticed anything was wrong. Had Azotay been assigned as Wakete's security detail, such a breach would never occur.

Luckily for them, he had no intention of taking the old man here. Should the carver go missing in the middle of the show, it would attract attention. Should one of his team bungle the grab—entirely possible with the band of misfits he had to work with—then that would also attract attention. No, Azotay had a plan for capturing Ben Wakete, but that was for a different time.

Today was all about finding out more about the Warrior who guarded his prey.

Azotay wandered closer to Ben's table, stopping here and there to admire this trinket and that.

The Warrior returned and handed a bottle of water to the old man.

"Thank you, Adrian," the carver said.

Adrian? Not the name he'd expected.

Azotay wandered closer. He had to time it just right in order to get what he needed.

"As you can see," the old man said, twisting open his water, "I am still here."

"Pure luck." The Warrior's voice sounded somewhat familiar.

"You are a cynic, Adrian Gray," said the carver. "You always see the worst in people."

"That's my job, Ben."

Azotay slid closer and bumped into a woman who'd stopped in the middle of the traffic flow to rummage through her purse. She squealed. Toppled.

Adrian swept forward and caught her before she hit the floor. He remained bent over, assisting her in finding her footing. Which was exactly what Azotay needed. He veered closer to the couple, just another passerby checking out the commotion.

He saw it.

His breath caught, his heart skipping to double time. Could it be? Could it really be after all this time?

Adrian stood and glanced around. Azotay timed it that when Adrian's gaze slid over him, Azotay turned at that moment to look at another display. But not before he'd gotten a good look at the face of the man who called himself Adrian Gray.

Dark brown eyes of a Warrior. Black hair. Olive skin tone. Nothing unusual there. Even the tiny mole behind his left ear could have been dismissed. But the scar—the small, hook-shaped scar that cut across the bottom of one eyebrow and curved along the edge of his eye, faded now but still visible up close. The hair would never grow over that pale line again. No one would even notice it if they weren't looking for it. But with that and his fighting technique, and the distinctive kick that had felled his opponent . . . Add all that together, and the truth could not be denied.

After more than twenty years, he'd finally found Atlas.

CHAPTER TEN

As soon as they entered the cabana, Darius went to the storage cabinet, pulled a set of keys from his pocket, and unlocked it. He slid the familiar wooden box off a shelf and set it on the small table.

"The stone is still here?" Faith asked. "I thought you would have had it under armed guard."

Darius shrugged. "Since we're going to be working with it all the time, I moved it down here."

"I just thought you'd have it in a safe or something. I mean, this is the Stone of Igarle, a stone of incredible power. Everybody's after it."

"Normally we keep it in a vault, but I think it's fine to leave it here while you're working with it. Besides, with the security in this house, no one could get past the gates to make it this far, even if they knew it was here."

"I'm surprised your family lets you get away with that."

"They trust me." He smiled. "And I trust you."

A simple statement, yet warmth flooded her body. She glanced down at the box, more to compose herself than anything. "Your sister might disagree."

"Don't worry about her. My family put me in charge of this project, and besides, I'm the oldest. Baby sister has to do what I say."

She glanced at his face. The mischievous glint in his eye and the way his lips curved in that little-boy-with-his-hand-in-the-cookie-jar way made her insides go all squishy. They had work to do with this stone, and it was no time for melting glances, but she couldn't deny the lift in her confidence at his support in the face of his family's suspicion.

She stood on tiptoe, cupped his face, and kissed him.

His cane hit the carpeted floor with a muffled thump, and he grabbed her hips, tugging her closer. Her brain shut down, her body flaring to life at his touch. What started as a gesture of gratitude quickly exploded into something more. He took over the kiss with a mastery that made her shiver all the way to her toes. He knew what he wanted, and he wasn't afraid to demand it. Yet she knew she was safe with him. Knew she could trust him. Knew that if they dropped to the floor right now and made love, that it would be more than just mindless sex.

She could fall in love with this man. Maybe was already halfway there.

She broke the kiss. His quickened breaths swept her damp lips, his eyes burning like blue fire. His arousal pressed against her, but he had control over his body. And patience. He was waiting for her, letting her set the pace. And she tumbled the rest of the way into love with him.

She laid her hands flat against his chest, putting inches between them. "The stone."

"Yeah." He closed his eyes and leaned forward so their foreheads touched. "Like I said, a hell of a chaperone."

His heartbeat thudded beneath her palm, strong and vital. She curled her fingers as if she could capture it. "The sooner I get the stone stabilized, the better."

He opened his eyes, and that intense blue gaze sent a ripple straight to her core. "Guess we'd better get to work then."

He stepped back and slowly bent to retrieve his cane. Tilted forward

"I've got it." She steadied him with one hand on his shoulder and crouched. She looked him in the eye as she straightened, handing him the cane. "Just for the record, this has nothing to do with pity and everything to do with the fact that if you go down, you're too darn big for me to pick up."

The frown that creased his brow smoothed away, and his mouth quirked in a grin. "Is that so?"

"Of course it's so. Look at you. You're this big muscular guy, and I'm this skinny girl. No way I'd be able to get you up, not without a crane or something."

He laughed. "I suppose you're right."

"Glad you realize that." She propped her hands on her hips. "And while you're feeling so agreeable, there's something else I want to say." She leaned in. "Just because people feel badly that you got hurt does not mean they think any less of you, or find you lacking."

He shrugged, his expression closing. "Some do."

"Then they're idiots." She rolled her eyes. "I saw you kick some Mendukati ass, cane and all. You're a scary dude. And that's all I'm going to say."

That startled another laugh from him. "Okay."

"Now we have to clear room for a circle over here." She gestured toward the area where he'd clearly worked his healing rituals a couple of days ago. "Do you want to take the chair or that wooden chest?"

"I can take the chest. You grab the chair."

"And slowpoke gets the candles."

He raised his brows. "Oh, is it a race?"

She grinned. "Do you want it to be?"

"Scared I'll win?"

She hooted. "You're on, Montana. Loser has to clean up the candles."

"Deal."

They moved into position. She grabbed the back of the chair with both hands, and he bent to grasp the handle on the side of the chest. "Ready, set . . . go!" he said.

She tugged the large, armless chair backward across the carpet. The piece was clearly well made and matched the couches elsewhere in the room. And was heavier than it looked.

He tilted the wooden chest up on its edge, pushed a button with his thumb, and began to drag the thing across the carpet. Its wheels left grooves in its wake. Wait . . . wheels?

Having only moved about a foot, she dropped the chair back on its legs with a thump and propped her hands on her hips. "Hey, that's cheating! You didn't tell me that thing had wheels."

"You didn't ask." From the far side of the room, he grinned. "But just to show you what a good sport I am, let me help you with that." He walked over and gripped the chair just under the seat. "You lift your side, and I'll lift from the bottom. One . . . two . . . three!"

She lifted the chair with her hands on either side of its back, and he hefted one-handed from the bottom. She stepped back several steps, the chair much lighter with his help. They set it down at the edge of the room. "No wonder you took the chest. I thought you were crazy."

He shrugged and tapped his bad leg. "Since this thing, I've had to make tasks easier so I can manage them by myself. I'm strong enough to drag that chair, but not to lift the chest, which would normally take two hands and balance. Not to mention the box is full of stones. So I got one with wheels, like luggage."

She chuckled. "Why you think anyone would pity you, Darius Montana, is beyond me." The arrested look that crossed his face made her want to hold him, but they had work to do. "I lost the race, so let me move those candles, and I can set up my safety circle."

"How 'bout we both grab the candles?"

"No, no." She held up her hands. "Not only did you win our little race, but you had to come back and help me with my part. The least I can do is collect some candles." She pointed at the chair. "You can sit over there and lord it over me while I toil."

"Toil, huh?" But he sat.

She started gathering the candles.

· · · · ·

Darius leaned back in the chair and admired the view of Faith's butt as she bent down to gather the candles. The past few minutes had been one surprise after another, not the least of which was Faith dragging his demons about pity into the bright morning sunlight.

And that kiss.

He didn't know which threw him more, the fact that she'd made the first move this time, or her declaration that his injuries didn't lessen him as a man in her eyes. He wanted to believe her words, and her freely offered kiss—not to mention her enthusiasm to his response to that kiss—seemed to back up what she was saying. But he still couldn't connect to her empathically.

How had she blocked herself from his empathy? Was the stone guiding her actions? Had it not retreated after all?

Finished with the candles, Faith fetched the box Ben had sent her and brought it to the space they'd cleared. "I need to sit on the floor and make a circle. But first I need to make sure I can connect here." Setting down Ben's box on the carpet, she slid off her sandals and sat cross-legged in the middle of the space. Then she removed her silver ring, placing it on top of the box.

And his empathic senses exploded with the essence that was Faith.

Happy. Secure. Determined and focused. A bright citrusy tang on the tongue tempered by the warm, cinnamon-like notes of arousal. He glanced at the ring. Wondered.

She leaned forward, laying her palms flat against the floor, and closed her eyes. A quiet hum erupted from her throat. The same echoed in his mind. Then she nodded and glanced up at Darius. "The closer I am to the earth, the better. I'm going to set the circle to give me a buffer, but not enough to block the stone completely. That thing has been acting like a spoiled kid. As soon as I can clear some of that negative emotion, I should be better able to talk to it. But I'm going to need your help."

"Whatever you need. Except sitting on the floor."

"No, you can stay in the chair. I'm the only one who needs to be close to the Earth. The last couple of times the stone trapped me, you were the one who led me out. I need you on standby to do that again. If something happens where I am not responsive, and even you can't find me, put this ring on me." She picked up the ring and held it out to him.

He got to his feet and took the ring from her. "What does it do?"

"Offers me a layer of protection. It's never failed me yet."

That she was trusting him with this knowledge set her on edge. He could taste it, like Texas chili searing his tongue. But like cool sour cream, her faith in him tempered the worry and soothed the assertive fear. "Okay."

"Once I'm set up here, I'll need you to bring me the stone."

"You got it."

"You might as well have a seat. This is going to take a little while." She reached into Ben's box and pulled out the packets of crystals. Opening the plastic pouches, she set out the various stones in a wide ring around her.

Setting her ring on the table beside him, Darius sat back in the chair and prepared to follow her into the chaos of the stone.

. . . . .

Connected to the Earth's energy, Faith tuned the stones surrounding her so they formed a filter of sorts. She'd been thinking about this since the incident last night. Since the Stone of Igarle was a stone of incredible power, she would need a matching source of power to help her clear the negative energy from the crystal. The only thing even close was the vortex energy all around her.

Since she'd first connected to it the other day, she'd sensed the vortexes humming constantly in the background of her mind. In the hands of a normal Channeler, the energy would be unstable. But under the direction of an elemental Earth Channeler like herself—a Stone Singer—she should be able to funnel enough energy in a controlled stream to help clear the Stone of Igarle.

If her plan didn't work and she got sucked into the stone again, she had Darius as a backup. And in the event he was compromised like last night, she had Ben's ring, designed to block her from any Atlantean power, corrupt or otherwise. If she could wear the ring to work stone energy she would, but in addition to blocking her from other Atlanteans, it also stopped her from using her abilities, as if she were sealed up in a plastic bubble. No power in, none out.

As she wore the ring this morning, the short walk from her room to the cabana had seemed eerily silent without the familiar murmur of the ancient rock around her and the constant hum of the vortex energy.

The gems around her vibrated on their own frequencies that only she could hear. Her tattoos flared, the minerals in the ink joining the choir. She reached deep into the Earth and anchored herself, Earth song surging up through her roots and erupting from her throat to blend with the other harmonies. She wove protections for herself in case the Stone of Igarle tried again to suck her into its dark places. Opening her eyes, she continued to sing but sent Darius a mental message.

Bring me the stone.

He got up and removed the stone from its box. He crossed the room to her, and by the time he'd reached her, the bloodred pyramid had turned completely clear. He handed her the stone.

She gripped the pyramid between two hands.

Seer, it whispered, before tendrils of crimson swirled into it, like blood dripped into clear water.

He is a Seer. I am the Stone Singer, she sent.

Singer. Once again, it tried to connect with her mind, but with the vortex energy behind her, she was able to hold it back.

Shadows consume you, she said. *I can help.*

Ja-Red, the stone whispered. The name of the Stone Singer from Atlantis.

Ja-Red is no more, she said. *I am Faith. I can help you.*

So much to say, no one to listen.

I am listening, but first I must clear the path.

So much to say!

You can say it to me . . . after *the path is cleared.*

She waited what felt like a very long time before the stone answered her. *Very well.*

Clearing the negative energy was like trying to bathe a squirming dog with one hand while attempting to scrub an oven with the other. She sang the shadows away, scraped at the black despair and negativity that coated everything, illuminated the dark corners with light. The stone shied away from her sometimes, like a small, muddy child who did not want to wash, but she forced it to her will.

It seemed like forever, but finally she had removed a couple of layers of negative emotion, enough that the tarlike muck had faded to half of its previous volume.

Ja-red, the stone lamented.

Tell me about Ja-Red. Tell me about the last day of Atlantis.

Images slammed into her mind. She became Ja-Red.

. . . . .

He rose from the bed of his mate, awakened by the shaking of the Earth and the cries of the frightened. Leaving his beloved Kindin wrapped in the bedclothes that even now smelled of their loving, he grabbed his garments from the floor and hurried out of his dwelling to the street.

Agrilara, he mind-spoke, *what's happening?*

To the temple! Even her mind-voice sounded frantic. *Selak is trying to perform the Sortu-Ka!*

He broke into a run, leaping over obstacles and pushing past fleeing citizens without a glance. He kept his gaze on the temple. Thunder boomed, and lightning split the sky. Huge waves dwarfed the buildings nearest the harbor, smashing down on them as if they were eggshells. The city shook as if Poseidon himself pounded his fist on the base of the world.

And Selak, that arrogant statesman, was trying to perform the Sortu-Ka.

Everyone knew only Seers could perform that ritual. It was they who were selected by the Creators to be the voice of the people. Not Channelers. Not Warriors. But the Channeler Selak had raised dissent among the citizens, questioning the old ways, making the denizens of Atlantis, especially some of the Zaindari—those gifted with special abilities by the Creators—believe the Seers were trying to enslave Atlantis.

It was all fabrication and trickery, a political maneuver so Selak could seize power.

But to go this far, to actually attempt the Sortu-Ka? Heresy! No wonder Poseidon was angry!

Ja-Red burst into the great chamber of the temple. Agrilara was already there. And Selak, that madman, had already begun the Sortu-Ka. He had the Stones of Ekhia in the triangle frame, and he'd activated them. They had faded from crimson to clear, and red swirls of energy danced in their sparkling depths. Agrilara looked over at Ja-Red, her blue eyes wide and damp.

He's started the ritual, she mind-spoke. *My abilities are in stasis.*

The stones always neutralized the abilities of any Atlanteans who handled them, and their field of power grew to anyone surrounding them during the Sortu-Ka. The only exception to this was the Stone Singer. It was up to him to stop Selak.

He shouted for Selak to stop. Rushed for the frame. Reached tattooed hands toward the stones.

And Selak blasted energy through the stones, through Ja-Red, snuffing his life force and leaving Faith a helpless ghost to observe.

A mad scramble. The temple began to crumble. Those in the great chamber grabbed what they could and ran. Selak lay in the wreckage, laughing.

A young Warrior snatched up the Stone of Igarle. Fled from the temple. Found space on a boat and watched as the great city of Atlantis sank into the sea forever.

· · · · ·

Faith came back to herself with a gasp, her heart pounding. Darius crouched in front of her. "Faith, are you all right?"

She nodded, swallowing as she realized she was in Arizona, not Atlantis. She licked her dry lips. "I could use a drink," she managed.

Darius straightened and went to the small fridge behind the bar. He pulled out a bottle of water, unscrewed the cap, and brought it to her. "Here. Drink slowly."

She ignored him and chugged several swallows before stopping. "Thanks."

He sat down in his chair and bent forward with his gaze on hers. "You've been gone for three hours."

"What?" She glanced at the clock. It was after twelve. "It only felt like a few minutes."

"Hours." He reached out and brushed her cheek, his fingers coming away damp. "You're crying."

She nodded. Sniffed. Took another drink of water.

"What happened in there? You didn't seem to be lost like before, so I didn't go in after you."

"Give me a minute." She swiped the back of her hand across her wet face. And noticed her fingers trembled. She curled them into fists, images from the stone's memory lingering in her mind. The devastation. The loss. And the lie.

Especially the lie.

She took a deep breath, then another and another until her heart rate slowed. Darius waited, his patience like a warm blanket on a cold night. He was so different from the other men she'd known. Other Atlanteans, especially. She felt like she could tell him anything, and it would be okay. She sipped some more water, and when she decided she could talk without sobbing, she set down the bottle.

"It took me to Atlantis," she said.

"Took you?"

She shook her head. "Sorry, I'm still rattled." She breathed in again, then out. "Not physically took me. It showed me Atlantis, through the memory of the last Stone Singer who had balanced the stone. A young man named Ja-Red."

"I'm sorry." He squeezed her shoulder. "That must have been horrible, seeing the destruction firsthand like that."

"It was horrible, but amazing, too. I *saw* it, Darius. I saw Atlantis as it was, not as we speculate it to have been." She rubbed her face with both hands. "And I felt him die. Ja-Red. He was trying to stop it."

"Stop the destruction? How can you stop an earthquake?"

"By shutting down what was causing it." She got to her feet and paced. "The Stones of Ekhia caused the destruction of Atlantis. No, that's not exactly accurate. Let's say *misuse* of the stones caused it."

Darius sat back in his chair, a frown on his face. "So it wasn't just a tragic natural disaster?"

"Nothing natural about it. Someone caused it."

"Using the stones."

"Yes." She swept a hand through her hair and kept pacing, one hand on her hip. "I'm trying to process this, trying to accept what I just saw. Because if it's true—and it has to be, since the memories are stored in the stone—then everything I believe, everything every Atlantean believes, is based on a lie."

"What are you talking about?"

"Selak. He destroyed Atlantis."

"Who's Selak?"

She stopped pacing to stare at him. "Are you serious? You don't know about Selak?"

He shrugged. "I told you, I know very little about the history of Atlantis. Until recently, I thought my ancestor was the only survivor."

"Hardly. The entire island of Santutegi was founded by Atlantean refugees."

"What?" He leaned forward. "Santutegi, where Jain Criten is from? That Santutegi?"

"Yes. You could call it the homeland of the Atlanteans. It was founded by Selak."

"So the guy who blew up Atlantis founded the new home for its people?"

"Oh, yeah. He's a hero, like George Washington is to the United States. He's revered. There are statues of him and buildings named after him."

"I don't get it. Why would the guy who caused the destruction be revered?"

"Because until this moment, no one knew he caused the destruction. The history books say he was the leader of the refugees because he was the ranking council member, the *only* council member, to survive." She held his gaze. "He told everyone the Seers got greedy for more power, abused the stones, and destroyed the city."

"Wow." He slumped against the chair back. "That takes balls."

"Don't you see? That's what the Mendukati believe. It's what drives them: 'The Seers blew up our utopia, so they all must die.'"

"What about the Seers who survived? There must have been some. I know Agrilara, my ancestor, survived because I exist."

"I saw her. Ja-Red knew her."

"No way."

"She was beautiful. Blond hair and those gorgeous blue eyes all of you have. She called Ja-Red to come to the temple to help try and stop Selak. Once the stones were activated in the Sortu-Ka ritual, only a Stone Singer could disrupt that. When Ja-Red attempted it, Selak killed him with an energy backlash." She cleared her suddenly clogged throat. "Sorry. He was a nice guy, in love with a young man named Kindin. Anyway, about the Seers who survived. Santutegi history talks about a disease that only seems to affect Seers. There was some kind of plague that killed a lot of them off."

"Handy, considering they thought the Seers had blown everything for them. I can't imagine Seers would have been very popular in the new place."

"I have a feeling—and this is not based on any fact—that they might have been killed."

"What does the stone say about that?"

"Nothing. This stone never made it to Santutegi. It left Atlantis in the possession of a young Warrior, who ended up somewhere else. I broke off the memory at that point. However, and this is what is bothering me, the Mendukati's mission is to get rid of the Seers. They truly believe the Seers destroyed Atlantis in some kind of power grab, and they're determined to set things right."

"By wiping the Seers off the planet? Great."

"Don't you see? It's not just the Mendukati. Every single Atlantean believes this. Everything I was told, everything I believed, the entire history of my people, was a lie." Her eyes stung as she looked at him, her certainty about her place in the world crumbling beneath her. "So where does that leave me? Who am I?"

"Hey, hey." He rose and came to her, pulling her into his arms. "You're still you. Still Faith Karaluros. That hasn't changed."

She buried her face in his shoulder, her hands pressed to his chest. He smelled like soap and laundry detergent, with a hint of chlorine, and his arms around her made her feel safe in a precarious world. "There's something else. Something I haven't told you."

He eased her back so he could see her face. "Tell me now."

She hesitated. "You asked me once about Michael's death."

"I figured you'd tell me when you're ready."

"Guess I'm ready. Michael was trying to steal my power from me." She sighed, staring at the front of his shirt and seeing that day on the hilltop in her head as if it were yesterday. "We were on a mission to capture a family of Seers. But I found out too late that he never intended to capture them. He wanted to kill them. He wanted *me* to kill them. When I balked, he tried to seize control of my power. I fought for it, and it chose me. The backlash killed him." Her composure slipped. "I felt that in the vision. Backlash of energy. That's how Ja-Red died, and that's how Michael died. How *I* killed him." Her lower lip trembled as she fought to keep steady. "It's a horrible, painful way to die."

"I thought your powers didn't work on other Atlanteans?"

"They don't. I was supposed to cause a rock slide to stop the van. Then we'd capture them."

"I see." He smoothed his hands along her back. "And you had no idea killing them was the real plan?"

"Of course not!" She stiffened. "As soon as I realized what he was up to, I tried to leave. But he stopped me. He tried to . . . to . . ."

"Okay, okay." His gentle hands seemed to create a soothing calm within her. "You got away. You won."

"But I killed him." She gripped his shirt.

"Sounds like a clear case of self-defense. If he had succeeded and taken over your powers, those Seers would have died, right?"

She nodded. "There were little kids. And a dog."

"Well, yeah, the dog seals it." He brushed a kiss over her

forehead before tilting her chin up so he could see her face. "You did what you felt was right, and you saved lives. It was a terrible accident."

"I never meant to kill him," she whispered, taking solace in the calm understanding in his eyes.

"I know you didn't." His lips quirked. "And you saved the dog, so extra points."

That startled a laugh from her. "Thanks."

"Hey, this is what I do. Peacemaker." He rubbed her upper arms. "You steady?" She nodded, and he released her. "I'm going to put the troublemaker away." He stepped away and picked up the stone. The pyramid lightened from crimson to clear in his hand. He walked over to the wooden box sitting on the table and replaced the stone, then locked it back in the storage cabinet.

She watched him, so assured even with a disability. How was he able to calm her just by his presence? "You're an amazing man."

He laughed and came back to where she stood. "Not really."

"Yes, really."

He nodded at her circle of gems. "You going to clean up your toys? Or do I have to send you to bed without dinner?" He grinned that mischievous little-boy grin again, and her heart thumped. Falling in love? Ha.

She was already gone.

She propped a hand on her hip. "Maybe you should just take me to bed instead."

CHAPTER ELEVEN

Darius searched for the right thing to say. With the stone put away and her ring across the room, his empathy was in full form. He could sense that she felt off balance and vulnerable from what the stone had shown her. Guilt about Michael's death still weighed on her. And while she was attracted to him as much as he was to her, he didn't want her to regret what might happen between them.

Especially since he had deliberately kept secrets from her.

"That's not what I expected to hear," he said, knowing she was still waiting for an answer.

"What's the problem?" she asked. "We talked about this chemistry between us the other day. We both acknowledged it."

"Yes, but you also said you weren't ready. You're feeling a little vulnerable after that trip into the past, and I don't want you to have regrets the morning after."

She approached him, hips swaying and eyes soft. "All my life, people have been telling me what to do, and while I appreciate the gesture, I've made up my mind. There's something powerful between us, Darius, and I want to find out more." She linked her arms around his neck. "Now are you going to kiss me, or what?"

He cupped her face in his palm, stroking a thumb across her cheek. "I want nothing more than to make love to you, Faith."

"That makes two of us." She leaned in closer, her lips a breath away from his.

"Wait a second. There's something I have to tell you."

"Talk fast." She eyed his mouth. "Time's a-wasting."

"This pull between us . . . it's not just attraction." He cupped her head between his hands. "It's the mating bond."

"What? No." She stepped back, and he let her.

"Yes. We're destined mates, Faith."

"Look, if you don't want me, just say so. You don't need the elaborate story."

He'd hurt her. "I didn't tell you to put pressure on you."

"You mean it's true?" At his nod, she spun away from him. "Then why did you tell me? You know I can't stay. You know that when all this is done, I mean to get as far away from the Atlantean world as I can."

"Which is why I told you. The mating bond pushes us toward each other, and the sex would be incredible. But there is no law that says we have to walk down the aisle."

She gave a short laugh. "I should say not."

"If we're going to end up in bed, I want you to be sure. Remember, I'm not exactly strong in the long-term relationship department myself." He caught her hand. "I want you all the time, Faith. Every time I look at you."

"You're good at hiding it."

"Am I?" He sent a pulse of the desire he'd been trying to keep in check along the mating bond. She gasped, her cheeks turning pink. "That's the mating bond, the link between us. It's been getting stronger every day. It's how I found you when the stone had you trapped. The Stones of Ekhia may shut down normal Atlantean powers, but they have no effect on a link like this." He took a step closer. "Believe me when I tell you that I want you badly, Faith, but what I don't want is to be the next man to hurt you. You need to be sure."

．．．．．

He'd left the decision in her hands. Part of her wanted him to decide for both of them, to sweep her off her feet and seduce her so that later, if things went sour, she could blame him. But that wasn't the way to handle an affair. She knew the notion was just a knee-jerk reaction to having been manipulated all her life.

He was asking her, adult to adult, what she wanted. No one had ever really asked before.

She studied his face, so familiar to her now since they'd spent most of the past several days in each other's company. She knew she trusted him in a way that made no practical sense, given her past experiences, but maybe that was the mating bond he talked about. The little pulse he'd sent to her had illuminated the bond, and she recognized it from when she'd been trapped in the stone's coils. The silver path that had led her home.

To Darius.

Why was she hesitating? She'd already recognized her growing feelings for him.

"It bugs me that me wanting you might be the result of this mating bond thing," she said. "I refuse to be manipulated anymore, even by a mystical link."

"Like I said, you're under no obligation to do anything. We can continue as we were, ignoring it except in emergencies, like if the stone decides to act up again."

"Stones Behaving Badly." She chuckled. "Think we could get a reality show going?"

"I suspect the audience would be limited." He smiled, but it was a bit forced. She could see the tension in his shoulders, and her reservations weakened. Her answer mattered to him, more than whether or not he would get laid.

She mattered to him.

She already knew that Darius was a man who cared passionately about things. And she wanted to be one of those things. She wanted to make love with him, to be cherished for who she was, not what she could do. Darius had proven himself her safe harbor time and again in their short acquaintance. He would not hurt her. She could trust him.

"Yes." She walked to him and wrapped her arms around his neck. "Yes, I want to make love with you. Right now."

He slid his arms around her, his cane pressing along her buttock and thigh. "If you're hoping I'll sweep you off your feet and carry you to bed, you're going to be disappointed."

His tone was playful, but she caught the concern that lingered in his eyes. Darius, worried about rejection? For some reason, his wariness reassured her even more. She had equal power here.

"How about we forget about all those romantic clichés and just do what works for us?" She brushed a kiss to his lips. "Is your room close?"

He grinned, the shadows fleeing from his gaze. "Yeah."

"Let me just put these stones back, and we can go." She stepped away and began to gather her safety circle, scooping up the stones and dropping them back into the box without bothering with the plastic bags. The entire operation took minutes, but it seemed like an eternity when she'd finished and turned to face him.

He'd clearly been checking out her backside while she'd squatted down, and he didn't even look guilty. He looked—hungry.

He'd dropped his mask, his need stark on his face, his eyes burning with it. Had she really thought him a patient, controlled man? There was nothing controlled about the way he looked at her as he held out his hand, the demand unspoken.

She took it and followed him from the cabana.

· · · · ·

They hurried along the length of the pool with the furtiveness of a couple of teenagers, glancing around them in case anyone was home. But the pool and its deck chairs were deserted this Friday afternoon, and they reached the door to Darius's cottage without seeing a single soul.

He tugged her inside and shut the door behind them, clicking the lock. She barely glanced at his living room, focused completely on him. He leaned his cane against the wall, her scent tickling his senses. "Tell me you're sure."

Her lips curved, and she laid her hand against his thudding heart. "What do you think?"

He took that hand and guided it around his neck, pulling her against him. "I think you're beautiful."

She blushed. "You're not so bad yourself."

He laughed. "I'm the one with the dents. If I were an appliance, I'd be in the clearance section of the store."

She stroked his cheek with her free hand. "I think you're the most amazing man I've ever known, dents and all."

The sincerity in her words intoxicated him like top-shelf bourbon. She looked at him as if he could leap tall buildings, arousal simmering in her eyes. It sparked his own hunger.

He kissed her, relishing the sweetness of her mouth, the ever increasing desire that reflected from him to her and back again, intensifying each time. The bond between them swelled, lengthening, strengthening.

It wasn't the only thing.

He slid his hand beneath her shirt, started to pull it out of the way. She broke the kiss and put her hand over his, stopping him.

"I'm not very experienced." Her voice sounded lower than normal. Husky. Sultry. And sexy as hell.

"That's okay." He slipped his fingers below the hem of the shirt and traced the flesh of her waist along the edge of her jeans. She didn't stop him this time.

"I've only been with one man." She bit her lower lip, an earnestness coming through that humbled him. "I don't want to disappoint you."

His heart softened. "That won't happen."

"You don't know that." Her doubts crowded in, dampening a

bit of her ardor. "I was so young when I met Michael, and since him . . . well, there's been no one."

"Don't worry about that."

"No, listen to me. I want you to understand." She stared into his eyes, her own stark with honesty. "I never had the inclination. Figured I was a failure at romance, at being a woman. And you— You're so strong. Protective. You always know the right thing to say. It's like you can read my mind." She swallowed hard. "You make me feel like a woman the way no man ever has."

With every word of her heartfelt sentiment, the yoke of guilt tightened around his neck. Here she stood in his arms, pliant and willing, and he was deceiving her by not telling her the full truth about his abilities. She'd been manipulated all her life by everyone, even her husband. Was he any better?

"I just wanted to tell you that." She pulled away a little, her insecurity whittling away at her earlier confidence. "So you would understand if, you know, it isn't as good as you expect."

He put a finger to her lips. "Stop talking like that." He couldn't stand how she doubted herself, denied her very allure as a woman. He knew he should probably stop this now, before it was too late. But if he backed away after that poignant confession, it would only make her think she was right, that she wasn't attractive enough for him.

He couldn't let her think that. But neither could he take advantage of her when he hadn't told her the whole truth. So if he couldn't walk away and he couldn't in good conscience indulge himself, there was only one option.

Today would be all about her.

"I think you're beautiful and sexy and fun." He held eye contact as he said the words and reflected a little of his own hunger along their bond. "You feel that? You do that to me, Faith. I want to take you to bed and make you feel so good, you'll know for certain you're the sexiest woman on the planet. Because you are, to me."

Her lips parted, her cheeks flushing and her eyes bright. "Promise?"

"Hell, yes."

She took the edge of her shirt and jerked it off herself, dropping it on the carpet. Her pale pink bra cupped her delicate breasts, her waist a gentle curve, her belly smooth and flat. She waited, half excited, half nervous.

He took her hips in his hands, bending forward to press soft kisses along her throat and down, nuzzling the succulent flesh that pushed up from her bra. She arched into his touch.

He took his time, savoring the taste of her, her answering passion bursting on his tongue like tart berries. Slipping a finger beneath the edge of her bra, he teased her nipple. Arousal shot through her, reflected to him. He pulled the material out of the way. Bending his head, he captured the tip of her breast in his mouth and sucked. She cried out. He let her nipple slip out of his mouth and blew gently. The taut flesh grew even stiffer. A shiver rippled through her.

He slid his hands into her hair and captured her mouth, pressing her back against the wall. Her body heated and sparked beneath his touch, singeing him physically, empathically. She filled his every sense with her need, intoxicating him. He wanted to give her more. Give her everything.

He ripped his mouth from hers. Staring into her eyes, he caressed her cheek. "I want you in my bed."

She nodded and licked her lips. "Yes." Her voice sounded hoarse, her breath coming in pants. He held out his hand, and she placed hers in it. She was so delicately built, he felt like he was holding a butterfly in his grasp as he led her into the bedroom.

He yanked the covers off the bed one-handed, tossing them to the floor, and led her to the edge of the mattress. She started to sit, but he stopped her. "Not yet."

She obeyed, watching him with a question in her beautiful green eyes. And trust. She believed he would take care of her.

Which only reaffirmed his resolve to make this the best experience of her life.

Desire ran hot through her veins like lava, flooding his senses and making his head spin. He pushed the bra straps off her shoulders. The cups gaped. He reached behind her and unfastened the bra one-handed, tugging it down her arms and baring her completely.

"You are so beautiful." He cupped one slight mound in his palm.

"I'm small."

"No." He caressed the soft flesh. "You're gorgeous. Look at how you respond to me." He swept his thumb along her nipple. She jolted. Gasped. He leaned in, covering her whole breast with his hand as he touched his mouth to hers. "I want to see all of you."

A long, low sigh swept from her lips across his. Her surrender washed over him like a warm tide. He tugged at the waistband of her shorts, and she helped him pull them down, her lacy scrap of panties going with them. They pooled around her ankles, and she kicked them off.

He took a step back, regarding her from head to toe. "You look so sexy."

"Good thing I didn't put my sandals back on."

"That would have been even sexier." Her eyes widened, and he grinned. "Oh, come on. Haven't you ever gotten your kink on?"

"Not like that."

"We'll have to change that. But later." He gestured at the bed. "Lie down."

"What about you? You're still dressed."

"Yeah, and it kind of gets me hot." He helped her get settled in the middle of the mattress. "There's something really sexy about a naked woman and a fully dressed man."

She slid him a glance that singed his good intentions. "You'd better plan on taking those pants off at some point."

He nearly lost control right then. "First I'm going to make you come a couple of times."

Her eyes bugged. "A couple of times?"

"Sure." He sat on the edge of the bed and skimmed his hand along her body from collarbone to belly. His fingertips grazed the dark hair between her thighs. "I'm a gentleman. I think I told you that before." He leaned down to kiss her. "And gentlemen always let ladies go first."

She smoothed her hands over his chest. "At least take off your shirt. I've been dying to touch you since I first saw you in the pool."

Her sincere yearning strained his resolve. How long had it been since a woman had genuinely been turned on by his body?

He yanked the white polo shirt over his head and tossed it across the room, leaving him clad in just his jeans. His erection strained against the denim, bold and unmistakable. "Better?"

"Yes." The word ended in a hiss of pleasure as she threaded her fingers through his chest hair. "You're so furry."

"So are you." He stroked a finger between her legs.

She made a little sound, part gasp, part catch in her throat. Her eyelids slid halfway closed.

"You like that, sweetheart?" He stroked her some more, each touch sending another jolt through her system, mirroring back to him and feeding his own hunger. She spread her thighs wider in answer.

The sight of the moist, rosy flesh nearly did him in. She wanted this—him—so badly. His senses whirled as if he were drunk. And he was . . . on her. He wanted nothing more than to bury himself inside her and take them both to ecstasy. But if he did that and she found out he'd been keeping secrets from her, ecstasy would turn to heartbreak very quickly. And he didn't want that, for either of them.

He focused on her reactions, making her the center of his world. Kissing her mouth, her neck. Teasing her breasts with his tongue until those pink peaks strained hard and tight. He worked his way down her body with his lips and tongue, discovering what she liked, what she didn't. Her fevered responses washed over him in waves, telling him what had no effect and what drove her wild.

He nibbled her belly and then deliberately skipped over her sex to tease her thighs with his tongue. She whimpered and raised her hips, silently begging for his attention at her core. The scent of her arousal tortured him. He couldn't resist those damp folds, so hot and swollen. He spread her thighs wide and dipped his head to lick her there.

She cried out, clawing the mattress, and lifted her hips to his mouth, so turned on it made him desperate to drive her higher. Everything she felt echoed back on him, made him want to give her more until they were both insane with it.

He found her clitoris and rubbed his tongue against the sensitive bud. He could feel the pressure building inside her, climax hovering just beyond her reach. He kissed and nibbled, licked and sucked, tension stretching so taut it might snap. . . .

She came with a little scream, her body shuddering, cream bursting on his tongue. Her pleasure flooded through the mating bond, making his head spin and his cock even harder. He clenched his eyes shut and rested his head on her belly, waiting for her to come back to earth.

They'd only begun.

. . . . .

Faith shivered as her body slowly came back to normal. Darius's head still rested on her thigh, and she stroked his hair, content to drift. Her body hummed with satisfaction. He lifted his head to smile at her, and her heart did a slow turn in her chest. The way he looked at her. Touched her. Talked to her. He was like no other man she'd ever known.

She was definitely falling for him.

He kissed her thigh, his goatee tickling the sensitive flesh. She jumped and he grinned at her, a wicked curving of the lips that melted her insides and any inkling of rational thought. He brushed his facial hair along the inside of her thigh, then nipped her. She yelped.

He laughed. "Ready for more?"

"More?" she squeaked.

Still grinning, he shifted his body until he lay beside her, his head propped on one elbow. "Just let me know when you're ready. There's more where that came from." He drew a circle around one still-sensitive nipple, sending a jolt straight to her loins.

She groaned. "My whole body feels like pudding, and you want to go again."

"Sure I do." His grin faded, his gaze hawklike in its intensity. "I loved watching you come. Tasting you. I could do that all night, make a meal of you."

He gave her that look again, like she was a buffet and he was a starving man. She wanted to just open to him and let him take his fill. The bond between them throbbed like a live wire, conveying quite clearly how aroused he was.

"What about you?" She trailed her fingers down his hair-roughened chest to rest on the snap of his jeans. Her thumb brushed the heat of him, hard and ready beneath the denim.

He gave a hoarse laugh and lifted her questing hand to his mouth to kiss the palm. "Today is about you, sweetheart."

"If it's about me, I can do whatever I want?" The idea piqued her mischievous side. "What if I want to touch you?"

He lay back and spread his arms. "Touch away."

She scrambled up onto her knees and swept her palms over his torso. "I've been dying to get my hands on this chest since I saw you swimming that time. I could barely remember my name."

"Sure it had nothing to do with the hot dream you had the night before?"

Her cheeks heated. Even though she'd just climaxed harder than she'd ever done before, her body sprang to life in response to that teasing light in his eyes. He seemed relaxed and in control, nowhere near the wild arousal that held her in its grasp.

She wanted to change that.

She stroked her hands over his shoulders. "Look at this upper body. Your muscles are amazing."

"Spending a few years in a wheelchair will do that."

She stopped her exploration. "Oh, Darius."

"That and swimming."

She accepted the change of subject without missing a beat. "You're an amazing swimmer." She trailed her fingers along his ripped abs. "Look at this tone." She bent forward and swept her tongue along the bronzed flesh. Grinned at him. "Tasty, too."

"You want to play?" He hauled her up along the length of his body as if she weighed nothing.

"That's not fair. You're stronger than I am." She pushed against his chest and straddled him. "Well, this is an interesting position."

"Yeah, it is." He reached up with both hands to caress her breasts.

His hardness pressed against her bottom, imprisoned by his jeans. She wanted to explore him, to make him as mad with desire as he'd made her.

Taste him.

She swung off him, his hands falling from her breasts as she landed beside him. Before he could react, she'd leaned forward and flipped open the snap of his jeans.

His features tight, his eyes burning, he reached out a hand.

But it just settled on the top of her head as she pulled down his zipper and jerked his jeans and boxers out of the way to free him.

"You don't have to do this." His voice sounded like sandpaper. "Today was supposed to be about you. Giving you pleasure."

"This gives me pleasure." She stroked a hand down his stiff cock. "So hard and yet such soft skin. Like steel encased in silk."

"Poetic." He shuddered as she swept her fingers along his length, across the tip. "Sweet mercy, you're killing me."

"Payback." She leaned forward and took him in her mouth.

His back arched. He cursed, his voice rich with tormented pleasure. He slid his hands into her hair, holding her still but not hard enough to hurt her. His reaction sparked answering wildness inside her. She closed her eyes and focused on his wordless cues. The way he lifted toward her, the inventive, sometimes unintelligible profanity he muttered.

The way he held her hair out of her face in a gentle grip.

The mating bond flowed between them, throbbing and molten. His escalating excitement flared her own. She was ready for him again, damp and hot between her legs. She would die if she didn't get him inside her, right now.

She glided her mouth up his length one last time and licked the tip before sitting up. He made a sound of protest. His eyes drifted open, and a low groan vibrated from his chest as she straddled him and took him inside her.

She closed her eyes as he settled deep, the delicious friction stealing her breath.

He gripped her hips. "This wasn't the plan."

She moved up and down, slowly, enjoying the feel of him. He tightened his grip but didn't push her away. A smile curved her lips. "Oh, did you want me to stop?"

Breath hissed from between his teeth. "I'll die if you do."

"Me, too." She closed her eyes and indulged herself in him.

· · · · ·

He should stop her. He knew it. But he couldn't.

He might have summoned the strength to pull away. He'd resisted the physical before. But the emotional . . . Even if he weren't an empath, their mating bond linked them so strongly that everything she felt was magnified back to him, flooding him with every sensation. He was swamped with her pleasure, drowning in how badly she wanted him. How she thrilled at the way he filled her. He could only hang on as she rode him and whipped both of them to the hot, sweaty finish that had her throwing back her head and wailing her release seconds before she collapsed on him.

Her climax ricocheted through him, pushing him over the edge with a harsh groan as he exploded inside her.

They lay that way for a while, replete and panting, sweat drying on their bodies. He toyed with her hair, their situation niggling at him. He'd have to tell her everything. It was the only way he could in good conscience continue their affair. But first he had to let his family know he was going to tell her. He'd agreed to the deception for their collective safety, but since he'd gotten to know Faith, he knew she wasn't part of some Mendukati plot to infiltrate their home and kill them all. His family wouldn't be inclined to agree, but they would eventually accept his decision. He wouldn't accept anything less. Faith was too important to him.

She stirred. "So." Satisfaction soaked the word. "This mating bond thing. Pretty intense."

"Yeah." He caressed her buttock. "You realize we didn't use any protection."

"Dang it." She let out a long sigh. "I wanted you inside me so badly I didn't even think of that."

"Me neither. And I have condoms in the drawer, too."

She lifted her head and regarded him with eyes half closed like a cat before a warm hearth. "Well, well. Check you out, Mr. Prepared."

He stroked a hand over her tousled hair. "I take precautions when it's warranted. Condoms seem like a no-brainer, and not just because of pregnancy."

She folded her hands on his chest and rested her chin on them. "Lucky for you I've been living like a nun these past few years."

"Still, we should be more careful if we're going to keep this up."

The corners of her mouth curved just a little. "Isn't that your department?"

He chuckled and squeezed her buttock. "Don't you worry about that."

"Worrying requires thinking, and that's just too much work right now." She closed her eyes and snuggled against his chest. "Let's just drift for a while."

"If you want. But I have to move. I've been in this position for too long, and it's messing up my back. Happens sometimes."

Her head popped up again. "Oh, sorry." She rolled off him, disconnecting their bodies and landing beside him. "Is this better?"

"Help me get these jeans off." He shoved at the pants still tangled around his ankles. She helped him, peeling the denim off his legs and casting it aside. His socks followed.

"Good thing you took off your shoes." She turned back to face him. Her gaze fell on his scarred knee, and her grin faded. Gently she touched the puckered flesh, traced it. She leaned forward and brushed her lips over the scar.

His breath caught. Tenderness shone in her eyes, soaking his empathic senses like a warm compress on a throbbing bruise. She really didn't care about the scars. She wanted him, all of him. Cared about him. Didn't see him as some kind of damaged goods.

He swallowed past the hard lump in his throat and turned on his side to face her. "Turn over."

She obeyed, rolling on her other side with her back to him. Hooking an arm around her waist, he pulled her against him and settled his semi-hard cock in the cradle of her buttocks.

"Mmmm." She wiggled her butt against him. "Nice."

It was more than nice. He inhaled the scent of her hair and stroked his palm over the softness of her belly. Her satisfaction vibrated through him like the purring of a kitten who'd found a prime spot in the sun. He knew she was happy. He'd made her happy. Two wounded people finding a moment of contentment together.

He closed his suddenly moist eyes for a moment. He could easily fall in love with this woman.

Cuddled together, they dozed, the world outside and all its dangers forgotten.

CHAPTER TWELVE

The growl of her stomach woke Faith sometime later. She squinted against the sunlight peeking through the blinds. Unfamiliar room. Where was she? Something heavy draped across her body. An arm—a muscular, hairy arm. Darius. Memory returned.

The scent of their coupling lingered in the room. She stroked his strong fingers where they rested against her belly, his olive skin a stark contrast to her pale complexion. If anyone had told her even last week that she would not only take a lover but that he would be a Seer as well, she would have thought them crazy. Yet here she was. Lucita would be proud.

Her stomach gurgled again.

"That's loud enough to wake the dead." Darius's chest vibrated against her, his voice a drowsy rumble.

"It was past noon when we came in here. What time is it now?"

She felt him shift, probably to look at the bedside clock. "After two. No wonder you're hungry."

"We missed lunch."

"Did we?" He turned her onto her back, those sexy lips curved in a smile made all the more wicked by his mustache and goatee. "I beg to differ."

Her cheeks heated. She lay in bed with him naked, not even a sheet for modesty, both of them sticky and sweaty from intense sex, and yet that grin of his still turned her insides to mush. "That doesn't count as far as my stomach is concerned."

"How 'bout the other parts?"

She gave him a playful slap on the shoulder. "Cut that out."

"Never." He took her hand and kissed it, held it. "For what it's worth, I could eat. I bet I can rustle up a couple of sandwiches from the kitchen."

"My hero."

"Yeah?" He chuckled. "I always wanted to be the hero. Usually that's Rafe's job."

She twined their fingers together. "Why's that?"

"Well, he was always the physical type. Me, I'm the talker."

"Ah, right. Peacemaker. Negotiator."

"Guilty. You know those action movies where there's the badass hero who charges in to save the girl, and he's got this partner who hangs out in the van feeding him intel and all that? Well, I'm usually the guy in the van." His smile dimmed. "More so these past few years."

"Since the accident."

He nodded.

She leaned up to kiss him. "Let me tell you something, Darius Montana. You've saved my butt a couple of times now from that hunk of rock, and you didn't have to move a muscle to do it. So in my book, you're already hero material."

"I think the mating bond is more responsible for that than I am."

"Modest, too."

"Truthful."

"That's refreshing. I haven't run into many honest people, especially men."

"Glad I can stand out." He untangled himself from her and rolled over, sliding his legs over the side of the bed so he could sit up on the edge of the mattress. "I'm going to call Lupe and have her make us some food to go." He glanced over her shoulder at her. "Unless you want to go up to the house to eat?"

"No, I kind of like being away from all those prying eyes." She sat up. "Did I say something wrong?"

"What do you mean?" Using the edge of the nightstand, he pushed himself into a standing position and paused as if testing his balance.

"You seem funny."

"I'm fine. But my cell and my cane are in the other room."

She scooted on hands and knees to the edge of the bed. "I can run and get them for you."

He held up a hand. "No. I need to do this on my own."

"Why won't you let me help you?"

He pressed his lips together as if debating his response, and for a moment she thought he wouldn't answer her. "This is something I need to do for myself. My body and I have been engaged in this battle for over five years, and I can't let anyone else fight it for me."

"So me running into the other room to get your cane is fighting your battle? I thought it was just me helping someone I care about."

He gave her a tight smile. "I appreciate it and believe me, when I need help, I'm not afraid to ask for it. But this is a daily ritual for me. Getting up. Walking across the room under my own power. It's important to who I am that I be as independent as I can. Please tell me you understand."

"Oh, I understand. I'm an independent person, too." She grinned, hoping to lighten the mood. "Blame it on the fact that I'm starving. The faster food comes, the happier I'll be."

He laughed. "Noted. Your appetites are not to be ignored." He tweaked her chin. "As I found out earlier."

"You're terrible." She shifted to sit on the edge of the bed. "Well, if you're going to check out the food situation, do you mind if I use your shower?"

"Go ahead. There's a cabinet in there with fresh towels, but I have to tell you I don't have any girly shower gel in there."

"Then I guess I'll smell like you."

He winked. "I think you already do."

"I'm ignoring you."

She started past him for the bathroom, but he caught her arm and pulled her near enough to kiss. The playful embrace quickly heated, the mating bond flaring to life like gas-soaked cotton. She wrapped her arms around his neck, loving the friction of his hairy body against her smooth one, and leaned into the kiss.

His knee buckled, and he stumbled, catching himself on the nightstand. She shoved her shoulder beneath his arm until he steadied. "Sorry about that," she said. "Guess I'm just overly enthusiastic."

"Yeah." He managed a smile. "Next time you pounce on me, make sure we're already in bed."

"I didn't pounce, you grabbed. I was just on my way to the shower."

"Uh-huh." He swatted her butt. "Get in there while I call Lupe."

She stuck out her tongue.

He tweaked it with his finger. "Later, sweetheart. I've got to get your food."

"Fine. Guess I'll see about that towel." She marched to the bathroom. Though she couldn't see him, she delayed by rummaging in the towel cabinet, listening to the shuffle of his footsteps as he made his way across the room. She heard the creak of the door as it opened and finally, the familiar thud of his cane.

Content that he wouldn't fall, she grabbed a fluffy towel off the top of the pile and turned toward the shower. As with the rest of the Montana estate, the bathroom even in this tiny guesthouse was more luxurious than most five-star hotels. Black and white marble vanity with gold fixtures. Mottled gray tile on the floor and walls. A shower the size of a minivan.

But also rails around the toilet and when she opened the shower door, handrails installed there also. A marble seat was part of the enclosure. Stark reminders of the challenges Darius had to face every day.

She started the water and stepped into the shower.

. . . . .

Darius pulled on a pair of shorts and a T-shirt and made his way barefoot to the house. With any luck no one would be around, and he could collect the food from Lupe and get back to the guesthouse without seeing anyone.

He didn't want to think about the implications of what had happened, and he certainly was not in the mood to entertain the questions of his often nosy family.

He spotted the bag sitting on the table through the glass doors. Lupe knew a tray wasn't the best option for him, so she'd gotten into the habit of using her canvas shopping bags whenever he called up for food. He slid open the door and stepped inside, intent on grabbing the bag and getting back to Faith as soon as possible.

"Well, hey there, big bro." Dressed in running shorts and a sleeveless shirt, Rafe leaned against the counter with an iced tea in his hand. "Haven't seen you all day."

"I've been working."

"Yeah?" Rafe sauntered toward him. "With Faith?"

"Yeah. That stone is a bitch." Darius held up the bag. "Got to get back. I just came to grab lunch."

"Did Lupe make her chicken salad? I love that stuff." Rafe peered into the bag.

"I don't know. I just called up for food."

Rafe looked from the contents of the bag to lock his gaze with Darius's. "You know you're not fooling anyone, right?"

"I don't have time for guessing games, Rafe. If you've got something to say, just spit it out."

"From the sight—and smell—of you, I'd say you slept with the Stone Singer."

"That's none of your business." Darius turned to leave.

Rafe blocked his exit. "It is my business, but not for the reason you think. I just want to make sure you're okay."

"Why is everyone so worried about me? First Tessa and now you. You do remember I'm older than both of you and fully capable of making my own choices?"

"I'm not coming down on you about this, Dar, really. Tess is definitely not one of Faith's fans, but she's been sheltered most of her life. Me, I've been out there. I've met the scumbags of the world, and while I may question the wisdom of getting involved with someone as important to our cause as the Stone Singer, I don't get the scumbag vibe from her."

"Glad to hear someone agrees with me."

"Cara likes her, too, and that goes a long way with me." Rafe swirled the ice in his tea. "I'm just saying be careful. Don't get your heart all broken, Powder."

Darius scowled. "I'm touched that so many people are looking out for me."

"Translation: mind your own business. Message received." Rafe gave a little salute and stepped out of the way. "Give my best to Faith."

Darius brushed past him and slid open the door. Paused. "I appreciate the concern, Rafe."

"We've got to watch each other's backs," came the reply. "You know I've got yours."

Darius gave a nod. "Same here." With a wave to his brother, he headed back to the guesthouse.

At least that was one family member who would support his decision to tell Faith the truth.

When he walked into his living room, he found Faith waiting for him, dressed in her clothes from earlier but with her hair damp from the shower. She was watching TV, but clicked it off and stood when he came in. He kissed her and handed her the bag.

She set it on the coffee table and dug into it. "This looks fab-ulous!"

"You'll find soda and water in the mini-fridge behind the bar." He stripped off his shirt. "Make sure you save some for me. I'm going to shower."

"No guarantees," she said, unwrapping a sandwich. "I'm pretty famished."

He paused in the doorway to the bedroom. "You do want me to keep up my strength, don't you?"

She paused mid-bite. Her eyes brightened as her interest bubbled through the link. "Heck yeah."

"Then save me some food." He headed for the bathroom.

He'd just finished shampooing his hair when the shower door slid open and Faith stepped in.

"This looks handy." She regarded the seat in the stall with gleaming eyes.

Darius swept his hair back with one hand while gripping the rail with the other. "What are you doing in here? I thought you were hungry."

"I am." She eyed him up and down. "I thought we could put that seat to good use. If you're up to it."

He reached for her.

. . . . .

They had eventually made it to the bed. Faith lay in Darius's arms watching the sky darken through the windows of his bed-room. They lay spoonlike again, his arm around her waist hold-ing her close. For the first time in forever, she felt safe.

"I've always dreamed of this." She idly stroked his fingers resting on her stomach as the sky darkened from rose to purple.

"Of wild shower sex?" He sounded sated and content.

She chuckled. "No, of a place like this, your house. A place where I could be myself without having to watch my back all the time. A place where the Mendukati can't find me."

She sighed. "That's what I'm going to do with the money your family is paying me—build a secure house where I never have to be afraid again."

He didn't reply for a moment. "Maybe you could just stay here."

She tried to look behind her, but she couldn't see his face. "What? I can't stay here."

"You could, if you wanted to." He traced his fingers down her arm. "If things worked out between us."

Hope rose for just a moment, then practicality slammed it down. She gave a little laugh, hoping the forced humor would cover the momentarily foolishness. "You just got me into bed a couple of hours ago, and now you're talking about living together? Moving a little fast, aren't you?"

"I guess I am getting ahead of myself." His sigh breezed over her cheek, and he pulled her closer. "Sorry."

She should push him away, set some boundaries, but she just couldn't. They lay quietly, wrapped together and listening to each other's heartbeats.

"This place is safer than it used to be," he said several minutes later. "Criten got in here a few weeks back. We didn't even know he existed, much less to set up security to keep him out. That was a close call."

She seized on the change of subject. "I heard about that. Fractured neck?"

"Yeah. They took him out of here on a stretcher."

"So Cara told me. He's back in Santutegi, nursing his wounds. Word on the street is that the Seers ambushed him and stole the stone."

"That's the word, huh?"

"Obviously that story is incorrect, like everything else to come out of Santutegi. Still, at least Criten is temporarily benched. That's probably why he sent Azotay after me."

He rolled her onto her back, his brow furrowed. "Who's Azotay?"

"You've never heard of him?" When he shook his head, she went on, "He's Criten's hit man. His fixer. If he sends Azotay after you, you're pretty much toast."

"And this Azotay is chasing you?"

"Yes, he's here. Well, in New Mexico, anyway. He's the one who sent Corinne and Erok to get me. If you hadn't come, I don't know if I could have held them off."

He sat up. "Why didn't you say anything about this before?"

"About Azotay? You knew the Mendukati were after me."

"The Mendukati, not this hit man. You say he's in New Mexico?" Darius reached for his cell phone on the nightstand.

She sat up. "Who are you calling?"

"Adrian. He called this morning to tell me he and Ben had been attacked by a bunch of Warriors." He opened his contacts and selected one.

"What! Is Ben okay?"

"Yes, he's fine. The show is over tomorrow, and I've sent the jet to bring them here afterward." Darius turned to sit on the edge of the bed, his back to her. "Gray. What do you know about a guy named Azotay?"

Faith frowned at Darius as he listened to Adrian. Why hadn't he told her about Ben being attacked? He had to know she'd want to know the instant he did. She crushed the sheets beneath her fingers. Though Ben was in the company of a very capable Warrior, she knew Adrian wasn't invincible, and the Mendukati—Azotay—could very well capture Ben and use him to try to force her over to their side.

Was that why Darius hadn't told her? Did he think she might defect before she was done analyzing the stone? Was that the real reason he'd suggested she stay?

"Faith." She jerked her head up and realized he was handing her his phone. "It's Adrian. He wants to talk to you."

She took it and brought it to her ear as Darius got up and headed for the bathroom. "Hello?"

"Hey, Faith. I don't want to leave Ben for long, so I'll keep this short. Have you ever seen Azotay? Can you describe him?"

"No, just heard about him. Dark hair and dark eyes. They say he has a scar across his throat where someone tried to kill him. That's all I know."

"I've heard the same, but I'd hoped you'd actually seen him yourself."

"Sorry, no."

"Okay. Listen, don't worry about Ben. He's my number-one priority. We'll see you tomorrow night."

"Yes." She tightened her fingers on the phone. "Be careful, Adrian. These guys are ruthless."

"I know. See you tomorrow." He hung up.

She stared at the phone for a moment before setting it down on the nightstand. Darius came out of the bathroom. "What did he say?"

"He wanted to know if I've ever seen Azotay." She sat back against the headboard and hugged a pillow against her body. "I'm so worried about Ben. If anything happens to him—"

"Hey, now." He sat on the edge of the bed and reached out to touch her hair, his dazzling blue eyes soft. "Adrian Gray is a badass. You know that, right?"

"He's a Warrior, which is good, but Azotay has a band of Warriors with him, which is bad." She rested her chin on top of the pillow. "Why didn't you tell me, Darius?"

"I forgot."

Her eyes bugged. "How could you forget something so important? Didn't you want me to know?" She flung the pillow aside. "Or were you worried it might distract me too much to finish the work with the stone?"

"What? No, of course not."

She shoved herself off the bed on the opposite side from where he sat. Why had she even allowed herself to hope, even for a second, that he was different from everyone else? "Maybe you thought I might give in to the Mendukati's demands if they got hold of Ben? Steal the stone or something?"

"Faith, where are you getting this?" He came around and took her by the upper arms. "Sweetheart, he called me at six thirty this morning. I had every intention of telling you."

"Then why didn't you? Darius, we've been together all day."

"I know, and I don't have any better response than it slipped my mind."

"Slipped your mind!" She pulled away from him. "My only family is in mortal danger, and it slipped your mind?" She spun away from him and stalked the room, hunting her discarded clothing.

"Faith, wait. I said wait, damn it!" He took her arm as she rose from picking up her panties off the floor. "You're acting like I deliberately kept this from you."

"Didn't you?"

"No, I didn't."

She shook him loose and turned her back. Jerking on her underwear, she faced him again, hands on her hips and half naked. "Then explain. And I'd better believe it, pal."

His face darkened. "You're not going to use this to push us apart, Faith."

"Now what are you talking about?" She bent to scoop her jeans off the floor.

He folded his arms and watched her, his expression stony. "Gray called early this morning. I went for my swim, showered, got breakfast. I planned to tell you when you got down to the cabana."

"Why didn't you?" To her horror, tears stung her eyes. She

blinked furiously and tugged on her jeans, hoping she could stop the betrayal of emotion before he saw it.

"You were late." His voice had softened.

"So? I overslept." She turned, searching for more garments. Anything to keep him from seeing the angry-scared-embarrassed moisture welling up.

"You were late, and I was scared for you. I thought the stone had captured you again."

"Oh, come on."

"It's true. I thought it had sucked you in, that it was too late to save you. And then you came walking out, wearing those tight jeans and that cute pink shirt, all excited about the stuff Ben had sent you. You looked so beautiful, and I was so relieved that I completely forgot to tell you about Ben."

She slowly faced him as he spoke. The catch in his voice, the genuine concern in his eyes, his posture, all indicated he was telling the truth.

"Then you started working with the stone," he continued, "and you were gone so long, so deeply caught by its memories. I was afraid I wouldn't get you out. Then when you did come out . . ." He stopped.

She'd thrown herself into his arms, into his bed. Her shoulders relaxed.

"Honestly, Faith, I just got distracted by everything going on. Is one mistake really enough for you to write me off already?"

"No, it's not. I'm sorry. You're right. A lot happened today." She swiped a hand over her face. "I've just gotten so accustomed to people trying to use me for their own goals that I guess I've gotten hair-triggered."

He reached out a hand, and she took it, allowing him to pull her into his embrace. Part of her demanded she should stand firm, not be fooled by tender words and earnest apologies. But if she went through life trusting no one, suspicious of everyone, she'd end up a very hard, embittered, and lonely woman.

"You know you're still naked," she said against his chest.

"You know you're overdressed."

She pulled back and met that steady, blue-eyed gaze. "Let's do something about that, shall we?"

"Works for me." He watched as she stripped off her jeans and panties. "By the way, in the interest of full disclosure, there's something else I need to tell you."

She tossed her clothes aside, braced for bad news. "All right."

"I want to tell you now so I don't forget and get in trouble again." He waited for her smile to continue. "Tomorrow morning my family has a private ritual they're doing up in the temple. Entertain yourself, sleep in, go swimming or something until I come get you. Then we'll work with the stone."

"Okay." It seemed odd that he'd go out of his way to tell her about such a personal family thing. She was a guest here, not a permanent resident. But the fact that he'd felt the need to mention it only reminded her how much his family distrusted her. One more obstacle that proved a permanent relationship with him was just a fantasy.

"Hopefully the thing will be over fast." He rested his forehead against hers. "Then we can take another whack at that stone."

"Work, work, work." She shook off the negative feelings and focused on the hot, naked man before her. "Let's play."

"Race you to the bed."

. . . . .

Sometime after midnight, Faith left Darius's place and headed back to her own room. She swung by the cabana and picked up her ring, which she'd forgotten earlier. She slipped it on her finger. Though it had been the wedding ring from her doomed marriage, she still cherished it because Ben had made it for her. And its protective powers had shielded her from the Stone of Igarle's consciousness until she was ready to deal with that tricky hunk of rock.

She only wished the ring could protect her from the complications of her relationship with Darius.

Okay, so she'd flung caution to the winds and slept with the man. Was it the smart thing to do? Probably not. She was fairly certain she was risking heartache by following her emotions rather than exercising caution. If she were smart, she would have kept things purely professional with Darius so she could leave at the end of the job with her bank account full and her heart whole.

But the revelations today had shaken the very foundations of what she thought she knew, and he'd been right there, steady Darius. Always sympathetic. Always extending a hand to help. Always so darned attractive. Going into his arms had seemed a natural thing, and making love with him had felt like coming home.

She had to dig deep and find some objectivity, some way to seal up her emotions in a safe place so that she could keep control of their relationship. Enjoy the affair, the sex, the closeness, not mourn for a permanent romance that probably wouldn't work out anyway. She wasn't going to stay, no matter the sweet fantasies she'd conjured. She lived in the real world, and eventually she would have to leave the bubble of the Montana mansion and return to it.

But as she slipped through the sliding doors to the kitchen, she wondered if she would depart this place whole, or if she would leave her shattered heart behind.

· · · · ·

Darius knew when Faith slipped out of the guesthouse to return to her room, though she clearly thought he was asleep. He'd followed her empathically until suddenly the connection cut off. He jumped out of bed and went to the window. She came out of the cabana and headed for the house. The motion lights around the pool flicked on as she walked, gleaming off something on her hand.

That ring again, the one that blocked her from his powers.

He watched her until she disappeared into the house, then turned back to his solitary bed. It would be so much easier once he was able to tell her the truth about his abilities, especially that his empathy worked on other Atlanteans. That was something he had in common with her late husband, so she might not take that news well. She might even see their sexual encounters as some kind of attempt at manipulation, but he was convinced he could make her understand his side and the promise he'd made to his family for everyone's safety.

Tomorrow was Rafe's Soul Circle, and Darius would need all his energy to aid his brother in getting through the ritual intact. Once Rafe was safe, Darius could approach the family about telling Faith the truth. Maybe then, once he'd come clean about his empathy, he could start coaxing Faith toward a more permanent relationship. Because that's what he realized he wanted.

He'd fooled himself into believing he could have a brief, casual thing with his destined mate, even justified it with the idea about solidifying the mate link as another defense against the Mendukati. But the more time they spent together, the more he came to understand that temporary wasn't enough. He wanted Faith in his life permanently.

He loved how she tried to be so tough all the time, to handle everything on her own. How she accepted him and his damaged body as they were. She'd been used and manipulated her entire life, orphaned young and betrayed by her husband. Everyone wanted a piece of the Stone Singer. Only Ben had shown her the love she so deserved. It was no wonder she had such trouble trusting people.

He wanted to earn her trust. To laugh with her, to share her burdens. To look at him with love.

He was an empath, and his power was to see into the heart. Now when he looked into his own, all he saw was Faith.

. . . . .

The Mendukati had been suspiciously absent over the past twenty-four hours. Adrian didn't trust it. Another man might relax his guard, thinking they'd abandoned their mission. If creating that assumption was their intent, it had backfired. He remained even more vigilant because of their absence. Because he knew the Mendukati did not just go away.

Von was monitoring the Mendukati's movements, ready to send in the cavalry at the first sign of trouble. If Adrian and Ben weren't leaving tomorrow, Adrian would have already abandoned their "under the radar" strategy and given Von the go-ahead to send some more Warriors. As it was, in a few short hours they'd be safe in Sedona.

Blessed Ekhia, the sun, had set hours ago. Clad only in a pair of running shorts, Adrian made his way to the area he'd cleared in the untouched desert surrounding the hotel. Steps away from the hotel's parking lot, he could see the window of the room he shared with Ben. The light from the TV flickered, like others in the motel. Ben had promised to stay put while Adrian performed this ritual, and from this vantage point, Adrian would see any-one approaching the room. He could be there in moments if Ben was threatened.

All his strength and cunning would be required to keep them both alive until they got to Sedona tomorrow night. For that, his mind and heart needed to be clear and focused.

He turned his face to the star-studded sky. Brilliant Ilargi, the moon, had risen already, only half revealed. In another few days she would bloom in full glory. He murmured the appro-priate words as he stepped into the sacred space he'd prepared. Soft sand, still warm from the day's heat, gave way beneath his bare feet. With the ease of a lifetime of practice, he crouched into the first position, arms bent, hands poised. Then he began to dance.

Beneath Ilargi's light, his body twisted and coiled, extended and stretched, a parody of battle. One movement led into another, each an integral part to an ancient song: graceful, controlled, balanced. The wind and the night were his music; Ilargi, his audience. The rite brought peace to his inner self. Reminded him of who he was. Reminded him why he was.

His muscles warmed; his soul calmed. He danced to keep his skills sharp, to keep his mind focused, to keep himself connected to the Earth.

And as always, he danced for victory in the battle to come.

CHAPTER THIRTEEN

When Faith headed downstairs just before nine the next morning, she found Darius in the foyer with a man she'd never seen before. He looked to be in his late thirties, with black hair, bronzed skin, and strong bone structure that hinted at Hispanic or Native American heritage. He was dressed in jeans and a muscle-clinging black T-shirt with a buzzed hair-cut that could be either military or trendy. He looked up as she descended the stairs, his dark brown eyes speculative and alert.

Definitely military.

She glanced at Darius, and her stomach gave a little flip at the warmth in those gorgeous blue eyes. She'd missed his arms around her last night.

Warrior? She flicked her head slightly toward the newcomer as she sent the telepathic message.

No. Human, he sent back.

"Faith," Darius said aloud as she got to the bottom of the stairs, "this is Rigo Mendez. He works on my father's security team and is going to keep you company this morning."

"I see." Faith held out a hand, and Mendez shook it. "So you're the babysitter."

"I wouldn't say that," Mendez replied.

"Not a babysitter," Darius said. "Just someone to talk to. It's rude to leave a guest all alone."

"Uh-huh." She had to admit that it pinched just a bit that he didn't trust her to entertain herself. She'd thought that Darius, at least, understood she wasn't the bad guy.

This wasn't my idea, just so you know, he sent. *Having Rigo here gives my parents a sense of security that they need right now.*

Wow, it was like he could read her mind. Or maybe he was just really intuitive. She wanted to stay annoyed at him, but who could fault a guy for trying to make his mother feel safe? Her heart melted just a little bit more.

"So," Mendez said, and she realized that from his non-Atlantean perspective, her telepathic conversation with Darius must have seemed like awkward silence. "What did you have planned for this morning?"

"First, breakfast," Faith answered.

"Lupe made muffins," Darius said. "Banana nut, I think."

Mendez grinned, the flash of white giving a softer aspect to his stern visage. "My favorite. She must have known I was coming."

"She must have," Darius agreed. He glanced at his watch.

"I need coffee," Faith announced. "How about you, Mr. Mendez?"

"Rigo," he corrected. "Sure, I could go for a cup."

"Okay then." Faith looked at Darius. "You'd better go. We'll be fine."

"You sure?" His lips curved in a private message just for her. "I could stay a couple more minutes."

Her insides turned to warm goo. Aware of Rigo's perceptive gaze on them, she ordered her organs to solidify and managed a calm response. "We'll be fine. You'd better go before you get in trouble."

"Right. Take care of her, Rigo."

"You know it," the other man replied.

Darius turned and began to climb the stairs, one fist gripping his cane and the other clenched around the bannister. He made good time, but the slow, steady pace indicated it wasn't easy.

"Let's go grab that coffee," Rigo said. He added in a murmur, "Don't watch him; it will just tick him off."

"Right." With effort, she turned away from Darius's arduous climb and walked with Rigo to the kitchen. "You'd think they would have installed an elevator for him to use," she said as they arrived at the coffeepot.

"Oh, they did." Rigo waved a hand, indicating she should go first. As she poured her coffee, he continued, "When he was in the wheelchair, he had to use it. Once he got on his feet, he refused. He climbed those stairs no matter how hard it was or how long it took."

"Sounds like him." She added vanilla creamer to her coffee while Rigo poured his. "He's a stubborn man."

"Sounds like you've gotten to know him pretty well after a couple days' acquaintance." Sharp, dark-eyed gaze upon her, he took a swig of coffee, straight black.

She raised her eyebrows. "Is this the interrogation part of our time together?"

"You're blunt."

"I grew up in what was basically a military camp. Not a lot of chatty types." She indicated his biceps, where the letters of a tattoo peeked out from beneath the edge of his sleeve. "I'm betting that says *Semper Fi*."

He slid the sleeve up with one finger to reveal the whole tat. "Good guess."

"It was the haircut. And the way you walk. Everything about you screams 'Marine.' "

He shrugged.

"Right. You am what you am." That startled a laugh from him. She smiled back. "Since we're going to be hanging out together, what do you suggest?"

"It's up to you. I'm just along for the ride."

"Okay then. First things first: muffins."

"I'm down with that."

. . . . .

Darius was sweating a little as he reached the *tenplu* on the third floor of the house. The family temple, a rooftop garden, and the vault holding all their Atlantean artifacts took up the entire uppermost floor of the house. This was where his brother Rafe would go through his Soul Circle. If all went well, Rafe would emerge from the ritual with more control over his powers than ever before.

If he failed, Rafe would be gone forever, replaced by the primordial warrior Rafe became when he allowed his abilities full rein—the Hunter.

Darius paused before entering the *tenplu* to catch his breath. He looked down at his cane. Rafe had lost control of his Hunter five years ago, resulting in the injury that had left Darius in a wheelchair. He hoped history didn't repeat itself.

Especially since his love life had taken such an interesting turn.

A Seer and a former member of the Mendukati. Who could have foreseen such an unlikely pairing? His mother said he and Faith were bonded as mates, and she was never wrong. Rafe had found his destined mate in Cara, and she anchored Rafe, something his brother had needed for a long time, especially today. The Soul Circle tested one's control over one's abilities, which meant pushing them to the limits. Rafe hadn't had a whole lot of control before Cara came along, and his link with her might be the only thing to save him if something went wrong. They were a truly bonded couple, and their happiness poured off them like rainwater, soaking any room they were in together with the bliss of true love.

He wanted that for himself and Faith, but would it be possible to overcome the deception that had been in play since the day they'd met?

"Darius, what are you doing standing in the hallway?"

He looked up and saw his mother in the open doorway. She wore the large, faceted crystal pendant around her neck that marked her as *apaiz nagusi*—the high priestess. The chain, made of orichalcum, an ore found only in Atlantis, shone red-gold against her black shirt. She focused her power through the clear quartz.

"Well?" she pressed. "Are you coming in or did you plan on participating from the hallway?"

"Sorry." He stepped through the door she held open for him. "I was thinking."

She patted his arm and closed the door. "I know you must be nervous."

"A little. But Cara seems to keep him stable, so I'm holding on to that."

"I'm glad." Maria smiled. "Your brother needs your support."

"I know. Listen, after all this is over, I'd like to talk to you and Dad about Faith."

"What about her?"

"I need to tell her the truth." His mother opened her mouth to speak, but Darius rushed on. "You said she's my mate. I can't keep lying to her. I know she means us no harm."

Maria sighed. "We will discuss it—after the ritual."

"Thank you." Darius tugged his own focus stone from beneath his shirt, a solid two-inch triangle of green moss agate on its own orichalcum chain. "I'm ready."

"Good. Everyone's here."

He looked up and saw that she was correct; he was the last to arrive.

"Sleep through the alarm, bro?" Rafe asked. Dressed in a

T-shirt and jeans, he stood at the edge of the massive sandpit that split the room, hands on his hips and a smart-aleck grin on his face. The clear quartz focus stone hanging around his neck glittered in the morning sunlight streaming in the windows.

"You should talk," Darius shot back. "I was up and swimming laps when you finally rose from your beauty sleep. I saw you stumble into the kitchen for coffee."

"I expected you to sleep in a little," Rafe said, glancing at Cara beside him, "given recent developments."

"Rafe!" Cara smacked her fiancé's arm and hissed, "That was supposed to be a secret!"

"What secret?" Tessa asked, looking up from watering the plants lining the edges of the room. "What developments?"

"You tell us, O Knowing One," Rafe shot back. "You're the one who makes all the prophecies."

"Rafe," Cara warned.

"You think you're safe because I can't read other Atlanteans?" Tessa put down the watering can and strode over to Rafe. "Let's put that to the test."

"Here we go." Cara buried her face in her hand.

"Bring it, sis." Rafe folded his arms and smirked.

"Children," their mother said, "this is not the time for nonsense."

"It's not nonsense." Tessa's eyes widened as she peered closely at Rafe. "Darius and Faith? *Mates?* Are you nuts?"

"Hey, since when can you read me?" Rafe demanded.

"Oh, Rafe." Cara looked up, her expression revealing the exasperation Darius knew she felt. "She didn't read you, she read me. She *always* reads me." She turned a scowl on Tessa. "Which is very rude, Tessa. If we're going to be sisters, you have to cut that out."

"Sorry. I like to know what's going on. Darius and Faith? No way." With a shrug, Tessa turned to Darius. "Tell them."

"Tell them what?" Darius asked.

"Tell them it's ridiculous."

"What's ridiculous?"

"Dar." Tessa narrowed her eyes. "Don't play dumb."

"Who said he's playing?" Rafe said.

"*Children,*" their mother said again, this time through gritted teeth.

"You and Faith, a romance, destined mates. Tell them it's crazy," Tessa said.

Darius shrugged. "Maybe not as crazy as you think."

"No way." Tessa's eyes bugged. "Tell me you're not falling for that . . . that . . ."

"That what?" Darius set his jaw. "Finish it, Tess. I know you've got some ax to grind regarding Faith."

Tessa folded her arms. "She used to run with the people who are trying to exterminate our family."

"Briefly," Darius said. "She broke off from them years ago."

"Maybe."

"No 'maybe' about it. She's here to help us, Tessa, and she wants nothing to do with the Mendukati. It wouldn't kill you to be polite to her."

"I don't trust her."

"Why, because you can't read her?" Tessa's sudden flash of guilt told him the truth. "That's it, isn't it? Every woman Rafe or I have dated was human, and you could read them. Judge them. But Faith is Atlantean, so you have no idea what she's thinking. And it's driving you nuts."

"Someone needs to know what she's up to."

"Darius does." Their father spoke from the other side of the room, near the light switches and temperature controls. "His powers do work on Faith. He'd tell us if she was up to something."

"And while I, too, am nervous about having her here," their mother added, "I know what I know. I don't want to believe Darius's destined mate is a true danger to us."

"So she is his destined mate? That can't be right." Tessa wrapped her arms around herself and turned away.

"It is what it is," Maria said. "Now please shake off that negative attitude so we can work some energy. Rafe, are you ready?"

That quickly, every person in the room sobered. Rafe nodded. "Let's do this."

Cara laid a hand on Rafe's arm. When he looked at her, she stood up on tiptoe and brushed a kiss to his lips. "I'm right here. Make sure you come back to me."

"You got it." Bending his head, Rafe gave his fiancée a harder kiss than she had bestowed on him. Turning, he faced the sand.

"John, if you will," Maria said.

His father turned a dial, and the sunroof in the ceiling slowly opened to let in the sunlight. The open space was as wide as the sand below it and only six feet long, though the sand itself extended the width of the room. The sunshine poured in and hit the stones they'd placed on the seven three-foot-high rock pillars that made up the most sacred part of the *tenplu*.

Each of the colored stones sitting on a pillar represented one of the seven chakras: red tumbled ruby, bright orange carnelian, yellow tiger eye, green moss agate, blue turquoise, dark indigo amethyst, and light violet amethyst. Darius stood along the edge of the sandpit with his mother and sister as Rafe stepped into it, walking forward until he stood between the pillars. As one, all four Montanas turned their faces to the sun. The warm light streamed over them, touching their focus stones, warming them.

And as one, they began to sing the chant to initiate the Soul Circle.

. . . . .

Faith and Rigo had settled at the kitchen table with their coffee and muffins when Lupe came into the kitchen from the laundry room.

"What is this?" she demanded.

Faith paused in lifting the muffin to her mouth. "Oh, were we not supposed to eat these?"

"Don't be ridiculous." Lupe threw up her hands. "Why do you think I made them?"

"Because you know they're my favorite?" The affection in Rigo's voice startled Faith, as did the mischievous look in his eyes.

Lupe blushed and waved a hand at him. "You. Don't try to sweet-talk your way out of this, Rodrigo Mendez."

"Could I? Sweet-talk you, I mean?"

"Bah!" Lupe addressed Faith. "This one, such a charmer. Of course I made the banana nut for him. But is that all you intend to eat?" She whirled back on Rigo. "A man like you, a muffin will not hold you for long. I'll make you eggs. That's a good breakfast."

"Oh, Lupe, you don't have to do that," Faith said.

"Three or four of these, and I'm good." Rigo held up the muffin.

"You need protein. Especially you." She pointed at Rigo. "No arguments. How do you want your eggs?"

"Over medium," he said.

"Scrambled," Faith said in response to Lupe's lifted brow.

"Ten minutes," Lupe said, and pulled a frying pan from the cupboard. She muttered beneath her breath in Spanish as she collected eggs, cheese, and nonstick spray.

Rigo lifted his cup to his lips and met Faith's gaze over the rim, his eyes full of mirth and crinkling at the edges. She felt her own lips twitching and quickly took a gulp of coffee. Minutes later, Lupe slid a plate of steaming scrambled eggs sprinkled with cheese in front of Faith and a plate with two fried eggs in front of Rigo. She slapped a bottle of hot sauce beside it.

"Now, this is breakfast," she announced. The buzzer from the dryer went off, and she headed into the laundry room, still muttering to herself as she left.

Faith glanced down the hallway to make sure she was gone. "I don't know about you, but I feel like I've been schooled."

Rigo grinned, took the cap off the hot sauce, and splashed some on his eggs. "Lupe makes her thoughts known, that's for sure."

"If I keep eating like this, I'll have to hit the gym after I get back home."

"There's one here. I'm sure the Montanas would let you use it." He cut into one of the yolks. Yellow goo oozed out.

"Maybe I'll ask Darius." She scooped up a forkful of eggs.

"Good idea."

Out of nowhere, her tattoos flared like freshly seared brands. Her fingers spasmed. She dropped her fork with a clang. A scream tore through her mind like a sharp blade through a sheer veil. She whimpered and grabbed the edge of the table with contorted fingers.

A stone, splintered, out of balance. Energy being forced through distorted channels. Hot, so hot. Can't hold it all. Throbbing, throbbing. The wail ripped from her throat, scraping her vocal cords like gravel. Agony. So much. Too much.

Have to . . .

Make. It. Stop.

It flooded her mind like acid. She swept her arm across the table. Plates and silverware crashed to the floor. Someone grabbed her wrist. She saw a face. Rigo. His lips moved, but there was no sound.

Another wave seared into her mind. Her body jerked. Rigo was saying something. She couldn't hear him through the deranged shrieking in her head. She yanked her wrist from his grasp and leaped to her feet. She had to find that stone, save it. Stop the screaming.

Rigo grabbed her elbow. Tried to hold her back.

The Stone of Igarle had been whispering to her all morning, urging her to heed its call, to connect again and discover the secrets of the ages. She'd ignored it earlier, but now she reached for it, tapped it with a feather-light touch for the power she needed, and shoved Rigo away one-handed, the force of the ancient stone behind it. Mendez flew across the room, smacked his head on the stainless-steel fridge and slumped to the floor, dazed.

Faith ran for the stairs.

She followed the scream of the damaged stone to the third floor. Her throat vibrated with the hum of the Stone of Igarle, and the ancient crystal seemed to shield her somewhat from the mind-splitting wail of the fractured stone. With her connection to one of the most powerful crystals in Atlantis fueling her, she shoved open the double wooden doors and took in the scene with a glance.

Bright sunlight pouring in from an open sunroof. Seven pillars with seven colored stones glowing, all healthy. John in the far corner, Darius, Maria, Tessa, and Cara standing alongside a sandpit. And in the pit—Rafe.

The mind-searing screech came from the stone he wore around his neck. She could see it clearly now, feel it, a jagged shard of crystal hanging from a chain. It glowed as he fed power through it, but the channels were warped. This stone did not belong to him, yet he forced it to his will.

And was killing it.

She threw her hands up, tattoos burning like lava, and sang a short, harsh song with the power of Igarle behind it. Every stone in the room flared, then winked out.

The screaming in her mind cut off. Silence.

Rafe stiffened and collapsed in the sand, and the room exploded with panicked voices as the entire Montana family turned and looked at her.

CHAPTER FOURTEEN

Faith managed to remain standing, even as her legs trembled with the aftereffects of the ancient power she had channeled. She wanted to lie down in a quiet corner somewhere, but the fear and rage in the faces of the people in front of her had her stiffening her spine. She wouldn't let them see her weaken.

"What do you think you're doing?" John Montana strode forward. "You were told to stay away from here!"

"Hold on a minute." Darius came to stand beside Faith. "Let her explain."

"Explain? Seems obvious to me. She just burst in here and shut down every stone in the room with a wave of her hand." Tessa glared at Faith. "Know who else can do that? Jain Criten."

"Criten sucked the energy out of Rafe's focus stone when he forced his way into our house, and he nearly killed us all." Maria gripped her pendant. "That she can do this, like *he* did . . ."

"Hold it right there!" Rigo swept into the room, his pace measured and a two-handed grip on the gun pointed at Faith. "I'm sorry, sir. She got the drop on me. It won't happen again."

"See that it doesn't," John said.

"I told you she was dangerous," Tessa said, eyes narrowed. "How'd a little thing like her take out Rigo?"

"What is wrong with all of you?" Darius demanded. "Lower the gun, Rigo. Faith doesn't want to hurt anyone." He looked at his family. "She came to warn us, didn't you, Faith?"

"Yes," Faith said. She could see by his expression that he was willing to hear her out, but the rest of his family looked like they wanted to go out and find a strong rope and a sturdy tree.

They're afraid of you. The whisper in her mind came from the Stone of Igarle.

"Rafe's crystal is unsafe," Darius announced.

"What do you mean 'unsafe'?" Maria demanded.

"I mean he can get hurt if he keeps using it. Right, Faith?"

"Yes, that's right." Faith frowned. "How'd you know that?"

Darius ignored her question. "Seems to me that's a good enough reason to do what she did." He didn't break gazes with his father. "Tell them the rest, Faith."

Puzzled by his grasp of details she hadn't told him but grateful for the ally, Faith gestured toward Rafe as Cara helped him get to his feet. "Rafe's crystal is fractured, warped. Every time he uses it, he damages it more, and one day it's going to lash back on him. I could hear it screaming." She closed her eyes, as if that would tune out the painful memory.

"Screaming?" Tessa said. "What do you mean 'screaming'?"

"In my head." She opened her eyes. "I can craft Rafe a new one. But he can't keep using that one."

"Out of the question," John said. "How do we even know you're telling the truth, that this isn't a trick?"

"Because *I* know," Darius said. "It's no trick, Dad. Something is wrong with Rafe's stone. Maybe we should let Faith examine it."

"Absolutely not," Maria said. "What do we know about Stone Singers, after all? She might destroy it."

"What would you like me to do with her, sir?" Rigo asked.

"Put her in the safe room," John said. "And this time do a better job of keeping her contained."

"Keeping me contained?" Faith's heart sank as she glanced at Darius. "I thought he was just supposed to keep me company."

"He was." Darius frowned at his father.

"I gave him another set of orders," John said. "I told him to watch you in case you tried something. And you did try something."

"Dad, you don't understand," Darius said.

"I understand plenty!" John pointed at Faith. "This woman just ripped away the power from every stone in the temple. The family is defenseless now!"

"What was she supposed to do?" Darius demanded. "Let Rafe continue using a fractured stone for his Soul Circle? She just told you the stone was screaming in her mind, tearing her apart, yet she still managed to get up here and save us from ourselves."

"That's exactly what it felt like," Faith murmured.

"Is that the act of an enemy?" Darius regarded his family. "Let's put the Soul Circle on hold for now until we find out what's going on."

"We have no choice," Maria said. "She drained the energy out of all the stones. We'll have to recharge them all before Rafe tries again."

"I didn't drain them," Faith said. "I put them to sleep."

"Looks like you drained them to me." Tessa put her hands on her hips.

"Well, you're not a Stone Singer, are you?" Faith mimicked Tessa's pose. "I put them to sleep rather than let the lot of you continue to destroy them with your ignorance."

"Ignorance!" Maria's eyes bugged.

"Yes, ignorance. It's clear as day Rafe's stone was not created for him. Every time he uses it, he fractures it a little more."

"Damn it, Darius, how could you let this happen?" John demanded. "You were in charge of her, and you've done a miserable job of it."

"I was afraid of this," Maria said. "What were we thinking, allowing one of them into our home?"

"She's trying to help," Darius said. "She's not like the others."

"The hell she isn't." His father put his arm around his

mother's shoulders. "I thought she just talked to rocks, but apparently she can use them as weapons as well. She's dangerous. Take her, Rigo."

Mendez came forward. "Come on, let's go."

"Hey!" Darius stepped in front of Faith. "We're not locking her up. She just saved our asses."

"That's not your call, son," John said. He nodded at Rigo.

"You're making a mistake," Darius said.

"The only mistake we made was letting her into our home to begin with," John said. "The safe room, Rigo."

Rigo moved to Faith's left, keeping his handgun trained on her. He pulled a set of plastic hand restraints from his pocket. "Put these on."

"Oh, come on!" Darius glared at his father as Faith took the strip of black plastic and slid one wrist through the loop. "Isn't this taking things a bit too far? I know you're all scared—"

"Damn right we're scared. Here, let me help." Tessa came forward and pulled Faith's other wrist through the open loop of the restraints, then locked them with a yank. She gave Faith a smug smile. "There. Now I'm not so scared anymore."

"Gee, thanks," Faith said through gritted teeth.

"She's not our enemy!" Darius appealed to his father. "Dad, there's a reason everyone is looking for her, and we just witnessed it. She can manipulate the energy in stones."

"All the more reason to keep her locked up until we know the truth," Tessa said. "Dar, I can't believe you're buying into her little innocent act."

"It's not an act. She is innocent in this. Don't you think I'd know if she wasn't?"

"I think you're a little too close to this," Tessa shot back. "Too emotional. I knew it was a mistake to put an empath in charge of someone like her."

"You all put me in charge of her *because* I'm an empath, remember?" Darius shouted.

"Excuse me?" Brother and sister looked at Faith as if they'd forgotten her presence. And maybe they had, given the expressions of guilt on their faces. "Did you just say Darius is an empath?"

"Rigo, get her out of here," John said.

Rigo tugged her toward the door, but Faith dug in her heels. "No, I'm not leaving. Not until you explain this."

"As if you have a choice," Tessa said.

"There's always a choice," Faith said.

Just go along until I can get this sorted out, Darius said into her mind. *Don't do anything to make matters worse.*

Not feeling real cooperative right now, she sent back.

I know.

"Yeah, you do know, don't you?" she said aloud. She met his gaze for a moment, steeling her heart against those beautiful— lying—blue eyes. She turned to Rigo. "Let's go, jarhead."

She didn't protest further when Rigo led her out of the room. And she didn't look back.

．　．　．　．　．

Darius watched Faith exit the room. He could sense her feelings of betrayal, and it ate at him. He should have been the one to tell her, to explain.

"So you really believe this screaming stone stuff?" Tessa asked.

The doors closed behind Faith and Rigo.

"Dar?" Tessa prompted. "You don't seriously believe all that hooey, do you?"

"Yes," Darius said. "I do."

"Oh, please." She gave a snort of disbelief.

Darius spun to his sister. "Okay, let's take a look at what we have right here in this room. A girl who can see the future, a guy who can turn into a badass killing machine, a woman who can match anyone with a soul mate. Some people would find that stuff *hooey*, as you put it."

"Don't forget the dude who always knows what everyone's feeling," Rafe put in with a weak grin. "Mr. Lonely Hearts himself."

"Say that again when you can stand on your own," Darius shot back. "Listen, I know you're all scared—"

"Not anymore, I'm not," Tessa said. "Not now that Rigo has her locked up."

Darius leveled a no-nonsense look on his sister. "Pretend all you want, Tess, but you can't fool an empath. Yes, it's scary dealing with powers we're unfamiliar with. And Mom, I know this is hardest on you. Especially after what happened to your cousins."

His mother nodded.

"But let's remember something. Faith walked away from the Mendukati. She doesn't want to do what they are doing. Did it occur to you that she's scared, too? Of us?"

"Why would she be scared of us?" Tessa frowned. "We don't go around manipulating energy or stealing the power from people's stones."

"Her people are raised to believe that Seers are evil," Darius said. "We're the bogeymen in her world. They're afraid of us, which is why they hunt us. And yet she still came here, where she's locked away from the world and trapped with a houseful of Seers, to help us."

"Or to be the Mendukati's Trojan horse," his father said.

"Darius, what did you sense from her?" his mother asked. "Is she up to something?"

"As far as I can tell, she has no plans to hurt anyone."

"But how can we trust your opinion?" For once his sister had no hostility to her tone, only curiosity. "If what Mom says is true and she's your mate, wouldn't that affect your interpretation?"

"She has a point," Cara said. "Would you recognize ill will, or would you explain it away?"

Darius stiffened. "Look, Faith is a Stone Singer. There's apparently something wrong with Rafe's focus stone, and she noticed it. That's all that happened here, no stranger than Tessa having a vision in the middle of dinner."

"I don't know if we can trust what she says," his mother said. "What if this is a plan to weaken us?"

"You all put me in charge of her while she's here," Darius reminded them. "Do you trust *me*?"

"Of course we trust you, honey." His mother sighed and rubbed her forehead.

"Nonetheless, we're going to have a little chat with Faith. And I'm going to have more security guards placed in the house and on the grounds," his father said. When Darius opened his mouth to protest, his father held up a finger to silence him. "I know human guards may not be very effective against Atlantean powers, but it's better than nothing."

Darius nodded. "If it makes you feel better."

"It does."

"Fine. But I'll be the one to talk to Faith."

. . . . .

Faith made it downstairs with some effort. Her limbs shook, and she barely had the energy to put one foot in front of the other after the drama up in the temple. The Stone of Igarle still whispered in the back of her mind. She tried to sever the connection, but her reserves were low, and her feeble attempts yielded nothing.

Once she rested and recharged, she would have better control.

Rigo marched her to the first floor and then to a door behind the staircase. He opened it, revealing stairs going down into a basement of some sort. He flicked a light switch to illuminate the way. Gray walls formed a tunnel on either side of the descending steps, with a metal door at the bottom. "Let's go."

She went down, the noises from above them fading the deeper underground she went. When she reached the bottom, Rigo took hold of her elbow and punched in some numbers on a keypad. He placed his hand in a device mounted on the wall and looked into some kind of eye scanner above it.

The door clicked open. Rigo pushed her forward, not hard enough to make her fall but enough that she knew he meant business.

The first thing she noticed was that the safe room had no windows. There was another locked metal door to her left, and on her right was a small bathroom. There was a sink and countertop with cabinets above and below it, like a kitchenette without the stove and fridge. A coffeepot, nondairy creamer, and sugar packets were on the counter. A metal table and chairs sat in the middle of the room, and the table was bolted to the floor.

Rigo closed the door behind him and walked her to one of the chairs. He pushed her into it with a heavy hand on her shoulder. "Sit."

"What is this place, a prison?"

"A safe room." He pulled out the chair across from her and sat, his gun pointed at her.

"To keep me safe? Or to keep them safe from me?"

"I don't know how you did what you did back there," he said, ignoring her question. "But I'm onto you now."

The door opened and Darius walked in. For one second her heart leaped. Then she remembered.

"My father's on his way down," Darius said to Mendez, "but he said it was okay for me to talk to her first. You can wait outside."

Mendez narrowed his eyes. "I've got my orders. I stay."

"I thought you might need a bathroom break." Darius focused on Rigo, and through their link, Faith could feel him push something at the other man.

Mendez frowned and shifted in his seat.

"She won't leave this room," Darius said, "and I won't remove the restraints."

Rigo jumped from his chair. "Be right back." Grabbing his gun, he hurried into the tiny bathroom and slammed the door.

Darius pulled out a chair and sat down.

"What did you do to him?" Faith asked.

He glanced at the closed bathroom door. "Just asked if he needed a bathroom break."

"No, you did something. I felt it."

"Really?" He shrugged.

"I don't believe it." She stared at him as realization dawned. "You made him think he had to use the restroom."

"Well, he did." One corner of his mouth quirked. "I can't manufacture emotion from nowhere, but I can take an existing emotion and . . . ah . . . emphasize it. In this case, urgency."

"Is that what you did to me?"

His smile faded. "No. Never. Look, I came down here to say I'm sorry."

"Really." She leaned back in her chair. "Sorry for what? For lying to me, for taking me to bed under false pretenses? You're going to have to be more specific."

"For all of it." He sighed. "I didn't like it, either. I knew as soon as I met you that you weren't one of the obsessed ones, but my family has been through a lot. They were afraid, so they asked me to let them know if you might be a danger."

"I get it. Really, I do." She leaned forward. "This has been no picnic for me, either. I didn't know what to expect from the Seers. Guess I do now. Same thing I expect from the Mendukati: betrayal and deception." She slumped back in her chair. "I can't believe I thought you were different."

"I am different. Yes, I know it doesn't look like it from where you're sitting, but I told my mother this morning that I was going to tell you everything. Think about it. I'm an empath. Do you really think I could handle deceiving you after last night?"

Her lip curled. "I don't know what you can handle, Darius.

All I know is you've been spying on me, telling me only one side of the story."

"Here's the rest." He held her gaze. "I'm an empath, and yes, my abilities work on everyone, both human and Atlantean."

Her gut clenched. *Just like Michael.* "What exactly does it mean that you're an empath?"

"That I can feel the emotions of others. Everyone. Drives me nuts sometimes, having everyone else's feelings shoved in my face."

"And you can make people feel things."

"Yes and no. Like I said, I can only amplify an emotion the person is already feeling. Example: When Criten broke in here, Cara tackled him. One of his goons freaked out and took a shot at her. He was terrified for his leader. I just took that and amplified it so his terror overwhelmed him."

"Like you did to Corinne."

"Right. I just turned their own emotions back on them."

"And what about my emotions?" Her throat tightened as she asked the question. "You knew I found you attractive. Did you amplify those emotions, too? Make me ignore my own rules about getting involved and beg you to take me to bed? Was it easier for you to spy on me that way?"

"No." He touched her bound hands, but she jerked them out of his reach.

"Don't touch me," she whispered. "You forfeited that right when you lied to me."

He swiped a hand over his face. "I didn't want to do it, but the safety of my family was at stake. Can you tell me you wouldn't use your powers to protect the ones you love?"

"I told you, I get it." She reached for the stone all around them, the earth beneath them, humming a song to spin the energy into a new kind of Stone Shield, one that helped her hold the icy resolve that was her only hope of getting out of this with any dignity.

"I didn't mean to hurt you."

"But you did," she said as the walls of ice fell into place. "You won't anymore."

. . . . .

He'd certainly made a mess of this.

One moment Faith had been simmering with anger, betrayal throbbing like a bleeding wound. The next moment, all he got from her was . . . ice.

She'd done something. He could see it in her eyes. Somehow she'd shut him out. Mostly. And she wasn't even wearing her ring.

Rigo came out of the bathroom. A moment later Darius's father came into the room. Both men radiated suspicion and antagonism directed at Faith. Darius shifted to be closer to her. She didn't even acknowledge him.

"Well, Ms. Karaluros," his father said. "That was quite a show you put on."

"As I told you, Mr. Montana, there's a problem with Rafe's stone."

"So you say. But I have a problem now. We opened our home to you, treated you as a guest despite our misgivings, and this is how you repay us." He laid his palms flat on the table and leaned in. "Are you working for the Mendukati, young lady?"

"No." Her jaw tightened, and Darius could sense her struggle to hold on to the ice shield she'd adopted. "I'm sick to death of defending myself to you and your family, Mr. Montana. *You* came to *me*. *You* need *my* help to analyze that stone you've got. I was minding my business, living a nice, normal life until you and the Mendukati came after me."

His father reared back, his eyes lighting with the ire Darius had sensed bubbling beneath the surface. "You dare put us in the same category as those murderers?"

She held up her bound hands. "It looks the same from where I'm sitting. You both want the power the stone holds, but in order to get to it, you need me. Doesn't matter to you *or* them if I'm willing or not. Both of you will steamroll right over my wishes to obtain your goal."

"We offered to pay you." Darius recognized that terse tone in his father's voice.

"And they offered not to kill me. But neither of you trust me, neither of you will let me decide." Her voice lowered, roughened. "You don't seem to understand that I saved your son's life today. That stone was going to blow, and it would have taken him with it, if not everyone in that room. I did what I had to." She sat back in her chair. "You're welcome."

"Your attitude is not helping your case," his father said.

"And what will?" she shot back. "Kowtowing to the mighty John Montana? I don't care who you are or how much money you have. You judged me before I ever stepped foot in your door, and at the first misunderstanding—*your* misunderstanding, mind you—you have your guard tie me up and lock me in the basement. Not creating a lot of trust on my side, either."

"She's right, Dad."

Darius's father shot a sharp glare at him. "I haven't even gotten to you yet."

"Gotten to me?" Darius surged to his feet, balancing himself on his cane. "You asked me to spy on Faith empathically, like some kind of alarm in case she had a bad thought. And I did it, because I love my family. But you put me in a tricky spot, Dad, and now you're making things worse by thinking with your emotions and not your head."

"I am not thinking with my emotions!" John swung away from the table.

Darius raised his brows. "Did you forget who you're talking to?"

His father slowly closed his hand in a fist. Said nothing.

"Look, this is a sticky situation for all of us." Darius stepped closer to his father. He could feel the anger flooding his senses, but beneath that was a bone-deep fear that he recognized. "Faith is right. She didn't come to us offering her services, we went to her. You keep wanting to make her into some Mendukati spy, but the truth is she hates them as much as we do." He touched his dad's arm, waited for his father to meet his gaze. "I know this, Dad. I *know*."

"You're apparently involved with her. How can we trust your judgment?"

"Emotion doesn't lie. I sense the emotions and they are what they are. There's no data to analyze, Dad. No mission, no secret Mendukati mole. Faith was trying to help. She has abilities we've never seen before, and what we don't understand can be frightening."

"What she did, it was like him. Like Criten."

"We're both Channelers," Faith said. "We manipulate energy. That's all we have in common."

His father looked at Faith, jaw clenched. "Tell me exactly what happened today."

"Where did Rafe get his stone?" Faith countered. "The one he wears around his neck?"

"It was our grandfather's," Darius answered. "He was a Hunter like Rafe, so when he passed away, my mother gave Rafe the focus crystal."

Faith put her bound hands on the table. "The thing about stones like that is when they are created, they are designed for a specific person. That crystal may have served your grandfather well, but his power harmonics are completely different from Rafe's. The stone can probably sense that Rafe and your grandfather were related, and it's been trying to accommodate the new energy signature, but if he's been doing this for years, which I suspect is the case, those channels will have gotten frayed and warped. They are well on their way to fracture, which is what I sensed today."

"And if the stone had fractured," Darius asked, "what would have happened to Rafe?"

She swallowed, and he felt a little flutter of horror behind her arctic defenses. "The power would have backlashed into him, probably killing him."

Just like Michael.

His father paled. "Is this true?" he asked Darius.

Darius nodded. "That's what I've been trying to tell you, Dad. Look, if the toaster starts smoking because something got caught, what do you do?"

"Pull the plug." His father looked back at Faith. "That's what you did, isn't it? You pulled the plug before it exploded."

"Yes." Her shoulders relaxed. "I'm not your enemy, Mr. Montana. I came here to do a job. Let me complete it, and I'll be on my way."

"What about—?" His father glanced at him. "Never mind."

Faith spoke into Darius's mind. *My sentiments exactly.*

She hadn't hidden her emotions that time. Her distrust and hurt oozed from the words. Struck him in the heart like a well-aimed blade.

"Can you . . . what . . . reactivate the stones in the temple?" his dad asked.

"Yes. They weren't damaged."

"Good." John rubbed his chin. "I'm going to have Rigo release you, Faith, but I will be increasing security on the grounds. And I'll also require you to continue working with Darius on this project."

"Isn't there someone else?" She didn't even look at Darius as she addressed his father. "He's already proven that I can't trust him. I'd rather have Tessa. At least she's honest about her feelings for me."

John shook his head. "I can't bend on this. You work with Darius."

"Fine." She held up her bound hands. "Can I go?"

"Yes." His father signaled to Rigo, who removed the restraints. The team leader's face remained impassive as he shoved the strips of plastic into his pocket, but Darius could sense the suspicion beneath the facade.

Faith got up from the table, rubbing her wrists, and walked to the door. Rigo opened it for her. She left the room without looking back.

"Well." His father watched Faith go, then turned back to Darius. "This must be hard for you, based on what your mother says."

"What did she say?"

"That Faith is your destined mate and that you wanted to tell her the truth about your powers." He rubbed the bridge of his nose. "This is such a mess."

"You're right about that."

Rigo came to stand beside his father. "Orders, sir?"

"I want more men stationed around the house. And I want you to assign yourself to Faith, Rigo."

"Wait," Darius protested. "I thought I was supposed to be the one watching her?"

"You have personal feelings for the woman, son. Questions have been raised about your ability to remain objective." Darius opened his mouth to object, but his father raised a hand. "Having a third party there will put any of those questions to rest. Now let's get this done."

Rigo nodded and went after Faith. His father left the room next, leaving Darius to follow more slowly.

How was he supposed to win back Faith's trust with a chaperone watching their every move?

CHAPTER FIFTEEN

Rigo had caught up with Faith by the time she got to the patio doors. He slid one open for her, his face impassive but his eyes heavy with suspicion.

"Thank you," she said.

He nodded and followed her as she headed to the cabana. She could feel his gaze boring into her back.

"Faith!"

Faith turned at the shout to see Cara slipping through the patio doors. The other woman caught up to them at a jog. "Hey," Cara said. She nodded at Mendez. "Rigo."

He gave a nod of greeting but maintained his silence.

"He's not talking to me," Faith said, unable to stop the edge of bitterness in her tone. "You sure you want to be seen with public enemy number one, Cara?"

"Yes, I do." Cara laid a hand on Faith's arm. "I'm sorry about all that. The Montanas have gotten positively paranoid since Criten got in here back in September."

Cara's words were meant to be soothing, but Darius's betrayal gaped inside Faith like an open lava pit. "I understand where they're coming from." She shrugged, unwilling to let the pain show. "Not that it doesn't sting, but I get it. I was raised in a military lifestyle. Where's Rafe?"

"Resting. He said he was hanging on by his fingertips when you intervened. I might have lost him." Her voice caught on the last word, tears gleaming in her eyes. "You said he can't use the stone he has. That you can make him a new one."

"I'm sure I can."

"Rafe refuses to get married until he conquers this Soul Circle thing, and if it takes a new stone to do it, then he gets a new stone. I'll pay you whatever it takes."

Faith couldn't stop her lips from curving at Cara's passionate declaration. "Not necessary. Ben sent me a variety of stones. I can probably use one of them."

"Are you sure? Seriously, I can pay."

"Let me do this for you." Faith touched Cara's arm. "You and Rafe belong together. It would be an honor to help you achieve that."

"Wow. Thank you." Cara swiped a knuckle across her eyes. "Sorry for the waterworks. When do you want to do this?"

"How about now? It shouldn't take that long, but I need Rafe to be present."

"I'll get him." Cara darted off.

"Meet me at the cabana!" Faith called after her. Cara just waved a hand in acknowledgment. Faith turned back to see Rigo watching her, head tilted like he was trying to make sense of an Escher drawing. She shook her head and continued on to the cabana to get ready for Rafe's arrival, Rigo trailing behind her.

· · · · ·

Darius arrived at the cabana to find Faith and Rigo already there. Faith sat at the table, sorting through the stones Ben had sent her. The security man stood just behind and to the side of her, his brow furrowed as he watched. Faith looked up when Darius came in. Their gazes met; their bond flared. For an instant they were one. Then came the sear of hurt as she remembered, and she looked away, slamming down those defenses he'd sensed when he first met her.

"What are you doing?" he asked.

She didn't look up from the crystals she was sorting. "Cara asked me to make Rafe a new focus stone. I'm sorting out some that might be a good fit."

He stepped closer. He knew she was aware of his nearness, but she still did not look at him. "How do you know which ones?"

"I ask them." She indicated her selections, three colorless and one yellow. "Clear quartz and one citrine. The citrine surprised me, but it's good for enhancing the body's healing energy. For mental focus and endurance. Might be a good match." She lifted the gem and looked at it, humming softly. The melody echoed in his mind.

A sound at the door had him turning, had Rigo coming to attention. Cara and Rafe came in, holding hands.

"Cara says you can make me a new focus stone." Rafe held out the chain with his old crystal without letting go of Cara.

Faith took the chain and stroked the crystal, humming again in communication with the stone. Tenderness flowed from her as if she'd found a half-drowned kitten. "This was sung for your grandfather many years ago by Wei Jun." She lifted her gaze to Rafe with a sad smile. "He was the other Stone Singer besides me. He died recently."

"Sorry to hear that," Rafe said.

Faith set down the pendant. "Cara said you've been having trouble with this ritual for some time?"

Rafe's jaw tensed. "Yeah. I've never been able to get through it."

"This is why." She tapped the stone. "Your power was bottlenecked and unfocused. I will sing you your own stone of power that will enhance and guide your abilities, not hold them back."

A surge of hope came from Rafe, and Darius saw his brother squeeze Cara's hand. "That sounds great."

"These stones are willing to be yours." She swept a hand at the four she'd set aside. "Choose the one that speaks to you."

Rafe's eagerness vibrated like the engine of a vintage Mustang. He reached for the citrine.

She smiled. "I had a feeling about that one."

"There's something about it." He weighed the gem in his palm, then handed it back to her. "What do we do now?"

"You sit across from me." Rafe obeyed. "I'm going to balance and charge the stone," she said. "When it's time for you to imprint on it, I will hand it to you, and I want you to access your powers, let the citrine see you at the basic level."

"Okay."

Faith held the stone in her cupped hands and opened up to connect. The citrine responded like a flame to tissue, its energy young and eager as it charged along the connection. She tamed its wildness with gentle, guiding hands, her throat vibrating with its song. She told it what she wanted, then showed it. How it would no longer be just a pretty rock; it would become a stone of power.

The citrine responded with gusto, absorbing the energy she poured into it like a dry sponge in a bucket of water. It swelled with the power, glowing to her inner sight, pulsing and heavy with vitality.

Stone of power came the whisper in her mind.

Yes. You are a stone of power, molded to filter the energies of one.

Who? came the reply.

This one. Without opening her eyes, she held out her hand to Rafe. He took it, and she connected with him and the stone, forging the link between them until the citrine pulsed along with his heartbeat. Spreading his fingers wide, she placed the stone in his palm and covered it with her own. She sang the words to bond them, to show the citrine who Rafe was, to shape the channels for the power to flow.

The stone accepted Rafe, imprinted him upon it, sparked with exuberance at having purpose.

Faith opened her eyes and smiled at Rafe, sliding her hand away. "It's done."

"Seriously?" Rafe frowned down at his palm.

"Try it."

He focused, and the stone glowed, singing its joy as it funneled his energy. He jerked his gaze to her. "I can't believe it. There's so much there, power surging into me almost as soon as I reach for it. Like trading in an old pickup for a brand-new Ferrari."

"That's how it's supposed to be when a stone is sung for you alone."

Rafe got to his feet, the stone clutched in his fist. "I'm going to try this out." He looked at Cara. "Come with me?"

"Always." Cara had only a moment to smile at Faith before Rafe pulled her from the cabana.

"Will he be okay now?" Darius asked.

"As far as his stone goes, yes, he's out of danger." She picked up Rafe's discarded pendant, never looking at Darius. "Now let's see what I can do with this one."

She focused on the stone, on healing it, smoothing the warped channels and softening the rough edges. The crystal responded to her restorative energy, its power fluctuations calming.

If only she could mend her torn heart as easily.

"That should do it for now." She set aside the pendant and looked at Darius for the first time. "Now for the Stone of Igarle."

"Are you sure? You just sang two stones of power already."

"Get the stone, Darius. I want to make sure your family gets their money's worth."

Lips clamped in a hard line, Darius went to get the stone.

· · · · ·

The second day of the art show passed without incident, leaving Adrian even more on edge. He kept all senses open as he helped

Ben pack up his tools, materials, and unsold work. They loaded the truck and set out for the airport.

Dusk had fallen. Each second closer to sunset ramped up Adrian's adrenaline. He expected the Mendukati to make a move tonight because once they were on the plane to Sedona, the number of opportunities to grab Ben dwindled considerably.

It's what he would do.

But nothing happened on the ride to the airport. They got the boxes loaded on the Montanas' private plane without so much as a stubbed toe. Ben boarded, and Adrian waved off the luggage handlers as he hefted his bag and Ben's and headed for the stairs to the plane.

That's when the attack hit.

Three Warriors sprang from nowhere. He dropped the bags and spun just in time to block a strike from a guy with a black eye. Adrian punched Black-eye and sent him stumbling. Two other Warriors charged him. These looked to be the same bunch who took him on in the restaurant parking lot the other night. He sent one sprawling while the other took a swing at him. He blocked the blow and kicked the Warrior away.

Where the hell was Montana's security detail? Where was airport security, for that matter?

He could see airport personnel moving around near the hangar, but no one seemed to notice what was happening. The Whisperer. Had to be. Only a Whisperer could convince that many people that they didn't see anything. Which explained why only three Warriors attacked him. There had been four outside the restaurant that night.

No sooner had he taken out one than another came. He kept fighting, hoping to lay all three out long enough to get on board the plane. If they could just get airborne, everything would be okay. But these guys kept coming, three Warriors to one. Eventually they might wear him out. He needed an ace in the hole.

One got in a lucky punch and knocked him down. He hit the

pavement with a hard whoosh of air from his lungs. They scrambled for him.

He chanted beneath his breath, gathering power. The tattoo on his chest began to burn and throb. He yanked open his button-down shirt.

The Warriors grabbed him, one on each arm, and hauled him to his feet. Black-eye sauntered over, a smirk on his face.

"You don't want to do this," Adrian said in Atlantean.

"Oh, but we do," Black-eye said in the same language. "Azotay wants a word with you."

"Azotay risks the wrath of the Leyala," Adrian replied. "As do you." As expected, mention of the Leyala, the elite group of Warriors who handed out justice to other Warriors, made the grin fade. Black-eye shoved open Adrian's shirt.

The tattoo over his heart, three triangles connected at each base by a circle with an Atlantean symbol in the middle, rippled like living scar tissue and glowed.

Black-eye fell back a step. "Leyala," he whispered.

"Leyala," Adrian agreed. "You have been judged." He flipped backward, breaking the hold of the other two Warriors. Rather than attack him, they backed away. Black-eye charged him, fingers curled, aimed for his throat. Adrian blocked, grabbed Black-eye's arm and twisted it up behind his back. Black-eye thrust out his chest, back arched, trying to ease the pressure. He twisted, swung his fist up with the momentum.

Adrian slapped his left hand against Black-eye's chest and spat the Word of Judgment.

His tattoo flared, power surging down his arm into the other Warrior. Black-eye howled, jerking with spasms as if electro-cuted. He dropped to his knees, head lolling. Stayed there.

Adrian looked at the other two, who were inching away. "Take him." He strode to the plane, scooped up the bags he'd dropped, and jogged up the steps. Ben waited for him in the doorway, his eyes wide as he looked down at the Warriors on the tarmac.

"What did you do, Adrian?"

"Judgment." Adrian dropped the bags on the floor and turned to shut and lock the door to the plane. "Get buckled in. We're out of here."

"Okay." Ben took his overnight case and shoved it in the overhead compartment. Adrian did the same with his duffel bag, then dropped into a seat and buckled his seat belt. He hit the intercom to the cockpit. "Bob, let's get out of here."

"You've got it, Mr. Gray," the pilot answered. The plane began to move.

They'd been in the air for about fifteen minutes before Adrian's intuition flared. Warriors were not only stronger and faster than normal humans, they had the acumen and instincts to go with it. Warriors were masters of strategy and logic, and sensitive to the slightest hint of danger. Right now his senses were screaming that something was very wrong.

They should be heading west, but the sunset was on the right side of the plane, not in front of it. They were heading south.

Something was wrong.

"I'm going to talk to the pilot," he said.

Ben nodded, flipping through a magazine. "Would you get me a soda on the way back?"

"Sure." Adrian went up to the cockpit. He opened the door, and the pilot jerked his head around.

"You're not supposed to be up here, Mr. Gray."

"I'm getting drinks. Did you want one?"

"No, thank you." The pilot checked his dials. "You should have allowed a flight attendant."

"You're right." Adrian glanced at the instruments and saw his supposition was correct. "Are you aware you're heading south? Sedona is west."

"I know how to get to Sedona, Mr. Gray. It is my home airport."

"I know, which is why I'm wondering why we're going away from it."

Bob's face flushed red. "We're not going away from it. Clear skies all the way there. No reason to divert. We are headed to Sedona." He tapped the console. "It's right here, and if you were a pilot, you'd see that."

"I am a pilot." Adrian placed a hand on the back of the co-pilot's seat. Bob's forehead beaded with sweat and his hands trembled. Completely out of character for the normally placid man he'd come to know.

"Well, if you're a pilot, you can see for yourself we're on the right course." Bob waved a hand at the instruments.

"Maybe you should take a break, Bob. You don't look well."

Bob whipped around as far as the seat belt would let him. "I'm fine! Now get out of my cockpit, Gray. You have no business here."

"You seem sick. I could take over for you, make sure we get home."

"Is that what this is? You're trying to take over the plane? Hijack it?" Bob yanked out a gun and pointed it at Adrian. "Get out of here, Gray. Back to your seat."

"You don't want to do this, Bob." His instincts flared into battle mode, his senses becoming more acute, a dozen strategies playing through his mind. The Whisperer. He hadn't been with the rest of the Warriors sent to ambush him. He must have gotten to Bob.

The only way to break a Whisperer's compulsion was physical shock.

Adrian braced himself and swung. The door behind him opened.

"Hey, Adrian—" Ben said.

Bob pulled the trigger. Adrian's fist connected with Bob's

jaw. The bullet zipped past Adrian. Bob slumped in his chair, unconscious. The gun clattered to the floor.

Adrian flipped the switches to make sure they were on automatic pilot. Turned.

Ben slumped in the doorway, blood soaking his T-shirt.

"No!" Adrian sprang forward to kneel beside Ben. The older man's eyes were closed, his breathing labored. Adrian pressed his fingers to Ben's neck, found a pulse. Ripped open Ben's shirt. Bullet to the chest, oozing blood. Too much blood. Too close to the heart. "Damn it, Ben, stay with me."

The older man's breath wheezed through his lips, each shallow inhale and exhale pumping more blood from the wound. He remained unconscious.

"Don't you die on me," Adrian muttered. He found the first aid kit and taped the bandages tightly against the wound to try and stanch the bleeding. Then he turned to the pilot's console and flipped the oxygen control to manually drop the oxygen masks in the passenger compartment. Lifting Ben in his arms, he settled him in the first available passenger seat, buckled him in, and fastened the hanging oxygen mask over his nose and mouth.

Then he went back to the cockpit to fly the plane.

. . . . .

Coil by coil, bit by bit, Faith cleared more of the thousands of years of trapped emotions from the Stone of Igarle. She wouldn't be done today. Maybe another week if she could keep up the pace.

And if she could stand being with Darius for that many hours, every day.

She sensed him nearby through their mate link, could see him in the dark morass of the stone's black memories as a shining blue light, just like before. If his empathic powers really were neutralized in proximity to the stone, then it must be the mating bond that allowed him to stay connected to her, even when she was this deep in the rock.

Why him? Why did she have to always fall for a man who could use his power to manipulate her? First Michael and now Darius. How much of what she had felt for him, the constant sexual hunger, had been real? Or had it all been manufactured by him, the empath? She'd seen what he'd done to Rigo. He'd told her himself he could take a scrap of emotion that already existed and exaggerate it. Had he done that with her attraction for him? Blown it up into this craving that haunted her now, convinced her it was a mating bond? Would he really use her in such a way in order to get her to help his family?

Maybe those legends about Seers hadn't been as fabricated as she'd begun to believe.

She could hardly believe she still wanted him so much even after his duplicity had been exposed. What was wrong with her that she could not follow the path of self-preservation and keep her distance? Why did she long to be close to him, to feel his arms around her, to feel safe again? It made no sense. How could she ever truly feel safe knowing she could not fully trust him? Yet her heart urged her to seek solace in his arms.

She dove deeper into the stone, singing away its pain. Wishing she could do the same for herself. It was tempting to stay here, to allow herself to be absorbed into the rock, to become as hard and durable as it was. But part of her resisted the impulse. She might never come back out, and she would not let him see how much he'd hurt her.

He was an empath, so he probably knew, but as long as the Stone of Igarle kept his empathy turned off while she worked on the stone, she could have privacy in her grief for the love that might have been. Face the knowledge that she had been a fool . . . again.

Resign herself to a life alone. Why had she even dared to hope otherwise?

A cell phone rang from far away. The low rumble of voices.

Faith. Darius spoke directly into her mind. *You need to come back.*

Not yet. She wasn't ready to let go of the quiet, of the one place where she could be truly alone with her thoughts and emotions.

You have to come. It's Ben. He's hurt.

The song she keened stuck in her throat. The energy fluctuated, flared. She struggled to maintain some semblance of control, to calm the energy, even with her breath frozen in her lungs. Please, no. Not Ben.

Go, whispered Igarle.

She found the radiant blue pillar of light that was Darius and the link that led to him. What had once looked like a thread now resembled a swiftly running creek. She followed it, found him. Disconnecting from the stone, she gulped air as if she'd been held under water. A warm hand closed over her shoulder. She knew that touch. She laid her hand over his and opened her eyes to look at him.

Those gorgeous blue eyes, sober with concern. Even with all that had happened, she couldn't deny his soothing presence. That feeling that everyone would be okay as long as Darius was there. With the stone present, she knew he couldn't be using his empathy to make her feel this way, so it must just be him. Just Darius. Was she weak for wanting to believe he could really make everything better, just for now? For taking comfort that he was there with her?

"What happened?" she asked. "Where's Ben?"

"The hospital. He was shot. Adrian had the EMTs meet the plane when they landed."

She stood up, and his hand slipped away. "I'm going to the hospital."

"Rigo will drive us. Go get your purse, and I'll lock up the stone."

"Meet you out front." She ran from the room, Rigo on her heels.

Darius picked up the stone and put it in its wooden case, then locked it in the cabinet. Whatever pain hung between them, he knew Faith was going to need him.

Whether she wanted to or not.

· · · · ·

Faith ran up to her room and grabbed her purse, then charged out the door again. She met Tessa in the hallway.

"Faith!" Tessa grabbed her arm. "What happened? Someone got shot?"

"Yes. Let me go." She wrenched her arm free and ran toward the stairs.

"Wait!" Tessa fell into pace with her, then darted in front of her, forcing Faith to halt. "Who got shot? Faith, was it Adrian?" Her voice caught.

For the first time, Faith noticed how pale Tessa was, the anxiety in her eyes. Tessa's former hostility was completely absent. "No, it wasn't Adrian. It was my father-in-law, Ben." The tears sprang, unwanted. "Please, just let me pass. I have to get there. Have to get there in case—" She couldn't say the words, sucked in a shuddering breath.

Tessa squeezed her arm. "We'll go together. Come on, Rigo's pulling the car up out front."

Faith nodded and sprinted down the stairs, Tessa next to her. She didn't wonder about Tessa's about-face; there was time to consider that mystery later. All she wanted to do now was get to Ben . . . before it was too late.

CHAPTER SIXTEEN

Darius hated hospitals. So many emotions flying around, grinding against his empathic senses like unoiled gears. Grief, worry, fear, pain. They bombarded him as he, Rigo, Faith, and Tessa came through the emergency room doors. Faith's feelings were the most powerful of all, washing over him both because of her proximity and through their link.

Gray met them in the waiting area. He had a couple of bruises on that pretty face of his, and his dark eyes were somber. He was worried about Ben, but guilt and anger rippled off him. Guilt about Ben getting shot while under his protection, and anger at himself for letting it happen.

"It was Azotay's men," he said as soon as he saw them. "They ambushed us at the plane, but it was a half-assed attack at best. I didn't think much about it, just considered myself lucky and got us in the air. That's when the real plan became clear. They'd gotten to the pilot."

"Bob?" Rigo narrowed his eyes. "He's a good man. Was he hurt?"

"No. Your men have him in custody," Gray said to Rigo. He looked at Darius. "I don't know that we want to turn him over to the cops for this, at least not until we confirm what I suspect happened."

"What about Ben?" Faith demanded. "Where is he?"

"He went right to surgery. Still there." Gray pointed to the nurses' desk. "You're family, so they should talk to you."

Faith ran over to the nurses' desk.

"I would have thought they'd talk to you, Gray," Darius said.

"They did," Gray said, confirming what Darius had suspected. Adrian Gray was a Whisperer. It would be a simple matter to get the nurses to tell him what he wanted to know. "It doesn't look good." He clenched his jaw, guilt hammering at him.

As if sensing what he felt, Tessa stepped up to the Warrior and peered at his face. "Got some bruising going on there, Mr. Invincible. Guess you're mortal like the rest of us."

He touched her chin, his lips curving in sad, silent acceptance. "Didn't know you cared, princess."

Faith came back to them, her face white as gut-clenching fear swished through her. "Still in surgery. They don't know if—" She cleared her throat. "They don't know if he's going to make it." She raised terrified green eyes to Darius. "I don't know what I would do if something happened to him."

Her panic overwhelmed him, burning like raw jalapeño peppers on the tongue. He could sense fatigue, too. She'd spent too long in the Stone of Igarle, and her reserves were faltering.

"Let's get something to eat," he said.

She shook her head. "I can't leave. What if he comes out of surgery and I'm not here?"

He touched her shoulder. "Do you really want Ben to see you like this? You're pale, and you need to eat. I'm betting you haven't had anything since breakfast. I don't think you want him worrying about you, do you?"

Resentment flared, and she opened her mouth to argue. Then she sagged, and he felt the indignation fade. "You're right."

He took her arm. "I'll go with you, if only to make sure you don't pass out before you get there."

"Ha-ha." But she didn't shake off his hold. For a moment, all the negativity of the past few days no longer existed. She needed him now, and that need lived alive and well behind the walls of her angry defenses. Without further protest, she let him lead her toward the elevators.

. . . . .

Adrian watched them go, furious with himself for letting all this happen. He should have realized that a man like Azotay did not reach his current position without being a master strategist. But he'd been in such a hurry to get Ben away that he'd overlooked what should have been obvious.

"Hey," Rigo said. "You got the guy home alive. That's all anyone could do."

"I could have prevented him from getting shot."

"Maybe. Or maybe you both would have gotten taken out." Rigo shrugged. "I choose to look at the positive."

"Oh, no!" Tessa clapped a hand to the side of her head and swayed. "Not now!"

"Tessa?" Adrian caught her as her knees went out from under her. He dragged her to a nearby chair and sat beside her. "What's wrong?"

She was breathing fast. When she looked up, her violet eyes glowed, her expression far away. "One end begins another. Sacrifice is the only way to be free. That which was separated becomes one."

Rigo squatted down in front of Tessa. "What's going on?"

"Vision," Adrian said.

"O-o-okay. And that stuff she just said . . . what does that mean?"

Adrian held Tessa as she slumped forward. "We'll ask her when she's more lucid." He gave Rigo a considering look. "You must be wondering what's going on."

"After what I saw last September when that Criten guy infiltrated the house, I figure the less I ask, the better."

"You're probably right."

"But I do have one question. Will she be okay? She's not having a seizure or something, is she?"

"She'll be okay," Adrian said.

"All right, then." Rigo stood. "I'd better check in with my men, see what's up with Bob. I'll be outside." He headed out of the hospital, pulling his cell phone from his pocket as he went.

Tessa stirred in Adrian's arms. Groaned.

"Hey." Adrian stroked her hair away from her face. "It's all right. You're safe."

"Oh, no." She sniffed, and when she lifted her head all the way, he could see the tears welling in her eyes. "I've been so horrible to her. And all she wanted to do was help."

"Hey, what's this all about? What did you see?"

"Faith. I saw Faith. And pain . . ." She closed her eyes. "But I can't read Faith. I must be getting this from Ben."

"What? Was someone hurting her?"

"Not that kind of pain." She touched her chest. "Here. Pain. Anguish." She swiped both hands over cheeks damp from tears.

"Hey, it's okay. We're all okay."

"For now." She fell silent, and they waited together to hear the news.

· · · · ·

Faith and Darius got to the cafeteria. She looked at the food, but the mere thought of trying to choke down a meal made her gag. Darius seemed to sense that. Of course he did, with his abilities, but she couldn't even drum up any outrage at him reading her emotions. For once, she was glad of it. He settled her at a table with a bottle of water and a yogurt. The water soothed her parched throat, and the yogurt didn't require chewing, just scoop and swallow. Scoop and swallow. It was the most she was capable of right now.

He sat across from her, concern on his handsome face, and

she wondered if he really meant it, or if it was just an act. Had any of it been real?

"Do you really want to talk about that now?" he asked.

She gritted her teeth. "Cut that out."

"Sorry, it's a part of me, like seeing and hearing." He folded his hands on the table in front of him. "I never wanted to lie to you, Faith. I hope you believe that."

She scraped another spoonful of yogurt from the carton. "I don't know what to believe anymore."

"I didn't do it to be dishonest, or to manipulate you."

She jerked her gaze to his. "But you were dishonest. And maybe you were manipulating me, with all that talk of mating bonds and stuff."

"The mating bond is real." A pulse of warmth came to her through the link. "I didn't manipulate you, Faith. I swear."

She dropped the spoon in the empty container and shoved it away. "Then how do you account for all this? We just met a few days ago, for heaven's sake, and suddenly we're hot and heavy in your bedroom like a couple of horny teenagers."

"It was the mating bond. It's powerful, and it became more intense the longer we were together."

"Convenient. Well, playtime is over. Your father says if I want my money, we have to work together. So that's what we will do. Work."

"Faith."

Just her name, but the weariness and sorrow in the word sucked the anger right out of her. It was easier to rage at him than to think of what was going on in surgery. Of the possibility of losing Ben. Darius was trying to help her. She knew that. Even if he had lied by omission, she needed that quiet strength of his to get through this—damn it.

"I don't want to fight with you." She met his gaze. "I'm ashamed to admit I need you right now. I just can't go through this alone."

"I'm here." He covered one of her hands with his.

She turned her hand palm up and twined her fingers with his. "I don't know if things can go back to the way they were."

"You feel betrayed. I understand that. Now I need you to understand something, even if you can't forgive it. I made a promise to my parents before I ever met you that I would keep an eye on you while you were with us. You know how scared they are, how the Mendukati have been systematically murdering my mother's family."

"I do."

"And suddenly they were letting a former Mendukati agent into the house. They were terrified." He squeezed her fingers. "This whole thing was my idea. I talked them into it. But I knew as soon as I met you that you didn't intend to hurt anyone."

"Oh, Darius." She took a deep breath. "I don't know if I can deal with this right now."

"You're worried about Ben. I know."

"Just . . . and I know I have no right to ask this of you . . . but can we just get through this? Sort out everything else later?"

"Of course. Ben comes first."

Relief swept through her. "Yes."

"But Faith." He waited until she looked at him. "You can't keep running away from things forever."

She jerked her hand from his, dropping both into her lap. "What does that mean?"

"You've been running from the Mendukati, from the war. Now you're running from us."

She curled her hands into fists under the table. "I can't think about anything but Ben right now. And you know there might not even be an us, not after all this."

"We can get past this, if you're willing to stay and fight for it. Not run away and pretend it isn't happening."

"That's it." She stood, her chair skidding back with a loud

scrape. "Stone Bear—Ben—the only family I have, is up there fighting for his life." She sucked in a shaky breath. "And you want to duke it out about our affair. Some empath you are."

He stood and took her shoulders in his hands. "It was more than an affair. You know that, Faith. I started falling in love with you the first time I heard your song in my head."

"Stop it. Stop it." She jerked away from him, her throat tight. "Don't lie to me, not now."

"I'm not lying." He pulled her, still stiff, into his arms.

She should push him away. Chew on him some more about lying to her and then wanting to get her right back into bed. Words whipped through her mind, sharp and accusing. But his arms enclosed her, his heart a steady thud against her ear. His calm composure, that feeling that he could make everything all right, had her clinging to his shirt instead of pushing him away, burying her face in his chest instead of railing at him.

He said he could use a scrap of her emotions and enhance them, but if he were doing that now she'd be a ranting basket case. She didn't feel the least bit at peace. So these soothing feelings she was getting had to be just him. Just Darius.

For an instant, their connection felt like it used to, warm and irresistible, like a cozy blanket and hot chocolate before a winter fire. Safe.

Adrian's voice sounded in her mind. *You two had better get up here.*

They jerked apart, and one glance at his face told her Adrian had spoken to both of them.

"Ben," she whispered.

His face grim, he grabbed his cane with one hand and her with the other. They hurried from the cafeteria.

. . . . .

They got back to the waiting room to find Adrian looking grim and Tessa sitting in a chair with her face buried in her hands.

Both of them looked up as Faith and Darius entered. Tessa jumped up and came to Faith, wrapping her in a hug.

"I'm so sorry I was such a bitch to you," she whispered.

Uncertain how to react, Faith just said, "Okay."

Tessa pulled back to look at her. "I really am sorry, Faith. Darius was right. I can't read you, and it made me suspicious. Plus your past and . . ." She shrugged. "My family's been through a lot recently from people I can't read. I was scared."

This Tessa seemed a completely different person from the woman Faith had seen up to now, but she couldn't worry about Tessa's angle at present. Her mind was on Ben. "I get it. Thanks." Faith looked at Adrian. "What happened?"

"The doctor wants to talk to you."

As he said it, an older man in scrubs walked over. "Ms. Karaluros? I'm Dr. Flyte. I understand you're Mr. Wakete's daughter-in-law?"

"Yes." Without taking her eyes from the doctor, Faith felt for Darius's hand where he stood beside her. His strong fingers closed over hers. "How is he?"

"I'm very sorry. We lost him. The bullet nicked an artery, and he lost too much blood. He was diabetic, too, correct?"

"Yes," she whispered, her world crashing down around her.

"That didn't help." The doctor paused, seemed to be searching for words. "I'm very sorry," he said again.

Through the roaring in her ears, she heard Darius asking questions about claiming the body, paperwork. But she couldn't think about it yet. Couldn't comprehend.

Ben was gone. The Mendukati had killed him. All because of her.

The rage started as a slow burn in her gut, consuming everything. Ben was dead, a good man who had nothing to do with this stupid war the Mendukati had launched against the Seers. He'd sent her to the Montanas to protect her and so she could help. Well, she hadn't done much helping at all, had she? She'd fallen into bed with Darius and wallowed in her part in Michael's death while she stuck her head in the sand and pretended she had no stake in this battle.

She'd been fooling herself.

The Mendukati had taken her only family from her. They wanted war? She'd bring them one.

. . . . .

The plan had failed. Azotay paced in his cabin at the camp, going over the strategy in his head. Luka, the Whisperer, had put the compulsion on the pilot to see the instruments as heading toward Sedona, even though the coordinates had been set to land in Roswell, closer to the camp. A brilliant plan that should have worked. By the time Adrian Gray realized what was going on, they would have been caught.

Not only had the plane not been redirected, but the team he'd sent to try to take Wakete and Gray had failed as well. He had to admit he'd expected that and used it more as a diversion for Luka's part than the focus of the operation.

What he hadn't expected—and should have—was that Adrian Gray was a member of the Leyala.

Just the thought seared through his gut like acid. The Leyala. Those high-and-mighty pricks who thought they were above everyone else. They didn't recognize real talent. They'd rejected *him*, hadn't they? And look at him now. He was Azotay, right hand to President Criten himself, and the most feared man in the Atlantean world.

Soon to be the most feared man in all the world, when Criten collected all three Stones of Ekhia and used their power to return the Atlanteans back to their proper place—as rulers of mankind.

Azotay smiled, imagining it. He had power now, but it was nothing compared to what he would have.

Adrian Gray had sent back one of his best Warriors as a drooling idiot. Azotay had killed the man immediately. No reason for that one to be draining the resources of the Mendukati when he was of no use to them anymore. He'd instructed the other two who'd failed in the mission to dispose of the body.

In the meantime, he planned his next move. He still needed that stone, and the Stone Singer. He'd get them and kill the Seers, too, baseless scum who'd destroyed the perfect utopia, Atlantis. Who thought they were better than everyone else.

And he had special plans for Adrian Gray.

· · · · ·

Darius and Faith arrived back in Sedona late that night. His parents came to meet them as the four of them walked in the door. His mother came to Faith and took her hand.

"I'm so sorry about Ben," she said. "He sounded like a nice man."

"Thank you," Faith whispered, her voice hoarse from the sobbing she had done in the car.

"I can't believe it about Bob," his father said. "That sounds out of character for him."

"It is," Adrian said. He looked up as Rafe and Cara came down the stairs. "Hey, you two. Rafe, we can use you. Rigo's got Bob secured, and we're going to have a little chat. Thought you might want to come with."

"Anything you need," Rafe said as he reached the bottom of the stairs. Cara hurried to Faith and embraced her, her energy a soothing balm.

"I'm going, too," his dad said.

Adrian nodded. "Good deal." He looked at Darius, who hadn't taken his eyes from Faith. "Darius?"

"I'll stay here," Darius responded. *Where I'm needed,* he added telepathically. Faith's pain throbbed like a gangrenous wound. He knew he couldn't make it go away, but he could help, at least for tonight.

"Okay. Rafe, John, let's head over and see what's going on with Bob."

"I'm coming, too." Tessa fell into pace with them. "You can never have too many Truth Seers at an interrogation. And maybe I'll get a vision or something."

"Tessa—" her father began.

"She's right," Adrian said.

"Fine," her father said.

The three men filed out the front door, and Tessa paused in the doorway. "Faith," she called. Faith glanced over. "Be careful," Tessa continued. "This isn't over yet."

"I know." Faith started for the kitchen.

Watch over her, Dar, Tessa sent telepathically. *She's not thinking straight. She might do something dangerous to get revenge.*

I know, Darius sent back.

Ben's death is just the beginning, Tessa said. *I saw it. Watch your back. And hers.* She hurried outside after the others.

"Is there anything we can get you, Faith?" Maria asked. "Maybe some tea?"

"No, I'm okay." Faith reached a hand for Darius as she addressed his mother. He took it. "It's been a long day, and I think I'm going to turn in."

"Of course." His mother smiled sadly. "We can talk in the morning. Please let us know if you need anything at all."

"Me, too," Cara said. "I know how it feels to lose a parent. You let me know if you want to talk. Any time."

"Thank you," Faith said. She squeezed Darius's hand so tightly he thought she might hurt her fingers. *Get me out of here,* she sent telepathically.

"Let me walk you to your room," Darius said.

"Actually," Faith said, "I left something in the cabana. I need to get it."

"I'll go with you and unlock the door."

"Thanks," Faith said, and turned away, Darius at her side.

Once they were clear of the house, Darius asked, "What are you really doing?"

"Reading me again, Darius?"

"Worried for you," he corrected. "I know you're not as okay as you're pretending to be."

"Stop spying on my emotions."

"I can't help it," he countered as they approached the cabana. "You're basically shoving them in my face."

"Sorry if my grief annoys you." She sped up her pace.

"I didn't say that. Damn it, will you stop for a minute?" He grabbed her arm, forcing her to a halt.

She shook him off, tears glimmering in her eyes in the light of the lamps illuminating the pathway. "I can't stop. Don't you see? I've spent my life stopping. Waiting. Hiding from this very situation. I tried to take myself out of this battle between the Mendukati and the Seers, but the Mendukati brought it right to my doorstep. Well, they don't get to get away with this. Do you understand me?" Her voice broke. "I'm finally choosing sides. The Seers are going to win this war."

"Faith." He cupped her cheek. "I know you're hurting, but we can't go into this half-cocked. We have to have a plan."

"I've got a plan. But I need you to help me."

"What can I do?"

"What you've been doing. Be my anchor to this world. I'm going into the Stone of Igarle, farther than I've ever been. I think our answer might be there, on how to defeat the Mendukati. And the way I'm feeling—" She sucked in a shuddering breath. "The way I'm feeling, it would be tempting to stay in there, lost in the stone. Forever."

"We can do this in the morning. You need rest."

"No." She shook her head, and he dropped his hand. "I need to do it now while I'm mad enough to have the courage. I need to honor Ben. He believed in me, believed I could help you win this war. I have to do that now. It's the least I can do."

"I don't know about this, Faith."

"Listen to me, Darius." Her tone was steely, her gaze grim. "I am doing this, with or without you. At least with you I have a chance of coming back."

He wanted to argue, to threaten to lock the stone in the vault where she couldn't get to it. He worried about her emotional stability. He could feel the grief and anger and fear churning around in her. And he knew that she would find a way without him if he refused to help. Her powers were considerable, and she'd already proven she could connect with the stone without even having to touch it.

"All right," he said. "But when I tell you to come out, you come. If we need to pick this up in the morning, we will."

A flare of resentment, then acceptance. "Okay."

"Let's get the stone and see what you can find out."

. . . . .

Down at the guardhouse on the Montana grounds, Bob Millhouse was locked up in the detention cell John Montana had ordered installed after Criten's visit back in September. The pilot jumped up from his seat on the edge of the bunk as they came in.

"Mr. Montana! Thank God, sir. I don't know what's going on. Why am I being held?"

"Don't worry, Bob. We're going to get all this straightened out." Rafe's father glanced at Rigo, who had escorted them back to the cell area. "Open the door."

Rigo nodded and stepped forward to punch the code into the keypad on the lock, then placed his hand in the scanner to its right. Red lights turned green, and the lock clicked. Bob stepped forward, then stopped as Adrian, Tessa, and Rafe stepped into the cell, closing the door behind them. Bob looked at his employer. "Sir?"

"We all just want to go over what happened with you, Bob," Rafe's father said.

"Do you remember anything about the flight?" Adrian began.

Bob's brow furrowed. "No, nothing. Last thing I remember is chatting with a new baggage handler before I boarded."

"What did he look like?" Tessa asked.

Bob frowned. "I don't really remember. It's all kind of blurry."

"Look at me, Bob," Rafe said. The pilot complied, and Rafe slid his hand into his jeans pocket, touching the new focus stone Faith had made for him. He reached for the Hunter. The power flowed through the new stone more easily than ever in his life, like water from a faucet instead of mud through a straw. He looked into Bob's eyes, but all he saw there was confusion. "Tell me what happened, Bob."

"I told you, I don't remember." Bob wrinkled his brow in thought. "I know we were in Santa Fe, but now I'm in Sedona. Anything in between is a big blank. Did I pass out or something?"

Truth, Tessa whispered in his mind.

Rafe nodded. He'd seen the same.

Telepathically, he sent to Adrian, *I don't see any evidence of a Whisperer in his mind. Did you shock him physically?*

I decked him, Adrian answered. *He was getting out of control, and we were off course.*

That would do it. The Whisperer's influence is gone, but his memories are wiped from when he was under the compulsion. The authorities are going to want to investigate the shooting. Amnesia could raise questions.

I can fix that, Adrian answered.

"Bob," Adrian said. When the other man met his gaze, Adrian stared at Bob hard. After a moment, Bob's face slackened as

Adrian took control of his mind and began to Whisper. "There was an accident on the plane," Adrian said.

"There was an accident on the plane," Bob repeated. His vacant stare and monotone words indicated he was in some kind of trance.

"You heard Ben at the cockpit door and grabbed the gun. You didn't know who it was."

"Someone was at the cockpit door. I didn't know who, so I had the gun ready," Bob repeated.

"There was turbulence, and the gun accidentally fired. Ben was hit."

"The gun accidentally went off because of turbulence," Bob echoed. "The passenger was hit."

"There's going to be an investigation," Adrian said. "But your boss is on your side."

"There's going to be an investigation," Bob repeated. "Mr. Montana is on my side."

That ought to do it, Adrian sent to Rafe as he broke the mind connection with Bob. The pilot shook his head as he came back to himself.

I've never seen you do this before, Tessa said. *Is it permanent?*

No, never is. In the end he won't remember anything about the incident, but this should get him through the investigation.

Rafe gave his dad a nod.

"I'll have my men take you home, Bob," his father said. "I'm sure your wife is worried."

"Thank you, sir. I'm sorry about all this." Bob stood, seemingly normal again. Rigo unlocked the door, and Bob exited the cell, followed by Rigo, the Montanas, and Adrian.

Rafe's dad clapped a hand on Bob's shoulder. "Everything's going to be fine. Just make yourself available over the next couple of days for the investigators."

"I will," Bob said.

"Rigo, have someone see Bob home." Rigo stepped forward

and escorted Bob from the building. "Good idea giving Bob a memory he can take to the investigators," John said to Adrian. "That was smart thinking. They got to Bob, and if you hadn't been on the ball, you and Ben would have ended up who-knows-where."

"But Ben might still be alive," Adrian said bitterly.

"We don't know that," John said. "In my experience, you can never predict what these kinds of people will do." He glanced at his watch. "It's late, and I know Maria had Lupe make up a room for you, Adrian. Since you're staying, we'll pick this up in the morning. Plan our next move."

"All right." The three men and Tessa exited the guardhouse. A black SUV with one of Rigo's team waited for them.

You know, Rafe said into Adrian's mind, *it still freaks me out that you can do that.*

Adrian's lips curved in that cryptic smile of his. *But it does come in handy, doesn't it?*

It's still freaky.

Oh, and you morphing into a primeval warrior isn't?

Rafe took a long moment to reply. *Touché.*

They climbed into the car and headed back to the house.

· · · · ·

When Darius took the stone from its box, he hesitated before giving it to Faith.

"Are you sure about this?"

"We need a way to defeat the Mendukati so they don't hurt anyone else." Her lips pressed in a thin line, Faith held out her hand for the stone. "I'm the best chance we've got."

"I'll be monitoring you." He stroked her cheek with one finger but she pulled away. "Don't stay in there too long."

He sensed her conflict. She enjoyed his touch, but something inside her resisted, holding on to the hurt of his secrecy. He longed to be close to her, to make love with her, to share everything with her. She was his mate, whether she acknowledged it or not. The mating bond had only grown stronger over these past few days, especially when they'd come together physically. She didn't seem to care about his disability; she was genuinely physically attracted to him. The combination was irresistible to him.

As she sat down cross-legged on the floor in the circle of protection she'd set up, he asked, "What are you looking for in there?"

"Answers."

"About the stones? We know that you need all three to use their greatest power," he said.

She raised her brows. "I thought you didn't know much about Atlantean history."

"We have some scrolls from Atlantis. I can't read the language, but it illustrates pretty clearly that you need all three stones to do . . . whatever."

"The three together do bring the ultimate power," she said, "but each one individually can provide value, if there is a Stone Singer to link with it. I believe the more of them we have, the more we will cripple the Mendukati." She stretched, then settled into position. "I know one of them is in Santutegi. It's just a matter of locating it. One stone may be able to sense the others." She closed her eyes. "Okay, I'm going in."

He could tell it was a difficult journey. She started out singing under her breath, but as the hours passed, her voice got louder and louder, and eventually hoarse. He kept the connection between them wide open as she went deeper and deeper into the stone. Navigating had become easier since she'd cleared a good amount of the trapped emotions out of there. The stone acted less like a needy child and more like the ancient touchstone of wisdom it was supposed to be.

It was into the wee hours when she opened her eyes and looked at him. She was paler than usual, the green of her irises made more pronounced by the redness of fatigue and overexertion in the whites. She reached out a hand to him and he helped her up from the floor. She groaned as she unfolded her limbs from their fixed position. Clinging to his arm with one hand, she gave the stone back to him with the other.

"I know where they are," she whispered. Her knees buckled, and she would have hit the floor if he hadn't been holding her up.

"Faith." He shook her, but she didn't respond. He could see the pulse beating in her neck, see her chest rising and falling with her breathing. She was unconscious and exhausted. He touched their link and found it as vibrant as ever. She'd just pushed herself too hard.

He laid her on the couch while he put the Stone of Igarle back in its box and locked it in the cabinet again. Then he scooped her over his shoulder in a fireman's carry, his knee protesting, and made his way over the short distance to his room. No way could he make it to the main house, and he didn't want to wake any of the others.

Faith was his, and he'd take care of her.

When he reached his room, he put her on his bed, covering her with the sheet as she was. He stripped off his own clothes and lay down beside her, cuddling her slight body close to his. He closed his eyes and dropped off to sleep seconds later.

CHAPTER SEVENTEEN

Faith woke up snug and warm, a heavy arm around her waist. She smiled, still half asleep, and wiggled closer. The arm tightened and its owner gave a contented grunt. She opened her eyes. Not her room.

Darius's room.

She sat up with a jerk, Darius's arm dropping away. A glance beneath the sheets showed she still wore yesterday's clothes—thank heavens—but his bare chest indicated he might not be wearing anything. She remembered yesterday in a rapid picture show in her head. The Soul Circle. Rafe. Being locked up by Darius's dad. Released. Working with the stone again. Ben.

Her lips quivered as the last hit home like an anvil on her chest. Ben was dead.

"Hey." Darius's sexy morning voice rippled along her frayed nerves like a cold drink on a hot day.

"Hey." She paused, trying to figure out the right way to pose the question. Screw it. Just ask. "So what happened last night? Why am I in your bed?"

He stretched, that powerful, hair-roughened body practically begging to be licked like chocolate ice cream. His lips curved. "You worked yourself into unconsciousness last night. No way could I carry you up to the house, so I brought you here."

"Convenient."

"I thought so." His eyes glinted from beneath half-closed lids. "It's no secret I like you in my bed."

Her pulse skipped, but she made herself focus. "Yeah, well, that part of our relationship is over. This is business."

"You just keep telling yourself that." He stroked a finger along her inner arm.

"Cut that out." She yanked her arm away before she crawled on top of him and rode him until the world went away. "I can't deal with everything else and this, too."

He sighed. "*This*, as you call it, is just healthy sexual attraction between mates."

"Mates!" She shuffled backward on the bed, putting a little space between them. "I told you I'm not staying, especially after the way you kept secrets from me. I thought you understood that."

"Understood, yes. Agreed with? No." He tugged on the sheets she was wrapped in, reeling her closer to him. "If Ben's death taught me anything, it's that life is short and needs to be lived. So let me tell you straight out: I love you. I want you in my life permanently, any way I can get you."

"Are you crazy?" Though her heart leaped at his declaration, she leaned back, trying to put distance between them in the tangle of sheets. She was still reluctant to trust him. "This is war, Darius. War is no time to start talking happily ever after."

"I think it's the perfect time. We don't know what's going to happen. Tomorrow might never come." He gave a yank on the sheets, and she tumbled against his chest, her mouth inches from his. "Seize the moment today. Because today might be all we have."

He kissed her.

She allowed herself to enjoy it for one moment. His taste. That quick leap of her heart, the warmth blooming between her legs, the way her hands itched to curl into that furry chest. Then she made herself break the kiss and sit back. "This isn't a good idea. Ben is dead. We can't just let his murderers get away with it."

He sighed. "I know. And that wasn't what I meant." He tossed the sheets aside.

She braced herself for the quick hit of lust that a glimpse of his naked body would surely bring. Then she saw he was wearing navy blue boxers. Ignoring the pang of disappointment, she told herself she was glad he'd had enough decency to leave his boxers on. Really.

He reached over the side of the bed and picked up a pair of jeans, sliding them up his legs before he stood to button and zip. She allowed herself to admire the bunch and ripple of his muscular back. It would be so much easier if she could stay completely angry at him, if his secrets had killed the aching physical attraction. But no such luck.

Darius sat down on the edge of the bed. "Last night you said you 'knew where they are.' Where what is?"

"Oh, man, how could I forget?" She slapped a hand to her forehead. "I know where the remaining two Stones of Ekhia are located."

He stared. "What did you say?"

"One's in Santutegi. We knew that. It's heavily guarded in the palace vault." She pushed back the covers and got out of bed. "That one has been there since Selak himself brought it from Atlantis. The other has been missing since the cataclysm. No one knew where it was, where to look. Until now."

He propped his hands on his hips. "Where is it? If no one else knows, maybe we can get to it first."

"And have two out of three." She nodded. "Exactly what I was thinking. The one in Santutegi isn't going anywhere. We can go after that one last."

"We? I thought you weren't sticking around?"

"I'm seeing this through. Besides, you'll need a Stone Singer for the lost stone."

"I guess. So where is it?"

She smiled slowly. "Belize."

. . . . .

Three days later, Faith found herself on a boat in the Caribbean, heading for a tiny, uninhabited island off the coast of Belize. She, Adrian, Darius, and Rigo made up the team the Montanas had sent to recover the Stone of Gerlari—the stone of the Warriors—from the ancient underwater tomb where it resided.

"This sure is a pretty place," Rigo said, looking out over the clear turquoise Caribbean. "So this underwater cave is on one of these islands?"

"It wasn't underwater centuries ago," Faith said. "It was near the shoreline, but easy to access from the land. Good place for a tomb. Rising seas or earthquakes, maybe both, sank it underwater."

"And this is legal, right?" Rigo asked. "We're not grave robbing or anything?"

"Darius's father cleared it through his government contacts," Adrian broke in. "As far as they're concerned, we're just scuba diving."

Rigo nodded.

Darius was piloting the boat. He cut the engine and lowered the anchor. "Okay, gather 'round." The three joined Darius near the wheel. "We need to get in and get out as fast as possible. We don't know if Criten's men or this Azotay character is on our trail. The sooner we get what we came for and get back to Sedona, the better. You three navigate the cave. I'll stay on the boat as our home base."

"One of us can stay if you want to go," Rigo said.

"You three are in better physical shape than I am." He tapped his bad leg. "Better it be me who stays."

"Guess we'd better suit up then." Rigo turned to pick up his oxygen tanks.

Faith started buckling herself into the gear. Darius came

over to help her, lifting the oxygen tanks so she could get her arms through. "Are you okay with this?" he asked. "You said you've been scuba diving before."

"Once, on my honeymoon. I'll be okay."

"Rigo has extensive experience with this sort of thing, and I'm betting Gray does, too."

Her mouth quirked. "Is there anything Adrian can't do?"

"Haven't found anything yet."

. . . . .

Across the deck, Adrian was methodically donning his own equipment. Getting this stone before the Mendukati did was the goal. Then the Seers would have two of the three stones, and it would just be a matter of getting the third out of Santutegi. The harder they hit the bastards who murdered Ben, the better.

He still blamed himself. He should have been looking for a more complicated plot after the half-assed attack at the airport. But no, he'd gotten cocky. Figured he was smarter than they were.

His ego had cost Ben his life.

He missed the guy. He'd known Ben for years, seen him off and on, more often when Ben had been married to Alishka, his Atlantean wife. After Alishka had died giving birth to Michael, he hadn't seen Ben as often, not even for Michael's wedding. But he'd known about Faith. Ben and Faith had bonded over their love of stones. Adrian had known Faith was a Stone Singer, and as he pursued his agenda to return the Stones of Ekhia to the Seers, he'd also known he'd be coming to her at some point once a stone was found. Ben had trusted him to watch out for Faith, and he had, by hooking her up with the Montanas. He hadn't watched out for Ben, though. Ben was dead, and all that was left was to avenge him.

Criten's flunky Azotay had a lot to answer for. And Criten, too, if he ever came out of hiding. Hopefully the Mendukati had no idea what the Seers were up to. Hopefully, they thought all of them were still in Sedona.

Adrian Gray. The whisper in his mind made him pause. He recognized the voice, but he couldn't pinpoint from where he knew it. *I am Azotay.*

Damn it. So much for secrecy.

What do you want? he sent back.

I want you, Adrian Gray, for erron-ka. Meet me on the east beach of this island.

Erron-ka. Warrior's challenge.

The erron-ka was an ancient ritual, originally used when one Warrior wanted the lands or possessions or woman of another. Over the years it had changed to more of a battle to prove which Warrior was superior over the other. He hadn't fought one since he was a teenager. Had no desire to fight one now.

Time had just become of the essence.

"Azotay's here," he said to the others. "He just communicated with me."

"What! How did they even know we were here?" Darius demanded.

"I have no idea," Adrian said. "But they're here, so we'd better get moving. Get that stone and get out of here."

"Copy that," Rigo said. He put his regulator in his mouth and backed into the ocean with a splash.

Adrian Gray, you have not accepted the challenge.

Adrian ignored the voice and continued to get his gear on.

Adrian Gray, you will answer me!

Faith took her position with her back to the water.

Adrian Gray! Or should I call you Atlas Itzal?

Adrian froze. He hadn't heard that name in years. No one knew that name, or rather, no one *should* know that name. He'd been Adrian Gray ever since he'd reached manhood.

Answer me, Atlas. Will you come, or do my men kill your friends?

Adrian watched Faith launch herself into the water. She had Rigo to watch her back. If Adrian distracted Azotay by accepting his challenge, then they might have a better shot at getting out of here with the stone. He unfastened the tanks and shrugged them off.

"Gray, what are you doing?" Darius demanded.

"I'm going to meet him," Adrian said, stripping off the last of the scuba gear and dropping it on the deck.

"Are you nuts? This guy is a killer!"

Adrian smiled. "So am I." He headed for the side. "I'll swim over and cut across the island to the east beach. Keep him busy and hopefully buy Faith and Rigo some time."

"I don't like it," Darius said.

"Noted," Adrian replied, and dove into the water.

Azotay, I accept your challenge.

. . . . .

Faith and Rigo started swimming for the cave, expecting Adrian to fall in behind them. Instead he shot past them at a ridiculous speed, leaving a wake of bubbles behind.

She reached for him telepathically. *Adrian? What's going on?*

Going to confront Azotay. You two get the stone, and I'll see you back on the boat.

Going to confront Azotay? Her blood chilled. The Mendukati had found them.

Rigo swam to her and pointed to his wrist. They were running out of time. Pushing her fear aside, she nodded and fell in beside him as he swam for the underwater cave. The sooner they got the stone, the sooner they could get out of here.

The Stone of Igarle had imprinted a map in her mind. She took the lead, guiding them to the nearly hidden entrance.

The tunnel snaked into the solid rock, taller than it was wide. At one time it would have been a narrow, curving passageway that people would have walked through. Now it was a dark tunnel with no light. If not for the underwater flashlights they carried, she would have been lost.

The rock hummed around her, its song like a lullaby. Enveloped by the dark, surrounded by stone, Faith's fear fell away. The journey reminded her of her forays into the consciousness of the Stone of Igarle. There was something peaceful about the dark, about the stony corridor, that eased the pain of Ben's death that still seared her heart.

The tunnel curved upward—uphill, had the cave still been above the sea—leading them deeper into the Earth and closer to the missing stone. As she swam, she caught a glimmer of light ahead. She increased her speed. The glimmer became a glow that filled the water around her. She swam toward it, and her head broke the surface of a pool.

Rigo popped up beside her. They both tipped their heads back. The roof of the cave stretched up several stories above them. The illumination of the cave came from an opening on the side, halfway to the top. Just enough sunlight got in to cast reflections from the water onto the walls. Stalactites hung from the ceiling. Beside them was a wide outcropping. Dark openings in the wall behind it hinted at other passages and other caves.

Rigo pulled his regulator from his mouth and took an experimental breath. "A little stale," he said, "but the opening up top probably keeps enough fresh air circulating that we don't need our gear."

Faith took out her own regulator. "Any idea how to get on that ledge? I doubt there's a ladder."

He laughed. "You're right about that one. Let's get closer. Maybe there's enough rock that we can make our own ladder."

They managed to use submerged rocks to clamber up the edge of the outcropping, hauling themselves up and out of the water.

"These tanks are so much lighter in the water," she groaned, sliding her air tanks off. She set them out of the way.

"I'll just keep mine. They don't bother me." Rigo put his hands on his hips. "So, where do we start?"

"Give me a minute." She closed her eyes and reached out with her senses, the song of the rock all around her vibrating in her throat. All of it sang together, connected and alive. She searched for one melody that was different from the others. Thought of Igarle and its song. Looked for one like it.

She found it finally, a lonely tune, whisper-soft, ancient. She reached for it, stroked it in her mind, coaxed it nearer. *I am the Stone Singer.*

The stone responded, its voice crackling like tissue paper. *I am Gerlari.*

Gerlari, the stone of the Warriors.

Help me find you, she sent.

The images poured into her mind. The caves had been used for many things over the centuries: sacred rituals, burials and cremations, sacrifices, and even a source of pure water.

Turning on her light, she went into the left-hand cave, following the ancient whisper guiding her way. She stepped where she was shown to step and did not disturb anything else, though she would have loved to have more time to explore. Rigo was right behind her. She was aware of calcified pottery, some shattered on the floor, and the glimmer of the occasional crude mirror. Faces were etched in rock. In one corner, a pot sat trapped beneath a long stalactite formed by the calcification from dripping water ancient people had once collected.

The narrow cave opened into a bigger chamber. Here there were bodies.

Her flashlight caught on human bones that glittered. The first skull startled her, but she quickly realized that the diamond-like sparkle came from crystallization of minerals on bones that had lain untouched for over a thousand years. Skeletons leaned against the walls or were wedged in crevices. Some were very small—children, perhaps. Had these people gotten trapped in the cave with no way out?

Sacrificial victims, Gerlari whispered.

Faith shivered, disturbed by the very idea, and moved her light to the center of the chamber. A sarcophagus had been set on a dais in the center of the room. She slowly traced the carving on the lid, three triangles connected at the base by a circle with a squiggly line in the middle—the symbol of Atlantis. A survivor of the cataclysm had been laid to rest here.

"Help me," she said to Rigo. Both of them took a corner at the head of the sarcophagus. Leaning every muscle into it, they were able to slide the stone lid over enough for Faith to shine her light inside.

Red crystal glimmered between skeletal hands.

"I see it." She started to reach inside. The lid skidded. She and Rigo grabbed it and prevented it from crashing to the floor. They stood balancing the heavy stone, muscles straining. The idea was to reclaim the stone and leave the rest of the artifacts untouched.

"Wish Gray was here," Rigo said. "How are we going to get that thing out?"

"You grab it. I'll hold the lid steady."

"What? You couldn't possibly."

She smiled. "Yes, I can." She closed her eyes and reached for the energy of Gerlari. The stone had been packed away for eons, no human contaminating it, which meant it flared to life with as pure an energy as she had ever felt. Unlike Igarle back at the Montana house or Eraldatu in Santutegi, this stone remained as pristine as when it had been balanced by the last Stone Singer.

Its song burst from her throat, full and eerily beautiful.

Rigo jumped when she first started singing. She didn't know how much he knew about who his employers were, but he recovered quickly and just waited for orders. She channeled the energy of Gerlari, asked for its help. Moments later, invigorating power swept through her, activating every muscle with an adrenaline rush. She easily lifted up the stone lid so Rigo could grab the stone.

"Sorry, *amigo*," he said to the skeleton as he freed the stone from the clasp of the dead.

As soon as his hand was clear, Faith replaced the lid with a soft thud and brushed her hands together to get rid of the dust. "Let me see it."

Rigo handed her the stone. The instant it touched her hand, it flared to life, glowing clear with swirls of red in it.

"*Dios*," Rigo whispered.

"Where's your bag?" she asked.

"Right here." He detached a waterproof catch bag from his belt and opened it.

Faith placed the stone in the bag. "Hang on to that with your life. Now let's get out of here."

"Hell yeah."

They hurried out of the cave, following the dim glow of the main cavern. They burst out into the light. Two Warriors in scuba gear met them, pointing harpoon guns.

"I'll take that," one said, and snatched the bag from Rigo. He tucked the harpoon gun under his arm and opened the bag, glancing inside. He nodded to his partner.

"You." The partner pointed at Faith and then swung his finger to the other side of the cavern. "Get over there."

Faith glanced at Rigo. Don't try anything, she thought. Please don't try anything.

He tried something.

As Faith shuffled to the other side of the cavern, Rigo lunged at the Warrior who'd opened the bag. The guy went down, and the bag skidded aside. Rigo leaped for it.

The other Warrior fired. Rigo tried to dive out of the way,

but the harpoon sliced along his side before bouncing off the stone wall. He landed hard, groaning and pressing his hand to his side. The Warrior he'd tackled snatched up the bag with the stone in it and stood. Rigo shoved himself into a seated position against the wall. His head sagged forward.

"We should finish him," the Warrior with the bag said in Atlantean.

"No," Harpoon Gun answered in the same language. "We have our orders. Separate the girl from the stone and wait for Azotay." He jerked his chin at Rigo. "He might want this one for some reason."

"Very well." Bag Warrior folded his arms. "Then we wait for Azotay."

. . . . .

Adrian came out of the lush forest on the east beach of the island, as instructed. A man in black jeans and a black T-shirt waited for him. Adrian glanced around. He appeared to be alone.

"Ah, Atlas. So good of you to come." White teeth flashed through carefully groomed stubble. "I assure you, we are alone, according to the rules of the erron-ka. I would not have it said I cheated."

Adrian stopped several paces away and folded his own arms. "I'm here. And the name is Adrian."

"Oh, I think not." Azotay's dark eyes gleamed. "I think you are Atlas Itzal, son of Ezares Itzal and his wife, Nilara. I think you are a Warrior of Mneseus."

Damn, the bastard knew too much.

"You're mistaken." Adrian frowned. Something about Azotay seemed familiar, but he couldn't put his finger on what.

"I doubt that." Azotay pressed his palms together and touched his lips with the tips of his fingers, that gleeful grin still playing about his lips.

"And what about you, Azotay?" Adrian challenged. "I know that's not your name."

Annoyance flashed in Azotay's eyes. "It is now."

Touchy subject. Adrian filed that away for later. "So," he said. "You challenged me. Here I am. What now?"

"Now we battle," Azotay said, and lunged.

. . . . .

Rigo hadn't moved since he'd fallen.

Faith slanted a glance at the Warriors. They sat on a large rock, their harpoon guns across their laps, talking in undertones. The bag with Gerlari in it hung from the belt of the one nearest to Rigo.

Faith leaned against the wall of the cave and closed her eyes. She summoned power from Gerlari, the white-hot energy sweeping through her channels like caffeine, amping up her powers. The Warriors had no idea she could do that; they thought she needed to touch the stone.

Ha.

She guided the energy into the wall behind her, the same wall against which Rigo rested, and focused her mind-voice stream. Rigo couldn't hear her telepathic speech, but when she filtered the energy through it, the result was a soft vibration through the rock. Barely audible sound.

Rigo, can you hear me?

He didn't respond.

Rigo, if you can hear me, twitch your pinky finger. She nearly squealed when the finger flicked. *Are you okay to swim? Move one finger for yes, two fingers for no.*

His pinky moved again. One finger.

I want you to grab the bag and swim out of here. Bring the stone to Darius.

Two fingers twitched.

Don't argue with me. I'm going to cause a cave-in, and I need to know you're clear before I do. Take the stone to Darius.

Nothing. Then, he flicked one finger again.

When the shaking starts, you run for it, you hear? Grab that bag and get out of here.

The pinky twitched.

Here we go. Channeling both the power of the massive rock cave around her and the ancient stone Gerlari, she jabbed deep into the earth and ripped through the delicate stability of carefully balanced plates to poke at the fault beneath them.

The cave started to shake. Stalactites fell from high above, splashing into the water. Rigo jumped to his feet and sprinted, snatching the bag off the belt of the Warrior and jumping into the pool before the man could aim the harpoon gun.

The Warriors shouted, argued. One dove into the water after Rigo. The other turned the harpoon gun on her . . . until a huge chunk of rock fell from the ceiling and flattened him.

Faith held the integrity of the tunnel, watching Rigo's progress through the eyes of the Earth itself. She threw obstacles in the pursuing Warrior's way, rocks from above and below, crashing on the bottom of the narrow tunnel, churning up sand and debris to block his view and slow him down. Finally Rigo was clear. She slumped back with a weary sigh. She knew she wouldn't make it out alive. She'd known that the instant she'd thought of this plan. But as long as the stone was safe, as long as the Mendukati didn't get their hands on it, her life was worth the risk.

She sat on the floor of the cave, hugging her knees to her chest as slabs of rock crashed down around her. How ironic that she'd never wanted to be part of this war, yet she would be giving her life for it. She thought of Darius, of a love that had started in deception yet somehow still lodged in her heart.

Maybe they could have worked things out. Or maybe she

would have been on her own again. She didn't know which way it would have gone, but she would have liked a happy ending.

She'd never know now.

Water gushed into the chamber. She bowed her head and waited for the Earth to take her.

CHAPTER EIGHTEEN

Something was very wrong. Darius could feel Faith as if she were there beside him. She was afraid.

Faith, are you all right?

Darius. Even her mind-voice sounded weary. *I sent Rigo with the stone. He's wounded. Make sure he gets . . . back . . . safe.*

Faith!

She didn't answer. He connected through their link, but her energy felt weak.

He searched for Rigo. There weren't a lot of people in the immediate area, so he found him quickly. The ex-Marine was wounded and losing strength fast as he struggled to make it back to the boat. There was another man closing in on him, one of the Mendukati Warriors, based on his emotional signature.

Darius jerked off his shirt and jumped into the water in his khaki shorts. His daily laps paid off as he swam easily and quickly, closing in on Rigo and the enemy. As he neared them, he focused on the Mendukati Warrior.

You can't breathe. You might drown. Darius built the natural concern into a crippling fear that stopped the Warrior cold. The man surfaced not far away, choking and frantic, lost in his own terrors as he tore at his regulator. Darius continued on to the other dark head he'd seen break the water. Rigo was barely holding on. He'd lost too much blood. Darius grabbed him around the chest with one arm and started to tow him back to the boat.

Rigo clawed at his hand. "I can make it," he panted. "Faith is in trouble. Cave-in."

They were halfway to the boat. The fading mating bond urged Darius to go after Faith, but he could tell Rigo's strength was flagging. He continued to tow the other man to the boat.

Finally they reached it, and Rigo grabbed the ladder.

"Take my tanks," he said, breathing hard. He unfastened the air tanks and shrugged them off into Darius's hands. "I've got the stone. Faith needs you."

Darius glanced at the gauge to make sure there was enough air, then shrugged into the harness. "You get up there and rest. Gray should be back soon."

Rigo nodded and started to climb the ladder. Darius put the respirator in his mouth, pivoted, and swam for the cave entrance. He only hoped he was in time.

. . . . .

They were evenly matched, Adrian thought, countering a move by Azotay. Their sizes, their strength, and even their skills were on par with each other.

They danced up and down the beach, a blur of flying fists and leaping kicks. Little by little, Adrian gained on him. Azotay gritted his teeth and came back harder and dirtier. "Fair fight" was apparently not in his vocabulary.

"When I win," Azotay said, "everyone will know I defeated the great Atlas Itzal. I will be revered."

"You'll be bruised and bloody," Adrian countered. "And I told you, my name is Adrian, not Atlas."

"You don't call yourself Atlas *anymore,* you mean." Azotay dodged a blow, spun around, and pinned Adrian against a tree with a forearm to the throat. He shoved his face right up into Adrian's. "Not so high and mighty now, are you?"

Adrian gouged his thumb into the other man's eye. Azotay howled, stumbling back. Adrian followed, plowing his fist into

Azotay's jaw. Azotay sailed backward, landing with a thud on the sand. Adrian approached him, following the protocol of the erron-ka. "Do you yield?"

Azotay groaned and rolled over onto his hands and knees. "Do I yield?" He sprang to his feet and spun, flinging a handful of sand into Adrian's eyes. "No! I do not yield!"

Adrian stumbled backward, blinking at the sting. He swiped the sand off his face and brows with both hands, his eyes watering. He heard Azotay charging, ducked and rolled to the side, landing on his feet. His vision cleared a bit, though his eyes still burned.

Azotay strode toward him. "Now we are both similarly impaired." He flicked a hand at his own injured eye.

"You were the one who called erron-ka," Adrian said. "Time to end this."

Azotay chuckled, teeth flashing in a knowing smile. "If you can . . . Atlas."

Adrian smiled back. "I can." And he began to chant.

"Oh, so you fall back on your Leyala ways?" Azotay snickered, dancing backward. "You cannot continue the battle as equals without leaning on that Leyala crutch, can you?"

"You, Azotay, are responsible for the death of Ben Wakete." Adrian's tattoo throbbed on his chest, glowing hot beneath his wet suit.

"Wakete? I wasn't even there." Azotay's eyes widened in what seemed like shock. Then the surprised expression melted into amusement. "All right, it's true. I ordered Venkat to Whisper the human pilot. Brilliant, wasn't it?"

Adrian grabbed Azotay by his shirt and pinned him against a boulder. "Azotay, you have been judged." He raised his hand to lay judgment.

"You would do this? To *me*?" Azotay's dark eyes burned. "To your own brother?"

"What?" Adrian's concentration faltered.

"Yes, Atlas." Azotay laughed. "It's me, Gadeiros. Your twin."

Gadeiros? No, it couldn't be. He studied Azotay's face more closely. And saw it, in the eyes, the shape of his mouth. How had he missed it before? How could he not have recognized his own brother? True, they were fraternal twins, not identical, and also true, he hadn't seen his brother for some twenty years. Not since young Atlas had left Santutegi with his father to follow the ways of the Temple of Mneseus, and Gadeiros had stayed behind with their mother.

Not since he'd become Adrian Gray.

"What?" Azotay mocked. "No words for your long-lost brother?"

Adrian let the power fade. Lowered his hand.

"I thought not." Azotay shoved Adrian off him. Swung his fist.

Pain exploded in Adrian's jaw. And the world blinked into blackness.

. . . . .

Faith came to in darkness. For a moment, she couldn't figure out where she was. Then she remembered. The cave. The Stone of Gerlari. The Mendukati. She'd sent Rigo out with the stone and called down an earthquake on the Mendukati warriors.

She'd expected to die.

She reached out with her senses. Her stone shield had activated, perhaps a subconscious attempt at survival. It had sheltered her from being crushed by the falling rock. She could tell she was buried under some big chunks; the rock sang in her mind like a choir. She could breathe, so there was air for the moment. But she could hear the sound of rushing water. The earthquake she'd caused might have collapsed some natural dam that had been holding the water at bay.

She was okay for the moment, but if she wanted to live, she had to get out of here.

There wasn't much room to move. She closed her eyes and

reached upward into the stone around her with her power, trying to figure out how far she was buried. Each time she established one layer, she encountered another.

After four layers, she gave up.

She'd caused a landslide. There was a good possibility the rock had blocked the tunnel, as well, so even if she did somehow manage to get unburied, she might still be trapped in the cave. How ironic that the tomb of an ancient Atlantean Warrior had become her tomb as well.

Sacrificing herself had seemed like a good idea at the time, but now she realized she didn't want to die.

Ben's death still throbbed deep inside her. She'd loved him like a father—she could barely remember her own—and his loss left a gaping hole in her heart. But he'd wanted her to live, to find love and have a family. To be happy. She'd been so busy looking for betrayal around every corner that when love finally had happened with Darius, she'd used the first excuse that came along to push him away.

Yes, he should have told her that he was an empath and could feel her emotions. And yes, she had felt angry and betrayed when she'd found out. But she also understood his reasons. He'd made a promise to his family, and Darius kept his promises.

Shouldn't that be enough to forgive him? To set new rules for their relationship?

Fine time to think of that, when every second she exhaled more carbon dioxide into her little shelter meant less time she had to live.

Darius, I wish we had more time. She sent the wish telepathically, not really expecting to reach him. Not only was she buried under solid rock, but she'd expended most of her energy causing the earthquake. Her range was very short now.

Faith. His whisper swirled into her mind.

Her heart leaped. *Darius?*

I'm almost through the tunnel. Where are you?

Buried. She laid her hands against the rock as if that would help her reach him. *Did Rigo get back safely?*

Yes, he's on the boat.

She rested her forehead against cool rock. *Thank heavens.*

I'm in the cavern. The shaking has stopped, but rocks and soil keep falling from the ceiling. Where are you?

I don't know what it looks like now, but I was in the corner. Do you see the rock shelf?

The edge of it, he answered. *There's a pile of rubble nearly covering it.*

I was on the right. She stroked the rough stone as if it were his face. *I have air right now, but I'm not sure how much longer that will last.*

I will get you out, Faith. Believe that.

Her heart overflowed, curving her lips in a sad smile. Darius, always the optimist. *I don't know if that's possible.*

I'll make it possible. Remember how I found you when you were lost in the stone?

Yes. The glowing silver trail through the desolation of the stone's emotions, leading to the sentinel that was Darius. Excitement bubbled up. *Rigo took the Stone of Gerlari with him, but I think I can lead you to me if I use the other stones here.*

Give it a shot. Find the mating bond and funnel the energy through there.

What good will that do?

I don't know. She could see his smile in her mind. *But it can't hurt.*

Faith dove deeper into the stone around her, reaching for Darius with her faltering powers. She saw him finally, that blue light in chaos, guiding her home. And leading to that light was the winding silver path, like a river through the clamor of the different stone voices around her. She funneled all the energy she could from the rocks into that path. The path brightened almost to blinding at the influx of Earth energy. The stones felt excited, their interest like sweet anise on the tongue.

And where had that image come from?

We're connected, Darius said. *Without the Stones of Ekhia blocking my powers, you can share my empathy through the mating link, and I can share your abilities, too.*

The thought should have alarmed her, but she felt only relief. Working together, they might be able to free her. *I didn't know you could taste emotion.*

She sensed—sensed!—his amusement. *Welcome to my world.* He grew serious again. *We have to work fast. Water is filling up the cave. Do you still have your scuba gear?*

No. She wanted to bang her head against something. *It was getting heavy.*

Guess we'll share then.

Guess we will. If you can get me out of here.

I have an idea. Do you trust me?

She didn't even hesitate. *Yes.*

When Criten broke into our house, he shut down Rafe's focus stone, but Rafe was able to get an energy boost through his link to Cara. I wonder if we can try something similar here.

I've used up a lot of my stores already, Faith said. *I don't know how much I have left.*

But I have plenty. If I feed you enough energy, do you think you can make the rocks move away off your position? Maybe let you crawl out?

Worth a try.

Let's do it. Take what I send and channel it through you into the rocks on top of you.

Energy surged through the link and into her, filling up her reserves and overflowing into her normal power stores. It tasted and smelled like Darius. She wrapped herself up in it, like feeling Darius's arms around her, and absorbed it into her heart and mind. Then pushed outward.

The scrabble of dirt and stone reached her ears. The clack of a large rock being tossed aside.

Keep doing whatever you're doing, Darius said. *It's loosening the chunks so I can move them.*

She dove deeper into the energy, swimming in it, wallowing in all that was Darius. Sent it streaming into the ancient stone that covered her, pressing on the boulders and pebbles, urging it away. Finally a chink of light appeared above her through a small hole. She ducked away as soil rained down on her.

"Faith?" His physical voice this time, a little muffled because of the layers of earth between them.

"I'm here," she called back, a little surprised at how raw her throat felt.

He peered into the hole. "I see you. We have to move. The water's started to flow up onto this ledge."

The glimpse of those bluer-than-blue eyes was all the incentive she needed. She closed her eyes and focused the energy on the rocks around that tiny glimmer of light. Darius grabbed and heaved stone after stone. Finally he had widened the opening enough that she would be able to crawl out.

"Faith, let's go!" He reached in a filthy hand. She grabbed it and he yanked, giving her a head start on the climb. She was head and shoulders out of the pile, scrambling for footholds to push herself out, when she felt the rocks start to collapse beneath her.

"Darius!" She reached out her other hand. He clasped it and jerked hard on both. His muscles rippled and strained, his teeth clenched as he dragged her to safety with his entire body. He fell flat on his back, Faith sprawled on top of him. A moment later, the pile collapsed upon itself.

She blew out a hard breath and rested her forehead against his chest. "That was close."

"We're not out of the woods yet. This place is flooding."

She glanced over at the edge of the shelf, saw the pool had

already overflowed onto it and was inching closer. She scrambled off him backward on her hands and knees. "Yeah, let's get out of here before the tunnel collapses."

"Could you give me a hand? I'm like a turtle on its back with these tanks."

"Sure." She helped him get to his feet.

"We'll have to share the respirator."

"Ha. Fine with me."

"In fact, here." He shrugged off the tanks and offered the gear to her. "You take the oxygen, and we'll share it as we swim."

She shook her head. "No, they're yours."

"Don't let your pride cost you your life. I'm an experienced swimmer. I can hold my breath longer than you can." He gave her a half grin. "Just don't forget to share."

"As if."

He helped her fasten the gear. Once she was ready, they both waded into the pool and headed for the tunnel exit.

. . . . .

Azotay climbed onto the Seers' boat, alert for any cries of alarm. But nothing reached his ears except for the cry of seagulls and the quiet lap of the sea. He tiptoed along the deck, searching for the stone.

It was almost too easy.

Mere minutes after he boarded, he found a dark-haired human laying on the deck, a steady trickle of crimson streaming down his side. A small pouch hung from his belt. Azotay grabbed it, felt the points of a pyramid inside the waterproof material. He yanked the pouch free and poured its contents into his palm.

A ruby red crystal glittered in the sunlight.

He grinned and popped it back in the bag, then rose. He pondered killing the human, then decided against it. The fool was probably at death's door, anyway. With a shrug, he turned his back on the poor sod and jumped back into the ocean.

First he'd bested Atlas and now this. The stone was a victory for President Criten, and finally beating his older brother, after all these years, was a personal one for him.

Two stones down—the one in Santutegi and now this one—and one to go.

The Seers would soon know the wrath of the Mendukati.

. . . . .

Darius climbed on board the boat to find Rigo passed out on the deck, blood pooling along his side. Faith dropped to her knees beside the security man and laid two fingers on his neck. "He's alive. Do you have a first aid kit?" She unzipped his wet suit.

"On it." Darius retrieved the kit within minutes and handed it to Faith. "Is it bad?"

"I'm no doctor, but I'm thinking the first order of business is to stop this bleeding." She pulled out a wad of gauze and pressed it against the oozing wound. "Any sign of Adrian?"

"No." Darius frowned. "Where's the stone?"

"In a bag on his belt." She glanced down. "Damn it. The bag is gone."

"Maybe he lost it? Or hid it?"

"If it's in this area, I'd be able to sense it."

"Try it." Darius stared out at the ocean. "I have a bad feeling about this."

Maintaining pressure on the wound, Faith closed her eyes and concentrated. Long minutes passed. She opened her eyes and looked at Darius. "It's not around here. Not sensing it at all."

"I'm betting Azotay took it." Gray's head appeared over the side as he climbed up the ladder and stumbled onto the boat. His eyes were red and puffy, and he moved slowly.

"You're hurt. What happened?" Darius asked, making his

way over. Gray simmered with anger and chagrin and a whole kind of what-the-fuck-just-happened vibe.

"Azotay wanted to have a little chat." Gray stretched his neck, winced.

Darius knew he wasn't getting the whole story. "About what?"

"The usual," Gray said. "The Mendukati want all three Stones of Ekhia. It's how they think they're going to gain power over the human world." He rubbed his shoulder. "Azotay took me out long enough for him to sneak back here and steal the stone, or so logic would suggest."

"How did they even know where we are?" Darius asked.

"I don't know," Gray replied. "But you can be damned sure I'm going to find out." He glanced at the fallen Rigo. "I suggest we get Mendez to a hospital."

"I agree," Faith said, setting aside bloodstained gauze and grabbing fresh bandages.

Knowing he wasn't going to get anything more out of Gray right now, Darius nodded and headed over to start the boat. "Home, here we come."

· · · · ·

After a stop at a medical facility in Belize, where Rigo was stabilized and pronounced fit to travel, the trip back to Sedona seemed fast and anticlimactic.

Faith had taken comfort in the presence of the others around them. Alone in the cave together, everything had seemed clear about her and Darius. Then they'd waded back into the real world with its bad guys and heartbreak and war, and her certainty wavered.

He'd saved her life, but she'd never doubted that about him, not even when she'd discovered he hadn't told her the whole truth. Darius would always help those in need. No, she didn't fear for her life around him—just her heart.

She sat in the clearing where Darius had once come to find

her. The constant humming of the vortexes soothed her fretting mind. Here, among the giant formations of ancient stones, she felt at peace.

She heard his footsteps on the dirt path before she saw him. Felt a pulse along the mating bond.

"If you were trying to stay clear of me," Darius said as he picked his way down the dirt path with his cane, "then you're going in the right direction with this spot."

"I wasn't trying to stay clear of you." Much. "So, was your father very upset about Azotay getting away with the new stone?"

"He was not happy, that's for sure. Gray is putting together a plan to get all the stones back from Criten."

"Ha! Good luck with that one."

"That was my first thought, but if anyone can achieve something like that, it's Adrian Gray." He paused. "So why have you been avoiding me?"

She didn't even pretend not to understand. "Because I can't think when you're around. Everything gets confusing." She shifted over so he could sit beside her on the rock.

"Confusing, huh?" He settled next to her, hip to hip. "Most people tell me I'm peaceful to be around."

She gave a quick laugh. "The last thing you are, Darius, is peaceful. At least not to me."

He placed both hands on the top of his cane, his lips quirking. "I'm not sure if that's good or bad."

"Oh, don't smile at me like that, all innocent. I've seen you naked."

"Yeah, you have." He waggled his brows.

His clowning startled a giggle from her. "Cut it out. I'm being serious."

"So am I." He took her hand and lifted it to his lips. "I take you seeing me naked *very* seriously."

As usual his touch ignited the slow burn that lurked beneath her skin whenever he was around. Her instincts urged her closer to him, but she stood firm. They had to come to some sort of understanding.

"In the cave, I thought I was dead," she said, ignoring with difficulty the tickle of his mustache and goatee against her fingers. "I called down that earthquake to take out those Warriors and so Rigo could get away. And because I realized that I was okay sacrificing myself for the cause."

His fingers tightened around hers. "*I'm* not okay with you sacrificing yourself for anything."

"But when I thought about you, about never seeing you again, I wanted to live." She laid her free hand against his cheek. "What happened, keeping things from me . . . if this is going to work, that can't happen anymore."

"It won't." He turned his head and kissed her palm. "I had made that promise before I ever met you, and I owed it to my family to let them know I was going to tell you. Unfortunately, Rafe's focus-stone troubles brought everything out ahead of schedule."

"I understand." She glanced down at their joined hands. "I know I'm prickly. I don't trust easily."

He shrugged. "People have manipulated you your entire life. That's understandable. And I get how it looked like I might be doing the same thing."

"But it was worse with you. Because I thought you were different, that you were safe. And because I was already falling in love with you." His startled look said she'd surprised him, and the knowledge made her lips curve. "Didn't you know? I thought you were an empath."

"I'm not usually good at sorting out emotions directed at me." He took both her hands in his. "I loved once, and she left me when I got injured. I was sure no woman would ever love me again. Even when I finally got out of that wheelchair, I believed that."

She tilted her head. "Do you still believe it?"

"No." He shook his head. "Not since I met you. The wheelchair, the cane, none of it bothered you."

"Oh, Darius, that has nothing to do with who you are. If anything, it increases my admiration for you, that you're still able to live a full life with such physical challenges." She slanted him a flirtatious look from beneath her lashes. "Besides, I think we overcame any physical limitations just fine in the bedroom."

"Keep looking at me like that, and I'll show you how many limitations I can overcome."

"Big talk."

"True talk." He stood and pulled her into his arms. "You really love me."

"Yes. And you really love me."

"Yes. And you'll stay with us here? This could be your safe haven, Faith. The one you've been longing for."

"No, I don't think so." She leaned into him and placed her hand over his heart. "A house doesn't matter. *This* is my safe haven."

His lips curved in a smile. "That's the truth."

ACKNOWLEDGMENTS

The character of Ben Wakete was inspired by the Zuni fetish carvers of New Mexico. I had the opportunity to visit the Zuni Pueblo and meet two of their carvers, who took time out of their busy days to talk to me about their craft. I even got a demonstration in one carver's workshop!

There are specific families who carve fetishes, and entire books are written about them, including family trees. Fetish carving is an ancient tradition, tied to the religious beliefs of the Zuni tribe. While they do continue to carve special fetishes for religious purposes, they also carve some for sale at art shows and Native American festivals across the globe. As with any art form, there are those who try to counterfeit Zuni fetishes. If you are interested in purchasing one, your best bet is to get it from the artist himself.

You will not find Ben Wakete or the Wakete family in any fetish carving book, as their characters are completely fictional. Any errors regarding carvers or the art of fetish carving are mine.

Much thanks to Todd Westika and Jimmy Yawakia of the Zuni tribe for answering my questions and providing wonderful demonstrations of their craft. You can view their work and make contact with them on their Facebook pages:

Todd Westika
    https://www.facebook.com/pages/Todd-Westika-Carvings/
    155214678017202

ACKNOWLEDGMENTS

Jimmy Yawakia
https://www.facebook.com/pages/Jimmy-Yawakia/12231
3837916284

For more information on the Zuni tribe and how to visit the Zuni Pueblo:
http://www.ashiwi.org/